PRAISE FOR

Booth

BEST BOOK OF THE YEAR

USA TODAY • AARP • REAL SIMPLE

"*Booth* is a triumph! No one writes like Karen Joy Fowler, and in this gripping family saga, she has taken a piece of American history we thought we knew and told it slant. With wit, heart, and revelatory insight, she teases ghosts from their shadows, transforming the way we see the past, shedding new light on our troubled present."

—Ruth Ozeki, author of *A Tale for the Time Being*

"Fate, history, and chance collide in Karen Joy Fowler's riveting historical novel. . . . What elevates *Booth* is the granular texture of what's beneath the bald facts: the how and the myriad whats and whys, the truths. And there is also Fowler's trademark dark humor. . . . A massive achievement. In it, Fowler weaves history, family culture, and human cruelties into an insightful reckoning of a past that seems too much a prologue to our American present."

—*The Boston Globe*

"Masterful . . . A dazzling blend of fact and fiction with piercing echoes to today . . . Fowler's excavation of this material is astonishing in its breadth and specificity, treating events of historical record with the same detail and care as secret bedtime talks and plays staged in treetops."

—*San Francisco Chronicle*

"*Booth* doesn't hold anyone in judgment; like all the best literature, it seeks to better understand the human heart in all its flawed complexity. It's a haunting book, not just for all its literal ghosts, but for its suggestion that those ghosts still have not been exorcised from this country."

—*USA Today*

"Fowler's riveting saga explores these strains of familial devotion and sorrow connecting the colorful Booth brothers and sisters."

—*The Washington Post*

"An ambitious novel . . . Slow-burning and rich, it illuminates America's core contradictions."

—*People*

"[Fowler] weaves an intimate, engaging portrait of a tribe whose aims and alliances were always shifting, buffeted by tragedy (several beloved siblings died young) and fickle fortunes."

—*Entertainment Weekly*

"An epic novel, it's both the story of an eccentric household and historical saga zooming in on the tumultuous lives of each family member as the country catapults into civil war."

—*Real Simple*

"Solid research mixed with empathetic imagination enriches *Booth*. . . . An engrossing tale . . . Fowler's narrative is packed with drama."

—*The Christian Science Monitor*

"An epic story that captures the unstable passions that disrupt the Booth family and the disagreements that set the nation on fire."

—*CBS News Sunday Morning*

"Fowler returns here with an ambitious and consequential saga about a family with a monster in their midst."

—*The Philadelphia Inquirer*

"Fowler's gripping historical novel takes us behind closed curtains to reveal their scandals and disasters in a book that shows us how a family can be torn apart and stitched back together."

—*Virginia Living*

"An enjoyable novel that offers historical insights into life in the antebellum border states and also brings to life sibling interactions of both love and rivalry during a very difficult period of American history."

—*Bowling Green Daily News*

"*Booth* is a sad, astonishing, and beautifully written look at a complicated, secretive family that failed to save one of their own from himself. Highly recommended."

—*Historical Novels Review*

"Like the very best historical novels, *Booth* is a literary feast, offering much more than a riveting story and richly drawn characters. It offers a wealth of commentary about not only our past but also where we are today, and where we may be headed."

—*BookPage* (starred review)

"Razor-sharp . . . Fowler sets the stage in remarkable prose. . . . The nuanced plot is both historically rigorous and richly imagined. This is a winner."

—*Publishers Weekly* (starred review)

"The historical context [Fowler] offers is of a pre–Civil War America of deep moral divides, political differences tearing close families apart, populism and fanaticism run amok. The similarities to today are riveting and chilling."

—*Kirkus Reviews* (starred review)

"Fowler presents an omniscient, bird's-eye view of these lives, along with a nod to what could be apocryphal. The result is an engrossing portrayal of a nineteenth-century family living through the United States' most turbulent era."

—*Booklist*

"One could write an old-fashioned horror novel, but an even better way to terrify modern readers is to show them the parallels between a gut-wrenching period of American history and today, as Karen Joy Fowler does in *Booth*. . . . That's what makes *Booth* so unsettling and thrilling: the many parallels between the Booth family's era and the present day."

—*Shelf Awareness*

"Like Tolstoy before her, and Natalia Ginzburg, Karen Joy Fowler understands that the only way to write about history is as clattery, complex dramas of ordinary people and their families—they become the stuff of history later. *Booth* is a subtly devastating meditation. . . . Its world— dense, granular, intricate—is created with immense care and precision, and rendered in prose of limpid, lyrical beauty. This is her finest, most beautiful novel to date."

—Neel Mukherjee, author of *A State of Freedom*

"A splendid book, displaying a dazzling range of style, tone, and odd, true insights. Fowler is one of a kind."

—Minneapolis *Star Tribune*

"A playful romp through the Pacific Northwest at the end of the last century, mixing poetry and newspaper reports into a wild yarn."

—*San Francisco Chronicle*

"*Sarah Canary* is certainly an enchanted and enchanting narrative, and Karen Fowler has found her way from the details of what we take to be our history, our past, to the legend that is our true present. Her powers of evocation of character and consequence, her storytelling gifts, are exhilarating, and she has given us, at the beginning of her writing life, a work with the suggestive authority—and the evanescent, haunting power—of myth."

—W. S. Merwin

"Remarkable . . . A larger than life, magical realist Western that is funny, mysterious, and harrowing by turns . . . Its imaginative virtuosity and stylistic resources announce Karen Joy Fowler as a major writer."

—*Newsday*

"Part adventure story, part history lesson, part flight of marvelous fancy, *Sarah Canary* is among the very best novels I have read this year."

—*The San Diego Union-Tribune*

BOOTH

A Novel

KAREN JOY FOWLER

G. P. Putnam's Sons

New York

PUTNAM
— EST. 1838 —

G. P. Putnam's Sons
Publishers Since 1838
An imprint of Penguin Random House LLC
penguinrandomhouse.com

Grateful acknowledgment is made for permission to quote letters from Asia
Booth Clarke to Jean Anderson, 22 May 1865, BCLM Works on Paper
Collection, ML 518, Box 37, H. Furlong Baldwin Library, Maryland
Center for History and Culture, Baltimore.

The Library of Congress has catalogued the G. P. Putnam's Sons
hardcover edition as follows:

Names: Fowler, Karen Joy, author.
Title: Booth: a novel / Karen Joy Fowler.
Description: New York: G. P. Putnam's Sons, 2022. |
Identifiers: LCCN 2021048770 (print) | LCCN 2021048771 (ebook) |
ISBN 9780593331439 (hardcover) | ISBN 9780593331446 (ebook)
Subjects: LCSH: Booth, John Wilkes, 1838–1865—Family—Fiction. |
Booth family—Fiction. | LCGFT: Biographical fiction. |
Historical fiction. | Novels.
Classification: LCC PS3556.O844 B66 2022 (print) |
LCC PS3556.O844 (ebook) |
DDC 813/.54—dc23/eng/20211008
LC record available at https://lccn.loc.gov/2021048770
LC ebook record available at https://lccn.loc.gov/2021048771

First G. P. Putnam's Sons hardcover edition / March 2022
First G. P. Putnam's Sons trade paperback edition / February 2023
G. P. Putnam's Sons trade paperback ISBN: 9780593331453

Printed in the United States of America
1st Printing

Book design by Katy Riegel

This book is dedicated to three people who, as teachers,

exemplars, and advocates, changed my life.

All three are gone now, but my gratitude

will last as long as I do.

To Chalmers Johnson, Ursula Le Guin,

and Marian Wood.

America is false to the past, false to the present, and solemnly binds herself to be false to the future.

—Frederick Douglass

We cannot escape history.

—Abraham Lincoln

1822

The people who live there call it the farm, though it's half trees, woodland merging into dense forest. A two-story, two-room log cabin has been brought from a nearby acreage on rollers greased with pig lard. The walls are whitewashed, the shutters painted red. A kitchen is added on one side, a bedroom and loft on the other. The additions stand off the main room like wings. There is nothing special about this cabin with its low ceilings, meager windows, and canted staircase, and moving it was a costly business, every local ox and man hired for the job. This all left the neighbors with the impression that the new owner was a bit crazy, a thought they never had cause to revise.

The relocation puts the cabin beside Beech Spring, where the water is so clean and clear as to be invisible. But, and the neighbors suspect that this is the real purpose, it's also a secret cabin now, screened from the wind and the road by a dense stand of walnut, oak, tulip, and beech. Still, since everyone in the neighborhood helped move it, everyone in the neighborhood knows it's there.

The nearest neighbors are the Woolseys on one side and the Rogerses on the other. Bel Air, the county seat, is three miles away; the big city of Baltimore some thirty miles of rough coach road to the south and west.

Improvements are made. Orchards of peach, apple, and pear are planted; fields of corn, cane sorghum, barley, and oats; a kitchen garden of radishes, beets, and onions. A cherry tree sprig is set near the front door and carefully tended. A granary, stables, barn, and milking shed are built. Three large, black Newfoundland dogs arrive to patrol the grounds. They are chained during the day and loosed at night. The neighbors describe these dogs as savage.

Zigzag fences are erected or repaired. The mail is delivered on horseback once a week, thrown over the gate by a postboy, who whistles through two fingers as he passes, driving the dogs to a frenzy of howling and rattling chains.

A secret family moves into the secret cabin.

SIXTEEN YEARS PASS. The family grows, shrinks, grows. By 1838, the children number at nine, counting the one about to arrive and the four who are dead. Eventually there will be ten.

These children have:

A famous father, a Shakespearean actor, on tour more often than at home.

A paternal grandfather, skinny as a stork, with white hair worn in a single braid, his clothing also fifty years out of fashion, breech trousers and buckle shoes. He's come from London to help out during their father's long absences. He was once a lawyer, treasonably sympathetic to the American revolutionaries, enthusiastic for all things American. Visitors to his London house were made to bow before a portrait of George Washington. Now that he lives here, he hates it. He likens the farm to Robinson Crusoe's island, himself a marooned castaway on its desolate shore. He's rarely sober, which makes him less helpful than might have been hoped.

An indulgent mother. A dark-haired beauty with retiring manners, she'd once sold flowers from her family nursery on Drury Lane. She'd first seen their father onstage as King Lear and was astonished, when meeting him, to find that he was young and handsome. He'd had to perform the Howl, howl, howl speech right there in the London street before she'd believe he was the same man. "When will you spend a day with me?" he'd asked within minutes of learning her name. "Tomorrow?" and she'd surprised herself by saying yes.

During their brief courtship, he'd sent her ninety-three love letters, pressing his suit with his ambition, his ardor, the poems of Lord Byron, and the promise of adventure. Soon enough, she'd agreed to run away with him to the island of Madeira, and from there to America.

Perhaps adventure was more implied than promised outright. After they'd left their families in England, after they'd had their first child, after they'd arrived in Maryland and leased the farm on a thousand-year lease, after he'd arranged to move the cabin onto it, only then did he explain that he'd be touring without her nine months of every year. For nine months of every year, she'd be left here with his drunken father.

What else could he do? he asked, leaving no pause in which she might answer; he was a master of timing. He needed to tour if they planned to eat. And clearly, she and the baby couldn't come along. There is nothing worse than an unhappy, complaining shrew for a wife, he'd finished, by way of warning. He didn't plan on having one of those.

So here she's been, on the farm, for sixteen years now. For seventeen years, almost without break, she's been either expecting a baby or nursing one. It will be twenty continuous years before she's done.

Later, she'll tell their children it was Lord Byron's poems that tipped the scales. She'll mean this as a caution but she'll know it won't be taken as such. All her children love a good romance.

None of the children know that they're a secret. It will come as quite a shock. They've no cause for suspicion. Much like the secret cabin, everyone they know knows they're here.

Lincoln and
the Perpetuation of
Our Political Institutions

Is it unreasonable then to expect, that some man possessed of the loftiest genius, coupled with ambition sufficient to push it to its utmost stretch, will at some time, spring up among us? And when such a one does, it will require the people to be united with each other, attached to the government and laws, and generally intelligent, to successfully frustrate his designs.
—Abraham Lincoln, 1838

In January of 1838, Lincoln delivers, to the Young Men's Lyceum of Springfield, his first major speech. He is one month shy of his twenty-ninth birthday, recently reelected to his third term in the Illinois General Assembly. He's already been a farmer, a clerk, a postmaster, a surveyor, an army captain, and a lawyer.

Two horrific murders, the first of a black man, the second of a white, form the backdrop to this speech. The first was the lynching of twenty-six-year-old Francis McIntosh in St. Louis. McIntosh was tied to a tree and burned alive. A grand jury being convened, the judge instructed them not to blame the mob, but rather those abolitionists who had stirred things up. He called one out by name—the minister and newspaper editor Elijah Lovejoy. Lovejoy then fled St. Louis for Alton, Illinois, where the mob killed him anyway. In *that* trial, the jury chair had been part of the mob and the judge himself was called as a witness for the defense. In neither case was anyone found guilty.

The death of the white man, Lovejoy, has a national impact. This is allegedly the moment John Brown decides to devote his life to the eradication of slavery. But both murders affect Lincoln deeply. In his speech, he warns of two possible threats to the republic. The first is found in the lawless actions of the mob, the second in the inevitable rise someday of an aspiring dictator. The gravest peril will come if the mob and the dictator unite.

BOOK ONE

What's in a name? That which we call a rose by any other word would smell as sweet.

—W. Shakespeare, *Romeo and Juliet*

Rosalie

THE LIVING

Rosalie, the oldest daughter, is sitting on the steps that lead down to Beech Spring, watching her baby brother and sister make boats out of leaves. She is thinking of Ophelia, drifting in her sodden gown, her hair spread over the water, her face surrounded by flowers. She is dreaming of what it would be like to be beautiful and dead. The month is March, the year 1838. In July, Rosalie will be fifteen years old. She finds Love Tragic more satisfying to contemplate than Love Triumphant.

Rosalie is neither dead nor beautiful though the first is easier for her to imagine than the second. She resembles her father and her older brother, but in miniature, and with little feminizing of their features. Reclusive, reticent, stocky, she is not witty and graceful like the rest. Nothing is expected of her, except that she be a good girl and a help to her mother. She wants little attention and gets less—the most unremarkable child in this remarkable family.

The long winter is just coming to its end. The blackbirds have arrived, the robins are expected, and Rosalie feels the turn in her breath, in her bones. She is not quite happy, but surprisingly close to it. She feels light. Perhaps the bad times are over.

The moment she registers the feeling, it slips away. There is a palpable relief whenever Father leaves on tour. Mail day is the exception. By noon, Mother will be reading a letter from Father. The letter will be good or it will be bad. Mother will need her desperately or she won't need her at all.

The sky above the trees is pale and bare and skims in reflection over the flat surface of the water. It's not a warm day, but it's a dry one. Rosalie is wearing her shawl, her bonnet, and a pair of sturdy boots that were bought some years ago for her brother June.

At sixteen, June is the oldest child. He's off in the barley fields this morning, because Father has read an article on some new fertilizing technique and so it must be tried at once. Father is always impatient for the completion of projects in which he has no part. He often berates his own father for lack of industry. Father thinks Grandfather drinks too much.

Grandfather thinks the same of Father. They quarrel about this endlessly whenever Father is home, often from their customary chairs at the Churchville Tavern, where all such arguments can be fueled by the jolly god.

Rosalie doesn't know where her grandfather is just now. Since her little brother Henry Byron died, Grandfather is often hard to find, and mostly they don't look. He comes. He goes. Sometimes he misses a meal, but not often. He used to give the children lessons, but really this was just for Henry; none of the other children are promising enough to interest him. Not June, who is more brawn than brains, a handsome, genial disappointment they once hoped would be a doctor or lawyer. Certainly not Rosalie.

Upslope, Mother appears at the door of the cabin, stands looking across the lawn. Her arms curve around her belly, holding it up like a great globe. She can't put on her shoes now or hook the laces without Rosalie's help.

Her face is in the sun, her eyes closed to better enjoy the warmth. She looks tired, but peaceful. She looks, just for the moment, like a young girl. "Someone is having a busy morning," she says, "swimming about in there." And then, opening her eyes, aging instantly back into her cares and worries, "Don't let Asia play so near the water." She vanishes back into the dark cabin.

As if Rosalie is not watching every move Asia makes.

As if Asia will do anything Rosalie asks! Asia is the youngest, if you don't count the swimmer in Mother's belly. Two years old, but only recently named and Rosalie still isn't used to thinking of her as Asia. Her parents had settled on Ayesha, or maybe Sidney, unable to choose between the two. Then suddenly, a letter from Father. "Let her be called Asia," he wrote, "because God first walked with man on that continent. With Frigga for a middle name since she was born on a Friday." Mother wasn't entirely pleased so they surreptitiously call her Asia Sidney now, and will until she's grown enough to bear the full weight of Frigga.

In point of fact, Asia was born on a Thursday.

Edwin, Rosalie's little brother, is four. Edwin is crying, which he does the way he does all things, quietly. He's been trying to collect pebbles and seed pods to be passengers in his boats, but Asia keeps taking them and throwing them into the spring.

Rosalie comes to kneel beside him, pushes up her sleeve with one hand, and reaches into the cold water with the other. She's distracted momentarily by the magic of her fingers elongating and refracting. Asia cannot throw well. Edwin's pebbles are easily rescued. She hands three back to him, wiping her cold hand on the hem of her skirt.

This makes Asia so angry she can't even speak. She points to the water and sobs. She stamps her feet and screams. Mother comes to the door again. "We're all fine here," Rosalie says, but she speaks so softly that only Asia and Edwin hear her. What she says makes Asia even louder and angrier since it isn't at all true.

All two-year-olds have terrible tempers, Mother says, but the others didn't, not like this. In the face of Asia's fury, Edwin surrenders his boats and his pebbles. Asia has them all now. Her cheeks dry in an instant. Already she has the beauty Rosalie lacks, dark hair, dark, shining eyes.

So does Edwin, who comes to lean against Rosalie, his bony shoulder cutting sharply into her upper arm. He smells like the biscuits they had at breakfast. Mrs. Elijah Rogers, their neighbor, had to teach Mother to make biscuits and corn bread on the kitchen's hearth when she first arrived at the farm. Now she's teaching Rosalie. A childless woman herself, she dotes on the Booths, all of whom call her Aunty. "I don't think your mother had ever cooked before," Aunty Rogers once told Rosalie, either to let her know that Mother was a real lady or else that Mother had been strangely incompetent by Bel Air standards; Rosalie has never been sure which was being conveyed. Mother's biscuits are fine now, but not as good as Aunty Rogers'. Or, to be honest, Rosalie's.

"The frog is sleeping," Edwin says. This doesn't sound like a question, but is. He wants to be told he is right. Edwin only asks questions when he already knows the answers.

"Old Mr. Bullfrog sleeps through the winter," Rosalie says. "He only wakes up when summer comes."

"Old Mr. Bullfrog is very old." Edwin is feeding her her lines.

"Very *very* old."

"A hundred years."

Bullfrogs don't live a hundred years. They are lucky to make eight. Grandfather says so. And yet Rosalie cannot remember a summer out of earshot of the enormous, bulbous frog. On warm evenings, when the insects are humming and the birds calling and the water rushing and the wind blowing and the trees rustling and the cows bawling, still that deep, booming groan can be heard. Neighbors a mile distant complain of the noise.

"At least a hundred years. He saw the American Revolution with his very own eyes. He drank the tea in the Boston Harbor." Rosalie feels her voice strangling in her throat. Henry Byron had always been the author of Old Mr. Bullfrog's rich and consequential past.

Some neighbors once approached Father with a request that the frog be killed in the cause of peace and quiet. Father refused. The farm is a sanctuary for all God's creatures, even the copperhead snakes. Father doesn't believe in eating meat and once, Mother says, rose up in a saloon to point his finger at a man enjoying a plate of oysters. "Murderer! Murderer! Murderer!" Father said in the same voice he used to play Macbeth. Sometimes you think Father might be joking, but you never can be sure.

Asia has finished throwing all of Edwin's boats and stones into the water. She turns in his direction a face shining with triumph, but immediately clouds over with the realization that Edwin hasn't been watching. She steps towards them and Rosalie shifts Edwin to her other side so he can't be pushed about. His knees soften until he's sitting in her lap. Asia comes to do the same, crowding into Rosalie's arms, taking up as much room as she can. Heat pours off her. Rosalie feels Edwin becoming smaller.

"Do you want to hear about you?" she asks him. He does. It's his favorite story.

"On the night you were born," she says, "Father was in New York being Richard III."

Rosalie remembers it as a terrifying night, but that's not the way she tells it. She skips the difficulties of the birth, Mother's agony, the moment the midwife told June to ride for the doctor. She skips the icy ground and her fear that June was riding too fast and the horse would lose her footing, or not fast enough and the doctor would arrive too late. Mother had had six other children and never needed the doctor before.

Rosalie tells Edwin instead that there was a shower of stars that night, lasting more than an hour. How, just as June was leaving, a great meteor exploded over Baltimore—Rosalie throws open her hands to show the explosion—and June rode on while the sky above him rained down stars.

She says that Edwin is the family's seventh child and that he arrived with his caul still over his face. The caul has been saved in a small box in her mother's cupboard. It has the feel of a well-worn handkerchief. Edwin has been shown this, but he won't be allowed to touch it until he is older.

All these things, Rosalie says—the stars, the caul, the number seven—they mark Edwin as extraordinary. "This child will see ghosts," the midwife had said when the doctor had gone and she was again in charge. "He will never drown. Men everywhere will know his name." She took Edwin and swaddled him more tightly. There was something reverential, ceremonial, in the way she handed him back.

Before, Rosalie has always left out the part about seeing ghosts. Today she forgets. She feels Edwin stiffen at this news. So far, he's shown no evidence of greatness. He's an inactive, fragile, anxious boy.

The ten-year gap between Rosalie and Edwin is where all the dead children are.

ii
—

THE DEAD

Frederick was the first to die. He died away from home, off in Boston where Father had gone to try his hand at managing the Tremont Theatre. Mother had joined him there, taking Frederick, who was too little to leave behind. Ann Hall, their farm manager's wife, and Hagar, a servant with no last name that either she or anyone else knew, cared for the rest of the children in their absence.

In November, only a few months past Frederick's first birthday, he died. Rosalie hadn't seen him since the summer. She missed his first words and his first steps. She desperately missed her mother. She was five years old.

The how and why of Frederick's death have never been made clear to Rosalie—an accident, but nobody's fault, is what she gathers, or maybe an illness. Father's experiment at management had lasted only two months and then, when he'd gone off to New York to perform again, Mother had remained in Boston with Frederick for another few weeks, arranging the move back. When Mother finally came home, she came home alone.

Father followed soon after, bringing Frederick, or at least a little coffin and everyone said Frederick was inside. Rosalie remembers how Mother hardly spoke for weeks, how she no longer appeared at bedtime to check the cleanliness of their hands and necks, or to kiss the children she still had. She remembers Mother's grief as peculiarly listless. There were no bouts of uncontrollable weeping, only an endless silent stream of tears. It was as if Frederick had taken her spirit along with him when he went, leaving only a Mother-shaped husk behind.

Rosalie remembers the exact moment she first understood that she was responsible now for Henry and for Mary Ann. She shared a bed with Mary Ann and one night, as Rosalie was crying quietly to herself, Mary Ann also began to cry. She was only two years old and didn't have the words to tell Rosalie why, except that she said that everyone was always crying.

"I'll stop," Rosalie told her and made an unpersuasive, gulping attempt to do so.

"Mama," Mary Ann said, crying harder than ever. "Mama."

Rosalie understood, or else she imagined, that Mary Ann was crying because there were no more good-night kisses. She rolled Mary Ann towards her and kissed her on the forehead, exactly as Mother used to do, though wetter. Then she got up, moving quickly through the cold room to kiss Henry, too, because apparently this job now fell to her.

She remembers another time, when she was sent outside with Henry and June to play quietly in the winter air and not be underfoot. She'd laid her red mitten on the trunk of the large sycamore, only to have it stick to the iced bark, vivid as a wound there. Her hand slipped out, leaving her staring at her pale, naked fingers. There'd been five of them: June, herself, Henry Byron, Mary Ann, and Frederick, but now there were four. They were no longer a full hand.

She missed Frederick, who was a lovely baby with dimpled elbows and two sharp teeth. When he crawled about the cabin, his little bottom swung merrily from side to side. Rosalie would hear him in the mornings, babbling quietly to himself. He never woke up crying as Edwin and Asia now often did.

But the way Rosalie missed him was not the way Mother and

Father missed him. She was shocked that he could disappear like that, right into the ground. She was more unsettled by the information his absence contained than by the absence itself. If it could happen to Frederick, what was to stop it from happening to her?

A large family graveyard was built around his grave, railed in with wire and planted with althea and jasmine. Even a five-year-old could see that plenty of room had been left for all the rest of them.

Three years later, Elizabeth was born, bringing the number of children back to five. But Elizabeth was never as hearty as Frederick, and it worried Rosalie. Her nose was always running and often scabbed under the nostrils. Rosalie decided not to become too attached.

This turned out to be wise. One dreadful February both Mary Ann and Elizabeth died. Father was off in Richmond performing Hamlet. He told them later that a prankster had taken out the skull usually used for Yorick and substituted a child's skull instead. As soon as his fingers touched the tiny head, Father said, he was nearly felled by a premonition of doom.

Two days later, a messenger arrived at the stage, covered with dust and stammering in his haste. He told Father that Mary Ann was dead of the cholera and that the baby Elizabeth and eleven-year-old June had it, too. Father had run immediately from the theater, still in his costume and stage paint, packing nothing.

Meanwhile, Rosalie watched the household collapse into madness. She was now nine years old. June was ill and Elizabeth deathly ill. Mary Ann was dead and Mother deranged, defiant, suicidal. This was not the quiet defeat that accompanied Frederick's death. This grief was a war against the world.

Aunty Rogers came every day to help Ann and Hagar with the

nursing and consoling, but Mother couldn't be consoled. "Let me die," Rosalie heard her saying, every day, every hour. "Just go away and let me die." Rosalie prayed for Father to come. Mother wouldn't die if Father told her not to.

But Father's arrival improved nothing. Rosalie ran outside to meet him when he came galloping in on his black-and-white pony, still dressed in his tights and cape, thwacking Peacock's sides with the flat of Hamlet's sword. He dismounted, handed the reins to Joe Hall, the farm manager, pushed Rosalie aside without a look, and demanded to see Mary Ann, a week dead now and buried. "Show me," he said. "Show me," he shouted.

It was a bright, sunny, cloudless day. Mother appeared at the door, summoned from Elizabeth's bed by the sound of his voice. She stepped onto the grass. She was still in her nightdress, her hair gone wild. He was caked with make-up and dust, as if his face was melting away. Horrid half-replicas of her mother and father. Rosalie was frightened of them both.

And yet, she was also hopeful. Father would fix things. It was why he'd come racing back. She took Henry's hand, his fingers wet since they'd recently been in his mouth, and they followed Joe Hall, Father, and Mother along the path to the graveyard. Already Father was shouting that he could restore Mary Ann to life and this was a level of fixing things Rosalie hadn't known was possible. Her heart lifted. "Bring me a shovel," Father told Joe.

Joe didn't move.

But the shovel was right there, leaning against the railing. Three steps and Father had it in his hands. "She wouldn't have died if not for me," Father said to Joe.

"God's will," Joe said. "Nobody's fault."

"God's punishment," said Father. "I've fallen from my beliefs, been careless in my habits. And God noticed."

The ground was loose over Mary Ann's coffin, easy to move. He dug and Mother sobbed, begging him to stop; he was breaking her broken heart, she said. And while all this was happening, Ann Hall suddenly arrived to take Rosalie and Henry away. "We don't need to watch this," Ann said, even though Rosalie desperately wanted to. Why couldn't she be there at the moment Mary Ann opened her eyes?

She sat with Henry on the grass in front of the cabin, leaning against Ann's legs, until Father came stumbling up the path with Mary Ann's coffin in his arms. Mother floated behind him in her cloud of insanity.

Ann told Rosalie and little Henry to go upstairs. They ascended slowly until Ann was no longer watching and then they sat together on one of the upper steps. It was smooth and cold and sloped a little in the middle where people put their feet. "It's all right," Rosalie told Henry. "Father is fixing it."

They could hear Father talking to Mary Ann, but they couldn't hear what he was saying. They couldn't hear Mary Ann answering. And then there was a roar as Father's grief consumed the heavens and Rosalie knew Father had failed. She knew then that she'd always known he would, even though only a few minutes before, Father failing at anything had seemed impossible.

The dead child was the only child that mattered. Father refused to leave the coffin, even to go see June or Elizabeth. He refused to have Mary Ann reinterred. Late that night, when no one was watching, he slipped from the cabin with the coffin and the child, hiding her somewhere in the considerable acreage of the farm.

Joe was sent for and he searched through the dark for many fruitless hours until the dogs finally led him right. Neighbors came, their lanterns swinging over the lane in the black night—Mr. Rogers and Mr. Shook and Mr. Mason. They gave Father drink and then forced him into the bedroom, where he shouted and called them names. They kept him confined while Joe returned Mary Ann to the earth. Ann wasn't there to shield Rosalie. Rosalie saw it all.

JUNE SURVIVED, BUT Elizabeth died and Father's being there didn't stop it. He began a punishing regime of penance, putting stones in his shoes and walking long distances on them. Hagar cooked meal after meal that no one ate, scraping the food from the plates and into the run where the dogs were. Father canceled all his upcoming engagements. He wrote to his closest friend, Tom Flynn, saying he couldn't leave his wife or she would kill herself.

Somewhere, in the midst of this tumult and agony, Edwin was conceived. He was born in November that same year with the stars and the caul, all as Rosalie had said.

When Father returned to his tour, he found that he could now summon the passion he needed only with drink. He played Louisville, where he witnessed firsthand the exuberant slaughter of the passenger pigeons, the same thing that twenty years earlier had so shocked Audubon.

Young as she was, Rosalie had also been through a pigeon year. She knew that you heard them before you saw them, a far-off sound of wings, like a ceaseless thunder, and, inside that, a song like sleigh bells. They passed in one continuous mass overhead, an ocean of birds, blotting out the sun for hours. There was no sky when they flew over, only pigeons above, in ripples of color, blue, gray, purple. Droppings fell like snow.

The farmers had run outside to protect their fields and fill their larders. They simply shot their rifles into the air. There was no need to aim. There was no way to miss. The bird mass coiled into the air and rose like a giant snake when the shots began. The dead plummeted and the living fell on the oat fields, stripping them in minutes. In trade for their crops, the farmers gathered the bodies into bushel baskets, not even bothering to collect them all. A handful of shots resulted in more dead birds than anyone could eat.

But Father hadn't been home, so he was seeing this for the first time. He was greatly affected by the terror of the dying birds, which drowned out even the noise of the guns. They died in inconceivable numbers.

The next day he went to the market and bought whole wagonloads of dead birds. He purchased a coffin and a cemetery plot, and he held a public funeral.

A crowd gathered. "What madness prompts you to such carnage?" Father shouted in anguished tones. "To the sin of killing these admirable creatures, with their fair colors and soft, tunable voices? Oh, you men are made of stone! Where is your mercy?"

The crowd was amused at first. The mood sobered when he compared the innocent birds to Christ on the cross. Then he said that Christ had been crucified for the sin of eating meat—no crucifixion without the loaves and fishes was his reasoning. *Then* he said that the Hindoos had the only true religion. He was arrested on the spot.

"Currently imprisoned for telling the truth to scoundrels," he'd written his father, who'd read the letter aloud to Mother while Rosalie listened unnoticed. "When, when, when," Grandfather asked, "will he tire of these mad freaks?"

IN 1835 ASIA was born.

IN 1836, THE year Rosalie turned thirteen, they lost Henry Byron. They were in England at the time, the whole family plus Hagar but minus Grandfather. Much as he now hated America, still he hated England more. Besides, he said, he had work to do. He was translating *The Aeneid* into English. He was trying to retain its rhythms while reworking it as a play for Father to star in.

Grandfather had spent the weeks before their departure creating months of lesson plans for Henry—science and literature and philosophy. Henry could do simple sums in his head when he was only four. By five he could read Father's reviews in the newspaper and the news of the day as well. He would sit in a kitchen chair, reading aloud to the women as they cooked and cleaned, charming them all by lisping his way through words like *spectacle* and *glorious*. Sometimes Father's reviews described him as *inebriated*, a word Henry mispronounced without correction. Ann Hall told them that inebriated meant full of spirit, and for a long time, the children all believed inebriated was the very highest praise until Grandfather, in an unkind moment, told them otherwise.

The trip was Father's idea, a way to remove Mother from the scene of so much loss but also another chance for him to dazzle the British audiences. It was his third such try, and still they refused to love him, comparing him unfavorably to Edmund Kean, no matter how he bellowed and declaimed. Edmund Kean! Who at the very start of Father's career had tricked him into a contract to keep him in bit parts. Whose followers came to Father's shows only to riot in the pit, fight and shout, throw orange peels onto the stage, and create such cacophony that no one could hear the play. Edmund Kean, dead and gone and still his relentless nemesis.

Once again, Father was found wanting in both physical strength and understanding of character. Kean, the reviews said, had understood Richard III as a man of consummate address, energy, and wit. Father had played him with nothing but bluster.

Father wrote home that ". . . *entre nous*, theatricals in England are gone to sleep—with all their puffing of full houses." He complained of the London Tricksters.

Those months in London provided the only schooling that Rosalie would ever have. She made no particular friends, too quiet and awkward for that, but her teachers were fond of her. She surprised her family by doing rather well. Father went so far as to write Grandfather and say so.

Before the trip all the children had been inoculated against smallpox. Still Edwin and Asia suffered light cases. Hagar had to be hospitalized, but she also survived. But Henry's inoculation didn't take. He died and his death was more terrible than either Mary Ann's or Elizabeth's.

Henry Byron had been the best loved of all the children. He was a quick, thoughtful, charming child. Their shining boy. For Rosalie, he was her rock, her constant companion, their tight bond forged during the terrible time of the cholera.

He'd climbed trees, rode hell-bent on horseback, knew and loved everything about the farm, everyone who lived on or near it. The summer before his death, June, Rosalie, and Henry had spent the time after their chores in a long game of Camelot, a game made into a play in which they all performed. June was Arthur and Merlin, Rosalie was Guinevere and Elaine, Henry was Lancelot and Galahad. The narrative, all Henry's, was short on romance, but long on jousts. They played this game under trees so thick with leaves that Rosalie could remove her bonnet and crown herself with flowers, and no reddened cheeks or freckled nose would give her away at bedtime. They stole capes and wooden swords from Father's chests, went smashing about among the branches and roots.

"'Hie thee home to me,'" she would say to Arthur openly or secretly to Lancelot, and she went so deep into believing, it was hard to come back and be Rosalie again. Sometimes she wondered if she could have been onstage like Father had she only looked like Mother. It still seemed possible then that she might come into her beauty. If she did, she'd run away and join a troupe and be someone else every day of her life. They'd played this game in what Henry called the green light of the forest, and it kept them out of the sad, sorry house where children died.

One day Lancelot had been sent off into the trees on a quest. Five minutes later he'd reappeared. "Rosalie! June!" he'd called. "Come see!" Between the path and the forest was an open space that led all the way to the swamp and every inch of it was covered in wild lilies. It was Henry's idea that they pick some for Mother, an extravagance of lilies, as many as they could carry, to overwhelm her with the sheer mass of beauty.

"How lovely!" Mother had said and immediately taken them in armloads, more than she could carry in a single trip, to the graveyard.

Henry's own grave remained in England. There was no way to bring him home.

GRIEF HAS DESTROYED Rosalie's parents right before her eyes. No wonder Edwin was born so anxious. No wonder Asia was born so angry. It seems to Rosalie that God has reached down and scooped out the middle of her family as casually as if He were eating a watermelon.

iii

If all these deaths made June stolid, and Edwin anxious, and Asia angry, then what of Rosalie?

Rosalie has become cautious. Since Henry's death, she hasn't spoken above a whisper. She's the only child who suffered neither cholera nor smallpox, but one's luck will always run out eventually. Henry Byron's did.

She still goes to the Mount Zion church with Mother, but now it's a part she's playing, the pious daughter. This is not her first falling-out with God. One Sunday morning, when she was eight, she overheard two women talking about her. Such a shame about Rosalie, one had said, her voice low and sympathetic. Rosalie didn't understand at first. What about her was such a shame?

But then the other woman—And her mother so beautiful!

No girl knows she's ugly until someone tells her so and every ugly girl remembers the someone who first told her. Rosalie had gone home and looked in the mirror, hoping the women were mistaken. She couldn't really assess her own face and this kept hope alive until the years brought further confirmation. Still, it hurt and it seemed to Rosalie that God shouldn't have allowed her to learn this in His very own church. He shouldn't have made her look so much like someone she was not. Or, what if she looked exactly like who she was? What if it turned out she wasn't beautiful on the inside either?

Later, she'd come to see that these feelings arose from her own sin of vanity. She didn't exactly forgive God, but she did shoulder her share of the blame.

This time is worse. This time she'd prayed for Henry to recover and God had responded by sending the swarm of red sores that covered and swelled his eyelids, ringed the inside of his mouth and nose, made his death an agony. Rosalie wanted no further dealings with Him. She didn't even care that Henry was in heaven now. There was no excusing such a death.

So her carefulness is a secular matter, intended more for her mother than herself. One more lost child, Rosalie thinks, will do Mother in. Rosalie will not be that one more child.

And yet, she can't help but wonder just exactly how much grief her death would cause; she sometimes spends those moments before sleep trying to imagine it. Would Father dig her up? Would Mother wake the stars with her weeping? There is an odd pleasure in these fantasies. Rosalie returns to her coffin again and again in dreams.

Ironically, it irritates Mother considerably, her silly whispering, her refusal to go out and about in the world.

ROSALIE IS KNEELING on the dirt floor in front of the kitchen fireplace, trying to unbutton her little sister's dress so Asia can nap in her underclothes. The room is too warm and smells of burnt eggs because Asia threw her custard into the fire when Mother said she had to eat it all. The biscuit dough is resting in its bowl on the scarred kitchen table until Rosalie has time to roll it out and there is wet laundry waiting to be hung.

Rosalie hears the frantic barking of the dogs and feels the lash of anxiety this causes her. The mail has arrived too early. Half an hour later and June could have gotten it on his way in to supper.

Asia picks up her shoe and hits Rosalie with it, once in the arm and once in the face. It surprises Rosalie more than it hurts her. Mother comes to stand over them. She's too pregnant to kneel down herself; she would never get up again. "Go get the mail," she tells Rosalie, "and leave the naughty girl behind," which makes the naughty girl scream.

Asia sobs and kicks her feet. "No nap!" she tells Rosalie. "No nap! No nap!"

Rosalie pretends she hasn't heard either one of them. She continues to wrestle with Asia. "Rosalie," Mother says firmly. "You will go and get the mail." She pauses so that the next sentence will sound like a concession. Father is not the only one in the family with a sense of dramatic timing. "You can take the dogs."

The dogs are howling now—*Howl, howl, howl*, Rosalie thinks, because any child in this family can summon up a Shakespeare quote when needed. *Screw your courage to the sticking place.*

"I haven't finished the biscuits yet," Rosalie says.

"I can finish them." Mother's words are clipped and clear. At first she'd pretended Rosalie's fearfulness would pass. When it didn't, she'd tried to coax Rosalie out of it. "You used to love to play outside," she'd say and, it's quite true, Rosalie did. She used to love to play outside with Henry Byron.

She remembers wandering all over the farm, sometimes with other children, sometimes alone—into the dairy, the cider press, the barn, the murk of the forest, the edge of the marsh. She'd walked on paths her father told her the Algonquin Indians had made, and brought home arrowheads and tomahawks. She remembers these things with equal parts loss and alarm. How happy she'd been, that wild child. How innocent.

How careless. How defenseless.

Her coaxing having made no difference, Mother now turns

stern. This nonsense has gone on long enough. She gets Rosalie's bonnet from the wall peg, pulls it on over Rosalie's braids. She ties it, perhaps too tightly. She stands at the door until Rosalie goes through it.

Rosalie looses the dogs. It excites them almost past their endurance to be freed. There are two of them now, Veto and Rolla, the gentler offspring of the original savages, a trio who used to slip the property in order to rip out the throats of the neighbors' pigs, so that Father was forced to buy the bodies and, much to his horror, let them be eaten.

Veto and Rolla race first to the cabin, where Asia has continued to carry on and they are anxious to discover who would torment a child so. After that, they scatter and Rosalie has to call them back. They return, leap about her, the barking and Asia's crying both rising in pitch and volume and still Rosalie can hear her own heartbeat, banging away in her ears. She dislikes loud noises. They make her head ache.

She unties her bonnet, but it doesn't help. The gate is a quarter mile away. Mother is in the doorway, watching. "The mail won't walk itself here," she says, unkindly since it could easily walk here with June. When Rosalie returns, *if* Rosalie returns, Mother may wish she hadn't been in such a hurry for Father's letter. One never knows about Father's letters.

Rosalie takes a heavy step, and then another, and then another. The dogs pad along beside her, quietly now, but Rosalie can hear them panting, and she forces herself to concentrate on all the things she can hear, tease them apart: the four-note stream where they swim, a six-note mockingbird in the woods, a far-off woodpecker drumming for insects, the wind shuffling new leaves. Her staccato heart, beating, beating, beating.

She makes it past the beeches and out into the open. She tilts her head back, and the great blue wheels above her, a dizziness so empty she feels it sucking her straight up into the sky. There is so much noise. The world is shrieking and spinning around her.

She runs for the woods. Soon, but it doesn't feel soon, she's skirting the meadow of the family graveyard. The pink hibiscus is already budding on the iron railing. Mother used to tell her that those flowers were gowns the fairies wore when they went to fairy balls; the bare rings in the forest where grass never grows, their ballrooms. Rosalie wanted to pluck the blooms, waltz them in pairs in her hands, but Father said no. No trees felled nor flowers picked on the farm. In his presence, at least, the older children follow these rules scrupulously. The younger will turn out less compliant.

Mother believes that her dead children are all eating from golden plates and flying about on silken wings, but Rosalie knows otherwise. She feels the breeze-like fingers of the three children buried nearby. They touch her face, her neck, whisper excitedly about this living thing on the path. They weave about her, web her in, whispering about the things that she evokes in their memories: *churned butter honey biscuits warm milk bonnet ties when the wind blows little redcap little redbreast perhaps when you've taken a nap your little white cheek will be red didn't you ever dream of a house up on a treetop the sea you can never be sure of it.*

Stars, hide your fires, they tell her. *Don't leave us here.*

How shocked everyone would be to learn that the child who consorts with ghosts is Rosalie. She does this so that Mother won't have to.

Now comes a part of the path so dangerous that the ghosts don't follow. Rosalie has seen strange men here before, here where the path and the forest meet. She's seen dark figures draw back into the shadows as she passes, hide behind the largest tree, a massive trunk all sheathed in lichen. Maybe it was only one man and one time. She knows that people come to the forest to hunt. Sometimes the baying of hounds can be heard, or the crack of a rifle, sometimes a tree is hit and bleeds its golden sap, but no hunter would have felt the need to duck away at the sight of her. She gestures for Rolla to stay close, but Rolla ignores this and Rosalie can't risk raising her voice, calling attention to herself.

A few months back, Grandfather had taken her aside for a warning. Now that she's growing up, he'd said, she should know some things. Some hard truths. The forest is a place where girls disappear, and not just the pretty ones. Then things are done to them, the things all the more terrifying for being so vague. He mentions Alex Verdan, who farms nearby, and whom every child in Harford County, boy and girl, black and white, has been warned to stay away from. Not that she'd meet Mr. Verdan in the forest, but someone like Mr. Verdan. Why, Rosalie wonders, was she ever allowed to play there?

She's almost certain now that she's being watched. The very fact that she's running confirms it. She hears footsteps behind her, each one timed exactly to match her own, and if no one is there when she looks back that just suggests a preternatural cunning.

She reaches the gate, breathless and with her hair coming out of her braids and into her face. She's teary and phlegmy, because she still has to return and it seems unfair. Having made it here really should have been enough for Mother. She sits down on the walk beside the bag of mail, her back against the gate, the dogs crowding in close, flanking her protectively. The damp of the ground seeps through her skirt and two petticoats. She wipes her face with a petticoat hem.

All three of them are panting. Rosalie takes hold of Veto's ruff, pulls him in, his black fur and wet breath hot in her face.

She puts her head on the hard ridge of his head. He holds very still until she's breathing more steadily and can let him go.

To delay her return, she makes a fan of the mail in her lap. Five letters for her father, two of them from England in the same female hand. A magazine with articles about farming. Two play-bills for shows in Philadelphia and Boston. Three newspapers. Two letters for her mother, both from Charleston, but only one of them from Father. The packet is too thin to contain money. Mother will be sorry about that; there are always bills to pay. Rosalie holds the letter to her forehead to see if she can tell by touch alone what it might do to Mother. She cannot.

She's become so attuned to her mother's moods that there are times when Rosalie can't be sure what she's feeling belongs to her. Her mother complains that her back hurts, and Rosalie begins to feel an ache just below her neck, a cramping in her shoulders, a twisting of her spine. Is she really worried about Father's letter or is her mother worrying through her? Is she really the one too fright-ened to leave the house, or is that Mother who, for all her indigna-tion over Rosalie's timidity, can't let a child out of her sight?

She decides that she'll look for bluebirds on the way back. If she sees one before she gets to the cabin, Father's letter will make her mother happy and if she doesn't, it won't.

To the delight of the dogs and her own relief, June joins her on the path beside the graveyard. He hands her a stalk of cane sorghum and she puts it in her mouth, tastes the sweetness of its syrup on her tongue. In his company, the dead children are si-lent. Even the sky brightens and quiets.

"I hate farming," June tells her. His face is red from the morn-ing's work. "I *won't* be a farmer." Rosalie is the only one he can say this to. Running the farm is Father's plan for June since he shows no particular brilliance for anything.

The cherry tree at the front door is just budding. Father has had it grafted so the blooms will vary from one side of the tree to the other, and this year, the graft having taken and aged, they hope to have some red cherries along with the usual black.

Rosalie remembers how often she used to climb that tree. It was a balcony from which Juliet's speeches could be shouted down to Romeo. But there was a time when she was seated on a branch, her skirts rucked up, eating all the ripe cherries she could reach. Birds above her were doing the same, and making a joyful noise until suddenly they weren't. It took Rosalie a moment to notice how quiet the tree had become. She looked up and a large snake was twisting down the trunk in her direction, its tongue protruding as if it could already taste her. Rosalie nearly fell in her haste to get down.

"It was probably perfectly harmless," Mother said, but Rosalie knows better. Even in the old familiar places, in places you know and love, in your very home, peril is hidden like a serpent in the leaves.

There's a bird in the tree now, a jay, who turns sideways to pin her with a glassy eye. This is not the kind of bluebird she meant, but it is blue, so it's an unclear omen in the end.

iv

The letters to Father are stuffed into the chaos of papers on his desk, amidst the wigs, the hats, the bills, the journals, account books, and press clippings. Books by Dante, Shelley, Torquato Tasso. Shakespeare lies open, facedown on the clutter.

The letter from Father, Mother reads to herself and then reads again aloud to Rosalie and June. She sits in one of the hard ladder-back chairs, her belly resting on her knees. Even at mid-day, the windows are too small for the room to be bright. Mother holds the letter right up to her face.

About Charleston, he writes: "There is a greater suavity of manners than can be found in the Northern States—and were it not for the unnecessary and wicked treatment of the colored peo-ple the Carolinians would have few blemishes."

He is likewise impressed with the quality of the fruits and vegetables. The weather, he says, is wonderful, not too hot for an audience, not too cold for a night on the town. He boasts of the large turnout for his first *Othello*. He says he got fine reviews.

And then he includes this quote from a letter to the editor: "We consider him not only as the ornament and glory, but the victim of his profession." Mother's eyes flick to Rosalie. June is oblivious, but Rosalie understands her instantly. It's an odd quote and Mother is wondering what he means by including it.

He sends them all his love and an admonition to be sure the babies don't go outside without proper shoes. This is so impor-tant for their health! he says. "You see how your father is always thinking of you," Mother says, though it sounds as if he is think-ing of Edwin and Asia, not June and Rosalie. He sends no money.

The babies are supposed to be napping, but Rosalie can still hear Asia talking to herself up in the loft. She's getting louder and Mother is worried she'll wake Edwin, so Rosalie goes upstairs to lie down with her. Asia does everything wholeheartedly. When she sleeps, she sweats with the effort of it. Soon there is a damp spot on Rosalie's sleeve where Asia's head has been. It smells like sour milk.

By the time Asia is settled, June has already finished his dinner and gone. Mother is still at the table, her forehead on one bent arm, her food untouched. Rosalie can see the sharp line of white scalp where Mother's hair is parted. Rosalie's breath turns to thorns in her throat. "Mother?" Rosalie asks.

Mother raises her face. It's flushed and wet.

She hands Rosalie the second letter from Charleston, this one from Thomas Flynn. Flynn is Father's manager as well as his closest friend. He'd accompanied Father to Charleston at Mother's request, to keep an eye on things. His letter is an apology for having failed to do so. His handwriting is cramped and uneven. Rosalie has a hard time with it, but she does make it out at last.

As the boat took them down to Charleston, Mr. Flynn has written, Rosalie's father became increasingly obsessed with Elder Conway, an actor acquaintance who'd drowned himself several years back in these same Atlantic waters. Father asked to be alerted when they reached the exact spot, though of course no one knew the exact spot, but the captain eventually said they were now somewhere in the vicinity.

Father had waited for Mr. Flynn to be distracted, then gone out, swung himself over the upper railing, and dropped noisily onto the promenade deck. This didn't go unnoticed. A crowd gathered on the deck above, calling for him to climb back. He looked up at all their faces. "I have a message for Conway," he shouted and then he jumped.

He was half a mile behind the ship, floating in the frigid waters, by the time the captain could get the safety boat to him. Mr. Flynn said that Rosalie's father had scolded him for nearly upsetting the boat while pulling him aboard. "My goodness, Tom, you'll drown us all if you're not more careful," Rosalie's father had said.

"I hope my letter reaches you before you hear about this elsewhere," Mr. Flynn has written. "By the time we arrived in Charleston, there was already considerable press."

Mother watches as Rosalie reads to the end. "We have no secrets between us," Mother has begun to tell her, which certainly isn't true on Rosalie's side, and Rosalie wishes weren't true on her mother's either. There are things she's glad to know and things she'd rather not. Mother never says, "We have no secrets," to June, which sometimes makes Rosalie think she loves Rosalie best and sometimes makes her think just the opposite.

Father's attempt to kill himself is one of those things Rosalie would rather not know about, the second suicide attempt of which she's aware—a hanging first, a drowning now—and June is not. What would happen to them all if Father were gone?

She comforts herself that when he actually wants to die he'll be less theatrical about it, and she takes further comfort in the fact that he's incapable of being less theatrical. Her father would never waste the dramatic potential of suicide. It's a big scene; it demands a big audience.

"I must go to him," Mother says. She makes two attempts to rise before she manages it with her huge belly and her shaking legs. She packs her case. She talks to Grandfather and to Ann and Joe Hall. At the last minute, she decides to take Edwin along. Edwin, she says, will cheer Father. So the tractable child goes and the intractable child stays.

v
———

THE ENSLAVED

June and Rosalie are not left fending for themselves and caring for Asia alone in the wilderness with only their drunken grandfather to help. Far from it. By 1838, the farm is home to some forty people, most of them slaves who live in a scatter of cabins at the forest's edge. Father has leased these slaves from their owners to work the farm, but he also pays them wages directly and a handful have been able to buy freedom with that money.

Once, when Rosalie was nine or so, she heard Aunty Rogers say to Mother that the distance between owning a slave and leasing one was not so great. "In my house," Mother had said, "we respect the natural dignity of every single person God made." Rosalie was shocked by how angry she sounded. Suddenly it seemed as if Aunty Rogers and Mother were quarreling.

But then Mother asked about Aunty Rogers' bad knee, which, as luck would have it, was very bad on this particular day, bad enough to require a detailed description. "It cuts under my knee-cap like a knife," Aunty Rogers said, and then, feeling the insuf-ficiency of this, "like a ribbon of fire." The contentious subject of slavery was forgotten. Ann, who was working in the kitchen at the time, said that's a shame about Aunty Rogers' knee.

Ann and Joe Hall are more like family than Aunty Rogers, yet Rosalie doesn't think of them as aunt and uncle, only as Ann and Joe. Joe came to the farm in 1822, so she's never known a home without him. He's been a steady, comforting presence in her life.

In Father's absence, Joe runs everything. He sets out the work schedules; he plants the crops; he runs the dairy; he oversees the workers; he does whatever repair jobs need doing. Joe is very black and very tall, a giant well over six feet while Father barely clears five. "Well, I can't help but laugh," Aunty Rogers told Rosalie once, "when I see them two try to put their heads together."

When she was four or so, Rosalie asked Joe why he was so dark and he told her he was descended from the royal house of Madagascar. It had thrilled Rosalie to think that a lost prince was tilling Father's fields.

She continued to daydream about it. For a while she inked in the faces of royals on Father's playbills—Hamlet and Richard and even Othello, whom Father played darker than most, but never nearly as black as Joe. She'd imagined Joe restored to his kingdom, possibly through her connivance, the role she'd have in his court. She'd altered the stories she knew about King Arthur to fit, tried to think how Joe might prove his claim. He was terribly strong. Pulling a sword from a stone would be almost too easy. Possibly he'd kept something, a brooch his mother had pinned to his swaddling clothes, something he could now produce. Possibly he had a birthmark by which he could be identified as the rightful king, not something she could ask him, but not impossible. Rosalie loved to imagine the court gathered as she herself argued his case, their suspicions turning gradually to joy. Something would have to be done about his name, of course. She'd never heard of a King Joe.

As infants, all the children slept in beautiful wicker baskets Joe made for them. As youngsters, they trailed him about the farm like ducklings. As adolescents, they love him no less, but they begin to find his lack of education, his grandiose claims, and his interminable stories amusing. They entertain each other imitating his speech. As an adult, Asia will refer to him fondly as *faithful*. Their faithful old Joe.

JOE'S WIFE IS a slave on the Rogers estate. Not Aunty and Elijah Rogers, but the larger estate of Elijah's father, Rowland Rogers. With Father's wages, Joe is slowly gathering the five hundred dollars Ann will cost. Rosalie can't wait for this to happen. Then Ann will finally live here on the farm with Joe. Then their babies will be free born.

They have two children already, two girls—Lucinda and little Mary Ellen—both of whom belong to Rowland Rogers. Ann is pregnant again and this baby, too, will be his.

Ann and Joe do nothing but work, not just on the farm, but anywhere they can find a job—sewing, carpentry, fieldwork, and farming—but a day has only so many hours in it. The pennies are slow to accumulate. Rosalie hears Ann talking with Mother. It makes sense for Joe to buy Ann first, since that will mean freedom for any babies that follow. But the children would be cheaper, and, should Rogers have a bad harvest, he's more likely to sell them. So should they buy Lucinda as soon as they can or the baby as soon as it arrives? Or should they keep saving for Ann?

Mother tells Rosalie privately that she needn't worry about any of this. Mother is sure that Mr. Rogers won't sell Ann's children away. He's reckoned to be a generous man and a tolerant slaver by every white person in the neighborhood.

She seems remarkably oblivious to how much Ann hates him though it's obvious to Rosalie. Ann and Joe have been married for years, but Mr. Rogers never lets Ann stay the night here. And Rosalie knows that Mother knows that one day when Ann was working in his fields, he'd refused to send for her as one of her own children choked to death.

Ann and Mother are bound together by their dead children. Ann has two—the little boy who choked and a baby girl who died before she could be named. Both are buried here on the farm. In working for Mother, Ann has traded time with her living children for time with her dead. Their graves abut the family graveyard, but outside the railing rather than in.

Rosalie has never felt their presence, but then she wouldn't recognize them by feel or voice. It's possible they're there and just not interested in Rosalie. Sometimes she thinks she'll ask Ann if they speak to her, but she always thinks better of it. Mother must never learn about the ghosts.

So ROSALIE GREW up with slaves all about her. As a child, she swam with the children, climbed after them into trees, joined the pack following Joe Hall, their personal Pied Piper, as he went about his business. They were some of her first playmates, but their childhoods ended while they were still children and they were returned to the estates that owned them, to work the houses and fields while their parents remained in Father's employ.

She'd had one particular friendship, lasting nearly two years, with a little boy named Nelson. Nelson was, like Henry Byron, good at making up games and good at playing the games he'd made up. Nobody knew exactly how old he was, but probably younger than Henry and certainly younger than Rosalie. He would come into the yard some mornings after breakfast and whistle for June or Henry or Rosalie to come out—not a one-note, fingers-in-the-mouth whistle, though he could do that, too, but a whole stanza of a song Rosalie didn't know.

Many years later, quite grown-up, Rosalie will hear this song again, hear it played on the fiddle by a man in a Baltimore park, when she is out for a Sunday stroll with her family. The others will walk on oblivious, but the tune will come for her like a fist, knocking the breath from her lungs. That tune will bring back everything. Nelson first, of course, Nelson smiling up at her from the yard, and then, the sharp, cutting memory of Mary Ann, begging to be allowed to come along when Rosalie leaves her to run off and play, and of Elizabeth, her arms outstretched, her cheeks flushed, her nose running, her light hair sparse over her baby skull.

And finally, Henry Byron, lying with her on the grass, the

sound of bees all about them. Lying without her on his bed, the
sores rising on his face, his hands, his neck, everywhere, everywhere, even inside his eyes.

She asks the fiddler what the tune is called. No one notices
this uncommon behavior, Rosalie speaking to a strange man,
because no one ever notices Rosalie. "It's called 'Poor Rosey,'"
he says—and the surprise of this will stop her cold. Had Nelson
known that? Had he pitied her? Was he making fun of her? "Do
you like it?" the fiddler will ask, and she'll hear him, but only
after she's already walked on.

She'd liked Nelson and she'd thought he'd liked her. On rare
occasions, when June and Henry Byron were busy with something else and Rosalie wasn't, Nelson had never minded playing
with just Rosalie. It hadn't happened often, but it had happened.
Had they never really been friends at all? Rosalie hasn't had so
many friends in her life that she can readily give one up, even one
she will surely never see again. She needs to believe that Nelson
liked her as much as she'd liked him.

Nelson's head was periodically shaved to prevent or eradicate
lice, so when he had hair, it was short. His two front teeth hadn't
come in yet, which helped his whistling and showed as a gap
when he smiled. He smiled all the time.

He never wore shoes. "Course I have 'em," he said, "just don't
like 'em," which made Henry Byron realize he didn't like 'em
either. Rosalie's feet weren't tough enough to run around the
forest unshod, and June chose not to, but Henry and Nelson did
just that until one of the dogs made off with one of Henry's shoes
and returned it half gnawed, and Mother made him wear it anyway, because he never should have taken it off in the first place.
Did he want to end up with ringworm? she asked. And then said
that June and Rosalie should have known better than to permit

it. Because any misbehavior in a younger child was always the fault of the older. That was how a family worked.

There was one day with June off somewhere, when Henry Byron, Rosalie, and Nelson went down to where the Hickory Road crossed the creek. The sun was seeping through the trees, landing on the water in stars and sparkles. Squirrels were chasing each other through the high branches, rabbits eating in the grass. Henry got the idea to put a dam in, make a fishing hole. If they did it right, they wouldn't even need poles. They could just reach in and scoop the trapped fish out with their hands. "Then we build a fire," Nelson said, a bubble of spit rising through the gap in his teeth in excitement, "and roast 'em on sticks. Steal some 'tatoes from the bins, bury them in the coals. Eat like kings!"

They scattered to gather up logs to make the dam. Rosalie made a try at helping though the plan didn't inspire her the way it did them. She'd found a log, too heavy to pick up and it still had branches so she couldn't roll it. She'd managed to raise it just a little bit, which sent a dozen bugs, a hundred legs—centipedes, wood lice, white-as-ghosts spiders—streaming in the direction of her feet.

"Father won't let us kill fish," she reminded Henry, lowering the log to the ground again. "We'll be whupped if he finds out." Nelson's role was to be game for anything. Rosalie's was not. The fish are safe from her.

At Rosalie's suggestion, they have an egg-fry instead. She fetches three eggs from the henhouse, snatching them warm from their smelly nests, the chickens gabbling about her. By the time she returns, the boys have a fire going. Nelson has collected a pot and filled it with water. They eat the eggs hot from the shells. It's enough like being kings to satisfy them all.

Another day: Nelson had found a large patch of moss in a

forest clearing that he said was soft like a carpet, like the red Turkish rug by the fireplace in the cabin. He'd come looking for someone to show and found only Rosalie and he'd taken her to it, holding on to the branches like a gentleman so they wouldn't whip back and lash Rosalie in the face.

Better than a carpet, Rosalie agreed. Much better. Henry Byron had arrived then and the two boys built a makeshift lean-to over the moss, a house of sticks, just large enough for the three to sit together inside, arm touching arm touching arm. Rosalie could feel the damp cold beneath her. She could smell the smoky, sweaty odor of the boys on either side.

"We be dry here even when it rains," Nelson said, as if the sun weren't filtering right through the roof, dappling Rosalie's hands and his own face. Under the leaves, they made plans. The boys decided to be Indians. But Rosalie opted for the comforts of the Swiss Family Robinson. While the boys planned hunts and raids, Rosalie imagined bedrooms and ballrooms, water that dripped through hollowed logs so they could wash their hands and their dishes.

Henry Byron and Nelson were always rearranging the world— lugging in stepping-stones to make new paths across the creek to its little island, moving logs and branches to be dams and bridges, forts and teepees. They dreamt of escape, of leaving their chores and lessons, their houses and families, and moving to the woods. For Rosalie, the escape was very real, a temporary respite from Mary Ann and Elizabeth and the tedium of caring for babies. She never knew if it was also real for Nelson.

And then, Nelson stopped coming. This happened right around the time her sisters died, so she didn't notice at first, too busy with the calamity of seeing everything she'd known collapse. Too secretly ashamed of how tired she'd been of being the oldest girl, of how often she'd chosen to slip off with the boys into the trees instead.

When she finally missed him, Rosalie worried that Nelson had also died in the cholera. She sought out Ann in the kitchen to ask. No, none of the other children had died, Ann told her. About Nelson she simply said, "Sold."

Rosalie was relieved.

"Sixty-five dollars," Ann said.

Rosalie was impressed. At nine years old, she was unable to imagine his life much changed. She assumed that wherever he was, Nelson was building forts, streaking his face with war-paint mud, smiling his gappy smile. If someone paid sixty-five dollars, she thought, they must love Nelson very much.

But perhaps she had doubts, because of what she'd asked next. "He's happy, don't you think?" she'd said and then, to prompt Ann into the right answer, added, "Nelson's always happy."

"Children can snatch happiness from even the darkest times," Ann said. "That's God's gift, that's how God loves children. You grow up, you can't do that no more. You don't have that gift. God's taken it back."

And, just as they would again all those years in the future, Rosalie's losses crowded into her heart, a heavier weight than she could bear. Frederick and Elizabeth, Mary Ann and Nelson. Mother's happiness and Father's sanity. She was too big now for Ann's lap, but Ann sank into one of the dining table chairs and gathered her in anyway, rocking her and humming something church-like, as if Rosalie were still a child, which she now, in her deep unhappiness, understood for the first time that she was not.

She'd lost that, too.

———

AND STILL, EVEN with this all everywhere about her, Rosalie had given little thought to slavery—slavery was a thing that just was—until they'd made that terrible trip to England with Hagar accompanying them. One day in school Rosalie mentioned her. Hagar, Rosalie had said, was a slave. She could feel the shock this caused. "Not *our* slave," she'd clarified quickly, but the damage was done.

Soon there was a lesson in which they all learned that slavery was a decision a country made, and that a country could always make a better decision. No one should be a slave to anyone else, one of the other girls said during this lesson, and the teacher agreed. It wasn't Biblical, the girl said. "That's what we think, too," Rosalie told her, though she was pretty sure it was Biblical even if it was also wrong.

Back in America, back in their sad, depleted home, Hagar had unexpectedly asked Father for permission to return to the estate of Dr. Elijah Bond. She was owned by Dr. Bond, and had been raised on that large and prosperous property, though she'd been working for Father and Mother for years now.

Before England, Hagar had seemed happy enough. She used to sing in the kitchen as she worked. After, she was different, distracted and silent. No one, not even Rosalie for all her watchfulness, took note. They were all sunk in their own grief. Why wouldn't Hagar be the same? She'd loved Henry Byron, too.

No one stopped to wonder what Hagar's narrow escape from death by smallpox might have meant to her. No one thought about what the freedom of England might have looked like to a slave in Maryland.

Father's first response to her request was no. Absolutely, no.

Mother needed her more than ever. Besides, it was in Hagar's best interest to stay on the farm. "Why return to slavery?" he asked her, not noticing that she'd recently done exactly that. Here, on the farm, she was salaried and loved. It made no sense. He wouldn't allow it.

Grandfather stepped in. "If you believe in freedom," he told Father, which Father was always insisting he did, "you'll agree this is Hagar's choice to make."

The last time Rosalie saw Hagar, she was riding away in the back of a cart, her back stiff and her face still, like a figure carved in wood. But she did not return to slavery. Instead, she ran.

Her absence wasn't discovered for three days and by then, there was no tracing her. Dr. Bond demanded her full purchase price from Father, as he was the one who'd taken his eye off her.

Hagar was not the only missing slave Father was forced to buy. One day, Rosalie found a scratched metal plate, rectangular, with a number on it—37—and a broken chain looped through. It was in the barn, down among the hay bales. Rosalie had no idea what it was or how it could have gotten to the barn. She showed it to Grandfather, who said it was nothing for her to concern herself with. He took it from her and she never saw it again. She wouldn't know for years that what she'd found was an ankle chain, the number meant to identify the man who wore it. She wouldn't know for years that Grandfather had been helping slaves to freedom in Philadelphia, hiding them in the forest on the farm until they could be picked up and guided into Baltimore and beyond by the fugitive maroons.

Father would never have known about it either, except that one time Grandfather was caught and only Father's money kept him out of jail.

———

IN PRINCIPLE, FATHER disapproves of slavery, but not as strongly as Grandfather does. He was, on two occasions, a slave owner. He'd bought Joe Hall from Dr. Bond, asking Joe's permission first, as if good manners could mitigate the evil of it. "Work hard for me for five years," Father had said, "and I'll free you." And that's what happened.

Father's second purchase was a woman named Harriet when Rosalie was one year old. June was two and a half, and Mother, who had no idea how to live in the wilderness, desperately needed help. Once again, Father convinced himself that he was being generous. Father could convince himself of almost anything; he was his own easiest mark. He offered Harriet, currently a slave for life, that form of bondage known as term slavery.

These were the terms:

1) Like Joe, Harriet was to serve five years and then be freed.

   But as a woman, any possible children must also be considered.

   So . . .

2) Father would own any children she had until they turned twenty-four, at which time they'd be freed. And finally . . .

3) Father promised that none of her children would be sold anywhere outside the state of Maryland nor removed from Maryland after manumission.

Three days after this contract was signed, Harriet casually announced her intention to bludgeon Mother to death with a fence rail whenever the opportunity first showed itself. She was given her freedom immediately and dismissed from service. She was the last human Father bought.

Rosalie knows about Harriet because Aunty Rogers has told her. Poor Mother couldn't bake biscuits and she couldn't manage a slave. Aunty Rogers could have mentioned Harriet during that quarrel they'd almost had about slavery. Clearly Father and Mother's principles were more fluid than Mother liked to acknowledge. But it was enough for Aunty Rogers to know this; she didn't have to say it. Whatever Mother might claim to believe, they were still white women together.

vi

Back in 1838, in the absence of both her mother and father, Rosalie is almost able to relax. Spring is arriving in manageable pieces, like things seen in the shards of a broken mirror, heard from a passing carriage—birds, bugs, leaves, flowers, rain, clouds. A contented hum rises from the earth all around the cabin. Overnight, the cherry tree has burst into spectacular bloom. It is unseasonably warm.

Still no word from the great bullfrog, but the wood frogs are awake and in the evenings when Asia is in bed, Rosalie pulls her mother's ladder-back chair out onto the doorstep to listen to them. Under the willows, right where the stream turns to marsh, they call out in a chorus strangely like the sound of galloping horses.

She watches for omens, signs of how things are going with her father and mother in Charleston. One night, she sees an owl fall and rise again with something small and tender in its feet. It settles in a nearby tree to eat. Strings of viscera dangle from its beak. Rosalie decides she doesn't believe in omens. She takes her chair back inside. She avoids the graveyard even more than usual as the ghosts have begun predicting vague sorts of doom—*hunters with hounds with teeth like the wolf in the fold they loosed him with a single lash who'll make the shroud if it's not in the dark these violent delights have violent ends.* It's not even clear they mean to distress with these ominous mutterings. They themselves seem unperturbed.

When night comes, June entertains her with recitations by candlelight. He practices the big soliloquies with big gestures. On the rough wood wall behind him, his shadow throws out its arms. None of the children has ever been allowed to see their father perform. He wants none of them following him into the theater. But every surface in the house is stacked with playbills, clippings, gloves, wigs, and hats. No child has to go far to find Macbeth's dagger or Hamlet's cloak. Richard's hump lies often on Father's desk under his farm catalogues and a great many reminders of money owed. During the summers, when Father's at home, he reads to them every evening. He talks about diction, inflection, rhythm. He is training them all for the thing they've been forbidden to do.

June has started to dream of an acting career in Philadelphia, where he knows some of the company and has been promised his chance. This is as much against his father's wishes as his father's own acting career was against *his* father's wishes. There are other family traditions that June will eventually carry on as well, but he doesn't know what they are yet.

Rosalie sees that June is hoping to astonish Father with his success, and she sees that he won't. He speaks too quickly and his voice scales up when he wants to show a great emotion. This saddens her, but June will be all right.

He's too steady to belong in this family anyway. She thinks that she will miss him dreadfully when he goes. Not that he was ever much company to her, but at least he was there.

FATHER, MOTHER, and little Edwin come home. They arrive late at night when no one is expecting them. Rosalie wakes to the keening of the dogs. She wraps her shawl over her nightdress and goes barefoot downstairs to fix them something to eat. Edwin is sleeping, draped over Father's shoulder like a sack. She approaches Father, intending to kiss him, but he fends her off by handing her Edwin instead. She sees why. Her father's face is a ruin.

What happened is something like this: Her father climbed through the window of Thomas Flynn's room at the Planter's Hotel in the dead of night and attacked him with a fire poker as he slept. It seems he meant to kill him. Mr. Flynn fought back. He picked up a pewter pot from a nearby table and smashed it into Father's face, breaking his nose.

Everyone deeply regrets it all; the friendship is unaffected. Mr. Flynn is much more upset than Father. He'll never be able to speak of it without tears. He blames himself for the blighting of Father's career, though no one else appears to notice it's blighted. The bookings, the big audiences, the rapturous reviews continue.

Rosalie's father will never be handsome again, but no one minds that. What matters is his voice, which has always been the better part of his genius—melodious, capable of such shadings and subtleties. Without his voice, Father's acting is more craft and less genius.

He recovers quickly. Only a few days later, he is out and about, *The Baltimore Sun* reporting that "the mad tragedian has arrived in our city."

And in another paper: "Is this man a maniac?"

No one is able to explain to Rosalie what the fight was about. It seems none of them know. Her father says that he gave Iago's speech as he bludgeoned Mr. Flynn.

> And nothing can or shall content my soul
> Till I am evened with him, wife for wife,
> Or, failing so, yet that I put the Moor
> At least into a jealousy so strong
> That judgment cannot cure!

Until suddenly the story changes and now he thought he was Othello, and what he shouted was,

> Villain, be sure thou prove my love a whore!

Mr. Flynn's version, confided to Mother, confided to Rosalie, is considerably less Shakespearean. Mr. Flynn said Father was angry because Mr. Flynn was preventing Father from having a fair shake at Mother. Rosalie doesn't know what a fair shake is and she knows better than to ask. Mother didn't see the fight herself, but she thinks that poor little Edwin may have seen something. "He had the biggest, saddest eyes after," she tells Rosalie. Edwin always has the biggest, saddest eyes. "Like saucers. When I picked him up, he buried his head under my arm as if hoping no one would find him there."

Rosalie knows that her father, who is so tender that he weeps over dead birds and won't kill even the poisonous snakes, a man who can't pick a flower because to do so means the end of that fragrant blameless life—that this same father can be cruel when opposed. When opposed and drunk, he's dangerous. She knows that her mother, who treats him with extraordinary reverence, is also deeply afraid of him. Rosalie loves him very much and is deeply afraid of him, too.

These are things the other children do not know and do not feel, and Rosalie is very sorry to think that Edwin may be learning them at such a sweet age.

She asks Edwin about his trip to Charleston. "Such a big trip for such a big boy," she tells him. Fortunately, the only thing Edwin seems to remember is being put to bed among the costumes in Father's trunk.

vii

Broken face and all, Father is off on tour again before three weeks have passed. One night, something, a premonition or an unexpected noise—Rosalie doesn't know what—wakes her. She makes her silent way to the stairs and down. In the dark, she skirts the chairs and tables by finding the edge of the Turkish rug and sticking to it until she's at the front door, which she opens. She might be dreaming. The moon is high and shiny as a dime above the trees. Masses of stars have been carelessly tossed about it. The nearby owl calls. A raven launches into the air and Rosalie can hear the whomp whomp whomp of its wings. The world is black and silver. She can smell that rain is coming.

The dogs are lying at the front of the cabin. They rise suddenly, their hair stiffening. They bark and continue barking. Rosalie feels a panic in her chest. She goes upstairs for June, shakes him up, fetches Father's unloaded rifle for him. They stand together on the doorstep in their nightclothes, listening to the dogs.

Mother joins them in the doorway, Grandfather a moment later. Suddenly Rosalie sees how frail Grandfather has become. If they're about to be killed, he won't be the man to stop it.

Figures appear, emerging from the darkness and the trees. They clarify into a man, a woman, and an enormous number of children. The woman seems misshapen until she comes close enough that they see she's carrying a baby in her arms. Closer, and they see that all are dressed in the most outlandish fashion—theater costumes from completely different plays, dramas and comedies and Greek tableaus. One boy is wearing women's pantaloons, far too big. He holds them up with his hand as he walks. He's barefoot. The man is dressed in a long-tailed green velvet coat. The woman wears a toga with a shawl around her shoulders—half goddess and half Irish washerwoman. The dogs growl and snap, but the people come ahead regardless.

Rosalie has never seen these people before; neither has June, nor Mother. The man speaks first to June and his rifle. "You'd be young Junius," he says. "I'm your uncle Mitchell."

The woman looks past Rosalie's head to where Grandfather stands. "Hello, Father," she says. "Here we are. All the way from England, through such trials as you can scarcely imagine."

"I've no welcome for you," Grandfather tells her. "Keep walking." He steps back inside and closes the door. June and Rosalie have been left on the wrong side of it just as the rain arrives.

JAMES MITCHELL IS a man of no accomplishments and no employment. Long ago he was a bootblack who persuaded Father's sister to marry him. It's one thing for Grandfather to admire the democratic spirit of the American revolutionaries. It's quite another to see his daughter elope against his explicit command, and marry so far beneath her. Grandfather immediately disinherited her and, until this night, he hasn't spoken a word to her. Nor will he again.

They will soon learn that, sometime during that terrible visit to England, before Henry had fallen ill, Father had gone secretly to see his sister. Distressed by her circumstances, the extreme poverty and the abusive, drunken husband, he'd given her enough money to bring herself and her children to Maryland. This money came with the specific proviso that her husband not be one of the party. This money was meant for Jane Mitchell's escape.

Obviously, Aunt Mitchell has ignored these instructions. They made it to New York on Father's money, but arrived as paupers, with no luggage and no provision. On they came, sometimes on foot and sometimes on charity in a passing coach or wagon, to Baltimore. There, their only clothing in rags, they'd applied to the local theater company and, on the strength of Father's name, got the bits of costumes they are wearing plus directions to the farm.

Mother opens the door and lets them all into the house. The seven strange children have runny noses and blistered feet. Drops of rain are beaded on their greasy hair and streaking their cheeks. They smell awful.

Uncle Mitchell looks around at the cramped room, the dirt floor, the low ceiling. Even in charitable candlelight, the shabbiness is undeniable. He holds a candle in front of a picture on the wall, makes a show of looking it over—a barnyard scene, a boy feeding a horse from his hand. The rain taps lightly at first, then louder and faster on the roof. "Where will we all sleep?" he asks.

First they eat. They fall on whatever cold food and stale bread remains in the pantry and complain that there's no meat. "In the morning," Uncle Mitchell says, "I'll kill a couple of your chickens."

"You can't do that," June tells him.

"Don't contradict your elders and betters," Uncle Mitchell says. "I'll do as I please." There is no more conversation.

Mother has been upstairs organizing. Mr. and Mrs. Mitchell will take Mother and Father's bed. The Mitchell girls are sent to sleep with Asia, all of them laid crossways on the mattress like fence posts. June retires to the carriage house with Joe Hall so that the boys can have the bed he shares with Edwin. Rosalie and her mother sleep, or mostly don't sleep, on the rug downstairs. Rosalie wraps herself in Macbeth's cape for warmth. All night the rain starts and stops, starts and stops. Next morning, Rosalie's mind is muddled with fatigue.

The day that dawns is mild and sunny. Mother is able to open the doors and windows, air the cabin out. This season is always such a beautiful one on the farm—the trees in tender leaf, the air filled with the scent of jasmine and the songs of birds and streams. It's a shame that Father so often misses it. He is always deeply moved by nature resurrecting.

The older Mitchells are still asleep, and Rosalie takes the children as far as the spring so the house will stay quiet. Mother suggested the woods, but Rosalie sees no need to go that far, expose the new children to the curiosity of the dead ones. The Mitchells are all limping, feet raw and swollen. The boys are drowning in June's clothing. The girls are wrapped in woven blankets with their legs bare. A walk would be unkind.

Besides, Rosalie would have to carry little Charlotte and then Asia would demand to be carried, too. "I don't like them," Asia tells her, right where they can hear, and Rosalie whispers not to worry, the Mitchells will be gone soon enough. Anyone can see there's no room.

The cousins are silent with each other—Asia suspicious, Edwin shy; the Mitchell children huddle together, inert and unsettled. Mother brings her chair to the doorstep to work in the sunlight. She's collected the rags of their costumes to see which ones can be repaired and returned. She's already mending.

When Uncle Mitchell finally wakes they all join him at the table, where Ann Hall serves them bowls of bread and milk, eggs and cheese, potatoes and baked apples. Aunty Rogers, on Ann's appeal, has sent over a Dutch oven of corn pone, which Ann tells Rosalie and June quietly not to eat until they know their guests are sated. Rosalie doesn't begrudge it, though she loves corn pone. But she's never gone hungry the way the Mitchells have.

Uncle Mitchell thanks them all with a forced elegance. "We've had as warm a welcome as we might have thought only a happy dream on those long, desperate nights of long, desperate travel." He tucks in.

After some serious eating, Uncle Mitchell continues. "But as to the future, I'm sure you see that it won't do. We can't all squash together like this. We'll need our own rooms and beds."

"We thought you lived grander," he explains.

He helps himself to more of the corn pone, douses it with butter and sorghum. "But all this can wait until your lord and master's return. No hurry. We've surely known worse."

Rosalie has been watching the cuffs of June's Sunday shirt, dipping into the breakfast eggs as George eats them, staining them yellow along the edge. That stain will never completely come out, though it will no doubt fall to Rosalie to try.

So Uncle Mitchell's words take a moment to register. She

turns a shocked face to Mother. She hears the little *tchh* Ann makes when expressing disapproval. The Mitchells are here to stay.

As they have no money, Father will now have to support them all. "Until I find my feet," Uncle Mitchell offers, but that day will be long in coming. Since Mary Ann's and Elizabeth's deaths, money has been tight. Father still draws enormous crowds, but he sometimes forgets or refuses to appear or does half a play and then loses interest. Then the manager has to be fully recompensed for the ticket sales and the space. Or else he spends his earnings on drink, or spurious business ventures, or sudden charities before Mother can get her hands on it.

New sources of income are necessary. Mother will have to take produce into the city and sell from a stall. It offends June that she is forced to do this, but Rosalie suspects she won't mind regularly leaving the farm for a day and a night.

Aunt Mitchell, who managed to walk the thirty miles from Baltimore toting her daughter, is suddenly an invalid. She takes to her bed and treats her sister-in-law as a servant. If Father had stayed in England while his star rose, she and her husband would be people of consequence. She blames Mother that this didn't happen. "Your mother owes me," she tells Rosalie, "the life I might have had if she hadn't seduced my brother away from us," and when Rosalie says nothing in response, "Stand up straight! Speak up! I suppose you think this lisping and stooping is delightfully girlish, but believe me, you're not the girl to carry it off."

The whole neighborhood watches and wonders. Why does Mother put up with this? It's a mystery. "Mr. Mitchell," Ann Hall tells Aunty Rogers, who tells everyone else, "does not one lick of work. He won't even bend down to put a log on the fire."

Mr. Mitchell is quickly known and despised as an ill-tempered drunk. The neighborhood children, black and white, are used to roaming the farm, even into the cabin, where Mother or Ann can be counted on to give them something to eat. Now there is no food to spare and Uncle Mitchell shouts at them, telling them to get off the very property where they have lived longer than he.

Rosalie's cousins also seem to feel that their previous hardships entitle them to the easy life now. "Cousin Rosalie," George says. "Fetch me some milk." The milk bucket is kept cool in a small brick cave that the spring runs through. Rosalie has to put on her boots and bonnet to go and get it, and then take it back. His tone is imperious though he's two years younger. In fact, he's just the age Henry Byron should have been. Rosalie resents this unearned and inexplicable survival more than she can say.

"Cousin Rosalie," says Robert, who is younger still. "Go and tell your servant to make me an egg with a soft yolk."

One day as Rosalie is getting Asia ready for her nap, Uncle Mitchell arrives with a rabbit that he throws onto the dining room table. Its neck has been broken. "It just up and died," Uncle Mitchell says. "Fell at my feet. Hand of God. I thought it disrespectful to let it just go to waste. Tell your woman to stew it with some onions and potatoes."

Rosalie sees the great absence in the rabbit's eye. Murderer! Murderer! Murderer!

"You can have the tail," Uncle Mitchell tells Asia, who has never been offered anything she didn't immediately desperately want.

Mother says no to the tail and then Rosalie has to remove Asia, screaming, from the house until she can be calm again. But she says yes to the stew. She even eats it. Everyone but Rosalie has some. Is Rosalie the only one who remembers how Father said that falling away from his beliefs and eating meat was what killed Mary Ann and Elizabeth? The cabin smells of cooked flesh for days.

IN THE EVENINGS, while there's still light, Mother sits, more pregnant than ever, on a chair dragged outside so she can be under the cherry tree. The wind tosses white petals onto her dark hair, her shoulders, the hillock where her lap once was. She's busily altering Rosalie's day dress and June's Sunday shirt to fit one Mitchell child or another. Mother has always made Father's costumes. She's good at this work. Rosalie watches her favorite dress disappear and reappear no longer hers. She herself has been put to the task of hemming cloth into diapers, the dullest sort of sewing imaginable.

Mother has opened the trunks and Charlotte is already wearing Elizabeth's little gingham. It feels as much like a ghost to Rosalie as the ghosts do, seeing Elizabeth's dress toddling around without her. Next will be Mary Ann's apron that she so loved because it had birds on it. She was supposed to remove it when company came, but she never would. She'd made Rosalie tell her the names of the different birds cross-stitched on it—the robin, the cardinal, the wren, the blackbird—with the same diligence she'd applied to learning her letters and then, on seeing wings in the yard, would call out Apron Bird, because the issue of whether or not a bird was on her apron was more important than the name she'd taken such pains to learn. Rosalie had always known she'd see that apron on Asia someday. But to see it on Maria Mitchell . . . that would be unbearable. Surely Mother, biting off the end of her thread with her teeth, shaking out the finished dress, must feel the same.

It rains for two days and they all have to stay inside, knocking against each other. By the time Father returns, the house is crowded with resentments and deprivations. But instead of making the Mitchells leave, as both Rosalie and June assumed he would, Father gives them the carriage house. Joe Hall, who lives there like a bachelor in spite of having a wife and children—four, if you count the two dead ones, which Rosalie always does—is moved to the slave cabins.

The additional work falls hard on Rosalie, but hardest on Joe and Ann. They no longer have time for their extra jobs. The day on which Ann will be free recedes into the future. Even worse, the money they've been saving is secreted in the sill along the back wall of the carriage house and the move happens so quickly, they're unable to retrieve it. They can't recover their savings while the Mitchells live there. And the longer Uncle Mitchell spends in those rooms, the more likely he is to find it.

viii

In May of 1838, one month after the arrival of the Mitchells, the family's ninth child is born. The birth progresses easily and no doctor is needed. No stars fall from the sky. No caul sheathes the baby's face. It's a boy.

There's no two-year wait to name him. Grandfather is given the honors and he chooses the name John Wilkes. Grandfather's translation of *The Aeneid* will never be finished. This naming will be his last mark on the world.

When he was a young man, Grandfather had fled to France on his way to America to join the revolutionaries. He applied to John Wilkes, the radical parliamentarian and scandalous libertine, for a letter of support though he'd never met the man. Wilkes immediately informed his family, who had him arrested and returned home for the sedate life of the law. Grandfather's father was a silversmith who'd come to England through Spain. He sent Wilkes an intricate silver presentation as a thank-you for the return of his wayward son.

Grandfather's admiration was undiminished by this betrayal. Eventually he married John Wilkes' niece, who died giving birth to their third child. Back in Britain, there are other relatives also named John Wilkes. The name has revolutionary and familial significance. It's an ordination.

When Mother's labor begins, Father hastily takes himself off to the Bel Air saloon. He returns as soon as Joe brings him word of the safe passage. Father is rarely home for the birth of a child, but Johnny is only three hours old when Father first meets him.

He takes an unusual interest in the baby, in whom he finds, like poor lost Henry Byron, the best possible combination of his wife's beauty and his own brilliance. These things are being talked of even when Rosalie can only see a baby, no more exceptional than any other.

Edwin's caul and stars are quickly forgotten. He's not the only boy in the family now with a destiny. Johnny has one, too. It arrived on a colicky night, the whole house asleep except for Mother and Baby, sitting downstairs by the dying fire. They were wrapped together in a single blanket, John's little body hot against Mother's breasts. She was looking down into his flushed and fretful face, when on sudden impulse she'd said a prayer asking to know what his fate would be.

Instantly a flame rose from the ashes and, shaping itself into an arm, stretched toward the baby as if to knight him. In that flame,

Mother said, she could read the word *Country*, followed by Johnny's name. And then the arm fell back and faded away. This strange, unfirelike behavior taking place on their own little hearth has the whole family excited. It may be an ambiguous fate, but it's clearly a glorious one, a narrative of such power that Asia will write a poem about it one day, forgetting how angry she once was not to have been given a glorious fate of her own. She was less upset by her own lack of a destiny than by the fact that nobody had ever even bothered to ask the fire if she had one.

THE IMPACT OF Johnny's birth on Rosalie is profound. He's such a happy child. He calms her down; he bucks her up. One day, she is passing the graveyard, carrying him against her shoulder. *Oh, pretty!* the ghosts say. *Little pretty. Little darling.* They curl about him, blow gently to close his eyes, cool his cheeks. They suck at his milky breath. They whisper about the way he smells. *Clover,* they say. *Butter. Kittens,* but they are only being nostalgic. He smells like nothing of the sort. Still Rosalie takes note of how uninterested in her the dead children are while Johnny is in her arms. She notes the absence of their customary menacing clinging. They are all love.

Rosalie begins to take Johnny everywhere she goes and, with Johnny on her hip, she finds that she can go everywhere. She takes him to church and feels that her feud with God is ended. She takes him to the creek to see the fish and the snapping turtles, and the dairy to see the cows, to the cabins to see Ann and Joe, to the neighbors to see Aunty Rogers. Everyone is entranced with him.

A year passes. He's growing into a beautiful, charming, affectionate boy. He loves Ann in particular and can often be found in her lap or gripping her skirt in his fist, letting her drag him about the kitchen as she cooks. The farmhands tease Ann about her new white son.

Even envious Asia is besotted. She insists on holding him, sobs and screams if he crawls away. When Mother looks at Johnny, Rosalie sees in her face a desperate, hungering love. Father begins to make plans for him, the sort of plans they haven't heard since Henry died. And Rosalie allows herself to think that maybe, just maybe, the child who can heal her broken family has been born at last.

ix

Grandfather has had enough of the Mitchells. He packs his trunks and moves angrily out, freeing up another bed. He lets a small room in Baltimore and never sets foot on the farm again.

Six months later, he quietly dies, just after Christmas, alone in the night, of unknown cause. Father is off on tour, so an undertaker with offices near the Front Street Theatre takes charge of the body until Father's return. Father doesn't bring Grandfather back to the family graveyard, because Grandfather left the farm of his own free will and Father believes in freedom.

Instead he chooses a grave in Baltimore, puts up a stone with an epitaph in Hebrew that translates to—

> *I take my departure from life as from an inn—*
> *Thee I follow to the infernal kingdom*
> *Of the most renowned ruler*
> *Thence to the stars.*

Rosalie thinks that Grandfather probably likes having an epitaph only the highly educated can read.

Father plays Hamlet around the house for a few days, the bereaved and guilty son, but this doesn't last long. "It's a terrible thing," he'll tell June one night at the table, "to lose a father. But a father's death must be expected in the natural course of things. That's not the ghastly unnatural fiend who comes and steals your child."

A LITTLE SCHOOL for white children opens on the Bel Air Road. For most of its pupils, the shortest route cuts across the Booth property and Rosalie can see them from the kitchen window as she does her chores of washing up and churning or grinding the spices or slicing the onions; or from the lawn as she hangs out the wet laundry on sunny, windy days. The schoolchildren walk in clusters, with their slates and their books. In the winter, they pelt each other with snowballs. In the spring, they chase each other, the girls dashing, laughing, to the safety of other girls. This school will be a good thing for Edwin and Asia, Rosalie tells herself, and will relieve her from constant guardianship.

She herself is too old and too busy to think about school. She hardly remembers her time in the classroom in England. Henry Byron's death eclipsed most memories. But she does remember Father being proud of her, an occurrence so rare as to never be forgotten.

One morning, June asks Rosalie to come out for a walk with him. She would rather not. Johnny is sleeping and can't come with her. She'll be very exposed.

But June is insistent. He coaxes her out to the creek in the forest where they once were knights and ladies, kings and queens. The wind is up. The loose strands of her hair sting her face as they whip about it. Twigs and leaves tumble in the current below, bubbling around the rocks or landing in the deadfall piled on the banks. Once Rosalie could cross this creek, dancing stone to stone. Her spine has begun to curve just slightly, throwing her weight off-center, making her too clumsy to try. Mother thinks this is from carrying Johnny around and is making Rosalie shift him to her other hip, which doesn't work for Rosalie and she only does it if Mother is watching.

June pulls her into one of the fairy ballrooms, a bare patch of dirt ringed with trees and sheltered from the wind. "I'm leaving for Philadelphia tomorrow," he says. "I've been offered a place in the company there." And then, watching her face, "Oh, Rosie!"

Rosalie has long known this moment was coming, but now that it has arrived, it's worse than she thought, as if June has reached down her throat and strangled her from the inside. She and June are not even close, only he's all she has, the only sibling who doesn't require her care. "Henry had no choice in his leaving," she says. "They none of them had a choice." She won't beg for herself. "What about Edwin?" Edwin adores June.

"I'll be nothing if I stay. Edwin has you."

But why should this job fall to Rosalie? Maybe she, too, would rather not be nothing. "Take me with you."

She sees how June is startled. He comes and puts his arms around her, tries to stop her seeing that he doesn't want her, but he's too slow and she does see. "Could you even come?" he asks. "Recollect how hard it was for me just to get you here."

She realizes with an absolute clarity that if she doesn't leave her mother now, she will never leave her mother. "I could," she says. "I will." She means it. *Hie thee home to me,* she thinks and marvels that she just might be the one to leave. She's almost the same age Mother was when she ran away with Father. If Mother made it all the way to America, surely Rosalie can make it as far as Philadelphia.

Passing the graveyard on her way back to the cabin, she encounters opposition. The ghosts hiss and tangle her hair. *We won't let you,* they say. *We'll tell Mother.*

It does give her pause, the idea of leaving Mother at the mercy of her dead children. She puts this thought aside.

You won't go anywhere, they call after her. *Mother will stop you mother mother mother mother,* they repeat so often the word becomes nonsense, babble.

Rosalie spends the rest of the day with excitement and terror and guilt and anger building in her breast like a scream. Late that night, Mother comes and beckons her from her bed, down the stairs so they can talk without waking Asia. "June is going," Mother says in the voice of her dead children, her hand wrapped on Rosalie's wrist so tightly it will leave fingerprints. "Stop him."

So June has not told Mother that Rosalie is going, too. Clearly he never thought she would.

Rosalie will always believe that she would have gone if only June had said so. She herself can't say it to her mother's anguished eyes. And what would she have done all day in Philadelphia anyway? How would she have earned her way? It was never a feasible plan. It was no plan at all. She'll feel the thought of it, that moment of possibility becoming impossible, as it leaves her body and drifts away. What remains is cold and hard.

"Things will be much easier when June and Father are both sending us money," she says, loosening Mother's grip with her own strong fingers. This statement will come from that same cold hardness. She's angry to think that this might actually soothe Mother, angry that Mother just might trade June for money.

She expects that Father will be furious; she expects to hear many variations on the serpent's tooth, but he takes the news more cheerfully than she did. He writes that June will be back, and sooner than they expect. He waxes lyrical about farming and the rhythms of seed and harvest, the goodness of a simple life. The stage leaves a man empty, he says. There's a falseness right at its core.

And the hollow, fleeting camaraderie of the company is nothing compared to a family who loves you. June will see.

Months pass and he'll continue to say these things, in letters, in person. "Is June home yet?" he writes. "It's time for him to press the apples."

"Remind him to check the shoes on the horses."

"Time to plant the radishes."

"The gate to the pasture was loose when I last looked. The cows rub against it. Tell June and Joe to check all the fencing."

He'll stop only when they learn, and not from June, that he has married. His wife, Clementina DeBar, is a comedienne, a famed dancer of the Highland fling, and thirteen years his senior. She sends them a breezy letter announcing the event only after it occurs. A daughter follows so quickly that, despite a strong family resemblance, June will always harbor doubts that she is his.

IN FEBRUARY OF 1840, the tenth and final child arrives, a boy named Joseph Adrian, the name Adrian chosen in tribute to June's debut in *Richelieu* as the handsome Adrien de Mauprat. It's a part in which June fails to shine. "Competent" is the best his fellow players can muster. "Great in nothing." They whisper that it was only the Booth name that landed him the role. These whispers carry all the way to his father's ear, but too late—Joe is already named.

That autumn the family moves to Baltimore, ceding the farm entirely to the Mitchells in the winter months, returning only during the summer when cholera and typhoid sweep the city. They trade the playground of orchards, fields, and forests for streets and parks. They trade their neighbors, all of whom they know by name, for a busy, noisy city of one hundred thousand people.

The Mitchells move into the cabin. This has at least one happy outcome: Ann Hall will finally be able to re-enter the carriage house, where she'll find her money in the wall exactly as they left it. She'll hold it a mercy from God that James Mitchell was too lazy to ever even look about the place where he had lived for two whole years.

x

Grapes clover rye potatoes peaches parsnips the piebald pony and the white calf Father's chair and Mother's powders rain falling through trees leaves turning silver in the stream mushrooms like fairy houses and Joe's hands and Ann's skirts and the color of rocks when they're wet and lying against the black dogs fur in our fingers and Father in wigs shouting I had a dream which was not all a dream and Mother and Mother and Mother and look! How our sister comes through the forest her arms all filled with flowers.

Lincoln and the Cave of Gloom

Yes! I've resolved the deed to do,
And this the place to do it:
This heart I'll rush a dagger through
Though I in hell should rue it!
—Abraham Lincoln on suicide

That same winter, while the Booths are moving to Baltimore, Abraham Lincoln suffers his second nervous breakdown. He's in his thirties now, a fourth-term state congressman in Illinois, and for the first time, he can't rouse himself to make his sessions. He feels too heavy to move. His thoughts circle like vultures.

He's called off his courtship of Mary Todd. Whether this is the result or the cause of his depression is unclear. It would kill me to marry her, he tells his friends. But he knows that people think he's behaved dishonorably towards her and he's not certain he hasn't.

He may be in love with someone else—several of his friends think he's smitten with the eighteen-year-old daughter of a state senator. She has many such admirers.

He goes to a doctor, seeking medicinal solace. He writes—"I am now the most miserable man living. If what I feel were equally distributed to the whole human family, there would not be one cheerful face on earth." He loses weight he can ill afford. His arms and legs are sticks; his clothing flaps about them like flags on poles.

Under pressure from his friend Joshua Speed, he makes a visit to the Speed plantation in Kentucky. On the deck of his boat he encounters twelve Negro men chained together like "fish on a trot-line." This image will haunt him. Over the years he'll refer often to these chained men. He'll see the straitened way they are forced to walk, hear the clank of iron. He understands that they've been torn from their families and everyone they love. But in this first encounter, still sunk inside the miasma of his miserable self, what he thinks is that they seem, on the surface, happier than he. He wonders how this could be so.

Joshua Speed fears he'll take his own life, and begs Lincoln to promise otherwise. Lincoln tells Speed not to worry. He's not yet done anything to make himself a man worth remembering and he's determined not to die until he has.

BOOK TWO

If I chance to talk a little wild, forgive me; I had it from my father.

—W. Shakespeare, *Henry VIII*

Baltimore couldn't be less like the farm. Instead of frogs, choruses of drunks sing on the street after dark. Instead of birdcalls, factory whistles. Instead of the spring and the stream, trains and *The Baltimore Sun* presses run through the night. By the 1840s, Baltimore is the second-largest city in the United States. Everything here is modern as can be, what with the new railroad connection, the factories, and the harbor, the air pollution, the water pollution, and the noise.

Pigs roam freely. So do packs of young white delinquents. Gangs like the Gumballs, the Neversweats, and the Cock Robins own the streets. An editorial in the *Sun* claims that the citizens of Baltimore are more plagued by wicked boys than the people of any other city in the nation.

For six years the Booths live in a rented row house. In 1846, Father buys the roomy brick townhouse at 62 North Exeter Street. The new home has a modest elegance. A Franklin stove. One bedroom for the boys and another for the girls. A dining room. Fleur-de-lis wallpaper flocked in yellow.

Green shutters frame the windows. Mulberry trees shade the yard. There is a gazebo in the back, a high stoop in the front, and, most conveniently, the tiny Struthoff grocery right next door.

Early in the evenings, when it's warm and dry enough, when their mothers have had just as much noise and quarrel as anyone could possibly endure, the neighborhood children, all of them white, are sent outside to play together in the street.

It's a short walk from the stoop to the Front Street Theatre—a palatial, Grecian-inspired venue that accommodates an audience of four thousand, the entire bottom floor reserved for horses and carriages. The Jones Falls waterway runs right past the back door.

Baltimore boasts four premiere theaters and is known nationally for its enthusiastic audiences. It also has the largest population of free blacks in the country and they attend in considerable numbers, except for those plays, like *Othello*, that they are forbidden to see.

THE FAMILY HAS fractured.

Now there is the older set, most of whom are dead, only June and Rosalie remaining and only Rosalie remaining at home—a faction of one—the only child in the house who remembers, if barely, when their father was celebrated, wealthy, and sober. The only child in the house who remembers Frederick, Mary Ann, and Elizabeth. In truth, Rosalie, now called Rose, can no longer be counted a child. She's twenty-two by the time they move to Exeter Street.

And then there is the younger set, the city kids, the farm a mere summertime interlude in their urban lives. They choose city names for themselves: Edwin becomes Ned (or sometimes Ted),

Asia becomes Sidney, and Johnny is known as Wilkes. These three have become the beating heart of the family. They quarrel and criticize, ridicule and betray each other. Still they are each other's whole childhood, a tightly laced, insular group. "We only had each other," Edwin will say in later years. "We could only be comfortable with each other," is Asia's version of the same.

Mother may have been forced off the farm by the Mitchells, but she's landed somewhere she likes better. She misses Ann, but has an Irish servant now who comes to cook and clean, as well as a free black woman who helps Rosalie with the laundry.

For the younger children, Mother sees possibilities. They go to school. They take dancing and music lessons. They wear better clothes, which Mother makes herself. She aspires to the middle-class respectability she herself had as a child. She sets about finding and nurturing useful social connections that have nothing to do with the world of the theater.

Father remains a barrier to this. To see a play may be completely respectable. But to act in one remains suspect, actresses in particular merely a rank or two above prostitutes. Once Father's genius was enough to overcome society's disdain. But now his mad freaks are more famous than his brilliant performances.

Other children, on the streets and in the schoolyards, ask about him: Did he once climb a tree naked and crow from the branches like a rooster? Had he tried to raise a pony from the dead? A child? Did he keep a murderer's skull in his trunk and bring it out whenever he played Hamlet? Had he, as Richard III, refused to die at the end of the play, forcing the scene to go on and on until the audience gave up and went home? Had he shot a man in the face? Jumped from a boat? Held a funeral for a pigeon? Were other actors afraid to take the stage with him? Did he not believe in God?

Some of these stories are true, some are not. All are news to the younger set. Their father's genius is the fixed point around which the family revolves. It seems impossible that people who don't even know Father would know more about him than his own children. They deny it all, and they believe their own denials, turning to each other for support in this belief. They are cut by the gossip nevertheless.

They hold their Mitchell cousins in particular contempt. During the summers, back on the farm, they exclude the Mitchells from every game they play, filling the numbers when needed with any Hall child who might be about. If no one else thinks being a Booth is an important distinction, then they'll insist on it themselves.

Edwin

Now it's 1846, another March coming round. On this particular day, the weather has been shifting rapidly from snow to rain and back again. A layer of white covers North Exeter Street and then is washed away. Four crows sit on the thin, barely budding branches of the mulberry. Their shoulders are hunched. Occasionally one or another opens and closes its beak. Edwin imagines the small, unhappy sound he's too far away to hear. He's at the window, watching the street in the faint hope that something interesting will happen outside. Certainly, nothing interesting is happening inside.

Edwin is twelve now, Asia ten, and Johnny will soon be eight. Like every adolescent everywhere, Edwin's turning moody and aggrieved, but he's so quiet compared to Asia and Johnny that this has gone largely unnoticed.

Tomorrow Father comes home, all boredom banished for a familial mélange of nerves and excitement. The house wakes up when Father is in it, the threads that connect the family tightening like violin strings until they buzz. Everyone, perhaps even

Father, gets busy pretending that they follow his rules in his absence, as if there is a routine of cooking and cleaning and chores and school, and he merely drops into it.

He'll spend the next two weeks here at home, completing a run at the Baltimore Museum, where he'll be, on different evenings, Othello, Hamlet, Richard III, Kotzebue's Stranger, and Edward Mortimer in *The Iron Chest*. Mortimer first. Edwin's read the play and it's easy to imagine how well his father will inhabit that angry, haunted, guilty man. Edwin imagines himself in the part of the young orphan Wilford and has already memorized a handful of dramatic speeches.

This house is no house for me. Fly I will, I am resolved:—
but whither? His threats strike terror into me; and were I to
reach the pole, I doubt whether I should elude his grasp.

What's harder to imagine is playing Wilford opposite his father's Mortimer. He's watched for years as his father prepares for a part. Early on the day *The Iron Chest* opens, Father will start his transformation. Over breakfast, his posture will change, his gestures, his intonations. How deep does the transformation go? For the course of a day and an evening, is Father truly in love with a woman who is not Mother? Does he even have children?

Would Edwin be pretending to be Wilford, the fatherless orphan, while Father actually was Mortimer, the childless murderer? Is that what real acting is, that moment you stop pretending? And if so, can a person ever be sure, even offstage, even in the parlor of his own house, that he isn't simply acting a part? *All the world's a stage* and etc., etc. You don't have to be the son of a Shakespearean actor to have such thoughts. Everyone has them.

The curtains by Edwin's face are lace, white spiderwebs all the way from Nottingham, a source of much pride for Mother. They smell of dust. Edwin leans forward, breathes on the window, clouding the glass in front of his face. He puts one hand on the cold pane and draws its outline with the other. He erases it, sees the street beyond unobstructed again.

The O'Laughlen house across the street is shuttered; it looks tired and sad. Perhaps the O'Laughlens are away for the day. Johnny would know. William O'Laughlen is Johnny's close friend. Kate O'Laughlen is Asia's enemy; it's not clear to Edwin which of the two started the feud, but they are equally interested in maintaining it. Michael O'Laughlen is about Joe's age, but the two don't play together. Instead, Michael tags along after William. He'll do anything for Johnny's attention. He's a grimy little boy with messy hair and smudged clothes. I'd like to give him a good scrubbing, Mother says, but Edwin sees no point. It wouldn't last to sunset.

A carriage pulled by matching black horses passes, their necks arched, their steps high and careful on the slippery ground. The crows flutter down to peck through the pile one leaves behind.

He wonders if Father might finally let him see the play. Museum theaters are all about gentility. No alcohol is sold. No one who might make a lady uncomfortable can get a ticket. The fare is chosen for its uplifting content. The pit is called the parquet and the audience is made to understand that throwing things at the stage will not be tolerated. Surely he is old enough—he'll soon be thirteen!—to see his father act in such respectable plays in such respectable surroundings. It's a museum as well as a playhouse. Every schoolchild in Baltimore has been to see the fossilized mastodon jaw, the diorama of menacing jungle cats.

"Edwin!" His mother's voice is irritated. "You really must learn to listen. It's annoying to say something three times without an answer."

When he first took his place by the window, he was alone in the parlor. Now, without him noticing, the family has joined him. Rosalie is on the green settee with her sewing basket, tightening the buttons on one of Father's shirts. Little Joe sits on her feet, leaning back against her skirt, his thumb in his mouth. Asia has gotten the dominoes from the bookshelf and is trying to talk Johnny into a game. A game of anything with Asia has only two possible outcomes. She will win and crow. She will lose and rage. Mother is standing on the rug by the large stone fireplace, trying to poke the fire awake. "Someday someone will say something really important to you, something you really need to hear," she tells Edwin.

"Don't step in that hole," Johnny suggests.

"Look out below!" says Asia.

"That gun is loaded."

They're laughing at him. He can't decide how much he minds.

"Why are you drawing birds on the window?" Joe asks. He points. The pane has fogged again and the outline of Edwin's hand returned.

"It's not a bird." Edwin wipes it away, pulls the lace between himself and his family. It's a mere gesture towards privacy. The lace is too open to conceal him.

There's a man on the street carrying a large and heavy trunk. He makes it a few feet, puts the trunk down, mops the moisture from his face. Picks it up again and staggers a dozen steps forward. Puts it down. Once when Edwin was out with Father, they'd seen a man trying unsuccessfully to roll a barrel uphill.

"Sisyphus," Father had said. "Sisyphus in a cutaway coat." The man steps out of Edwin's sight. Edwin turns back to the parlor.

Johnny has, very wisely, refused the game. Asia throws a domino at him, close to his head. If she'd wanted to hit him, she would have. He's not that far away. "Go to your room, Asia," Mother says. "Right now."

But Asia is only getting started. She rises from the floor—her scowling face, her angry eyes, her wild, black hair. "I will not," she says.

Mother's tone remains patient. "It's time you started learning to be the young woman you're becoming. Look at Rose. She never pouts and sulks."

"Who wants to be like Rose?" Asia says. "Nobody." Asked and answered.

Edwin looks anxiously at Rosalie, but she seems intent on her sewing. Still, of course, she heard. Poor Rose! And Mean Asia for saying out loud what all of them think. Rosalie's spine has developed a kink so she's begun to stoop, a little like Richard III. She has to work now not to limp when she walks, a limp being something Father will not abide. Asia would have said more, but Johnny has cut her off, deftly, before further damage can be done. "Edwin daydreams too much," he is saying. "Asia must learn to control her temper. What about me needs fixing?"

This is interesting enough to silence even Asia. What will Mother say about her favorite, her perfect shining boy? The log in the fireplace collapses with a crack and a fountain of red sparks.

"You need to work harder at school," Mother tells him.

"I work like the devil," Johnny says. "I'm just no good at it."

"You're as smart as they come," Mother says firmly.

Shortly after this conversation, Johnny will tell Edwin that he's hit on a method of improving his schoolwork by envisioning columns of spelling words and problems in arithmetic as enemy soldiers. He does better thinking of them as foes to be fought rather than things to be learned. Edwin will think this a very clever way to get around not being clever.

"Me next," says Joe. "Now me."

Rosalie puts her sewing down, pulls him into her lap, rests her cheek on top of his head.

"Joe must learn to be more cheerful," Mother says, "and save his moping for when something is really wrong."

"I'd be happy if I was a seagull," Joe says. He's been flying about the house for several days now, flapping his arms and calling out, *"Scree, scree, scree."* This is the first time he's tried to explain why. Edwin would laugh if he were sure Joe was trying to be funny, but he might not be. Joe is a strange, morose little boy.

The tempest has passed. Asia does not go to her room. Johnny does not play dominoes. Only at bedtime does Edwin realize he never did find out what it was Mother said three times to him.

ii

Enter Edwin.

He's walking alone, carrying, in secret rebellion, a set of foils that belong to his father. June has been giving him and Johnny both lessons in fencing when he visits, not real fencing, but stage fencing, and Edwin is desperate to be better at this than his athletic little brother. He has a ways to go. The last time he and June fenced, Edwin missed his parry and took a foil right in the eye. The point had been blunted. Still, for days his mother feared he'd lose it, or if not the eye itself, then the use of it. The sclera turned red as a ruby, not merely veined with red, but a solid bloody mass encasing the iris. No more fencing for Edwin, Mother declared, while leaving open the question of whether Johnny was still allowed.

Johnny is enormously popular. He runs with a gang of young toughs who call themselves the Baltimore Bully Boys. He's good with his fists. Edwin, by contrast, studies the violin. He excels at his dancing lessons. He has in his mind the person he wants to be, artistic, sensitive, and maybe a touch eccentric. He creates this person daily with costumes and props, voice and posture.

He wears a short cape like Romeo. He wears his hair mussed and curly like Byron. He's been seen on the streets with a pet lamb. His teacher, Susan Hyde, a marmish woman with spectacles and corkscrew curls, adores him. Miss Hyde is renowned both for her gentle manner and for her firm hand on the rattan cane. Edwin has experienced both, the latter in no way eclipsing the former. In fact, in later years, Edwin will say it was the caning that made him love her.

If he meant to make himself a target, then he's bagged it. The Bully Boys would beat him up themselves except that he's Wilkes' brother, and they are forced to protect him instead.

His hair blows into his eyes and he swipes it back with his free hand. In the window of the house he's passing, a little white dog barks angrily at him. The factory whistle sounds. Trees rattle their branches and the wind carries the smell of pigs.

A boy, probably younger than Edwin, but definitely bigger, falls in beside him as he walks. This boy is wearing a flat sea cap and hasn't yet grown into his front teeth. They protrude slightly, the tips of them exposed by his lip. His face is a mass of freckles. Edwin doesn't recognize him. "I know you," the boy says.

People often recognize Father on the street. They stop to say hello and Father always says hello back, so at first Edwin thought his father knew them all. But Father soon put him straight. Everyone knows Tom Fool, Father had said.

Two more boys appear. They land on the ground, dropping from the branches of a tree like rotten apples. They're not large like the first boy; clearly brothers as they have the same blond hair, the same blunt nose. "Here's Ned Booth," the freckled boy tells them, "strolling down the street like he's the biggest toad in the puddle."

"I don't think that. I'm just going home," Edwin says.

"This won't take long." The boy indicates the foils he's carrying. "Let me see those."

"They're not mine."

"Maybe they're mine," the boy tells him. He takes Father's foils from Edwin's unresisting hands, looks them over. "What are they? Toy swords? Toy swords for toy soldiers? I don't want them, after all." He drops them into the mud. He steps on them a few times, snapping them sharply. "Now you have twice as many. You should thank me."

Edwin didn't ask Mother's permission to take his father's foils, because she would have said no.

"You should thank him," the boy on his right says. He has a fading bruise along his flat cheekbone, a peeling scab on his chin. This is not his first fight.

Nor is it Edwin's. He knows what comes next. He hasn't yet found a role he can play that carries him through this. If he runs, they'll catch him and beat him. If he stands his ground, they'll take it as provocation and beat him. If he surrenders, they'll see it as weakness and beat him. The large boy takes hold of the back of his jacket and twists the collar so that it tightens around Edwin's neck.

"I don't hear you," the boy on his right says.

"Thank you." To Edwin's horror, it comes out a sob though he's fairly certain he's not crying. He puts his hands over his face just in time to block the first punch. The second hits his shoulder. He takes a kick in the shin that buckles his leg out from under him. He falls onto the pile of broken foils and remains there, curled up like a dead leaf, his hands over his eyes, his shin a sheet of pain. Someone kicks him in the back.

A sharp, loud whistle. It's George Stout of the Bully Boys, arriving on the scene, whistling for reinforcements. George doesn't wait. "Leave him be," George shouts, wading in, landing punches right and left. The big boy with the freckles hits the ground hard.

More Bully Boys arrive—Theodore Hamilton, Stuart Robson, William O'Laughlen, trailed by his little brother, Michael. Even Michael has more fight in him than Edwin. The battle moves down the street and into an alleyway. The noise of it fades. Edwin doesn't follow to see how it ends.

He stands. He tests his leg and finds it working. He leaves, scooping up the broken foils, walking the way anyone escaping from a thrashing and on his way to a scolding would walk. He doesn't look to see if Johnny is about.

He'd hoped to delay Mother's knowledge of the foils, but by the time he arrives, Johnny has already raced home and told the whole story. It seems that George triumphed. Johnny is quite elated by the whole thing. Victory to the Bully Boys!

But also embarrassed. "He just stands there and lets people hit him," Edwin overhears him telling Rosalie. "The only fight he'll ever win is a pretend one. And even then, he'll only pretend to win it.

"When someone hits him, he cries!"

How amazed Edwin would be to know that as an old man, he

will look back on these days with longing. My wonderful childhood, he'll think. My short and wonderful childhood.

iii

Father arrives at last and in such an excellent mood that the decision not to tell him about the foils is mutually made without a
word being spoken. He kisses the girls, returns to kiss them
again. Little Joe is tossed into the air. He even helps carry the
food to the table for dinner, doing an impression of a Negro servant that gives Asia the hiccoughs, she laughs so hard. The children stand behind their chairs until Father has taken his place.

Dinner with Father is a one-man show. His abhorrence of the
theatrical life is much less persuasive than the glamour he casts
with every word, every gesture. Tonight he tells tales of Sam
Houston, the wild man of the frontiers, intimate of the Cherokee, hero of the battle of San Jacinto, governor, orator, and senator. Edwin looks across the table, hoping to catch Johnny's eye.
They've heard these tales so often—*if there be nothing new, but that
which is Hath been before*—but Johnny doesn't notice him and Edwin actually loves these old stories.

Sam Houston dressed like an Indian. Sam Houston's near
mortal wounds. Sam Houston's broken heart. There are few men
Father admires as much and once, long ago, Houston was his
closest friend. Like himself, Father says, Houston has *mind*. He
points to his own forehead.

He tells them how, in a fit of despair, Houston determined
one day to do himself in. How his hand was stayed by the sudden
appearance of an eagle. "'A spirit messenger,' is how the Cherokee tell it. Old Sam's a great friend to the Indian—speaks the

language fluently, which few white men can do. He even has a tribal name—Col-lon-neh. That means the Raven." Father is wiping his plate clean with a piece of bread.

Around the time Father knew Houston best, around the time they were riding the steamboats on the Mississippi, tearing up the saloons together, regaling the audience on the stools with inebriated extemporaneous speeches on liberty inspired by Homer and Shakespeare, the Cherokee changed Houston's name from the Raven to Big Drunk. Father doesn't tell them that part. Nor how comical the Cherokee found them, tiny Father in his flowered waistcoat and brass buttons, hulking Houston in his blanket and sombrero, stumbling drunkenly along the streets, roaring their politics and their poetry.

Without these details, it all sounds grand. Edwin thinks that he would also like a Cherokee name. Obviously, the Cherokee won't give him one. He'll have to do that himself. Obviously, it won't be in Cherokee since Col-lon-neh is the only Cherokee word he knows. But it can't be in English. Maybe Hebrew? How would you say "the Raven" in Hebrew? Father will know.

Father has moved on to Andrew Jackson, another one-time friend, dead now almost two years. This leads to a brief Byronic melancholy:

Let my pure flame of Honour shine in story,
When I am cold in death—and the slow fire,
That wears my vitals now, will no more move me
Than 'twould a corpse within a monument.

The bit elided in *this* account is the letter he wrote during his old friend's presidency, calling him a damned scoundrel and threatening to cut his throat as he slept. Possibly he was joking.

The Cherokee have a special name for Jackson, too—they call him the Indian Killer. This also goes unsaid.

Father soon cheers up again, complimenting Rosalie on the leeks and potatoes, which she did not cook, Mother on the fish. Yes, fish! Suddenly Father, who once thought it murder to eat an oyster, has decided they should all be eating fish. None of the children like fish, so this is nothing to celebrate. Plus Rosalie has told Edwin how Father once said that he'd killed Mary Ann and Elizabeth by eating meat, so Edwin wonders which of them is being put at risk this time on account of a cod he doesn't even want.

Himself, of course. He looks up from his plate to see Father gazing at him fondly. "I've made a decision about our Ned," Father says. He leans back in his chair, drawing it out. "Momentous." He is all twinkle and trill. At last he gets to it. "Ned will be a cabinetmaker."

This is a shot to the heart.

"He's very skilled with his hands," Father says genially, obviously believing Edwin will be pleased with the compliment and the plan. "Look how quickly he picked up the banjo."

Edwin knows three chords at most, can play five tunes. He has always, always wanted to be an actor and *everyone* knows this. One of his early memories is of sitting with Mother in Father's dressing room, asking her what that sound was, the thunder four thousand people make when they all clap their hands at the same time.

Father dislikes being opposed, so Edwin says nothing, even as his dreams cry out in their dying. The more Father talks of it, the more fixed it will become.

Edwin doesn't expect Mother to argue with Father. She never

has. She never will. All he expects of her is silence. Silence, and maybe, after Father has quit the room, sympathy. Instead, his mother speaks. "Jesus was a carpenter," she says.

Now Edwin is so angry he can hardly swallow. As if Jesus is remembered for his woodwork! "June gets to be an actor," he says throatily.

It's enough resistance to set Father off. His hands smack down on the table, making the plates rattle. He begins to rail about the sacrifices he makes, the long hard touring, the exhausting falsity of it all. "All so that you can have a real life," he says. "What pleasure you will take in making something fine, something you can touch and smell and see, the product of your own hands. I envy you, by God I do."

There is a long silence in which Asia stares at Edwin balefully. Father was in such a good mood; they were having such fun, and then Edwin had to go and ruin everything. "'A man must rule his family in his own way,'" Father says.

But what about Edwin's meteor and caul? What about the more than 240,000 meteors falling over the East Coast and all the way to the Rocky Mountains at his birth? Will no one here speak up for the stars?

More silence. Father pulls his bread apart with his hands and puts a corner of it into his mouth. His teeth have been paining him for some time now. He shifts the bread about, seeking a place where he can chew comfortably. Edwin takes a small, grim satisfaction in seeing this. "June acts," Father says finally, swallowing. "But June is no actor."

The conversation is over. The decision is made.

In fact, it's been a long time since anyone remembered Edwin's stars. They've been superseded by Johnny's fiery arm. Even though

Edwin's stars were seen all over the city while Mother was the only witness to Johnny's magical fire. Edwin's stars were in the paper!

> *At my nativity*
> *The front of heaven was full of fiery shapes.*

And why does Johnny get to be an avenger while Edwin has to see ghosts? Why does June get to be an actor while Edwin has to be a cabinetmaker? It's the unfairness that Edwin objects to.

iv

After dinner, Father leaves to call on his friend John Hill Hewitt. Hewitt is one of Baltimore's brawling poets, and once punched Edgar Allan Poe (another of Father's friends—he knows everyone!) in the face in a dispute over a literary prize. Father's supposed to be back home for supper or, failing that, before the children go to bed, but no one is surprised when he isn't. If Father has money and friends (the friends optional—strangers will do in a pinch), he finds his way to the closest bar.

Mother waits for him until supper is cold. Then, claiming a headache, she goes to lie down. Rosalie follows. The other children serve themselves and eat in silence. Joe begins to cry and can't explain why. Nobody tells the children to go to bed and so they don't, except for Joe, who falls asleep in the parlor and is carried upstairs, his legs spilling from Edwin's arms and bumping against the banister and doorframe.

Sometime after midnight, they hear Father stumbling up the stoop and hurry to their bedrooms before they're seen. They leave a telltale fire crackling in the parlor.

Father is trying to be quiet. They hear this. They hear the wind, whistling through a crack in the bedroom window. They hear doors opening and closing. They hear Rosalie making her thumping way upstairs. The boys' bedroom is icy and Edwin leaves his socks on when he gets under the covers. He shivers and his teeth rattle until he's finally warm enough to fall asleep.

IN THE MORNING, Rosalie makes the children breakfast and sees them off to school. Her eyes are red from crying, but she refuses to admit this, claiming instead to be coming down with a cold. Father has already left. Mother doesn't come out of her bedroom. A hushed gloom settles like a fog on the house.

The recent rain smeared mud and puddles of pig shit on the pavement. Edwin has barely left the stoop before he steps in something vile. He tries to scrape his shoe clean on the bricks, using some language he is not supposed to use, and the whole thing—his fouled shoes, his foul mouth—makes Johnny and Asia laugh.

They walk three abreast. "Mother is quarreling with Father," Asia says, as if she's the only one to notice. They assume this has to do with money. Father has spent his money somewhere and now Mother doesn't know how to pay the bills. They've all seen this play before.

The O'Laughlens are half a block up the street. "Wilkes!" they cry and he dashes ahead to walk with them. Edwin's friend John Sleeper appears. He says hello to Edwin and nothing at all to Asia, but he reaches over, takes her books from her. Sleeper is a tall, awkward boy with a messy head of curls. They walk a few blocks and then Sleeper hands her books back, as Asia's school is to the right and the boys' to the left.

School is school and everything there seems quite ordinary

and all as it should be. The fact that Edwin smells like pig shit is remarked on. Perhaps as recompense, Miss Hyde asks him to read aloud "The Wreck of the Hesperus." She finds his performance surprisingly lethargic, notes the shadows under his eyes, and sends him back home.

As he turns onto North Exeter, he sees a woman ascending the steps of his house. The brim of her black silk bonnet is so old-fashionedly large, it entirely hides her profile. He watches her knock. No one comes. He slows his footsteps rather than en-counter this woman at his own front door. She's leaning across the railing now, looking through the window into the parlor, which is very nosy of her and something he thinks she shouldn't be doing.

Harriet Struthoff is standing in the doorway of her next-door grocery, her hair falling from its pins, burlap apron over her shirtwaist. She calls his name as he passes. "Why aren't you at school, young master?"

"Miss Hyde sent me home, because I wasn't feeling well."

"You'll find the house empty," Miss Struthoff says. "Your mother took Rose and Joe to the farm this morning. She told me to tell you all not to worry. Everything is fine. But will you be all right on your own?"

"Are they coming back?" Edwin asks.

Harriet's older sister is calling for her. "Of course," Miss Struthoff says. The calling is more insistent. "Only I don't know when. Now, you come right over here if you need any little thing. Milk or bread or something sweet." She disappears down the steps into the store.

All this time, the other woman, the woman in the black bon-net, has been walking towards him. "You're Junius Booth's boy?" she asks.

Edwin admits to it.

He's never seen this woman before. She's old, but not elderly. Under the shadow of her bonnet brim, deep lines frame her mouth and cross her forehead. The bit of hair the bonnet doesn't cover is the color of rusty iron. Her accent is almost British, but with something mixed in. Edwin practices reproducing her accent in his head. He's good at mimicry. "Are you from England?" Edwin asks the woman. "I went to England once."

The woman responds with a sharp inhale of air. "When was this then?"

"I was a baby," Edwin says. The woman stares at him in a way that makes him nervous, so he goes on to say something he wouldn't have offered ordinarily. "My brother Henry died there."

"I hear you have a lot of brothers," the woman tells him, as if Henry was someone he could easily spare. She is still pinning him with those gimlet eyes. "I was hoping to speak to your mother."

Edwin makes it past her and up the steps. "She's gone to the farm." It's a relief to shut the door.

He forgets about the woman. Being alone in his house is so unusual he's not sure it's ever happened before. He walks from room to room, seeing how it feels to be alone in each of them, and sure enough, it feels different in the kitchen than it does in his parents' bedroom, different in the parlor than it does upstairs. He has a sense not so much of being alone as of being invisible, an intruder in his own body. As if, when no one is watching, he ceases to be.

He lies down on the settee and the last words he thinks before he sleeps are

"O father! I see a gleaming light, Oh say, what may it be?"
But the father answered never a word, A frozen corpse was he.

He wakes when Asia and Johnny return from school. They're as perplexed as he by Mother's sudden departure. "Something must be wrong on the farm," Asia says. "Maybe something happened to the Mitchells?" But whatever is wrong made Rosalie cry and she wouldn't cry over the Mitchells. Edwin thinks it must be Ann or Joe Hall. Perhaps Rowland Rogers has sold away one of their children. That would certainly account for the tears. But it wouldn't be a secret, no reason to keep it from the rest of the family, so this answer doesn't really work either.

NOTHING MATTERS MORE than family, Father always says. Edwin makes a private vow to find Asia and Johnny less annoying in future. This lasts barely an hour, which is when Johnny calls him into the backyard. He's grinning, the sun hitting his dark hair and turning it into golden shine. On the bench in the gazebo is a lumpy, jumpy, snarling flour sack. From it, Johnny carefully withdraws two cats. He's tied them together in such an ingenious way that if either one struggles, it will slash the other with its claws. One of the cats is gray and starving, the skin between its ribs sunk as deep as Edwin's finger. The other is black, plumper, a cared-for cat. Both are spitting and yowling, scrapping and bleeding. Father's rule, that no creature is ever to be injured, is less clear in the city than it was on the farm. It's less clear to Johnny than it is to Edwin.

Johnny is discriminating. He loves dogs. He hates cats. He loves horses. He hates squirrels. He sings sometimes to the frogs on the farm, but they all do that—"A Frog He Would A-Wooing Go," which Mother taught them, or, from Ann, "Down by the Riverside." An image from the time Johnny's horse Blackie bit him rises in Edwin's mind, Johnny's face so full of his hurt feelings. When Johnny loves, he expects to be loved in return. Edwin has no such expectations.

"Let them loose," Edwin says, "or you'll see Father's belt."

"Only if you tell," Johnny says, but he cuts the string with his pocketknife. The cats bolt, leaping the fence (the black one), climbing a tree (the gray).

Father appears briefly at dinnertime, but only partly as Father, and partly as someone midway between Edward Mortimer and the Stranger. He seems unsurprised by Mother's absence, speaks very little, only saying wistfully that the big cherry tree on the farm will soon be budding and how sad it will be to miss that. If they were Japanese, they would go to the farm as a pilgrimage. So many things would be different if they were Japanese, Father says despondently.

Edwin waits to hear what these different things would be, but Father is apparently done with the Japanese. There are still traces of his stage make-up, particularly in the creases around his eyes. His eyes appear widened by it, as if he's painted a kind of shock onto them. "We should all go to the farm," Father says. "We were safe when we were on the farm."

Then he heads to the theater again, leaving the children to manage their bedtimes for themselves. Staying up late in the sad quiet house has lost its allure and they don't do it again.

MOTHER, ROSALIE, and Joe return two days later. That evening, when Mother has shut herself in her bedroom, and Father is facing the opening curtain, Rosalie gathers the older children into the girls' room to finally tell them as much as she knows. The important point is this one: Adelaide Booth, Father's wife, has arrived from England and is hell-bent on destroying them all.

v

The children had always assumed that Mother was Father's wife.

vi

Rosalie says that someone must have told Mrs. Booth that Mother was at the farm, because straight to the farm she'd come, in a hired carriage with a Negro driving, and then on foot, right through the gate and up to the cabin door, where she'd stood in the yard in her big black bonnet, spewing such dreadful names at Mother that nothing on this earth would compel Rosalie to repeat them. She was glad, she said, that none of them were there to hear it.

But farmhands working in the fields heard it. Neighbors on their porches heard it. Children in their graves heard it. "You can't imagine the humiliation," Rosalie says. Joe Hall had to loose the dogs to keep her from coming right into the cabin, which she informed them now belonged to her, both the cabin and the house on Exeter, too, and they had no legal right to keep her out of either one.

ROSALIE IS SEATED on her bed, her shoulders against the wall and her head pushed forward by the knot of her hair and the stoop of her spine. Her skirt, crinoline removed, spreads limply over the covers like a brown puddle. Asia sits cross-legged at the foot, facing her, and Johnny is stretched out next to her, his head on his arm. Both are lying on some part of her skirt, holding her by her wings like a pinned butterfly as she talks.

Edwin has taken a seat on the floor, which is cold, and either because of that or because he feels coiled so tight with tension, there is a tremor in his legs. He has wanted to know what's going on, but now that he will, he wishes he wouldn't.

He pulls his knees up to his chest, wrapping them in his arms until they are still. The light in the room is golden—*The weary sun hath made a golden set*—and Rosalie's eyes shine with unshed tears; the bottom of her nose glistens. Edwin wishes he were older, the days about to come now safely in the past. *The weary sun hath made a golden set, And by the bright track of his fiery car Gives token of a goodly day tomorrow.* The someone who told that woman that Mother was at the farm? That someone was Edwin.

"I don't see why we should feel humiliated," Asia says. "It's not as if *we* did anything wrong."

WHEN THE SHOCK has abated slightly, the children try to remember if they were ever actually told that their parents were married. They were certainly never told otherwise.

There seem now to be only three possibilities:

1. It's all a lie and Father was never married to the woman calling herself Adelaide Booth.

This is the option Asia will choose. For the rest of her life, she will insist that Father and Mother married first and ran off to America after.

2. Father seduced and deceived Mother.

This is Johnny's pick. He will decide that Father tricked Mother with a false wedding, that Mother was as stunned as the rest of them to learn she was unmarried. It's a sentiment shared by their neighbors and friends. Mother has always struck everyone as every inch a lady. Father, on the other hand . . .

Johnny's attachment to his mother will deepen. His feelings about his father will, from this time forward, carry an undercurrent of blame and anger.

3. Mother knowingly ran off with a married man.

Edwin is surprised to learn that Rosalie isn't certain which of these options is true. He is even more surprised to learn that Rosalie is leaning towards number three.

Among the children, Rosalie feels the scandal most deeply. How often has Mother said she has no secrets from Rosalie? Mother is such a liar. Shame spreads like a fever through Rosalie's body, making her cheeks hot, her hands cold. She adds this to the many reasons she already has for not leaving the house.

Edwin's own position will shift about over the years. Sometimes, like Asia, he will insist that his father's one and only marriage was to his mother. Sometimes, like Rosalie, he will acknowledge Adelaide's prior claim, though dismissing her as an adventuress, thirty-two years his father's elder (she was, in fact, four years older). Asia saw her once, he will say. I never did.

This is a good reminder that no one in the world is a reliable source for their own story.

Lincoln and the Merry-Begotten

During the ride he spoke, for the first time in my hearing, of his mother, dwelling on her characteristics, and mentioning or enumerating what qualities he inherited from her. He said, among other things, that she was the illegitimate daughter of Lucy Hanks and a well-bred Virginia farmer or planter; and he argued that from this last source came his power of analysis, his logic, his mental activity, his ambition, and all the qualities that distinguished him from the other members and descendants of the Hanks family. His theory in discussing the matter of hereditary traits had been, that, for certain reasons, illegitimate children are oftentimes sturdier and brighter than those born in lawful wedlock . . .

—J. L. Scripps, interview with Abraham Lincoln

Lincoln's mother had died of milk sickness back when he was nine years old and his sister, Sarah, eleven. The family had then been living in southern Indiana. Up to this point, the hardships of Lincoln's life were, for the times, quite ordinary—occasional beatings, hunger, a remote and unappeasable father, endless toil, and all the perils of the wilderness. His mother's love had made his life tolerable. And then she was gone and he, at nine years old, helping make her coffin.

Fourteen months after her death, Thomas Lincoln left his children to travel to Kentucky to fetch home a new wife. He was absent so long, Abe and Sarah decided he must have died. A neighbor described them as all but nude, their clothing rotting away. They were lice-ridden, starving.

When the new stepmother arrived, she was shocked by what she found. The children were immediately cleaned, clothed, and fed. In a matter of weeks, the cabin had windows, a floor, tables, and chairs. She was good at making things better.

Prior to her arrival, his father had forbidden Abe's reading as a waste of his time. His stepmother encouraged his studies. "Abe was the best boy I Ever Saw or Ever Expect to see," she will write someday when the gifts she saw early are widely recognized.

Whatever native talents he has, Lincoln attributes entirely to his first mother's bloodline. That he was allowed to make something of them is the work of his second mother. He credits his father with none of it.

vii

Adelaide Booth begins to follow all of them, though mostly Mother, around Baltimore, shouting that Mother is a whore and the children bastard-born. She'll appear at the market where Mother tries to sell her produce. She'll appear outside the classroom just as the boys are leaving.

"I'll fall on your backs like a bomb," Adelaide cries out, trailing them through the streets, weaving through carriages and pedestrians, her contorted face obscured by her bonnet, her voice loud and spit-filled. The Bully Boys scatter when she appears, reconvene in her absence. They remain Johnny's staunch supporters, but their fists and fisticuffs are useless against this woman.

The nagging sense that he must be grateful to the Bully Boys for their continued friendship is a feeling new to Johnny and very disagreeable.

The more she shouts, the more room she is given on the sidewalks and streets. She moves through Baltimore in a private space created by her own fury. She follows Edwin and Johnny right into the schoolyard. "You brats. You ill-begotten vipers. You aren't clean enough to step on. I wouldn't sully my shoes." The other children stare and Edwin's not sure if they're staring at her or at him. He feels the heat coming into his face. "We should come a different way," Johnny says quietly, and after that they change their route daily. Mother hires a large black man to walk Asia back and forth from school.

Only Father is left unmolested. Mrs. Booth is not so angry that she'll jeopardize his earnings.

Sometimes she's accompanied by Father's real son—a man only a few years older than June, and named for Grandfather. Rosalie tells the others that Richard Booth has actually been traveling with Father for more than a year. How Father can have imagined he would pull this off without Richard ever getting wind of the family in Baltimore remains one of the mysteries that is Father. He was, perhaps, emboldened by twenty-five years of successfully keeping his bigamy a secret from almost everyone.

Edwin rarely looks at Richard straight on for fear Richard will look back, but he knows him as a tall, pale, fragile man, nothing like June, opposite to Father in every way. Can this really be Father's son? Edwin doubts it.

Richard never speaks, but his presence at his mother's side suggests his enmity. A half-brother Edwin never knew he had is his mortal enemy. It's Shakespearean, really.

viii

Most of the time, Edwin manages to ignore the situation. He has other things to think about. He's been offered a theater!

Only not exactly. Mrs. Robson, the mother of Johnny's friend Stuart, manages a local hotel, and she's told Stuart that if he and his little friends clean out the cellar, they can use it as a playhouse. Stuart has even managed to purchase a real set from the Kilmiste Garden resort, a painted backdrop—the plain room of a simple cottage, a fireplace, rough-hewn shelves with bowls and mugs.

Johnny and his friends are full of plans. They'll charge a penny apiece for the neighborhood children, two pennies for interested adults, and pay an organ grinder out of the proceeds. Their first play will be *Richard III*, with all the women's parts removed and the swordplay emphasized. Johnny is terribly excited about the whole thing. He expects to star. He makes the mistake of boasting about this to Edwin . . .

. . . who sees instantly that he needs to take over. Johnny can't play Richard III. He's eight years old! Edwin and his friend John Sleeper offer to join the troupe. The offer comes with a contract specifying their share of the purse. As an adult George Stout will remember these thirteen-year-olds as intimidatingly professional. Also fantastically condescending. The older boys steal the set. Johnny and his friends steal it back. It changes hands so many times, it falls to pieces before it can be used.

The older boys don't join the troupe so much as they take possession of it. Edwin will, of course, be Richard. Sleeper will be Buckingham. Johnny can be Richmond, a very important part, they assure him. The hero.

All of these boys will go on to have careers in the theater. While other children are playing mumblety-peg, ringtaw, and the game of graces in their spare time, those in the Booth orbit have long been putting on plays. To date, these have taken place in the backyard of 62 Exeter. But this new venture is a magnitude greater. The cellar is enormous and free from the vagaries of Baltimore weather.

Edwin just needs costumes. And a horse. There is plenty of room in the cellar for a horse.

He's happily mulling these things over when Rosalie calls for him to come down to the kitchen. He can tell from her tone that he missed her first call. Rosalie is always so quiet. Really, you have to be expecting her voice in order to hear it.

He descends the stairs, but in body only; his mind is still on his production. He finds Rosalie making biscuits just the way Aunty Rogers taught her. She's flushed and there's a dusting of flour in her hair and on her rumpled shirtfront. Baby Joe is at the table cutting the biscuits from the dough with the rim of a water glass.

She asks Edwin to build up the fire in the stove, so he adds sticks and stirs the whole thing until it's crackling. Edwin and Rosalie have a conversation that, because of Baby Joe's presence, takes place in abstracts. It dawns on Edwin that while he has been working to avoid all thought of their parents' treachery, Rosalie has been worrying over it like a dog with a bone.

"How much do you know about Lord Byron?" Rosalie asks him.

Edwin knows how often Mother has said that she ran off with Father because of Byron's poems. They've all only heard this for their whole lives.

He knows that one of Father's first gifts to Mother was an oval of Byron's face, his dark curls encircled by a thin golden wreath. A brooch, and Mother treasures it, though she never wears it. Her life has turned out less dressy. The brooch is kept in a cupboard drawer with Mother's other treasures, including Edwin's caul. He knows that Byron was poor Henry's middle name.

"I've read some of his poetry," Edwin says. "I know he and Father used to be friends."

Rosalie, it turns out, knows a great deal more. She tells Edwin about Byron's abandoned wife and the sister whom he treated as a wife, and his friend Percy Shelley and *his* abandoned wife, who killed herself while she was pregnant (unless she was murdered, by whom and for what reason Rosalie couldn't say), and also William Godwin, an anarchist who believed women were just as good as men but had one illegitimate stepdaughter who killed herself, and another who'd had an affair and a child with Byron, and also a real daughter who was that same Mary Shelley who wrote *Frankenstein* after running off with Percy Shelley. Oh, it was all a dreadful tangle and, as far as Rosalie can see, nothing but free love from top to bottom. Free love, she explains to Edwin in a scatter of flour, means that love matters more than marriage. Marriage is a prison in which love cannot be free.

Rosalie wipes her hands on an apron cross-stitched with fraying pieties—*Her price is far above rubies.* She has more flour in her hair now.

Abstract or not, Edwin thinks that Baby Joe shouldn't be hearing any of this. He thinks that Rosalie has lost her mind. She's so gullible. She reads too many books. He himself stopped listening about the time Byron was wanting to marry his sister. Where has Rosalie heard such nonsense?

It can only have come from Mother. Mother and Rosalie are prone to quiet, private conversations while they beat the rugs, hang the laundry, churn the butter. He's always assumed they were deciding what to make for supper. Now it appears they've been sharing licentious, depraved gossip instead. Mother! And Rose!

Edwin and Asia have, on occasion, performed the balcony scene from *Romeo and Juliet* and he's tried to make it as real as he can, but he certainly doesn't want to marry Asia. He pities the man who does. Nor does he want to discuss free love with Rosalie. Nothing could be more embarrassing. He needs to get back to his costumes.

"'Marriage from love, like vinegar from wine,'" Rosalie is saying now, because apparently this is something Byron used to say. She leaves no pause during which Edwin might extricate himself from the whole horrid conversation.

"Scree, scree," says Baby Joe, who has his own ways of escaping.

The way Rosalie sees it, pretty much everyone in London was abandoning their wives to run away with their sweethearts around the time that Father met Mother. It seems to have been quite the fad. Sodom and Gomorrah with tea.

She is either accusing Mother and Father or she is defending them. Edwin can't figure out which. He thinks that she's angry, although with Rosalie it's always hard to tell. She speaks quietly, but there is something in the way she is working the dough as if stabbing at it with her spoon. "We're no better than anyone else," Rosalie says, "for all Father's airs. A lot of people will think we're worse now. Practically everyone will think that."

It comes to Edwin then what Rosalie is really talking about. Two years ago, Father had taken them all to the circus, where Rosalie met a handsome policeman-turned-lion-tamer from New York named Jacob Driesbach. Driesbach worked without cages, no bars between his cats and an audience full of tender young children. As they watched, he wrestled a full-grown tiger to the ground. He invited several lions to sup with him at a large dining table. The best of manners were observed, each cat in its own chair, no cat commencing to eat until Driesbach, the host, did so. And all the while, he wore a glittering Arabian costume tight around the legs and his muscled arms bare. Naturally, Rosalie was impressed.

Afterwards, Driesbach asked to be introduced to the great actor Junius Booth. But Rosalie seemed to be his real interest. This unexpected and almost implausible turn of events ended in a time of closed doors and muffled sobbing as Father put a quick stop to the whole thing.

He'd said: That Rosalie was needed at home. How did she imagine Mother would manage without her?

That Driesbach was a traveling man and had, undoubtedly, left a trail of broken women behind him. Rosalie would be a fool to think herself so special as to have captured his heart.

That maybe lions were happier untamed.

That Driesbach was a sideshow performer, a creator of mere spectacle, not an artist, not a true player. Circus folk were beneath them. Rosalie should remember that she was better than that. Father would not allow her to so undervalue herself.

Rosalie should remember that she is a Booth. End of discussion.

Rosalie is remembering that now.

"Why are you telling me about Byron?" Edwin asks.

"Who else can I tell?" Rosalie asks him back.

That night, Father remarks that Rosalie's biscuits have never been so light. Lighter even than Aunty Rogers'. Rosalie's biscuits are lighter than air.

IN 1869, WHEN Harriet Beecher Stowe ignites a conflagration by accusing Lord Byron of incest in the pages of *The Atlantic Monthly* and a third of their subscribers leave as a result, Rosalie will remind Edwin that she told him so first and he didn't believe her. No one will believe Stowe either.

THE NEXT SURPRISING thing that Edwin hears is that the Mitchells are leaving the farm. Just days after Adelaide Booth's arrival, with the secret of Father's marriage now out in the open, the Mitchells are being thrown to the streets. Everyone had always wondered why they'd been allowed to stay, crowding the family out as they did, abusing Mother's hospitality, offering nothing in return for Father's support. Now the mystery is solved. Clearly, Uncle Mitchell had secured their place through blackmail.

Edwin has an early memory. He's a very young boy, returning to the farm in the dark on horseback, seated on the slope of the saddle, his father behind him. Even safe inside the warm circle of his father's arms, a night terror has been growing, scorching his lungs and whipping his heart. He hears an owl, the wind, the panting and hoofbeats of the horse. The sounds swell in volume. The whole dark sky is in motion.

His father dismounts and swings him down. "There, boy," Father says. "Your foot is on your native heath." And the terror lifts and leaves him. The farm is his home and he will never be afraid there.

He feels a longing for it all—the way the water smells, branches scraping like violin bows in the wind, cows calling to be milked, fireflies sparking in the grass. Swimming and riding, climbing into the interlaced trees, singing with the slaves and the freemen in the warm evenings, taking the paths to the swamp with the dogs, ever hopeful for squirrels, panting and racing ahead.

No Mitchells lurking about, spoiling it all.

THE MITCHELLS DISAPPEAR into the squalor of the Baltimore Ring Factory. Edwin will not think of them again.

But after Edwin's death, Baby Joe will take, as his second wife, Cora Mitchell, the daughter of one of the Mitchell cousins. The groom will be fifty-four and a doctor, the bride twenty-four and a socialite. The wedding will be a grand affair, with many newspapers taking note of the fact that the groom had two older brothers, the late Junius Booth Jr. and the late great actor Edwin Booth. No other brother will be mentioned.

ix

Richard III is finally opening in the hotel cellar. Johnny has passed on his chance to be Richmond. He's lost all interest, won't deign to attend, even though George Stout has told him that Edwin's horse, bought for one dollar and seventy-five cents—a bony white mare unimpressed with her own stardom—may well be Edwin's undoing. So far she's foiled his every vision by refusing to move her feet. If this had been the horse Richard sold his kingdom for, he would've lost England anyway.

The afternoon progresses with Johnny roaming listlessly about his bedroom. His friends are all either watching *Richard III* or performing in it. He doesn't exactly regret his decision. He's just at a loss for what to do instead, when, from the first floor, he hears his father shout. He hears the thunder of footsteps on the stairs. Father arrives in the boys' bedroom, holding the tatters of his Shylock costume. Edwin has cut the spangles from it to make himself a suit of armor.

Father's first thought is to blame Johnny. He grabs Johnny by the arm, shakes him hard. He draws back his fist. Johnny is no telltale; it's little Joe who serves up Edwin and he does this in a high, hysterical voice before Father's fist can land. Now that Edwin's been named, Johnny's willing to confirm it. He's in no mood to take a whipping on Edwin's account. He tells his father exactly where the rest of his Shylock costume can be found.

Father arrives at the cellar just as the final act is unfolding. Edwin is savoring the climactic moments. "'Hark, I hear their drum. Fight, gentlemen of England! Fight, bold yeomen!'" As he swings his sword, there's a commotion at the back of the theater, which could be an enraptured audience, but isn't. He sees his father coming, unconcerned with the hands and feet he may be stepping on. His face is splotched with rage.

Edwin drops his sword and dives for the cellar window. He makes it halfway through before his father seizes him by the legs. The window is at street level. The Negro who collected tickets for them at the play's beginning sees Edwin emerging and takes hold of his arms to help him out. Edwin finds himself stretched between the two men, kicking his legs in an attempt to free them.

Over the years, as performed by the Booth family, *Richard III* seems to have had a variety of endings, none of them good for Richard. Father needs only Edwin's bottom half in order to deliver a beating Edwin will long remember. It doesn't give him the same strange thrill he gets from Miss Hyde's cane.

x

Father pays Adelaide Booth the enormous sum of two thousand dollars and considers the matter at an end. Still Adelaide's attacks continue. Since Father refuses to recognize Richard as his only legitimate son, the courts will have to decide. Three years of residency in the country are required before Adelaide has standing. She and Richard move into a shabby tenement and start the clock.

Adelaide's next three years are filled with drudgery, ill health, and poor food. Richard takes on pupils—he has his father's gift for languages—but he's so mild that his students torment him, so timid that he often goes unpaid. Edwin might actually like Richard if he knew him. Of all Father's children, it seems possible that Edwin and Richard are the most alike.

But Edwin doesn't know him, knows only that Adelaide Booth is a street brawler and that they can't all be Father's children under the law. It is Richard against himself and June, Rosalie, Asia, Johnny, and Joe.

Back in her tenement, Adelaide drinks steadily. This and tormenting Father's other family, whom she refers to as the Holmes set, Holmes being Mother's maiden name, will occupy her for the next three years.

THE FIRST YEAR passes. Edwin is moved out of Miss Hyde's warm little classroom and into the tutelage of Louis Dugas, a retired French naval officer high on discipline and presentation. Edwin excels at history and literature. Nothing is done to fit him for a career in carpentry. That plan is thankfully never mentioned again.

He and John Sleeper enact a schoolroom performance of a scene from *Julius Caesar*, which his father comes to see and even appears to enjoy. Edwin's desire to act has never wavered. He has a suspicion that his talents will be best suited to comedy. By now he's grown into his own sort of popularity, which is to say that among his small circle of friends, in his quiet way, he is liked.

And then, a great change comes.

Edwin is already asleep—at fourteen, it seems he can never sleep or eat enough—when he's suddenly aware that his mother is seated on the side of his bed, patting his hand. "Come down to the parlor, dear," she says. She's whispering so as not to wake Johnny or Joe. "I need to talk to you."

Outside there is wind and rain. Inside, shadows.

Edwin rises and follows her downstairs in the dark. In spite of her stealth, Johnny comes, too. She takes the seat in front of the fire, Edwin and Johnny at her feet. Edwin seldom really looks at his mother, the woman so beautiful his father left everything to be with her. So he's surprised by how gingerly she lowers herself to the chair, surprised by how, even in the rosy light of the fire, he sees a slight sag of skin on her neck. She kept her looks through ten pregnancies, four heartbreaks. She's still beautiful, but the fading has begun.

Johnny puts his head into her lap and she smooths his hair. Edwin is the one she speaks to. "When your father leaves on his next tour," she says, "you'll be going with him."

Johnny raises his head. "I'll go."

Johnny is so much quicker than Edwin. Edwin hasn't even begun to take in what's being asked. "What about school?"

"You'll still go to school. Whenever you're home in Baltimore," Mother says.

What if you were suddenly offered everything you ever

wanted, but the offer came in a voice so sad, with a face so sorry, it made you wonder if you'd ever wanted it at all?

"I'll go," says Johnny. "Ned's better at school than I am."

"My love, you're much too young," Mother tells him. She will never send Johnny away. Edwin, on the other hand . . . To Edwin, it feels as if Mother is opening the front door and thrusting him out into the storm.

"Ned gets everything," Johnny says.

Edwin's face and hands are cold. The log in the fireplace falls with a whisper into ash. He moves closer to the fire and farther from his mother. One cheek warms; the other does not. He remembers how Mother once asked the flames to reveal Johnny's fate and he makes a silent prayer to know his own. No response from the reddened coals. Across the dark room, the lace curtains flutter suddenly as if a breeze or a ghost has entered.

"It has to be you," Mother says to him. She reminds him that June used to travel with Father sometimes, but now he has his own family and career. She'd thought Father was doing fine alone, but now they all know that Richard was with him and clearly, Richard can't be asked to travel with Father again. Father's truly on his own this time and only catastrophe can follow.

The family depends entirely on Father's wages. If he continues to miss half his curtains or to spend his money the very night he earns it, they'll soon find themselves on the street or in the factories. Edwin must go along and keep him out of trouble. This is a job no one can do, and there is no one but Edwin to do it.

Mother has made it clear that Edwin has no choice in the matter and yet he can feel how much she wants him to agree. He considers denying her this, and it's not her tragic face and voice that finally make him speak up. Face and voice are the actor's tools and anguish can be easily feigned. It's her hands, the counterfeit wedding band, the worn nails just at his eye level, resting on Johnny's black hair. Something about his mother's hands, red in the firelight, moves Edwin to a terrible kindness. "I'll go," he says.

For many years now, Rosalie's job has been to save her mother. From this day forward, Edwin's job will be the saving of the whole family. This is a job no one can do, and there is no one but Edwin to do it.

"No fair," Johnny says.

Lincoln and the Whigs at Sprigg's

Allow the President to invade a neighboring nation, whenever he shall deem it necessary to repel an invasion, and you allow him to do so whenever he may choose to say he deems it necessary for such purpose—and you allow him to make war at pleasure.

—Abraham Lincoln, 1848

Lincoln has married the woman he said it would kill him to marry. They have two young sons and he's come to Washington, DC, to represent the good people of Illinois in Congress. The city is unfinished, yet already decaying. The Potomac is choked green with algae and the smell of dead fish permeates. Dead cats rot on the streets. Still! Washington!

They take rooms at Ann Sprigg's boardinghouse, where more than twenty other Whigs are already in residence. Restless, ambitious, Lincoln wants to see and do everything. But Mary finds it hard to keep their young sons entertained. She quarrels with the other boarders, demands that Lincoln take her side in all things. He feels a guilty relief when she takes the boys to her family's home in Kentucky.

Sprigg's is known locally as Abolition House. Those slaves that work for Ann Sprigg disappear north with mysterious regularity. The Whigs residing there see the Mexican War as a mere ruse for expanding the slaveholding territories. James Polk is president. In a grand tradition reaching back through the centuries, he insists that war was forced upon him by unprovoked aggression. He seizes huge swaths of the West as recompense.

Lincoln takes to the floor of the House to accuse Polk of lying. He demands to know the exact spot on which the first gun was fired, the first blood shed. Wasn't it, in fact, on Mexican soil? The word *spot* is repeated many times during this speech. Later he hears himself referred to as "spotty Lincoln."

Back in Illinois, folks are surprised by his attack on Polk. Even those who opposed the war find his speeches close to treason. Lincoln is surprised in return. He supported every measure to fund and supply American troops without condition or argument. The Democrats cynically conflated that with support for the war itself.

Lincoln abhorred the war and admired the soldiers. How hard is that to understand?

There is a second principle at stake. The power to declare war rests only with Congress.

The *Illinois State Register*, which once supported Lincoln, now says that he has demeaned the courage and sacrifice of Illinois' fighting men. When the Whigs lose the seat, the paper suggests Lincoln's obituary—"Died of Spotted Fever."

xi

Almost the first thing that happens is Edwin nearly losing his father. The month is August, the year 1848, and Father has a weeklong engagement in Albany, playing Othello one night,

Iago another, Edward Mortimer, and then Sir Giles Over-reach. On the 18th, he is scheduled to finish the run with Richard III, performed as a benefit. That's when the real money should arrive.

Edwin is finding his way into this new life. He looks younger than his fourteen years, thin and pale, with hooded eyes. The women in the cast make a pet of him, treating him as more of a child than he feels, which he likes and dislikes in equal measure. These women are bold and loud and touch him often, stroking his hair, taking his hand and running a finger over his wrist. He might be less uncomfortable if his father weren't there, one moment paying no attention and the next, seeing everything. Father either disapproves or is amused. Knowing Father, it's probably both. Edwin can't tell which he dislikes more.

Edwin aims for an unimpeachable professionalism. He stands in the wings, reading along in case his father needs a prompt or a sip of water. He manages the trunks and costumes, the entrances and exits. Nothing distracts him. For years, he hasn't been allowed to see his father act. Now it seems he does nothing but. He begins to notice when his father tries out a new gesture or an intonation. He sees the parts that never change. He begins to feel that he can tell, as the audience clearly cannot, when his father is bored, which is often.

The afternoon of the 17th, Edwin goes out looking for newspapers. His father likes to take his tea with the day's death notices. He's made it about four blocks from the Eagle Hotel, when he begins to smell smoke. He doesn't think anything of this at first, but the smell grows stronger and soon he sees the smoke as well, coiling above the harbor, spreading, thickening. More and more people appear on the sidewalks. At first, they merely watch, asking each other quietly what is happening. Fire, of course. Obviously. But how big? How close?

Edwin couldn't say who starts the panic. One minute, everyone seems calm and the next, they are all shouting at each other, running back towards their houses or else up the street. Soon, like a flock of birds or a school of fish, they've settled on their singular direction, out of the city, away from the fire. A bearded man in a tall top hat seizes Edwin's arm as he runs past. "Come with me," he cries, and it costs Edwin a wrenched wrist to break free.

Edwin is running back towards the hotel, moving with difficulty against the flow as the pavement fills with people. An oncoming family—mother and father, each with a child in their arms and another on their back—forces him into the middle of the street, where the horses have caught the contagion of alarm. A few feet away, a young Negro fights the reins against a large white horse. While he grapples for control, an older white boy takes advantage of his inattention to lift three children into the back of his cart, climb aboard himself. The horse nearly steps on Edwin, who pushes his way back into the crowd.

More people, and now Edwin is losing ground. A bonnetless girl falls and several people step over or on her until a flushed, fat woman takes pity, leans down, and hauls her to her feet. This woman grabs for Edwin, too, forcing him to turn around, but he breaks loose again, only to be seized from the other side. "Let me go!" he shouts and his voice cracks and squeaks in the way it sometimes does now, which angers him so much he has to clench his jaw or his teeth will chatter.

"Ned, boy!"

He looks and the person holding his arm is his father. The relief of this makes him suddenly dizzy. He might have fallen himself, but his father's grip keeps him upright. His father is wearing Richard's hump and Othello's cloak. He carries a hotel pillowcase over his back like St. Nicholas, knobby with two crowns, as well as with some other bits of costumes that are easily carried—eye patches, Othello's earring, Iago's hose. Also letters from Mother and Rosalie, and a few of last week's reviews. Later, when he unpacks it, Edwin will see that his father took the time to cull the best of these. His father throws Hamlet's cape onto Edwin's shoulders.

The light has become so strange now, thin and blurred, and ash is falling like snow from the sky. For a few moments, Edwin has the odd feeling that he and his father are alone in a small, unhurried place, under a bell jar, while outside the glass, all is roil, cacophony, and dimly heard chaos. "Where are we going?" Edwin asks and he doesn't even have to raise his voice. He takes a shallow breath and the taste of smoke goes all the way down his throat and into his lungs.

His father ties a scarf over his nose and mouth, hands Edwin one to do the same. "Upwards. Mansion Hill," his father says, muffled as a bandit. Moments later: "Mark my words, it will turn out to be a woman caused it."

Mansion Hill proves to be a long climb away. Eventually, the crowd substantially reduced, they arrive at the old Kane estate, an elegant house of yellow brick, surrounded by stands of maple and pines, its once spacious grounds now cut through with roads and alleyways. From the gated entry, his father lowers his scarf and expounds authoritatively to the other evacuees about the methods the firefighters will use. All the ingenuity of man—the leather buckets, the horse-drawn pumps—will prove futile against the dreadful power of the great fire. "When God claps His hands . . ." his father says. He quotes William Blake.

Little fly,
Thy summer's play
My thoughtless hand
Has brushed away.

Am not I
A fly like thee?
Or art not thou
A man like me?

The contemplation of human frailty seems to please Edwin's father enormously. He turns then to another equally pleasurable narrative—the egalitarian camaraderie of the volunteer firefighters. Apparently his father had once missed a curtain call to join in a communal effort to quell a fire. Edwin has never heard this story before. Under his scarf, he smells his own breath and the smell is stale and unpleasant.

Far away, down by the water, an explosion sends shafts of fire into the air like red spears, which then fall back into the boiling cauldron of smoke and flame. This all happens behind his father, the fiery backdrop to his speeches. He doesn't turn to see.

His father says that in January, the New Theater in Vicksburg burned. He was supposed to be playing Iago. "I begin to think God doesn't care for Shakespeare," Edwin's father says. He passes a hand over his flattened nose.

He has his usual rapt audience. The others have only just figured out that the oddly dressed man before them is the famous, the infamous Junius Booth. They may be losing their homes and all their worldly goods, but what a story they will have to tell.

Father returns to extolling the firefighters. "Most satisfying thing I've ever done," he says, "fighting in a battle so worthy. Against so implacable a foe. If I didn't have my son here to watch out for, I'd be down there right now, surrounded by comrades in arms. A man has so few chances to prove his mettle. Don't ever let one pass you by, Ned." Ripples of flame behind him, the low black sky above. The devil never had a better setting.

A skinny old woman stands next to Edwin. She has a drooping eye, a twisted foot, and a walking stick. Edwin thinks that she has already proved her mettle, just by making the climb here. She taps his shoulder with her stick, then thrusts it upwards. "Maybe God is not such a philistine, after all," she says. The thick, dark clouds above them are not, as he'd thought, entirely smoke and ash. It begins to rain, lightly at first, then with gusto. Everyone moves to the shelter of the trees. They are wet; they are smiling; they are thanking God for His mercy. The wind has shifted and over the slow minutes, the red horizon vanishes, either drowned or hidden by clouds. Lightning appears as arrows in the sky.

The branches are a porous roof. Edwin shakes the water from his hair like a dog, Hamlet's cape plastered wetly onto his shoulders. "'There's a divinity that shapes our ends, Rough-hew them how we will,'" he tells the woman.

His father regards him amiably. "You're soaked through, Ned. We really should get you in front of a fire."

BY THE TIME the rain comes, the fire has lasted five hours. Much of Albany has been destroyed. There are ten fatalities, many more injured by flame or smoke inhalation. Six hundred buildings are burned, businesses and ships, the whole Hudson River waterfront reduced to cinders. But the firefighters have more than repaid Father for his admiration. The Eagle Hotel is gone, but Father's trunks have been saved. Rumors that a careless chambermaid started the whole conflagration are never proved.

Johnny is deeply envious when he hears. Secretly, he doesn't think he would have spent hours under a tree when there was a fire to be fought. Secretly, he is unsurprised that Edwin would choose to do so.

Edwin is left with a question that will continue to puzzle him for years. Was his father looking for him in the crowd that day, or was it simply chance that he and Edwin found each other? Mother was quite clear that Edwin's job was to take care of his father. Was taking care of Edwin also his father's job? Or had the weather vane stopped pointing that direction?

xii

For the next five years, on and off, Edwin travels with his father. He will, in time, reduce this grim and lonely interlude to a handful of stories, told and retold, more amusing and less painful with each recounting.

There is the time he'd forbade his father to leave their room and Father locked himself in the closet, staying there so long and so silent, Edwin feared he'd suffocated. After an hour of banging on the door and begging for reassurance, Edwin had just decided he must fetch the innkeeper and an axe, when Father suddenly emerged without a word or a look, and climbed into bed. Soon he was snoring away.

The time in Louisville, when he chased his father at full run for the whole of one night—really, Father's stamina was astonishing—up moonlit streets, down unlit alleyways, hysteria rising in his throat so that he couldn't tell if he was laughing or sobbing at all the ways his father failed to lose him.

The time he locked his father in their hotel room to keep him sober while Edwin prepared for his appearance at the theater, only to find on his return that his father had bribed the innkeeper to serve him mint juleps, which he'd drunk through the keyhole with a straw.

More time passes and Edwin will stop telling these stories. His father's oddities were most painful to Father himself. "It's not for the son to lay bare what the sire would have wished concealed," Edwin will say. "I have no interest in merely satisfying the curious or making the unskilled laugh."

EDWIN'S SCHOOLING CEASES—he will feel disadvantaged by this for the rest of his life. But he sees much of the country as they move from hotel to hotel, theater to theater. His father performs in Chicago, Boston, Cincinnati, New York City, Louisville, New Orleans, Mobile, Savannah. Edwin picks up regional accents, mingles with people in fair straits and foul, enslaved and free, immigrant and native. He hones his gift for invisibility. Mostly, he watches Father.

He learns that there is to be no escape. One March, an illness keeps Edwin home. Already he's become an interloper in his own family, awkward with them and they awkward in return. Johnny is mostly absent at this time, and so is Joe, both at school at the Bel Air Academy. Joe boards there. Johnny rides back and forth daily, leaving early and arriving home again late. It's hoped that this tutelage will keep him from getting into the kind of scrape no one gets out of. Johnny never intends to worry his mother, but he can't seem to help himself.

Mother, Rosalie, and Asia remain at home. Edwin sees how pretty Asia is, how tired Mother looks, how strange Rose has been allowed to become. He sees them all with outsider eyes.

Being ill fixes everything by giving everyone a role to play, and Edwin luxuriates in his sisters fussing about him, in clean sheets, damp cloths, hushed voices. Asia runs up and down the stairs with cups of tea made from mint she picked herself. Rosalie reads *Jane Eyre* aloud, sunlight streaming through the windows, casting a silhouette of tree branches onto the scarred wood floor. One passage hits Rosalie and Edwin very differently:

> I remembered that the real world was wide, and that a var-
> ied field of hopes and fears, of sensations and excitements,
> awaited those who had courage to go forth into its expanse,
> to seek real knowledge of life amidst its perils.

The sun is gone and Rosalie fallen quiet. Edwin realizes that he slept through the last bit and he opens his mouth to tell Rosalie she needs to read that again, but Rosalie speaks first. In her usual whispering voice, she says, "I begin to wonder if I'll ever marry."

Edwin closes his mouth. Surely this issue has been settled for quite some time, ever since the lion tamer, if not before. Rosalie is twenty-six years old (or maybe twenty-seven, Edwin has lost track). Is it really possible she doesn't know she'll never marry? She's told the Cole sisters the story of Jacob Driesbach and her forbidden love, and they were so moved that they each knitted a muffler for Rosalie to give him when they are finally together, one blue, one red. Rosalie keeps these in a trunk, wrapped in linen and scented with dried rosemary. They're a secret from Mother and Father, but no one keeps a secret from Asia.

Edwin used to feel that Mother was too indulgent with Rosalie, that she should have been forced to stand up straight, forced from the house and out into the world. His time with Father has made him reassess. Maybe Mother is the one keeping Rosalie at home. Maybe, with nothing but love in her heart, his darling mother has eaten Rosalie alive. This seems to be something parents sometimes do.

His throat is so sore it hurts to swallow. His nose runs constantly and has chafed from frequent blowing. His eyes itch, and fever makes his joints ache, turns his thoughts glassy and distant. But he's lying in his very own bed, cared for and carefree. Outside his window, the thin upper branches of a sycamore bob. A silvery squirrel is making its way upwards. Edwin's completely contented. "You can come and live with me," he says. "If you never marry." He even thinks he means this.

Meanwhile in Richmond, *Richard III* commences with Father nowhere to be found.

EDWIN WRITES:

Baltimore, April 8th, 1850

Mr. Sefton. Dear Sir: Will you be kind enough to inform me if my Father is in Richmond, and whether he is ill, for we've not heard a word from him since he left here. I see by the Richmond paper Friday that he was not announced to play that night. We feel anxious to know something about him. Answer this by return of mail and oblige Yours truly, Edwin Booth In Haste

Mr. Sefton answers curtly, by return post, that Father never arrived.

Edwin must rise from his sickbed, take the train to Virginia, and search. When Father is finally found at a nearby plantation, drunk and penniless, Edwin must borrow fifty dollars to get them to his next engagement. He never does learn who the mad arsonist in Rochester's attic is.

UNDER EDWIN'S WATCH, Father never misses a curtain. But keeping him from the saloons after the shows, when his adrenaline is high and his thirst powerful, is impossible. A typical evening commences with a gesture Edwin quickly comes to recognize, a sort of chopping movement with one hand, a sign that Edwin is to go away.

Instead, he follows his father through the darkened streets, always at a distance but always in sight, until his father chooses a door, a stool, a glass. The more his father has to drink, the angrier Edwin's presence makes him. He shouts for Edwin to go back to their room, threatens to leave him in one city or another, have him kidnapped into the navy or arrested or sold into an apprenticeship. "My jailor," he tells his latest crew of drunken friends, pointing an accusing, Shakespearean finger in Edwin's direction. "My chain, my manacles. I once offered to sell him for a fiver. No takers, more's the sorrow.

"'Cassius from bondage will deliver Cassius.' Get out!" he shouts, his famous voice perfectly tuned to the key of contempt. Huddled on a chair at the far end of the room, Edwin might pretend he isn't listening. He might even doze off to lists of his shortcomings, almost as if he were counting sheep. Acquaintances describe Edwin at this time as fragile and pale, his cheeks sunken, his eyes too old for his age. He never smiles, they say. He never speaks. He lives like a servant.

Sometimes his father gives him the slip and Edwin is forced to search, bar by bar, through the night. Sometimes the streets are deserted. Sometimes groups of men stagger by. Sometimes women in doorways call to him, tell him how pretty he is and to go home to his mother before it's too late. He begins to dream of running in a panic through dark streets in strange cities. In his dreams, he is not the pursuer. He is the pursued.

xiii

One August night in Boston, he visits seven taverns before finding his father. Gas lamps light the streets. His shadow stretches and shrinks across the pavement as he passes beneath them. The air is thick, mild, and windless, the stars brilliant. His father has just performed at the Boston Museum in the part of Shylock.

The villainy you teach me I will execute, and it shall go hard but I will better the instruction.

Edwin turns down a small alley and arrives at the famed Green Dragon. The round sign marking the tavern sways over the door. A man is just emerging and, mysteriously, appears to recognize him. He holds the door for Edwin and points towards the stairs. "In the basement," he says. "Rare form tonight," when in fact, Father's state of pixilation is all too common.

Edwin descends the steps. There Father sits in a winged chair, his cravat loose, his blue jacket off, his vest unbuttoned from the bottom to make room for his stomach. A felt hat cups one knee. Edwin has never seen this hat before. He prepares to be shouted at. Instead, his father raises the hat, waving Edwin in, sliding over so that Edwin can take the arm of his chair. "Ned, Ned, my boy," Father says, as if surprised and delighted by this happy meeting. "You'll want to hear this." His face is flushed, his eyes water.

What Edwin will want to hear is a story he's already heard about a hundred times, the story of Father's early feud with the famous actor Edmund Kean. Edwin doesn't mind. As with all Father's performances, Edwin watches for new interpretations of old lines. Father has an audience of three men, all seemingly well versed in the theater and hardly drunk at all. Edwin takes them for journalists, which might explain Father's warm reception. Just part of the show.

The basement is large, but brightly lit through a careful arrangement of hurricane lamps and mirrors aligned with other mirrors. Edwin can see his father's famous profile, like the head on a coin, with his flat nose and unkempt hair, reflected and repeating, smaller and more distant with each iteration, an endless line of Fathers. The pocked surfaces refract the light and wreath his head in rays and halos, as if he were a saint.

"Garrett here saw Kean as Shylock," Father tells Edwin. No introductions take place, but only one of these men is old enough to have seen Edmund Kean act. "In New York," Father adds, "not London," as if an important distinction has been made.

The arm of the chair grows less comfortable. Edwin shifts his weight, which his father takes as inattention. The reprimand comes in the form of Father's fingers, a vise closing over Edwin's arm.

Edwin recalls that Kean had gone to New York when the scandals surrounding his affair and divorce drove him from London, but found the audiences of the New World even more prudish than those of the Old. Father's own scandal is still more of a whisper than a roar and Edwin wonders at this. Perhaps his long-established madness has provided some inoculation. Perhaps being a famous atheist who carries a murderer's skull in his trunk has reduced bigamy and illegitimacy to the realm of ho-hum.

"Of course, Kean was a magnificent Shylock," Father says, all generosity. He raises his glass with such enthusiasm he splashes bourbon down his front, the smell momentarily eclipsing the cigars, sweat, and horseshit. Father drops Edwin's arm to pull out his handkerchief, pat at his vest. Edwin sees this for what it is—a nice bit of stage business creating a pause, a pause that could be filled by someone complimenting Father's own Shylock. No one does. "Perfect part for him. Being himself such a vengeful man," Father adds, the moment of charity over.

What follows is a convoluted tale of two theaters—Covent Garden and Drury Lane—the two most prestigious venues in London. Father was under contract at the first when Kean lured him away to play at the second. Kean professed himself quite dazzled by this new young talent. But it soon became clear that Kean's real motive was to forestall any competition Father might have provided. He was kept in supporting roles, frequently sent out to play parts he was unprepared for, and in all ways, at all times, meant to show to disadvantage against the great Edmund Kean. "He came not to praise, but to bury me," Father says.

First, Covent Garden declared Father in breach and when he left Kean's employment to fulfill that earlier contract, Drury Lane did the same.

At that time, Kean had a group of rabid supporters who called themselves the Wolves Club. Rumors began to circulate that they intended to drive Father from the stage. Kean responded by taking offense. The gentlemanly Wolves would never behave in such a way and the club had been long disbanded besides.

In the mirror, Father turns his head towards his own reflection. His dark eyes catch the lantern light and shine like a cat's in the dark. His voice sharpens. "*Someone* was baying for my blood," he says.

The reporters, if they are reporters, take a drink in sudden unison, as if choreographed. It strikes Edwin as strange, this Greek chorus of gesture, though he's noticed that life with Father often feels staged.

When Father performed next, in the role of Richard III, a mob awaited him, creating such a pandemonium that he couldn't be heard. He tried to communicate through placards—*Grant Silence to Explain* and *Can Englishmen Condemn Unheard?* The response was a continued din. Whistles blew, feet stamped, men shouted, women fainted.

The Wolves invaded the boxes. Driven back, they beat on the doors with their canes. Fisticuffs broke out and spilled into the street. Chairs and spectacles and noses were broken. The play proceeded briefly in pantomime, but eventually the company gave up and moved directly into the afterpiece, a farce in which Father did not appear. Father went home (to his wife, as Edwin now knows). The angry audience outlasted him by many hours.

Over the next week, though the number of Father's supporters grew at each attempt, his detractors continued to shout him down. Roses from his supporters rained down on the stage, orange peels from the Wolves. Every show was an occasion for riot until, finally, at long last, rioting became a bore for everyone involved.

Father empties his glass. Another appears at his elbow. He says that, when finally able to perform, his interpretation of Richard was well received.

Modest Father! Surely Father's Richard was a triumph. In fact, in London, Father has never ceased to be compared unfavorably to Kean. Rosalie would have known this, but Edwin doesn't and wouldn't believe it if he did. No role is so completely Father's own as that of the murdering and murdered king. Over the course of his long career, he will play Richard 579 times.

This story has been changed from earlier renditions, less by Father's artistry and more by context. When orange peels were the worst missiles being thrown, Father could make this story quite funny. But now it plays against the backdrop of the Astor Place riot in New York, a class war disguised as a disagreement over who was the better Shakespearean actor—the British William Charles Macready, representing the upper crust, or the American Edwin (for whom Edwin is named) Forrest, the workingman's choice. The melee left some twenty to thirty people dead; no one knows the number with certainty. Scores more were injured. Many were bystanders, some children, shot by soldiers firing randomly into the crowd. Macready was forced to escape in disguise while Forrest's followers tried but failed to burn down the hated Astor Place Opera House, built so that wealthy theater lovers wouldn't have to mingle with the lower classes.

The parts that used to be funny no longer seem so. No one mentions the riot, but there is a long silence in which each man attends to his own glass. When Garrett speaks again, he appears to have changed the subject. "Did you ever see Ira Aldridge act?" he asks.

"The African? No," Father says.

"I saw him play Othello at Covent Garden. He was glorious. And the audience knew it, if the critics did not."

Suddenly Edwin is having trouble following the conversation. An African? As Othello? He must have misheard.

"Kean was a great admirer of Aldridge," Garrett says, so he hasn't changed the subject after all. Clearly, despite Father's story, Garrett remains a great admirer of Kean's and wants Father to know this. "Do you know what Coleridge, the poet, said about Kean? Coleridge said that watching Kean act was like reading Shakespeare by lightning flashes."

"No, I never heard that before." Father's voice is mild and possibly only Edwin hears the sarcasm. Because *everyone* has heard that and if there were an exception, it would not be Father. Two days ago, on the street, a man had told Father that the weather was very fine. Father had fallen to his knees. "Your powers of observation astonish me," he'd said. "Fine weather indeed. And you the one to notice! I bow before you, sir." His tone then had been much the same.

Father begins the arduous task of standing up. "The hour grows late," he says although late is long over and early has come round again.

One of the younger men fetches Father his coat. "Edmund Kean's son Charles is also a fine actor," he says. "Which of your sons will take up your mantle, Mr. Booth?"

A long moment passes. Father says nothing, but after he puts his arm through the sleeve of his coat, his hand lands on Edwin's shoulder. If Edmund Kean has a son who acts, then by God, Junius Brutus Booth will have the same.

EDWIN AND HIS father walk back to their hotel together. The night has turned chilly. The streets are mostly deserted, the lamps dark, the moon down, the birds silent in the trees, the crickets silent in the grass. Edwin is so tired that walking is an effort, but so giddy with Father's sudden approval, he thinks he'll never be able to sleep. He shivers, which might be the cold and might be excitement. Father's hand rests again on his shoulder, but this is just to stay upright. Edwin notices for the first time that he's grown taller than his father.

Father seems to be regretting his earlier criticism of Kean. He tells Edwin now that no human being could equal Kean for the expression of jealousy or despair. Then he says that Edwin is to take the role of Tressel when Father next plays Richard III. Not the bit-part/no-lines Tressel that Shakespeare wrote—no, they are performing Colley Cibber's adaptation, which everyone in America so prefers, being considerably shorter and bloodier. In Cibber's version, the princes are murdered right there on the stage.

In Cibber's version, Tressel comes from the battle at Tewkesbury to tell King Henry, in several long, impassioned speeches, how his son has been killed at the hands of crooked Richard, Clarence, and the rest. Edwin only prays that his father will remember this offer come morning.

Later, in a letter home, Edwin will say that the actor meant to play the part was also the prompter and, finding his dual roles too demanding, he asked Edwin at the last minute to take his place. In this telling, his father knows nothing about it until Edwin visits his dressing room, already in costume and paint. This is a story that will collect details over the years the way a room collects dust.

The truth is that Father is not bringing in the audiences he once did. Despite Edwin's efforts, his father often performs drunk, which sometimes angers the audience so much they get up and leave—a shame, as Father usually sobers and improves as the play proceeds.

So casting Edwin is a novelty act—the son debuting on the same stage as his famous father. It's hoped this gambit will increase ticket sales.

But one can only debut once. "How did you do?" his father asks when Edwin returns to the dressing room.

"Well, I think," Edwin says.

Few in the audience agree. His performance was said to be lacking in emotion and understanding. Also nearly inaudible.

OVER THE NEXT year, Edwin appears onstage only seven more times but the roles he's given grow in length and importance. He begins to play the handsome young men—Cassio in *Othello*, Wilford in *The Iron Chest*, Laertes in *Hamlet*. Women in the street no longer tell him to go home to his mother. Now they tell him to come inside.

Sometime during this period, in pursuit of dreamless sleep, Edwin begins to drink.

Lincoln: Fathers and Sons

Eat, Mary, for we must live.
—Abraham Lincoln, February 1850

In February of 1850, little Edward Baker Lincoln, the second son of Abraham and Mary Lincoln, dies of pulmonary tuberculosis just short of his fourth birthday. He has been gravely ill for months. "We miss him very much," Lincoln writes in agonized understatement.

A third son, William Wallace, is born in December of the same year. Less than a month later, in January of 1851, Lincoln's father dies. Since leaving the family home at the age of twenty-one, Lincoln has mostly heard from his father only when money is needed. His primary interaction has been to grudgingly provide it. Now he receives three letters in rapid succession informing him that death is imminent. He only responds to the third when chastised for his silence. He writes to his stepbrother: "Say to him that if we could meet now, it is doubtful whether it would not be more painful than pleasant." He encourages his father to think of the joyful reunion he will soon have with those who've gone before.

He does not attend the funeral.

xiv

1851 is a busy year for the Booth family.

In January, in Boston, Father makes the papers again for one of his mad freaks and Edwin is helpless to prevent it. Father has awakened in an agitated state and by the time the evening show begins, Edwin is already exhausted. The play is, once again, *Richard III*, and Father performs with competence, but sometime during the final act he completely loses his wits. Exiting the stage, he finds his way blocked by a young woman named Hannah Crouse. Crouse is an extremely large girl, circus large, and makes a living exhibiting herself. She's come to the theater to see the genius of Junius Booth.

Encountering her in the stairwell, Father believes she's an apparition. He jabs her with Richard's sword to confirm this. When she screams, he attacks, calling her a demon, shouting for her to defend herself. It takes two stagehands to restrain him, which happens, fortunately, before real damage can be done to the terrified girl. Edwin is sent the next day with an apology and an invitation to another show. Crouse accepts neither.

The papers love everything about this story. It's reported locally and picked up nationally, Crouse's Christian name inadvertently becoming Anna in the telling. Edwin thinks that Mother will be mortified, but Mother has her own problems. In Baltimore, the local papers have finally taken notice of Adelaide Booth.

IN FEBRUARY, ADELAIDE files for divorce, accusing Junius of a twenty-nine-year habit of adulterous intercourse. To the disgraceful act of desertion, she writes, he added the insult of a large number of illegitimate children whom he persists in supporting.

Father is shocked when he learns she's gone through with this. He'd thought the princely sum already paid her had settled things. He's been largely able to ignore Adelaide. Few bring up his bigamy to his face. Edwin, too, has been traveling inside that courteous bubble, unaware that those at home have been less lucky.

In Baltimore, Adelaide's harassment had continued unabated. The illegitimacy of the Booth children is now a published fact along with "the dissoluteness of the father and the shame of the mother." Mother takes the abuse stoically, moving quietly on whenever and wherever Adelaide appears.

But on the streets, in the neighborhoods, at his school, Johnny defends them all with his fists. He could use Edwin's help, but Edwin is off larking about with Father and wouldn't be any good in a fight even if he were home.

This also happens in February: June's wife, Clementina De-Bar, the dancer and comedienne, has June and a seventeen-year-old actress named Harriet Mace arrested as they leave the theater. They are accused of the crime of "being entirely too familiar." June is charged with adultery, Harriet with fornication. June's bail is four hundred dollars. Harriet's is fifty. No one in the family speaks of it. They remain on good terms with Clementina, who comes to call whenever she's in the area.

IN MARCH, JOHNNY visits a gypsy encampment, seven covered wagons and a tent, in a field near his school. The field is full of pussytoes in first bloom and knee-high Indian grass. Three beautiful red horses lift their heads to stare at him. Chickens scatter. Pigs grunt. Black pots hang over cooking fires. Skirts and trousers hang over bushes. A small girl with braids so long she could sit on them stares from inside a wagon.

A man in a battered hat takes his pipe from his mouth to nod at him. He points to the tent with the stem, blows a long stream of smoke into the air.

The palmist is tiny and old, her hair all gone to seed, her blouse soiled at the collar and cuffs. Her hands are rough, her eyes bloodshot, one front tooth is gone. A key hangs from a chain around her neck, a key so large and heavy looking, Johnny wonders it doesn't unbalance her. Nothing in the tent would require such a key and he wonders about that, too.

The palmist looks at Johnny's hand for a long time before speaking. As soon as he leaves her, he writes down, word for word, what she said. Memorizing speeches has never come as easy to him as to the other sons of Junius Booth, but this one is hard to forget.

Ah, you've a bad hand; the lines all cris-cras. It's full enough of sorrow. Full of trouble. Trouble in plenty, everywhere I look. You'll break hearts, they'll be nothing to you. You'll die young and leave plenty to mourn you, many to love you, too, but you'll be rich, generous, and free with your money. You're born under an unlucky star. You've got in your hand a thundering crowd of enemies—not one friend—you'll make a bad end, and have plenty to love you afterwards. You'll have a fast life—short, but a grand one. Now, young sir, I've never seen a worse hand, and I wish I hadn't seen it, but every word I've told is true by the signs.

He reads this later to Rosalie and Asia. "I asked if she really expected me to pay her for this, but she took the money all right."

His sisters rush to reassure him. "What tittle," Asia says. "Sheep bleatings," says Rosalie. They honestly don't believe in this prophecy, but they feel sorry for him all the same. *I* wouldn't want to get that fortune, they each secretly think, as if Johnny's fate is entirely his own and nothing to do with them.

"She said I'd better become a missionary. She said she was glad not to be a young girl or she'd follow my pretty face anywhere," Johnny says.

He carries the paper with her words on his person for a long time. At least it will be grand, he tells himself.

IN APRIL, THE divorce is granted, with Father conceding that all of Adelaide's accusations are true.

Also April. Father is performing in New York City. Waking from a nap, he refuses to go to the theater and be Richard III yet again. "You do it," he tells Edwin. "I'm sick of it."

Lacking an alternative, the manager sends Edwin onstage in his father's hump, his father's outsized costume. No warning has been given the audience, whose applause falls away into a puzzled silence. Edwin begins tentatively. He tries to imitate his father's inflections, his gestures. To his horror, his boots squeak loudly on the wood planks. The audience laughs.

He performs his first scene rooted in place, just when his father would be striding the stage. He can think of nothing but that squeaking. Or maybe quacking. His boots sound like a duck. A stagehand meets him when he exits, standing in his stocking feet, holding his own boots out to Edwin. They don't fit the period, they don't fit his feet, but at least they are silent.

Onstage, the actors nearest him provide every possible support. Those offstage crowd the wings, watching in friendly, nervous sympathy. He can see their eyes, the way they clasp their hands together as if praying for him. The audience, too, begins to pity the young boy, so obviously out of his depth, drowning in his own sleeves. Edwin can feel the change when it happens. He can feel the moment they start wanting him to succeed. He rides that change; it lifts him.

He has them on the edge of their seats, wondering if he'll get through his next line, his next scene, his next thrust, his next parry. The play ends with Edwin's first ovation. He won it merely by surviving.

In May, on Johnny's thirteenth birthday, Mother and Father marry. Afterwards Edwin, Asia, and Johnny pretend to forget that Adelaide ever existed. They do their best to insist that the rest of the world do the same.

June, like his father before him, has abandoned his wife to run away with a younger woman. In July, he and Harriet run all the way to San Francisco, where they've been booked by the indomitable Jenny Lind Theatre. Destroyed repeatedly by fire, the Jenny Lind is being rebuilt yet again, even as they make their way to it.

During this same month, June's nine-year-old daughter, Blanche, is sent from the chaos of her father's abandonment to stay with the Booths in Baltimore. Blanche adores her grandmother. Her grandfather frightens her with his temper, his violence, his casual cruelty. One night, when the whole family has gathered for dinner, he suggests that Blanche isn't really a Booth, that Clementina was already pregnant when she tricked June into marrying her. No real Booth was ever so stupid as this one, her grandfather says, waving a spoon in Blanche's direction. He doesn't even say this to Blanche herself. The comment is made across her to her gorgeous teenaged uncle Johnny.

IN AUGUST, EDWIN and John Sleeper put on an evening's performance at the Bel Air Courthouse. The early program is high-minded, consisting of several Shakespearean soliloquies from *Macbeth* and *Hamlet*, but the audience prefers the minstrelsy that ends the evening—Edwin on the banjo, Sleeper on the bones, both of them singing Negro songs with their faces corked.

The response is so positive, they repeat the performance on a second night.

ONE OF JOHNNY'S friends at school is a boy named Thomas Gorsuch. The Gorsuch plantation, Retreat Farm, is near the school and Johnny's been a frequent guest there, eaten supper at that table, spent the night. He greatly admires Edward Gorsuch—"the finest of men"—so sober and prosperous, so little like his own father.

Two years earlier, four enslaved men had fled the Gorsuch plantation. Gorsuch fancies himself a kindly master. He tells everyone that they will return of their own accord.

He gets tired of waiting.

In September, Edward Gorsuch travels with a posse of seven white men plus his eldest son to Christiana, Pennsylvania, where he's heard that the men are being sheltered by another escaped slave, the abolitionist William Parker. Gorsuch confronts Parker on Parker's doorstep.

Parker orders Gorsuch away.

Gorsuch answers that he'll breakfast in hell before he leaves without his property. The white men attempt to force their way into Parker's house. They have warrants and a sheriff with them. The law, they say, is on their side.

Parker blocks their entry. He says if they take another step, he'll break their necks.

Meanwhile Parker's wife, Eliza, has opened a window on the second floor. From it, she sounds several loud blasts on a tin horn. The first shots are fired at her.

Neighbors hear the horn. They come at a run, they are armed, and in the subsequent conflict, Gorsuch is killed and his older son, Dickinson, badly wounded.

Johnny happens to be with Thomas when the news of his father's death arrives. Johnny's outraged to learn that a man can't even go and recover his own slaves in safety.

Cruel retribution comes for the black community in Christiana, but it doesn't dim Johnny's fury. Five white and thirty-eight black men are arrested, and still no one is found guilty of the killing. William and Eliza Parker have fled to Canada. Why has no one gone after them? If Johnny were only older, he thinks, he'd see to this himself.

The whole episode clarifies his thinking about slavery, which it turns out is not at all the same as his father's. He doesn't say so to Mother, opposition to Father always making her so uncomfortable, but he shares his views freely at school, where they are largely agreed. Slavery, Johnny tells his schoolmates, is the luckiest thing to ever happen to the Negro. He describes Retreat Farm as a peaceful, happy kingdom until robbed of its benevolent king. "I have seen the black man whipped," he will later concede, "but only when he deserved more than he got." Over the years, he speaks often of what happened at Christiana. So does the South.

So does Frederick Douglass, who'll say that Parker's action, more than anything else, led to the destruction of the Fugitive Slave Act. Others, later, will call the battle at Christiana the beginning of the Civil War.

FATHER WANTS A larger house for the family on the farm. He hires an architect, James Gifford, to build something in the currently popular Gothic Revival style. In October, work commences with the digging of the cellar, done on Father's instructions, in such a way so as not to trouble the nearby locust trees.

The new house will be pretty rather than grand, two stories high, with diamond-paned windows, a peaked tin roof, and a wide, pillared front porch. Asia names the house-to-be Tudor Hall. The old log cabin is to be given to Joe and Ann.

IN NOVEMBER, Edwin turns eighteen.

IN DECEMBER, June sends Father a letter. He says that Father could make a lot of money by coming to perform in California, where gold is plentiful and elevated entertainment scarce.

XV

In 1852, June has convinced his father to come West.

This story begins in a familiar way. No one imagines for a moment that Father can make the trip alone. June and his Harriet (called Hattie) make the long trip from San Francisco to pick him up, and another actor, George Spear (Old Spudge to his friends), joins them in New York. Old Spudge has the face of a clown—mobile mouth, pouches under his eyes, fringe of hair in a wreath around the dome of his head—and the voice of a tragedian. He can do it all.

Edwin is to be, at long last, left home. He'll resume his schooling, catch up to Asia and Johnny. He'll be able to finally accept an offer from the Baltimore Museum to join the company as a utility player, on salary, taking smaller roles and learning his craft. He'll remember who he is when he's not with Father—this will take time.

He will rest.

June has tickets on a steamer from New York to Panama. But at the last minute, Father refuses to board. He's too anxious; even drink won't steady his nerves. He insists he can't manage. He needs Edwin. The ship sails without them while Edwin is fetched up from Baltimore.

This is crushing. Edwin arrives in a bad mood and everything about the journey will keep him glowering. After insisting that Edwin is absolutely necessary, Father all but ignores him in favor of the raucous company and sentimental reminiscences of Old Spudge. June, too, shows little interest in him. Edwin's not spent time with Hattie before. She's dark-haired and beautiful. He can't help but notice this. Which makes it all the more offensive when she treats him like a child. Hattie is younger by some months than Edwin, yet she seems to think she's the same age as June. It's insulting.

Sometime during his earlier travels, Edwin's caul mysteriously disappeared from Mother's cupboard. He is naked without it. Anything could happen to him now.

THE PASSAGE ACROSS the Isthmus of Panama is about forty miles as the crow flies. This is the quickest route west, but still takes a traveler several perilous days. The Chagres River is full of snakes and caiman. Fevers are common and often fatal. Worst of all are the Derienni, highwaymen who rob and kill travelers on the trail. Edwin consoles himself that June and Hattie have crossed two times now and are voluntarily doing a third. How bad can it be?

It makes sense, given his age and experience, that June take charge of the trip and also of Father. Edwin watches June attempt to keep Father in line by continually reminding him of all the money about to be made. Good luck with that! Hattie's façade of good cheer is fooling no one and Edwin wonders why she bothers with it.

She makes several attempts to talk to him. She asks if Asia might ever want to act. She asks what role he'd most like to play. She tells him that when gold was discovered in San Francisco, the sailors all abandoned their ships to go look for it and now an uncanny ghost fleet floats about the bay. She's already not as pretty as when the trip started, her hair in oily braids, her fingernails torn and filthy. But her eyes are as lively as ever, her mood unsinkable. Edwin answers in uninformative monosyllables until she stops trying. For the whole of the trip, Edwin hardly speaks to any of them.

In some ways, their timing is providential. Back in 1850, the railroad had hired Randolph Runnels, an ex–Texas ranger, to deal with the problem of the Derienni. Runnels was a young man, but experienced in murder; he'd served in the Indian Wars. Two years earlier, a Pentecostal preacher prophesied that a call would come for him, asking him to travel in a strange land over a river of demons and monsters to battle a dark and deadly pestilence. It was the Lord's will that this call be accepted. When the railroad man arrived to fetch him, stammering out his request, Runnels said, "What took you so long?" His bag was already packed.

William Nelson was the American consul stationed in Panama City at that time. He met with Runnels and secretly empowered him to deal with the Derienni by whatever means he chose. Maybe take care of some labor unrest in his spare time. Runnels formed a society of vigilantes who called themselves the Isthmus Guard. In 1852, Runnels gets a message from Nelson. Now.

Next morning, the residents of Panama City wake to find thirty-seven bodies hanging along the seawall. These men were dragged from the brothels, gaming halls, and their homes in the night by masked members of the Isthmus Guard. In October, an additional forty-one men will be hanged.

The locals keep their distance from Runnels. If he speaks to them, which they desperately try to avoid, they look at the ground while answering. They call him El Verdugo, the Executioner, because, Runnels thinks, they don't know the fist of God even when it strikes them in the face.

The Booths travel the Isthmus in the period between these two mass lynchings. This is a period of relative safety for travelers, but no one has told Edwin this. Nothing that happens feels safe to him. He's more and more astonished at June and Hattie's willingness to repeat the trip.

Eleven days after leaving New York, they arrive at the mouth of the Chagres River. Crowds of gold-seekers mob the beaches—some of them coming, some of them going. Those on their way home can be identified by their infirmities and their filth. Some of them are filthy rich.

On the hill above the beach is the ruin of Fort San Lorenzo, its ancient battlements crumbling, the jungle thrusting greenly through the embrasures. Bits of old cannon are scattered on the sand below. The ruined fort is the first thing Edwin sees and the main thing he remembers of Chagres. They are passing quickly onwards. In Chagres, the threat of yellow fever is so high, many insurance companies carry a rider canceling the policy if the holder spends the night here.

June hires men to pole them in the dugout canoes called bungos up the river to Gorgona. The rain is nearly constant, hitting the green tunnel of leaves above them with a sound like rattling beads. Also constant: monkeys, mosquitoes, and malaria. The water of the river is gritty with mud and the current runs slow.

June, Hattie, and Father share a bungo. Edwin is with Old Spudge. Edwin feels as if he's stepped inside the pages of one of Rosalie's adventure novels. He's never imagined a place so alive, so crawling with every kind of creature; the landscape is in continual motion. Whenever the sun comes out, the colors dazzle—bright trees, vines, birds, butterflies. He hears the calls of parrots, the chatter of monkeys, the soughing river. Even the wildest vistas at home seem timid by comparison. Edwin finds himself constantly turning to catch the things he sees moving in the corners of his eyes. He's deeply unsettled by this, half awe, half fear.

And wholly uncomfortable. Rosalie has good reasons for preferring to read about adventures rather than have them. The men who pole the boat wear almost nothing, which makes sense in the heat and the rain, but is an option closed to Edwin. His own clothes stick to him. He sweats, he shivers, and rain drips continually from his hat brim onto his nose. The bottom of the bungo is always an inch deep in water; it seeps through his boots and into his socks, turning the skin on his feet a nasty ash color that itches horribly and peels in strips.

At night they debark to sleep, the men in a circle with Hattie in the protected space between them. As perilous as the trip is to the men, Hattie is that much more vulnerable. Edwin wonders about June's willingness to subject her to it. Is San Francisco so dangerous that Hattie couldn't have been left behind? When Edwin has a wife, he'll take better care of her. He won't ever let her get so dirty.

In spite of all the rain, parts of the river remain shallow, so they must frequently debark and go on foot, hauling the boat, which is as heavy as a tree. Their guides hold whispered conversations in languages Edwin doesn't speak. He begins to distrust them, their sidelong glances, their moments of suspicious, untranslatable levity. Edwin could have been at home, learning poetry and history and science. Instead he will die here unschooled, his throat slit in his sleep, and it will be all Father's fault. He only hopes Father survives long enough to regret what he's done to Edwin.

At a small beach, the guides pull out and disappear into the jungle without explanation, which tunes Edwin's terrors to a higher key. But they return with brandy that Father and Old Spudge immediately purchase. "Good for all that ails you!" Father says, his mood much improved, as if it no longer matters that they're all about to die. "'I would not have given it for a wilderness of monkeys!'"

Half an hour later, Father and Old Spudge are singing. They'd like to get us drunk, Edwin thinks. It's all going according to plan.

Whenever Father passes him the bottle, he takes only a sip. A sip that size hardly counts as drinking. The brandy burns on his tongue, lights up his throat. He would like to take another sip, but doesn't dare.

A small woman with braided hair and a pregnant belly appears with food, which they sit on the little beach to eat. "What's this?" he asks June. He's been handed a cluster of tubular yellow fruits.

"Bananas," June tells him. "They're good. You'll like them." A spider the size of a rat crawls out from between the stems. A log floating in the river opens its mouth. Its teeth are sharp and there are a lot of them.

Stew with a meat he can't identify is given Edwin in a wooden bowl. It's very chewy. Maybe iguana. He doesn't ask. He slips behind a screen of trees to unbutton his pants, his vulnerability in that moment particularly vivid. What will get him first? The alligators? The fevers? The guides? He spends much of the journey with his insides knotted in cramps, his shit an acidic yellow stream.

The party, still alive, reaches Gorgona three days later. Gorgona is named for its many poisonous snakes. Hammocks are strung for them above a rocky terrain crowded with hasty graves, many quite recent. The rain has washed some of the crosses down to the riverbank. A few float on, continuing the journey for travelers who didn't.

As the day moves into twilight, the high pitch of mosquito wings rises in volume. It's their last day with the guides. Edwin watches them sharpening their machetes. "Stay awake tonight," he tells June, and June says he will, but doesn't. Father sleeps and snores. Old Spudge sleeps and farts.

"Edwin!" says June from his hammock. "You're snoring!" which is ridiculous. Edwin is the only one who hasn't closed his eyes. Below him on the ground, creatures he can't see move purposefully about the gravesites.

In the morning, much to Edwin's relief, their guides leave them. Then it's onwards on mules, threading through the tight and towering gorges, up to their fetlocks in mud. June is comically enormous on his mule, but Father is just the right size. Edwin's mount has a striped blanket for a saddle and a backbone sharp as a blade. Every step is an injury. He remembers, for the thousandth time, that he never wanted to come on this journey.

Such a joy to arrive in Panama City! Their first impression is glorious—a vista of red-tiled roofs and oyster-pearled cathedrals. On closer look, the streets are filthy, the walls rotting, the stench of the harbor unbearable, and the city crammed to bursting. They must share a room with more than forty other travelers. Hattie is separated from the men for the night, sequestered with the rest of the women, though Edwin can still see her, a red scarf over her hair, across the ramshackle wall of boards that segregates the sexes. The smell of sickness is thick in the air. They are right on the edge of cholera season, anxious to move quickly on.

At the harbor, they can only reach the canoe that will take them out to their steamship on the backs of locals who've been paid fifty cents apiece to carry them through the tepid water. Edwin is larger than the man he rides, which embarrasses him. He boards the *California*, his clothes stiff with salt.

But after the Isthmus, the flea-infested ship feels like floating opulence. They dine on cold salmon, broths, and crusty breads.

Father takes a seat under the skylights in the dining salon and hardly moves from it. He tells stories. He recites poems. He drinks. Edwin spends most of his time napping or eating, or staring from the deck at the dolphins following them up the coast, the wonderful arc of their leaping. "You will be amazed by San Francisco," Hattie says, appearing suddenly at his side. The ocean air has turned her cheeks pink, her eyes bright. Edwin looks at her briefly, looks away. She is with June. They are in love.

The voyage lasts another seventeen days, but the hard part is over.

xvi

A crowd meets them when they dock in San Francisco, a crowd made up mostly, but not entirely, of theater folk. The harbor smells of bilge water, fish, and fried oysters, and the bay is filled with the ghostly, decaying ships Hattie told him about. The *California* noses in beside a ship from China, its decks packed with more men than you would think could fit below.

Father's reception is magnificent. A man in a plaid waistcoat lifts his top hat in an extravagant gesture. "Welcome the greatest actor in America!" he shouts as Father comes down the gangplank. The man leads the crowd in a cheer, as if conducting an orchestra.

Edwin follows, raising his eyes to the hills, past the shacks and mansions, all the way up to where white clouds coast across the sky. He turns to see the island of Alcatraz, all stone and scrub, the impossibly long-winged pelicans riding the air in great circles above it. The next thing he hears is his own name. "Welcome Edwin Booth! The most beautiful man in the city!"

There is no overstating how startled Edwin is by this. Startled first to be noticed at all. Startled second to be identified as beautiful. He's been petted by women in the companies. He's been told he's pretty by women in the streets. This feels different. He's both pleased and appalled.

He's eighteen years old and California will soon make him, by his own accounting, a drunk and a libertine. About this period, he will later write: "Sin was in me, and it consumed me while it was shut up so close; so I let it out and it seemed to rage and burn more fiercely than ever."

San Francisco has everything he needs—women and drink at a price he can afford, theaters and roles to play, and June. Especially June. He never establishes the closeness to this brother that he has with Rosalie, Asia, Johnny, and even Joe. But June took charge of Father while they crossed the Isthmus. He can keep right on doing that. Edwin's been sprung.

"Father doesn't care about me," Edwin tells June. "Never has." He sheds those years of watchfulness like a snake shedding a skin. He doesn't recognize himself.

Now he's the one who shows up to rehearsals inebriated and unprepared. Now Father is the one stewing and scolding. A visible tension crackles between the two, evident to the whole company, who find Edwin sullen and rebellious. He's to play the part of Richmond—*the weary sun has made a golden set*—and Father is impatient with his lethargy. "Point to the setting sun," Father says. "Don't just mouth your lines. Do something!"

Edwin throws his hand mockingly into the air. There. "When can we go out?" he asks. "I want to see the city." June sides with Father. Edwin, he says, must get serious. He's not a genius like their father. He's not so talented he needn't work.

Once being an actor was the thing Edwin wanted most in the

world. Now he acts because it's all he knows. Perhaps if he hadn't spent those formative years with Father, he would, like most adolescents, have tried on this personality and that until he found the one that fit best. He might have learned to be comfortable in the role of Edwin Booth. Instead, Edwin has come to prefer being someone, anyone else.

Traveling with Father has been his burden, but also his apprenticeship. He's learned, better than anyone, that for a few magical moments, you trade in bad food, bad beds, and bad times.

Still, there are magical moments. Edwin knows that, too.

THE MONEY JUNE predicted doesn't materialize. Early critics are kind—*The San Francisco Daily Herald* describes Father as "a splendid ruin," "magnificent even in decay." But as the tour continues—up to Sacramento, where floods close the theaters and the heat is unbearable, and back to San Francisco, where he performs so drunk that he falls onstage repeatedly—the reviews sour. Father lasts two months. He's brought in no money, but still demands payment in full from June, an exorbitant sum that all but wipes June out. He leaves San Francisco one foggy morning with heavy pockets and bad feelings on all sides.

Edwin doesn't go with him. He's never been allowed to be an irresponsible young man before and he's gotten a taste for it. If June can stay in California, why not Edwin? He goes with his father, through a wispy fog, as far as the gangplank, terrified, almost certain that at the last minute, Father will refuse to board without him. Sure enough, there is some fuss about the baggage that makes his heart stop. Father asks a deckhand to carry his trunks. The man says that he won't. "I'm no flunky," he says.

"Then what are you, sir?" Father asks.

"A thief."

In an instant, Father is in character, his favorite character—Bertram from the play with the same name. "Take my hand, then, sir," he shouts, "for I'm a pirate."

This makes the deckhand laugh, clasp Father's arm, and haul him in. He hoists Father's trunk into the air, balances it on one shoulder, leads Father below deck. The ship is called the *Independence*.

Soon Father reappears at the rail. Fit and flush, he stands with his hand raised as the ship steams away, quickly disappearing into the fog. Edwin stays until Father has vanished. He's left with such a strange feeling, as if he's forgotten something he should have remembered, but doesn't know what it is. This feeling will last the rest of his life.

xvii

Edwin thinks he now has something he's long wanted, a tomorrow unformed and unknown, and then another after that, and then another, all entirely his to choose. It's exhilarating. It's terrifying. It's something only an eighteen-year-old could believe in.

He joins a troupe managed by two British newlyweds—Dan and Emma Waller—and sets off with them for the mining camps. His father's friend Old Spudge travels with him. The Waller Company has respectable actors and big plans. But it's a rung or two below what Father would find acceptable, a rung or two below what Edwin is used to. The Waller Company is not so grand they won't do a tableau of the Bear Flag Revolt with a live bear. But it suits Edwin not to be compared to Father while he's still learning his trade.

His sullenness left when his father did. He's ready for any-thing, wild to have the sort of adventures he'll live to regret.

The company plays in Yuba City, Nevada City, Hangtown, Grass Valley, Rough and Ready, Red Dog, and Shirt-tail Bend. There are two unmarried women in the troupe, both only slightly older than Edwin, but they make it clear that they prefer each other's company to his. The Wallers behave like newly-weds, a level of cooing Edwin feels they are too old—well into their thirties!—and too British to indulge in. He spends most of his time with Old Spudge.

Edwin works hard to perform well. He has moments of par-ticular triumph. In Grass Valley, his Iago is so persuasive that one drunken miner draws a gun and shoots, shouting at Edwin, "You're a sneaking no-account cur and you'll get what's coming to you!" Edwin dives to the stage along with the rest of the cast, and the play only continues when everyone in the audience has voluntarily disarmed.

His father left in October. In November Edwin turned nine-teen, and now it's late December. The company arrives in Downieville, a town of fifteen hotels and twice as many saloons. Downieville sits at the fork of the Downie and Yuba Rivers, the mountains cupped like hands around it. The trail in is too steep for carts or wagons. Only the horses can manage it.

In the spring, the sound of rushing water would have been deafening. In December, ice has narrowed and muted the rivers. Edwin shakes the horseback out of his legs by walking down to the banks with Old Spudge. The air is icy, the sky low. Edwin pulls his hands into his sleeves to warm them.

Old Spudge is telling him a story, something he'd read in the newspapers back when they were still in San Francisco, long before he ever thought to find himself in Downieville. "There was a woman lynched here, the first woman ever to be lynched in California. It stuck with me," Old Spudge says. "Terrible story.

"Juanita Something or Other. Twenty-six years old. And little. Slip of a girl. Stabbed a miner, popular fellow. Lots of friends. So they dragged her from the courthouse by her hair all the way to the river here. Rigged a scaffold. That's when Juanita really showed her sand. Put the noose around her own neck, shouted, 'Adios, señores,' and jumped into eternity. That's the reason I remember it so well. Because of the sand." Old Spudge's eyes, barely visible beneath his hat and above his scarf, are red and watery. He loves a woman with sand.

By all reports, Joe Cannon had tried to break Juanita's door down the night before she killed him. He went back the next day, either to apologize or to finish what he'd started; here reports vary.

The press had mostly taken the woman's side. She had every right to defend herself, they said. Mob action (and against a woman!) was a stain on the whole state. She would still be alive today if she'd been white, they said. It was the newspapers that gave her that operatic ending. They also changed her name. She was never Juanita. She was Josefa.

What Old Spudge is trying to tell Edwin is that they'll soon be performing *Othello* for a lynch mob. Edwin might want to calibrate his Iago accordingly.

But the play never happens. Instead, only a few hours later, a tremendous blizzard arrives. The town is buried in ten feet of snow. It would be nice to think Josefa sent this. Adios, señors.

The situation becomes dire. Food is running out and the

miners dig through the snow to the store only to find that the shelves are empty. Dan Waller holds a meeting in his hotel room. It's larger than the room Edwin and Old Spudge share, and redolent of pipe smoke and a recently emptied chamber pot.

The women gather together on the rumpled bed. Edwin stands by the window, looking out at the white undulation of the yard, the air filled with whirling snowflakes. The curtain is red and velvet and cold to the touch.

Dan tells them to pack up and quickly. He's a big man with a thick mustache. He plays the heroes, but without his make-up, he looks more like a no-nonsense barkeep. "No one here has food to spare for us," he says. "So we should get as far as we can before nightfall." The wind and snow are so thick, Edwin thinks they'll be traveling blind. Cold, hungry, and blind.

Grass Valley, their destination, is forty miles away. It's good they left the wagons and sets there. Otherwise, they would have had to abandon them here.

The three women ride their horses, wrapped in coats and blankets. The four men lead, forcing the path. The road out of Downieville begins with a steep climb. The men must stamp the soft snow down with their boots, through drifts as high as their waists. Edwin's breath is shallow and painful, the air so cold it rattles like nails in his lungs. He keeps his eyes down, blocking the wind and snow as much as he can with his hat brim.

Their progress is agonizingly slow. Edwin imagines days passing, the sun moving unseen overhead, the moon waxing and waning, the seasons turning on their wheel while on the ground below, Edwin takes one step and waits and then takes another. He wonders if he might freeze mid-step. He wonders if his hands might actually be warmer if he took off his gloves, curled his icy fingers together. He tries it and they aren't. He warms them under the saddle blanket of his horse while he walks beside. Surely he would be warmer if they could only walk faster. The wind dies down, which is a great mercy.

But now the daunting horizon of mountains is visible ahead.

Edwin wonders how the women are doing. He wonders if they're frightened as well as cold. He thinks about Dan's wife, Emma. No one would say she was pretty, but she has an expressive, compelling face. She commands the stage—Edwin can see this without understanding how she does it. He thinks about this a lot. He makes himself think about it now. He trips over an exposed branch. Maybe Dan has lost the road. Maybe they won't be found until the snow melts in the spring. His scarf is wet and icy from his own breath and sometimes freezes to his cheek. He can't be sure he still has toes.

The horses exhale loudly, unhappily. When they started, Old Spudge tried to urge them onwards with songs—"Old Dan Tucker," "The Pope He Leads a Happy Life," and "Whar Did You Cum From?" Now, except for their footsteps, the troupe is silent. No birds call. No water runs. Edwin tries to conjure the heat of Panama, how hard it was to breathe that thick cloying air. He tries to remember it so vividly he feels it, but he's not that kind of actor.

They trudge forward. On the way in, they'd passed an abandoned miner's cabin and Dan had hoped to reach it before nightfall. But they've been walking now for some time in the moonlight, and they don't know if it's still ahead or if they missed it. On a downward slope, they come instead on a different cabin, a ruin really, only a corner still standing. But there's a bit of roof overhead and under the collapse of the walls, some wood dry enough to burn. They make a fire and gather around it, drinking boiled snow for supper. Edwin hangs his scarf near the flames and the ice in it steams away.

The fire suffers from the limitations of fires—one's back can be warm or one's front, but not both. With the help of blankets, Edwin thaws and as he does so, his body begins to shake. He shivers more uncontrollably now that he's warmer than he did while walking. His teeth rattle and he's never quite warm enough to sleep.

In the morning, they begin again. They've been walking now, on and off, for twenty-eight hours.

Then, a miracle. They come down from the mountains. The snow thins on the ground and the sun shines. They're all able to ride the rest of the way. Edwin's a good, bold rider and the minute he swings into the saddle, the whole affair becomes a grand adventure, something to write home about.

Later, he's settled on a chair in Grass Valley, in the Golden Gate Saloon, with his legs stretched in front of him, dry and warm, a meal in his belly, a drink in his hand, and a fire at his feet. He's in a comfortable, dozy, immortal mood. In his nineteen years, he's survived fire, water, plague, and ice. He was born with a caul. What can possibly hurt him? He might just sleep in the chair. Or he might rouse himself, go and see if he can find the girl he visited last time they passed through.

He does neither. Instead, Edwin picks up an old edition of *The Sacramento Weekly Union*.

He reads that his father died on November 30th.

Today's date is January 12th.

NIGHT FALLS. EDWIN is wandering, sobbing, drunk and alone, along the main street in the bright moonlit snow when he sees his father coming towards him. His father wears no costume, but is dressed as himself in his stained coat and shabby hat. Edwin stops to wait for him. "'Cut off, even in the blossoms of my sin,'" his father says. A bobbing lantern shines through his body. "Honestly, I'm sick of it. You do it."

As the light grows brighter, his father dims, finally vanishing completely. The man holding the lantern is Old Spudge. "I'm here to fetch you back, boy," he says.

Edwin has just seen his first ghost. It won't be his last.

xviii

All that night, Old Spudge sits with Edwin, patting his knee, while Edwin cries. The next morning, Edwin leaves the Waller Company without a word. He leaves Old Spudge sleeping in the parlor, his head fallen forward onto his chest, his feet on the ottoman, his sparse hair sticking up like a rooster's comb.

The trip back to San Francisco proves almost as hard as the one in from Downieville. The horses all belong to the Wallers, so Edwin goes on foot again. It snows. It rains. When the sun comes out, he's no better off, the light so bright against the snowdrifts as to burn his eyes. He's always cold.

Every thought, every memory is painful; his mind exhausts itself looking for a place to land that doesn't hurt. He took no money with him when he left. By the time he reaches Marysville, he hasn't eaten in two days. He's gaunt, sickly, and silent. People meeting him for the first time fear his mind is gone. Out of pity, they take up a collection, buy him food, a seat on the coach to Sacramento, and passage on from there. Edwin hardly notices these things happening to and around him.

June and Hattie are living as man and wife in a small house on the steep slope of Telegraph Hill. The kitchen overlooks the endless noise, motion, odor, and color of Portsmouth Square. Edwin arrives there in mid-January. He's planning on going home to Baltimore. He imagines June will want to go home, too.

But June's had more time to get used to the idea of Father dead and even when the news was fresh, it didn't unmoor him in the same way. He'd promptly written his mother and also sent a letter after Edwin, a letter that never arrived. And then, that very night, June had returned to the stage.

He can see now that Edwin is not at his best, but only Hattie is genuinely alarmed for him. Hattie is eighteen, sensitive, and sympathetic. June is thirty-one, stolid and established. He claps Edwin on the back, says that Father wouldn't want to see him this way. He then leaves for work. Hattie finds a shawl for Edwin's shoulders, washes and patches his clothes, sits with him to make sure he eats three entire pieces of toast dripping with butter and drinks a cup of strong coffee. Her voice is commanding—sit down, drink this—but also gentle. The maternal behavior that Edwin found so objectionable in Panama, he now craves. He only worries that too much kindness will make him cry so hard he will never stop.

That evening, by candle, fire, and moonlight, June shares the details of Father's death as he knows them. Shadows jump about the room. There's a loud rain outside, and occasionally a drop falls through the chimney, lands with a hiss on the fire. Hattie reaches out and takes Edwin's hand. Her skin is so much warmer than his. He wishes to take that warmth in, but fears the opposite is happening. Hattie's hand cools as he holds it.

Everything he hears adds to Edwin's pain. Father died on

board the *J. S. Chenoweth*, never having made it back to Baltimore. Someone was with him at the end, but it wasn't the son who'd been tasked with caring for him. It was a stranger, a young man named James Simpson. Simpson had recognized Father on deck earlier and then a few days later, noticed his absence. He'd made his way to Father's cabin, where the smell of sickness was overpowering.

Simpson had the cabin and linens cleaned, sat by Father's bed, and asked what else he could do. Father was already past coherence. "He spoke but I could understand nothing," Simpson said. "Only that he had suffered a great deal and been exposed to much." Simpson was holding his hand when he died. Father's last words were "Pray, pray, pray."

Later Edwin will learn more of those final weeks. At some point while re-crossing the Isthmus (and probably drunk), Father had been robbed of all the money he'd made June give him. Penniless and disoriented, he'd gotten as far as New Orleans on the charity of strangers. There he'd taken an engagement at the St. Charles Theatre, where he performed over six nights and earned more than enough to get back to home. His reviews had been excellent, many noting his remarkable vigor and energy.

But sometime after boarding the *Chenoweth*, he'd fallen ill. He'd told no one, but remained in his cabin, drinking copious amounts of water drawn straight from the river. It may have been the water that killed him. It may have been the lack of prompt medical attention. Had Edwin been with him, he might very well have lived. Edwin certainly thinks so. He never forgives himself.

In spite of the raving and drunkenness, the violence and temper, the Booth children all adored their father. Edwin immediately rewrites his stories from the road. He insists, with no evidence, that on that night in New York when he first played Richard III, Father came secretly to watch, that he was proud of what he saw. Edwin deeply regrets telling June that Father never cared about him. So he wasn't Father's favorite? He was always the one Father needed and that should have mattered more.

At night, in search of sleep, Edwin loops through their final parting—how Father laughed and said he was a pirate, how the ship and his figure disappeared into the fog. He revises this memory, works it and works it, until it becomes a reluctant parting on his side. Until he can make himself believe that this really was the case, that these really were his feelings, he can't fall asleep.

June has a letter from Mother, a letter written to the two of them, which he gives Edwin on the day after his arrival. Edwin takes it to the small attic he's sleeping in. He wants to read it in private. He sits on the floor beneath the tiny window, where the light is best. His knees are bent, his back hard to the wall. The handwriting is his mother's, but also not exactly. Edwin thinks her hand must have been shaking, the words themselves seem to shiver. This letter tells both of her boys not to come home. She writes that the funeral is already over, that the family will rent out the Baltimore house and move back to the farm. Her own desires, she says, are not to be considered. The boys must remain where they are and make the best of their opportunities.

There is one point on which Edwin is quite mistaken. He believes that his father died a wealthy man. Years will pass before anyone tells him otherwise.

It seems to Edwin that the casting-out, which began on the night Mother first told him he'd be traveling with Father, is now complete. They will bury Father without him. They will live on the farm without him. He feels certain that under similar circumstances, Johnny would have been told to come straight home.

But maybe Johnny wouldn't have failed the family so disastrously. Mostly what Edwin finds in this letter is more evidence of his despicable selfishness. His own mother can't bear to look at him. Hamlet was less guilty.

A FEW MONTHS before Father's departure, Edwin had promised him to play Hamlet someday. Father thought he looked the part and that, a few years further into his career, with work and diligence, he might creditably carry it. June is certain that Edwin isn't ready.

But keeping that promise is now the only thing Edwin can still do for his father. He nags and begs and barters until June gives in. On April 25th, 1853, he plays for the first time the role that will come to define him. He wears the somber costume, the dark tights, the short, black cloak. The somber demeanor comes easy. Old Spudge is there to cheer him on in the role of Polonius.

Whenever Edwin remembers, he throws in a gesture. *Don't just mouth your lines. Do something!* Mostly he forgets. June is unimpressed with his performance and won't allow a repeat.

But a young critic, Ferdinand Cartwright Ewer, leaves the San Francisco theater in a fever of excitement and goes to his newspaper offices to write a long review. Edwin Booth, he writes, has made Hamlet "the easy, undulating, flexible thing" Shakespeare intended.

Tastes were changing. Edwin's Hamlet, as it developed over the years, was subtle where his father had been theatrical, contained where his father had been expansive, and natural where his father had declaimed. As Edwin aged, his Hamlet would become less agonized and more stoic—the embodiment of a good man enduring. This was a Hamlet who knew how his story would end, but moved forward anyway with courage and dignity. June may not have liked it, but Ewer says, in that very first review of Edwin's very first Hamlet, that, in concept if not in polish, Edwin has already surpassed his father.

Lincoln and Clay

Having been led to allude to domestic slavery so frequently already, I am unwilling to close without referring more particularly to Mr. Clay's views and conduct in regard to it. He ever was on principle and in feeling, opposed to slavery. The very earliest, and one of the latest public efforts of his life, separated by a period of more than fifty years, were both made in favor of gradual emancipation of the slaves in Kentucky. He did not perceive, that on a question of human right, the negroes were to be excepted from the human race. And yet Mr. Clay was the owner of slaves. Cast into life where slavery was already widely spread and deeply seated, he did not perceive, as I think no wise man has perceived, how it could be at once eradicated, without producing a greater evil, even to the cause of human liberty itself.

—Abraham Lincoln, 1852

Junius Brutus Booth is not the only luminary to die in 1852. The Great Compromiser, Henry Clay, Speaker of the House, Secretary of State, lawyer to Aaron Burr, and fierce critic of Andrew Jackson, a man whose shadow stretched from the presidency of Thomas Jefferson to that of Millard Fillmore, also dies. Lincoln, who has been out of office now for three years, is given the honor of eulogizing him at the Illinois state capitol. Henry Clay is Lincoln's ideal politician, a person who seeks common ground, a person who brokers peace.

To that end, Henry Clay was the architect of multiple compromises that both limited and sustained slavery, most recently the Compromise of 1850, a complicated legal elaboration triggered by California's desire to join the Union as a free state and dealing with the territories annexed from Mexico by Polk's war. Four years later, the Kansas-Nebraska Act, also authored by Stephen Douglas, will bring Lincoln roaring back to politics. Until then, he is riding the judicial circuit, making a name for himself as a stump speechifier, and retiring in the evenings to read his beloved Burns, his Byron, his Emerson.

Meanwhile, at home:

One morning, the neighbors are treated to the sight of Mary chasing him, half-dressed, from the house with a broom. A housemaid whispers over the back fence that Mary once hit him over the head with a wooden board as he was reading the paper, blackening an eye and swelling his nose. That she both strikes and underpays the servants so that the only ones they can keep are the ones Lincoln secretly bribes to stay. That she cries continuously.

In spite of this, he misses her when he travels. He can see how unhappy she is and that's a condition with which he has considerable experience and endless sympathy.

BOOK THREE

For such as we are made of, such we be.

—W. Shakespeare, *Twelfth Night*

The Booth family is gratified by the depth and breadth of national mourning for Junius Brutus Booth. Every American paper reports Booth's death and most include long eulogies. But one response is memorable for its brevity. Rufus Choate, a storied trial lawyer turned Whig congressman, a man famous for his soaring and sustained bouts of oratory, says simply, "There are no more actors."

If Father's legacy once seemed tainted by drink and madness, it no longer appears so. Death has burned everything else away and only genius remains. Wires and letters for Mother pour in from everywhere. Some come from people Mother knows, but far more from people she doesn't, people once touched by a chance encounter or a long-ago performance. For the children, there's a comfort in the sheer number of these letters, in seeing their father recognized as a great man. The further comfort is to see Mother recognized as his wife, themselves as his children. Father has died without leaving a will and the courts are not so settled on the matter. Richard Booth, now a married man with

four children, sues on the grounds that he is Father's sole legitimate heir. The entire estate amounts to $4,728.99.

He even claims Father's costumes, but, since she made them
all herself, the court awards these to Mother. A few years later,
Mother will give them to Johnny. A few years after that, Edwin
will destroy them, one by one, in the furnace beneath his theater.
It will take Edwin more than three hours to burn them all.

ALTHOUGH FATHER EARNED a thousand and eighty-four dollars in
his final New Orleans engagement, only five hundred of that
makes it home. Father's salary ceases, of course, and the rents on
certain properties in England now go to Richard.

Mother decides that the only way forward is to let the place
on North Exeter and return to the farm. This is complicated by
the state of the new house there. Tudor Hall is only recently
completed and the architect, James Gifford, not yet paid. Gifford
removes the heavy tin roof. He lets Mother know that, until his
money arrives, the unmaking of Tudor Hall will continue.
Mother gives him most of what's left in the coffers and the house
is re-roofed. They must manage to support themselves now on
the rent from the Baltimore house and the yield from the farm.

AT THE TIME of Father's death, Asia is seventeen, Johnny four-
teen, and Joe twelve. Once again, the family cracks and shifts.
The gravitational center that was Father is gone, with June and
Edwin flung all the way to California and Johnny and Joe to a
boarding school in Catonsville, some seven miles southwest of
Baltimore. St. Timothy's Hall is the sort of school that charges

top dollar for a regimen of cold, exertion, and hunger, a basic program of toughen-up. Mother selected it.

The rector, Reverend Libertus Van Bokkelen, comes from New York and is a secret abolitionist. The students are none of the above, proud Southerners one and all, many from prominent families. One of Johnny's classmates is the nephew of Robert E. Lee. St. Timothy's has everything Mother wants for her highest- and her lowest-spirited son—a good education, military discipline, and social connections. She doesn't care that these connections are with slavers.

Johnny makes friends quickly. He will do so all his life. And yet, he hates the school. *Something is rotten in the state of Denmark,* he writes in his first letter home. The classes are too hard for him, the rules too strict, the conditions too punishing. Only socially does he excel.

Meanwhile:

Off in California, Edwin is recovering his vim and his vitality.

He's moved in with a friend of his father's, an actor named Dave Anderson. Anderson is an older man, but not the parental sort. He doesn't provide the guidance or guardianship that Old Spudge did. After his grim and isolated adolescence, Edwin is finally having fun.

Using only boxes and tree boughs, Edwin and Anderson have knocked up a small, rickety house out in the dunes towards the end of Mission Road. Edwin refers to this house as the rancho and himself as a ranchero. His letters home are filled with those amusing adventures that won't distress his mother—pranks and pratfalls.

He's having plenty of the distressing sort as well. Once, up in Sacramento, he wanders off drunk, falls into the river, and nearly drowns. A passerby almost doesn't stop, mistaking him for a pile of laundry washing about in the current. Then he sees a hand floating at the end of a sleeve. He dives in, drags Edwin to the riverbank, and runs to a nearby saloon for help. Edwin's missing caul comes to the rescue. After an anxious interval, he's revived with slaps and shouts and brandy. More brandy is purchased to toast his narrow escape.

He's working now in a new company June has formed. Mother is solaced to think of them taking care of each other. In fact, they're seriously at odds. June has no patience with Edwin's drinking. Having always been careful himself around alcohol, he has no intention of continually rescuing Edwin if he won't be the same. June takes small roles, or no roles at all, in order to avoid comparisons, let his unseasoned little brother shine. When Edwin repays this by showing up late, unprepared, unsure of his lines, and unconcerned about any of it, June demotes him back to bit parts.

Edwin has a lot to learn, June thinks. June is very full of himself, thinks Edwin. How happy they are, think Asia, Johnny, and Joe. Those deserters. What lives they are leading!

Asia

i

For a brief time, a few hours though it seems much longer, Asia is the only member of the family who knows that Father is dead. The captain of the *Chenoweth* had telegraphed Mother to say that Father was very ill and she must come at once to Cincinnati to meet the boat. Mother departed immediately, leaving Asia and Rosalie to determine for themselves just how concerned they should be. Rosalie reminded Asia that there'd been many similar alarms over the years. Still, after a short period of dither and delay, Rosalie had decided that Johnny and Joe must come home from school. She'd gone off to fetch them.

So when the second wire arrives, Asia is the only one home. She reads it. She puts it on Father's desk. She puts some of his other papers on top of it. For one mad moment, it seems like a secret she can keep. Maybe the rest of the family need never know. Father is so rarely home.

Even better would be not knowing herself. If only she'd gone with Mother, she'd be on a train right now, traveling in the same anxious ignorance the rest of them are enjoying. She'd be worried, but not much. She'd be assuring Mother that Father is indestructible, which is what she really believes, even now, even after the wire.

Instead she's been left to deal alone with the fact that Father will never again walk in the door, bringing all the noise and excitement of the great world with him. In his absence, the house has always felt inconsequential to Asia, a place of petty concerns and niggling quarrels, no one in charge and someone's feelings, usually hers, perpetually hurt by one careless remark or another.

Nothing will ever be the same, she thinks, which sounds more like a line from a play than something a person says, and yet how true it is. All is lost, she thinks next, which is less true but not untrue. She thinks that she's performing grief rather than feeling it. What she feels is nothing.

She stands for a long time looking out the parlor window, where Father's death has not changed the view. The clouds are low and unbroken, a gray lid set over the city. A strong wind is ripping the few remaining leaves from the trees, tossing them into the air, trapping them against the fences and the snowdrifts. A man passes on a plodding bay horse. Another, on foot, keeps his hat on his head with his hand. There was no reason for Mother not to have taken her along. Father would have been pleased to see her face.

She turns back to the room. The flocked wallpaper she'd always found so cheerful now seems dingy. She remembers how, shortly after moving in, an actress friend of Father's came to visit. "This isn't a house," she'd said. "This is a home," which pleased Mother so much that roses came into her cheeks. Asia sees that the house is shabbier now, a little worn, a little worn-out.

The fire is dying so she goes to put more wood into it. A

splinter drives into her palm and when she pulls it, a drop of blood sits like a bead in her hand. Her blood. Booth blood.

She sees Father seated, right there, in his special chair with its cushion of yellow flowers and winding blue stems. They fight over this chair when he's gone, the only chair in the parlor with arms. He's reading to them from the paper. The bits he finds funny he reads in the crude accents of the comic character John Lump. The bits he finds sad he gives high polish. He lowers the paper and looks directly at her. "Are you sure that we are awake, Asia dear?" he says. "'It seems to me that yet we sleep, we dream.'" And then grief finally arrives, so that there is no speaking through her sobbing throat and all she can do when Rosalie returns with the boys is to dig out the telegram, streaked ever so lightly with blood, and fling it at them.

AT SEVENTEEN, ASIA has a strong and stormy nature. These are the things that matter most to her: the Booth name and reputation, her brothers Edwin and Johnny, and beauty. Asia wants everything in her life to be beautiful—the objects in her home, her clothing, her thoughts. She gets Rosalie to help her cover the parlor wallpaper with white drapes in anticipation of the arrival of Father's body. She removes every object from the room except for a statue of Shakespeare. It's a stark set. Father's final performance.

The body arrives with Mother. Asia and the other children meet her carriage, watch it carried in. Mother lifts her veil, her round face sagging with exhaustion. Asia has come outside without her shawl. She shivers and her breath clouds the air. A trembling anxiety overtakes her, peaking when she looks through the glass lid set in the coffin over Father's face. She turns to Johnny and sees that his thoughts are the same as hers. Her blood begins to pulse wildly. This isn't what a dead body looks like. "He's not dead!" Asia says. Her voice is rising. "Let him out! Wake him up! He's not dead." She's the one screaming, but Johnny is the one Mother goes to, so ashen and shaking that he might topple into her arms.

Asia can't calm herself. She runs upstairs, slams the door, and yanks her crinoline off so desperately that it tears. She collapses onto the bed, undone by grief or maybe terror. For the longest time, no one comes after her. When she finally stops shaking, she's too exhausted to move again. She tries to take a deep breath and discovers that she can't.

The door opens, but it's only Rosalie. "Mother sent for Dr. Smith. He's here now. He says Father is dead," Rosalie tells her. There's something in the tone of Rosalie's voice that Asia doesn't like, but she can't say for sure what it is. Rosalie has a gift for the seemingly innocent insult.

Dr. Smith enters the bedroom. He takes Asia's hand, feels her wrist. His fingers are cold and damp. "Your father has passed," he says. "There can be no doubt of this." The lenses of his glasses are so filthy she wonders that he can see.

He pours something brown and bitter into a small metal cup. He makes her drink it all though the taste is horrid. Then he leaves. Rosalie helps her out of her dress, which falls to the floor and remains there, a small hill of rumpled black wool flung over the crinoline.

When Asia wakes, it's nighttime. Sweat, or maybe drool, has stuck her hair to her cheek. Rosalie's bed is empty and the house is quiet. She rises, wraps herself in a shawl, and moves through the dark to the downstairs. Mother's door is closed. The coffin has been moved into the pure white room and moonlight streams through the window. The stage is set for ghosts, but thankfully none appear.

For three days, visitors pay their respects. Asia avoids the parlor she worked so hard to make beautiful. She never sees her father's face again.

THE STRUTHOFF SISTERS bring cakes and cordials from their grocery so Mother has something to offer the mourners. The neighbors on the other side are the Brownes. They've never been friendly, but they also come, a couple in their seventies, Ann Browne dressed in a severe, unornamented black, her husband, Elisha, whiskered and wizened.

Something about the way Mr. Browne holds his arms, rubs his hands, has always reminded Asia of a fly.

"Fetch your mother," he tells her. The Brownes bring no food or flowers. They won't enter the parlor, won't sit at the dining table. Asia leaves them standing in the entryway, staring past her into the hallway, where a large doily drips from a small table and a painting of Niagara Falls hangs on the wall.

Asia gets Mother. The hand rubbing begins. "I'll get right to it," Mr. Browne says, his voice high, his lips cracked inside the nest of his beard. "Your loss is the price to be paid for sin. This has been a sinful house."

His wife is looking down at the rectangle of light cast on the floor by the transom and never lifts her eyes. "We've come here as Christians," she says.

Asia had assumed they'd come to pay their respects. Her anger has always been a dark turbulence, quick to rise, slow to dissipate. She feels it taking hold of her and Mother must feel that happening, too, because she reaches over, takes Asia's wrist in her hand, and tightens her grip. Asia is quietly being told to be quiet.

She tries. She shakes her mother off, steps away into the hall to look at the painting of Niagara. It's a wilderness without people. The water is translucent, green with white foam; the trees are bright with autumn colors—red, gold, brown. When Asia was little, when she was upset (as she so often was, as she still so often is) she used to imagine herself into that painting, that cathedral of nature and peace. She tries to recover her gift of transportation now. She surrounds herself with nature's beauty.

"Rejoice," Mr. Browne says. He licks the corner of his mouth, his tongue flicking quickly out and back again. Maybe not a fly, after all. Maybe a snake. "God has given you a second chance. Renounce your sinful ways and beg His forgiveness." Mrs. Browne takes a pamphlet out of her reticule and hands it to her husband. He passes it on. "There's help here if you only open yourself to it. Repent. God loves a sinner."

It's a Methodist tract. Mother returns it. "We're Episcopalians."

Asia turns back. "We will never need *your* help," she says, her voice sharp. Mr. Browne looks at her. Asia looks back, though she knows he'll think her bold for doing so. If she had the power to match her feelings, he would burst into flame. He's the one to first look aside.

In fact, courtesy of a few years at a convent school, Asia is leaning towards Catholicism. She finds God in the silver candlesticks, the light filtered through stained glass, the murmured hush of the Latin Mass. If she were Rosalie, she'd take the veil, marry Christ. None of this is any business of the Brownes. Nothing about her family is any business of the Brownes.

"You've said what you came to say," Mother tells them. "You can go now."

They leave the pamphlet behind. Asia burns it in the kitchen stove.

THE FUNERAL TAKES place on December 11th at the old Baltimore Cemetery. The burial will have to wait for warmer weather and softer ground. More than a thousand mourners, young and old, black and white, join the family and the coffin as they move through the icy streets. The size of the crowd is a relief to Asia. Father was so respected. A great man. How many people will come to Elisha Browne's funeral?

She's freezing. Even with a cape, her black dress is too thin for the weather. She reaches out for Johnny's hand with her gloved fingers. She's lost the feeling in her thumbs. She thinks that she'll never be warm again. Father was the fire that warmed them all.

The cemetery paths have been shoveled, but snow covers the ground and lies in hillocks on the graves. Tombstones rise from the white drifts. A marble angel spreads its wings over the frozen world. Midway through the service, snow begins to fall again, thick, wet stars that land and melt on hair and hats, gloves and Bibles. At a distance, a local band plays a dirge composed for the occasion. The music is soft and faraway.

The coffin is set on a bier in front of the mausoleum. The reverend begins. "I am the Resurrection and the Life." Asia huddles between Johnny and Joe. Rosalie holds on to her mother. All are sobbing. Asia's handkerchief is a sodden ball.

The black mourners must watch from outside the cemetery walls, the white crowd the paths inside. Some say later that they saw Adelaide Booth, standing at a distance, silent as a statue and heavily veiled. Others insist she was never there.

EDMUND KEAN HAD his Samuel Coleridge, but Junius Booth his Walt Whitman. Thirty-six years after Booth's death, Whitman will still be mourning. He will write:

> The words fire, energy, *abandon,* found in him unprecedented meanings . . . For though those brilliant years had many fine and even magnificent actors, undoubtedly at Booth's death . . . went the last and by far the noblest Roman of them all.

ii

Life without Father begins with Mother going mad. Rosalie moves into Mother's room and for several weeks Asia sleeps alone. Rosalie has been through Mother's grief before. Asia hasn't and is horrified to see it. It's so unrelenting in its need for compresses, teas and soups, kisses and quiet. She can't take physical care of Mother since Rosalie has that role tightly wrapped up. She can't take emotional care of Mother; only Johnny can do that and he and Joe are already off at school.

Her own feelings of loss seem to hardly count in the face of Mother's extravagant grief and (even though she's just lost her father!) no one is paying her any attention at all. Hours go by without anyone saying a word to her. She eats her solitary meals, the sound of Mother's weeping coming through the wall.

The boys come home for one final, cheerless Christmas in

Baltimore and then, in the thickest part of winter, they remain to help with the move to the farm. They can't all fit in the cariole, and Johnny and Joe must ride alongside. The women's skirts fill the carriage, dishes and lamps squashed between the hoops and petticoats, the valises and blankets.

It's full dark by the time they arrive. The wind rustles through empty branches. No stars show, just one bit of bright cloud pulled like a curtain over the moon. Something dashes across the lawn at the front of the house. Asia thinks it's a rabbit, but it's gone before she really sees it. The snow crust crunches underneath her shoes as she steps down from the cariole. A black child she doesn't recognize unhitches the horse, takes the reins from Johnny and Joe, and leads the horses away, clucking softly. "Thus begins the winter of our discontent," Johnny says, for Asia's ears only.

She finishes the quotation in her head. *Made glorious summer by this son of York*. Why leave off the hopeful part? The windows of Tudor Hall glow yellow with lamplight. Someday this will feel like home, Asia thinks, and then how welcome a sight that light will be.

The Halls have already unpacked for them and made it comfortable, fire in the fireplace, tapers on the tables, lamps in the windows. Furniture in the rooms, dishes on the shelves, clothes in the wardrobes. The walls and floors are clean and new and every room smells of freshly sawn wood.

Ann Hall and Aunty Rogers are waiting with a supper Asia is too tired and too sad to eat. She watches as the two women hug her mother, each holding on long enough to bring Mother to tears. "It'll be all right," they tell her. "Everything will be all right," but they, too, are crying even as they say it. They hug the children next, all except for Joe who ducks away, hightails it up the stairs before anyone can lay a hand on him.

"What a beauty you've become," Aunty Rogers tells Asia, as if she hasn't said this same thing to Asia every time she's seen her for the last two years. Most recently, at Father's funeral.

Aunty Rogers holds her at a distance for a better look, then pulls her close so that Asia's skirt flattens at the front, bells out over its hoop behind. "You've got the Booth eyes. Same as Edwin." Aunty Rogers has doused herself liberally with a fashionable scent—bergamot and lemon. Ann smells of butter and sugar and cinnamon and is warmer to the touch.

Asia feels Father's absence here as acutely as she feels it anywhere. Even though he never set foot in the finished house, he's a tangible, erroneous emptiness. She remembers his excitement as Tudor Hall began to rise. "The only way I could ever be happy in a city," he'd once told her, "is if we didn't have to share it with anyone else. If we had the whole place to ourselves and no one ever knew we were there."

Later that night, the wind picks up outside. Asia hears it gusting around the house, whipping the trees, rattling the windows. But she's in her new bedroom, under the covers, warm and dry and safe inside the house her father had built. Rosalie is back in their shared bedroom, at least until Mother needs her in the night.

Asia speaks to Rosalie across the darkness between their beds. "Do you think we'll be happy here?"

At first Rosalie seems to be asleep; she takes that long to answer. Finally the whisper comes. "I doubt it," Rosalie says. "I can't think why we would be." So, as is often the case with Rosalie, Asia is sorry she asked. The effort of countering her family's continual gloom is exhausting. Tudor Hall is Father's last dream, his last gift. She decides to love it. Rosalie can do as she likes.

ASIA AND ROSALIE:

Twelve and a half years separate the family's two surviving girls. At the time of their father's death, Rosalie is almost thirty, Asia just seventeen. There is nothing to suggest that they were close, though all those years of sharing a bedroom must have produced an intimacy.

Two sisters have seldom been less alike.

Asia is much the better educated. She's been to a convent school and also a college for girls, where the standards and expectations were stringent and masculine. Competition was encouraged. Domesticity disparaged. The girls, addressed only by their last names, were told not to be soft. They played all the games of the rougher sex—ball, quoits, archery. Asia excelled at mathematics and science.

Rosalie attended school for only a few months in England. She thinks she liked it, but doesn't remember for sure.

THE FARM WAS Rosalie's first home. As a child, she ran about with the other children who lived there. She sees how hard Ann and Joe work, every minute of every day, to buy their very own daughters, their very own sons.

She remembers her grandfather's lectures—

—that freedom is God-given while the law is man-made. So any law that gives one man the ownership of another is a moral deformity and abhorrent to God.

—that, in fact, the word *owner* should never be used when speaking of slavery, as no man can ever truly own another.

—*Quaeque ipse miserrima vidi et quorum pars magna fui,* as Grandfather would say, though Aeneas said it first. *With my own eyes, I have seen heartbreaking things and even been a part of them.*

Rosalie has read the recently published *Uncle Tom's Cabin* and wept her way through it.

Asia barely remembers her grandfather. She grew up in the white neighborhoods of Baltimore and the only blacks she saw regularly were the women who did the laundry and the men hired to walk her to and from school. On the farm, she makes a visit every Monday out to the cabins, like a lady of the manor. "They flock around me," she writes to Jean Anderson, her dearest friend back in Baltimore. "I really think I am *beloved* by the poor and the black."

ROSALIE IS PAINFULLY SHY. "The Talmud sayeth, 'Allah sent ten measures of garrulity to earth and the women took nine.' Rose thinks I got my share and hers, too. For a fact nature cheated her tongue of its right and my brain of its wisdom," Asia says.

In a year or two, Asia will start referring to Rosalie as an invalid.

She'll say that her sister has suffered from early childhood with an unspecified ailment. All her siblings routinely call her "Poor Rose." They use the phrase so often Poor has all but become Rosalie's Christian name.

Exactly what is so pitiable in her remains unclear. She isn't housebound—she makes occasional trips to Baltimore, visits friends and goes shopping. But she is reclusive. She prefers books to people and spends much of her day seated. When she walks, she's slightly askew, which gives rise to rumors of drink.

Asia, on the other hand, is in constant motion, a tomboy who hikes and climbs trees. She dances across the streams, balancing on stones and logs in her full and inconvenient skirts. She and Johnny often ride together, galloping and jumping the horses— sidesaddle for her—the two of them singing loudly as they go.

"NOT HANDSOME, BUT NOBLE," one neighbor says of Rosalie. It's the closest thing to a compliment on her looks that Rosalie ever gets and that only the once. Meanwhile, Asia is rarely mentioned without someone noting what a beauty she is. She has black hair, a thin face, enormous eyes.

Asia makes conquests. Dan Burke asks for a daguerreotype of her, her hair parted in the middle, smooth in the front, clusters of curls in the back. George Mattingly, shown the image, sends her a poem entitled "Miss Asia's Picture." Jesse Wharton publishes his verses to her in the *Harford Gazette*. Henry Lee presses a silver ring into her hand and spins stories of a life together in a vine-covered cottage. Sleeper Clarke has loved her since she was eight years old.

Many nights Rosalie drifts to sleep thinking of her lost love, her forbidden love, Jacob, the lion tamer. The relationship was so brief, provides so little fodder, that it requires novelistic augmentation. Years have passed and she no longer knows which memories are real and which a dream. Nor does she even understand that she's made things up. In her mind, all of it is real.

THERE IS, HOWEVER, this one thing Rosalie and Asia have always had in common. They share a conviction, held by their mother and Father, too, when he was alive, that the important people in the family are the boys.

iii

Many things on the farm have changed since they lived here last. The trees are taller and so are the Booths. Asia has the strange, disorienting sense as she walks through the property that both her feet and the ground are farther away than they should be. The creek runs narrow through its iced edges when it once seemed wide and fast to Asia. The logs spanning it, the bridges June and Rosalie, Henry and Nelson made as children, are hollow with decay and wouldn't hold Asia's weight. The bullfrog is gone.

But the most profound changes are invisible to her and concern the Hall family. A few years back, Rowland Rogers died and his slaves, including Ann Hall, went to his son Elijah, husband of the Booths' beloved Aunty Rogers. Around that same time, Joe and Ann finally had enough money to buy Ann's freedom. They now have two little girls, Asia and Susanna Hall, born free as a result, and they've managed to buy their littlest boy, Joseph, for one hundred and ten dollars. But the oldest four—Lucinda, Mary Ellen, Pinkney, and Nancy—remain in bondage.

The Hall family resembles much of Baltimore in this respect. Baltimore has the largest community of free blacks in the nation, but mixed amongst them are term slaves, bound until they turn twenty-five, or thirty-five, or older still. And also slaves for life. This was far from the worst thing to come out of slavery, but the complicated, unnavigable family dynamic in which some siblings were free and others were not was surely a terrible evil.

Three of Joe and Ann's children remain the property of Elijah Rogers. The fourth child, Nancy, lives farther away on the estate of an elderly spinster named Elizabeth Preston. Nancy is five years old.

Ann Hall knows Aunty Rogers intimately and she wants to believe that her oldest children are safe now from sale. But there is no way this particular fear can ever be put entirely to rest, no way for Ann not to be conscious of this in each and every interaction that she and Aunty Rogers have.

Tudor Hall is the place where the two women meet most often, Ann working there daily and Aunty Rogers a frequent guest. Asia, who spends a fair bit of time with both, assumes that the two women like each other. There's no evidence to the contrary, even if she were paying attention, which she isn't. Rosalie might notice a shift in their relationship, but not Asia.

What Asia does see is how kind and helpful with Mother they both are. Maybe Mother spends more time at the graves of her dead children than seems advisable, maybe her handkerchief is never completely dry, maybe she seems determined to wear her widow's black until the day her own death takes her. At least her hysteria has passed. She faces each day with a stoic, if afflicted, determination. This leaves room, at last, for Asia's own griefs and grievances.

Her resolution to love her life on the farm is already forgotten. Tudor Hall is smaller than their home on Exeter. They're too often trapped inside by weather, bumping against each other, snipping and snarling and without the boys to intercede or lighten the mood.

Asia spends the winter plagued with mysterious abdominal pains, a sharp stabbing whenever she shifts position quickly, so she keeps her movements timid, walking about the house like an old woman.

Liberal doses of iodine do nothing. Mother prescribes a laxative, which Asia refuses to take. The only doctor she'll consider is the one they used to see in Baltimore, Dr. Smith, though she never liked him before. "His hands are always so cold," she once told Rosalie. "And his breath smells like something has died in his mouth." But now, unless she's allowed to make a visit back, see her friends, Mother can just watch her suffer. Our Lord fits the shoulder to the cross, Asia tells herself, a favored saying of the nuns at her old convent school. She tacks a picture of Job over her bed, begins a quilt in the Job's tears pattern, and prays for fortitude.

Quite simply, Asia is lonely. There was a round of parties for her when she left Baltimore—dances, teas. Her friends were inconsolable. But Asia's increasingly sure that, in the midst of their unbroken gay lives, they don't really miss her all that much. She sits at her desk, writing sorrowful letters—"Why haven't you written me back? I think you have forgotten me." She's long understood that no one will ever love her as much as she needs to be loved. She thinks she was born knowing this.

Her own feelings of love, she writes to Jean, are the best and purest of emotions. At seventeen, she writes that she's already known the sort of love that will last her lifetime. She won't divulge the object, only the exciting assertion that nothing can come of it. This is couched as a confession. Back when they were little girls at school, Jean and Asia had promised each other never to fall in love. They solemnized the pledge by trading rings.

They also promised never to marry and to that vow Asia insists she is constant. "It isn't so awful, being an old maid, is it, Jean?" she writes as only a woman who knows she'll have many offers can.

iv

Months pass, the calendar turns. Spring arrives to work her
magic. The branches of the cherry are budding with tender
leaves. Flocks of orioles and mockingbirds gather there. The
leaves grow and the blossoms open and soon the foliage hides the
birds completely so that the tree itself appears to sing. Violets
bloom and scent the forest floor. Daffodils unfurl above the green
spears of their stems. Spring turns gracefully into a green and
golden summer. Father's body is taken from the mausoleum and
buried at last in the ground of the Baltimore Cemetery.

On a tonic of flowers and sunshine, Asia recovers her health.
She acquires a beautiful black Thoroughbred and names her
Fanny. The good weather allows her to ride daily. Fanny is fast
and smooth. Asia comes home from one such ride, breathless
and flushed, to learn from an excited group of children that an
urgent letter has arrived on horseback from the rector of St. Timothy's Hall.

Mother is sunk into Father's old blue-and-yellow chair, seemingly incapable of speech. Light from the window falls on her.
Even dressed as she is, in all her desperate black, she's the brightest
thing in the room. Behind her in a shadowed corner, the spinning
wheel sits, lightly coated in dust. Asia remembers Father once saying that there was nothing more beautiful than a young woman
spinning though a young woman playing the harp was a close
second. Father used to insist that all blankets at the farm be made
from their own sheeps' wool. But no one has touched that wheel
in years. Asia has never learned how to spin nor does she wish to.

Mother waves the letter at Asia who takes it from her fingers
and silently reads. Van Bokkelen has an ornate hand and the very

paper he's used is weighty with importance. He begins by apologizing for the shock he knows this letter will bring. But duty compels him to tell Mother that a rebellion has taken place on the school grounds. A number of students have left the school and set up camp in the nearby woods. As of the date of this letter, he writes, the boys remain at large, refusing to return to their classes. They're patrolling the perimeter of their camp, day and night, with rifles they stole from the armory. They've threatened to shoot if forced back.

Van Bokkelen says that Mother will be pleased to hear that Joe, whom he pauses to praise as a diligent scholar, did not take part in this insurgency.

But Johnny did. In fact, Van Bokkelen suspects Johnny of being among the instigators. A group of their fathers have agreed to meet tomorrow at the school and force the rebels back to class. A suitable punishment for the miscreants will follow.

Sincerely yours, Libertus Van Bokkelen.

Mother's head is bowed so that Asia can see how the gray has threaded through her dark hair. Mother used to be so pretty that Father, on an extravagant whim, once commissioned the famous Thomas Sully, who also did Jefferson and Lafayette, to paint her portrait. Asia feels a sudden stab of pity over the way beautiful women grow old. She kneels and puts her head in her mother's lap. Her mother's hand comes to rest on her neck. Asia feels the calluses on her fingertips.

Of course, Mother must miss Father desperately. *Love alters not with his brief hours and weeks, But bears it out even to the edge of doom.* Asia believes in her parents' perfect marriage, no matter what Rosalie says. She believes that Father was a tender, solicitous husband, that the marriage was a Great Love. Mother will never find such a partner again and yet she's young to be alone. You would think four sons would be an insurance against such abandonment, but where are they? Just when she needs them the most, she must make do with her daughters.

Asia also knows that Mother is worried about money. Beside her on the settee is an old dress of Rosalie's, a blue-and-black plaid. If Father hadn't died, it would now be in the scrap basket. Instead, Mother has turned it to the fresher fabric on the inside. She redid all the seams, moved the buttons, and is just replacing the collar and cuffs. She should have tightened the sleeves, but she didn't, so they puff unfashionably. It's a sad dress for sad occasions and Asia hopes never to see Rosalie wearing it.

And now Mother must add Johnny to her list of worries. "If only he would keep out of scrapes," Mother says. "He's such a good boy at heart."

"What do you think the suitable punishment will be?" Asia asks.

"I suppose the rector means to cane him." Mother gets up heavily from her chair. She leaves Asia sitting on the floor with the letter. Asia reads it again. She decodes it. "I intend to beat your brother. Sincerely yours."

Over a dinner of last winter's vegetables—beets, carrots, and potatoes, all fried in butter in a single pan so that every bite is stained pink—Mother tells Asia and Rosalie that she'll be going to Catonsville tomorrow along with the fathers even though she wasn't asked. She'll insist on speaking directly with the rector and she'll also have a talk with Johnny. Joe Hall will take her in the cariole and they'll leave before dawn and be back midafternoon.

Next morning, Asia wakes to the sound of a horse whinnying in the dark. She hears the cariole rolling over the stones in the lane. She hears Joe sweet-talking the horse. She leaves Rosalie sleeping and descends the stairs to the dark and empty house.

All day she wanders. She goes to watch the children swim. She rides Fanny and brushes her afterwards, hooks the mud from her hoofs. Fanny puts her ears back and gives Asia the side-eye, but still lets this happen. Asia picks an armload of bluebells and arranges them in vases for the dining room and parlor. She holds the dustpan for Ann Hall when she sweeps. She writes a letter to Jean. She keeps herself as busy as one can be when there is absolutely nothing to do.

Midafternoon comes and goes with no sign of Mother. Asia wonders what's happening in Catonsville, but idly. God knows, Johnny's been in trouble often enough before. God knows, this won't be his first beating. The rector's letter makes Johnny look bad, but they haven't heard Johnny's side yet. No doubt he has one. Asia can't believe he would rebel in this fashion unless driven to it. She does know that he hates Van Bokkelen, whom he refers to dismissively as Van, with passion.

Dusk and Mother is still not home. Asia becomes anxious. She imagines an accident with the cariole, a shooting at the school, some other catastrophe causing the delay. Sometimes she thinks Mother must be injured; sometimes she thinks it's Johnny. She sits, waiting on the porch with Rosalie, and every moment that doesn't bring the cariole is increasingly stressful. Mosquitoes circle, and Rosalie notes aloud, slapping her arms, that they prefer her blood to Asia's. "Your blood isn't sweet enough," she says, as if this is a time to be joking, with Mother lying broken in a ditch somewhere. The chorus of the wood frogs begins. Three rabbits streak across the grass. An owl in the beech tree swivels his head to watch them, biding his time. The cariole appears in the lane leading to the house.

Joe Hall takes off his cap and waves. Nothing seems to be amiss. Asia transitions quickly from relief to irritation, that she should have been made so frightened for no reason. The surprise then is to see Johnny and Joe in the cariole alongside Mother. Joe Hall goes around to the back, picks up their bags. "Pretty evening, Miss Asia," he says, "Miss Rose." He steps past, takes the bags into the house.

Asia shouldn't have been surprised. The school year was all but over anyway. Johnny and Joe's return is only premature by a handful of days. But this will mark the end of Johnny's academic education, an endeavor he never took to and will not miss.

He's all smiles. When Asia goes to hug him, he stops her at arm's length, holding out two closed hands. "Pick one," he says. Long ago, he'd inked his initials onto the back of his left hand with such force they became a permanent tattoo. She touches the JWB with one finger and he turns his palm up, opens his fist, to show her an early firefly. A moment later, it sparks and the hand he holds out to her fills with yellow light.

"IT WAS RIPPING," Johnny tells Asia. She's seated on the foot of his bed, his stockinged feet in the bowl of her skirt. Joe is asleep and they keep their voices low, but even in a whisper, Asia can hear Johnny's pleasure. If Mother has given him a set-down, it doesn't seem to have disturbed him.

Nailed to the wall over Asia's head are the antlers of a large deer. If she looks up, she'll see a variety of weapons dangling from the forked tines. The sword of Damocles and his pistol and his dagger, too.

"We just decided we'd had enough of the horrid food—bread with mold and meat that was all gristle. We complained, but no one cared. So a bunch of us snuck into the armory and stole some rifles. We killed Van's own chickens, and forced the cook to fry those up for us. We made camp in the woods, just like soldiers, with a fire and the stars. It was maybe the best time of my life."

"I'm glad you're home," Asia says. "I've missed you so much." She waits for him to say that he's missed her, too. It hurts sometimes that Edwin has chosen to stay away. Asia wants to hear Johnny say he's glad to be home.

"Mother wouldn't let me be whipped." Johnny lies back, hands behind his head. "The other boys are all in for a walloping. I mean, I don't want to be whipped, but it don't sit comfortable that I get off free when I did all the same things they did. I certainly didn't ask Mother to come charging to the rescue."

Asia slides out from underneath his feet and stands. "I'm sure you can find someone local to whip you," she says sharply. It took a minute to land, but now she's smarting from his assertion that the best days of his life were days that didn't include her.

"Have I made you cross?" Johnny asks. "What did I say?"

Asia forgives him. "Nothing." She leans over and kisses him on the top of his head. His hair smells of smoke and tobacco. "I'm just glad you're home is all. Everything is so quiet and lonely with only Rosalie around."

Johnny's return marks the beginning of a period of great intimacy between these two siblings. For the next few years, no one will be closer to Asia. He closes his eyes, speaks in a drowsy voice. "We did some target shooting out in the woods. Turns out I'm quite a decent shot," he says, his tone affecting a modesty the words themselves don't convey.

NOW THAT JOHNNY is fifteen, he says that he's too old to be Johnny. He asks, in future, for the simple dignity of John. The family remembers this for about a week and then reverts back, but Johnny never tires of correcting them and eventually the change is made.

John and Joe have both been removed from St. Timothy's Hall and are currently gentlemen of leisure. But then one morning, soon after their return, while the family is gathered at the breakfast table, Mother says that the time has come for the boys to start running the farm. Starting today, she wants them to follow Joe Hall around, helping him out when they can, but mostly learning what tasks need doing and how and when. "You have such a beautiful day on which to begin." Mother's tone is falsely cheerful. She is not the actor Father was. "A perfect day to be outdoors."

It *is* a beautiful day. The sun is rising, turning the clouds pink and yellow. The birds are loud, the cows sociable, the horses high-spirited. John and Joe don't refuse. They don't say much of anything. They sponge up the rest of their eggs with soft pieces of bread and leave the house together. In short order, they're back, bright with excitement. They've decided that the very first thing they must do is build a boys-only shelter where they can rest and recover from their vigorous farming.

Because Father isn't there to stop it, they cut some trees to clear the ground where their shelter will go. All morning, Asia hears the forbidden sounds of an axe.

The boys return for dinner, tired, but happy and full of plans. They'll move the enormous antlers that currently grace their bedroom wall to the new shelter. They'll need chairs and maybe a table, which John will make. Maybe Asia could make them a quilt. "We've started the foundation," John says. "But we don't know where to put the door." John wants it facing the main road so they can keep an eye on the comings and goings. He likes the thought of passersby seeing them there, kings of their own domain. Joe wants it on the opposite side, facing the sunset so they'll know when to come home for supper. Mother says that she can see the merit in both proposals.

Midafternoon, and the boys are back again. Asia gasps when she sees them from the window, limping their way up the lawn to the porch. She calls for Mother and Rosalie, her voice so shrill, it brings them at once and Ann Hall, too. John is leading Joe by the arm. The boys' faces are mottled, misshapen, black with bruising. Joe's eyes are swollen into slits.

"There was a nest of hornets," John says. He's breathing hard, bent over, hands on his knees. "Like a plague in the Bible. They came right for our eyes."

"Hornets," Joe repeats with difficulty. His face is still swelling.

Ann Hall mixes dirt with water from the pump to make a poultice. She puts this on John's face, Rosalie daubs it on Joe's. Mother forces castor oil into both boys and sends them to bed. "Hornets," she says to Rosalie, and Asia can tell that information has passed between them but she herself doesn't know what was said. This happens often.

Around this same time, Joe is afflicted with the first visitation of what will become a recurring malady. For six days, he's sunk into a misery so deep, he's unable to eat or to speak. The diagnosis is melancholic insanity. Then the fit passes, leaving Asia unsure how much of it was merely performance.

The shelter is never finished. Soon after, despite the expense, Joe is sent off to a boarding school in Elkton, where he'll be enrolled for the next four years.

Months will pass before John confesses that, unable to agree as to the orientation of the door, he and his brother had argued furiously and then fallen on each other with their fists. When they'd finally exhausted themselves and calmed enough to see the damage, they knew they'd be in trouble. The hornets were a story they'd concocted together.

John's forthright if tardy confession is disarming. Asia writes to Edwin: "Those wicked boys! Of course, Mother knew. Knew from the moment she saw them. I'm just glad they didn't escape completely. I'm just glad about the castor oil."

John was quite impressed with Joe and says so repeatedly. Despite the difference in size, despite John's years of Bully Boy brawls, his little brother fought him to a draw.

"Nobody won in the end," John says, but it's hard to see it that way. After all, Joe was the one Mother sent away. This is a thing worth remembering when, years later, Joe disappears into the ether without a word to anyone, causing his mother no end of worry and heartache.

v
—

In good weather, Asia goes riding nearly every day, mostly in the morning before the heat comes on. She rides in the neighborhood lanes, between the cabins, into the cool of the woods. She jumps Fanny over streams and logs. She rides into Bel Air to pick up the mail rather than wait for the postboy to deliver it. She is getting to know the neighborhood. She is getting to know the neighbors.

She doesn't like them.

Miss Woolsey flags her down one morning. The Woolseys own the blacksmith and wheelwright shop on the road to Bel Air as well as the farm abutting the Booths', a tauntingly prosperous piece of property. As rich as they are, no one will marry them and they all live together, two sisters, three brothers, their parents long dead. The oldest, William Woolsey, is a local philanthropist, who's paid for Harford's good opinion by funding many improvements to the county roads. Simultaneously, inch by inch, he's been moving his property line. In this way, he's quietly purloined a piece of the Booth fields.

They could take him to court, but he owns all the judges.

The sister who stops Asia is slightly older than Rosalie. On this morning, she's wearing a gray silk dress with a tatted snowdrop shawl over her shoulders. Her hair spreads like great wings at the sides of her face. Pleasantries are exchanged on the subject of the weather, the pleasing aspect of Tudor Hall, the sad fact that Father was never able to live there. "How well we remember your father!" Miss Woolsey says and Asia dismounts, expecting to hear something of Father's career, his celebrity, his genius.

Instead Miss Woolsey recounts a story about the death of Father's pony Peacock. How Mother was made to wrap herself in a white sheet like a toga, and to sit between the dead pony's legs as Father marched about them in a circle, shooting his rifle into the air. "Your poor mother!" Miss Woolsey says. "She was that terrified! And no one ever able to do a thing to stop him when he took one of his queer turns." Throughout this account, the smile never leaves her powdered face. Asia thinks that Miss Woolsey is surely too young to have seen any of this. She thinks that Miss Woolsey's teeth are too large for her mouth. Miss Woolsey has teeth like a rabbit.

And yet, clearly Miss Woolsey imagines this preposterous story will amuse Asia. Asia climbs back into her saddle, adjusts her skirts about her ankles, and gives Fanny's reins a quick shake. She canters off without another word, which is rude, and no doubt, Miss Woolsey will call it so to all and sundry, but less rude than what Asia would have said if she'd spoken.

Similar conversations follow, ambushing Asia in places and times where she'd thought herself safe. So many of the neighbors now wish to share their recollections of Father, the closest, Asia thinks, that they will ever come to greatness, yet they rarely acknowledge his iconic roles, his towering genius. Most never even saw him act.

No, they all want to repeat the old salacious stories Asia had hoped were now forgotten. The things they say are fantastical, completely untrue, and yet there they stand, all of them swearing to have witnessed it personally. Asia hears again the story in which Father tries to raise his pony from the dead, but also of his attempts to do the same for his daughter. In this second story, Father digs up Mary Ann's grave, opens her coffin, slices into her arm, and drinks her blood.

Asia finds Rosalie in the kitchen, sitting with Ann Hall and her daughter Nancy. Old Mrs. Preston has just sold Nancy to Joe and Ann for a dollar and Ann has scarcely let Nancy out of her sight since. Slowly, laboriously, Ann is gathering in her children.

Nancy's seated at the table, her little head wrapped in a green scarf, eating a large piece of bread with sugar on it. The two women are seeding tomatoes, both of them up to their elbows in gore, great pots of water steaming on the stove. Asia doesn't want to talk about blood-sucking in front of little Nancy, so she pulls Rosalie into the parlor, repeats the story about Mary Ann, and appeals to Rosalie, as an eyewitness herself, to refute it. "There was no drinking of blood," Rosalie says, and then returns with her heavy step to the kitchen. This is the saddest excuse for a rebuttal Asia can even imagine. Its smallness makes her angry. If his own children don't vigorously counter these tales, who will?

The job falls to John. "I can't understand why it pleases sensible people to concoct ridiculous stories about great actors," he says on one occasion. And on another, "Don't bring damnation on yourself by swearing to the truth of your anecdotes." On a third, he laments the effort forced on him, to laugh politely in the right places while pretending to believe a great whacking pack of lies.

A relatively benign story in which Father is fishing, falls in, and has to leg it dripping wet for the theater, makes John explode. "If you'd actually known my father," he says, "you'd know he never fished. He considered fishing a kind of murder." Asia feels that John has successfully shown up the raconteur as a liar. But he's also, unwittingly, added to the general sense that their father was some kind of lunatic.

AN OLD ACTING friend of Father's suggests that Asia and John write a biography. "Someone is bound to do it soon," he says, "so you must be there first. Otherwise, these ludicrous tales will be set down as real."

Asia is instantly enthused. She's a good writer; she enjoys it. She has a hundred memories of Father's kindness, his generosity. She remembers how he once made her apologize to a servant for some careless words. How he forced her to sit at the bedside of a Negro woman as she lay ill, forced her to kiss the woman's hand on leaving. How he might bring the dirtiest beggar into the house to be fed.

She begins that very evening, by writing down everything she remembers of the first time she saw her father onstage. She was a girl of ten, and one day, she was given permission to call on a schoolmate named Pearl. Pearl was beautiful. Every night, her mother wrapped her shiny brown hair around her fingers and tied it with rags to make long sausage curls. Pearl was older by months and taller by inches, the daughter of traveling actors, with a confidence and sophistication beyond her years. Asia desperately wished for her approval. She also wished for her hair.

Pearl was staying with her parents in a boardinghouse frequented by actors as it shared a wall with the Baltimore Museum, which was a museum set inside a theater or else a theater set inside a museum, depending on where one's interests lay. The easy access between the boardinghouse and the theater meant that an actor might slip home for a cup of tea at intermission and be back when the curtain next rose. Asia was about to learn that access between the two buildings was even easier than she'd imagined.

An afternoon of dolls and tea parties came to a late end and it was already full dark before Mink, the hired man, arrived to take Asia home. "Why don't you go see your father in *Richard III* instead?" Pearl suggested in a whisper.

Asia knew her father was performing that night, but hadn't realized he'd be right next door. It made no difference. "I'm not allowed."

"What a baby you are, Booth!" Pearl seized her hand and Asia let herself be pulled. "Asia is staying the night," Pearl called down to Mink. "You can go." And then, in case her mother came to her bedroom door to investigate, said loudly, "Let's go up and kiss the dollies good-night."

They climbed the staircase past the doorways of the rented rooms. The steps were high and hard for Asia's short legs and by the time they reached the garrets, she was gasping. "How much further?"

"To the loft." Pearl had already gone ahead. Asia could see her petticoats swinging above the bottoms of her buttoned shoes. At the top of the final staircase, there was a little square door, so small Asia would have to duck and wiggle her way in. Pearl slid it open and pushed from behind. Asia found herself in the dark upper gallery of the theater, up behind the cheap seats, in amongst the rough crowd.

The stage was tiny beneath them. "Take up the sword again, or take up me." Her father was kneeling before a beautiful woman, his voice like music.

The woman answered him. "No! Though I wish thy death, I will not be thy executioner."

Her father stood. "Then bid me kill myself, and I will do it."

"Isn't he wonderful?" Pearl whispered. "He will make your hair stand on end before he's done." She reached out for Asia's hand.

Asia, wearing her cloak, was horribly hot. Her hand, in Pearl's, began to sweat. But she didn't care. Below her, past the forest of men's heads and ladies' hats, there on the stage, all wrapped in light, was her father not being her father. Asia felt so many things—pride, wonderment, the sorrow of the characters, the majesty of the language in her father's mouth, her anxiety over not having gone home and the punishment that would surely follow. And more. Her body was too small to contain it all. Pearl stayed with her right through Richard's death.

But the minute the applause began, Pearl sprang away. "I'm supposed to be sleeping in my bed," she said. "I'll catch jesse if they find out I opened the trap. I'll be whipped for sure." She turned to exit back the way they'd come. But she wouldn't let Asia follow. "No, no," she said. "My mother mustn't see you! You go downstairs with the crowd. Your father will come out eventually through the big doors to the street. Wait for him there. It couldn't be simpler." And she left just that quickly, fastening the little door behind her.

Asia had never in her life been out alone, not even in daylight.

She was always with family or else with a man hired to see her safely on. She was small enough to be stepped on in the crowd as she made her way down from the gallery. She was so buffeted about by the women's hoops and skirts that she could hardly keep on her feet. So she stood, hugging the wall, until the crowd was past.

But as soon as the upper floors emptied, a workman appeared, moving quickly through, extinguishing the lights on the middle floors as fast as he could. Asia had to run to follow him, and she wasn't fast enough. Even the sound of his footsteps vanished and only the faintest light remained.

"Don't be an infant," she imagined Pearl saying, but Pearl's words without Pearl had no effect. Asia was in the museum proper now, the stage still three floors down. She had to move from the staircase on one side of the building to the staircase on the other, right through the exhibits, in order to keep descending. This was a place every schoolchild in Baltimore knew well. She'd seen the collections many times with schoolmates and teachers. She'd stood and gazed in wonder on the fossilized jaw of the North American mastodon. But never alone and never at night.

The passageway she fled down took her straight into the taxidermied leopards, panthers, and lions, all posed with their mouths agape, their teeth sharp and shining.

Gasping, she went another way and there, grinning at her, was the skeleton of a man seated in a cane chair. Even in the daytime, even in the company of her classmates, she'd found these things frightening. In the dark, they were a horror. She ran on, lost in a maze of passages and doorways, cases and stairs.

By the time she found the doors to the outside, the crowd was entirely gone, the dark street empty except for one hack. Her father, swathed in his winter coat, hat, and muffler, was just climbing inside.

"Father!" she called, her voice catching. And again, louder. "Father!" till he turned.

"Who are you, child?" he asked.

"Asia. I'm Asia," and he reached out his two hands to lift her in.

Of course, there was trouble to follow. Mother had been frantic over her absence. Going to Father's performances had been expressly forbidden. What if she had been two minutes later, missed Father completely? What might have happened to her then?

There would be no more evenings with Pearl, although Pearl's family moved on soon after, so those would have stopped anyway. A whipping was coming, but who would deliver it? Her father, who seemed to be in a good mood and might go easy? Or the murderous Duke of Gloucester?

The boys were all in bed and the house hushed. Since she'd missed supper, she was given a piece of buttered toast to eat while she awaited the belt. She couldn't manage a bite.

Her father ate lightly after a performance, only gruel and pickled beets. "I acted well tonight," he told Mother.

So it was only acting? Asia couldn't quite believe that. For days after, she would see Richard in her father's face. His blue eyes would go black. His kindly face would seem a mere mask over Richard's scowling ambitions.

A day later, still suffering the effects of her spanking, Asia stood on a chair to pull the Cibber from her father's shelf. She skimmed through until she found that first line—*Take up the sword again, or take up me.* She read the scene, then read it again.

When next she was required to perform a piece at school, that was the one she picked. An odd choice for a ten-year-old girl— Richard making his desperate love to Lady Anne—but when she stood at the top of the staircase, which was where all school performances took place, her classmates crowding the steps beneath while she shouted her lines above them, she heard the schoolmaster applauding. "Well done, little Booth. Well done," he said. "Just try that last bit again with a touch more longing."

MANY OF FATHER's papers, playbills, reviews, mementoes of various sorts, and, best of all, letters remain in trunks in the attic of the Exeter house. The letters Father wrote are scattered over the globe, but the ones written to him are neatly organized, tied in bundles according to date. What history those trunks contain! Asia and John tell Mother that they're writing a book. She seems to approve. They ask her to bring the trunks to the farm when she next goes to town and she promises to do so.

On the day this finally happens, John and Asia have ridden out to the rocks at Deer Creek, a tributary of the Susquehanna River. In years past, tournaments with armor and tilting have been held here. June and Rosalie attended these as children. John does so now.

Asia is riding without a saddle yet not astride. This takes concentration and balance, particularly at the trot, but Asia has these things to spare. She leans into Fanny's neck. The way Fanny smells is just about Asia's favorite thing in the world.

John's horse is also black, a fast colt named Cola di Rienzi after the Roman dictator, or more accurately after Cola as romanticized by Edward Bulwer-Lytton and Richard Wagner.

Unexpectedly, the Booths have the popular spot all to themselves. Asia strips off her stockings, hoists her skirts, and wades. Some of the rocks shift about as she steps on them. There is always the thrilling chance she might fall in. The heat and humidity are so high today, she almost wishes for it. She lets her hem dip, an inch, then two.

John bends from the waist, submerging his entire head. He stands again, shakes like a dog. They sit together on a rock in the shade. The water that drips from John's hair onto his shirt evaporates quickly.

They talk about their futures. John says that he wants to do something important, something with weight and consequence, something that will leave a mark. Asia can have no such hopes, but she is excited to think that someone might read the book about Father. In her own small way, she wishes to add esteem to the Booth name. John is not so interested in that. "No," he says, "I want to be known for something more than simply being Father's son."

The creek is clear right through to the bottom, a wavering lens that makes the submerged stones oscillate in size. The sun and the sound of the nearby waterfall are lulling Asia to sleep. "'Men at some time are masters of their fates,'" John says, thinking perhaps again of the gypsy's curse. And then, "Did you ever think that growing up so steeped in Shakespeare's plays has left its mark on us? That maybe our dreams are bigger than other people's? I know I can't be just a farmer. I can't be buried my whole life out here where nothing ever happens."

It's so normal for Asia to dream for John instead of herself that she doesn't even notice doing it. A book about Father doesn't strike her as a big dream. But John, of course, John will be extraordinary.

They return home, contented, logy with sun, water, horse, and dreams. To her surprise, Asia sees smoke coming from the chimney. She points this out to John. The day is so hot. It makes no sense.

They send the horses to the stable and go inside. There they find Mother, red and sweating in the sweltering room. She's pulled her chair next to the fireplace. Father's trunks are open, the bundles of letters piled about Mother's black skirts. She is reading every letter. And then, when she finishes, Mother is feeding every letter into the fire.

vi

Nothing Asia or John can say stops the slaughter. Asia pleads, she shouts. She sobs in her fury and her disappointment. There, literally up in smoke, goes her chance to be someone more than what she is. "Leave us *something*," she begs and so Mother begins to tear off the signatures—Tom Flynn, Robert Elliston, the famous blackface performer Daddy Rice—and hand these to Asia prior to burning the letters to which they were attached. The only thing these signatures offer is the certainty that a fascinating wealth of information is now ash. "I will never forgive you," Asia tells Mother and she means it as only Asia can. She has an unforgiving heart, Shylock's heart, John once told her, and she wishes it weren't true, but knows that it is. She may let go, she may move past, but she never will forgive.

For several days, the only person she talks to is John. If Mother enters a room, Asia immediately quits it. John is less devastated—he has other dreams to sustain him—but equally angry. "It was a kind of murder," John says, which is exactly what Asia also thinks. "A homicidal mania."

"Oh, for heaven's sake," Mother says eventually. "I can tell you anything you need to know for your little book," but Asia has already made a different plan. She writes to those friends of

Father's she knows well, asking them to send her what they remember, along with any playbills and reviews they might have
kept. It occurs to her that Father's sister may have had her own
letters and memorabilia. Aunt Jane has recently died, but Uncle
Mitchell is still in Baltimore, cast off by his children and living a
grasping existence in a squalid garret. Asia decides she would
rather talk to her drunken, miserly, contemptible uncle than to
her mother.

It is now 1854. June is prospering in San Francisco. He and
Hattie have had a baby girl. Her name is Marion Rosalie Edwina
Booth.

Edwin is booked for a fall tour to Australia and Hawaii arranged by the British actress and manager Laura Keene. His letters are full of excitement and plans. "I will make a fortune," he
promises, "and then I will lose it all before I return."

Lincoln and the Kansas-Nebraska Act

We were thunderstruck and stunned; and we reeled and fell into utter con-
fusion.

—Abraham Lincoln's first response to the
Kansas–Nebraska Act, 1854

Prior to the admission of Kansas and Nebraska into the Union, the federal policy was to keep the slave and free states in some sort of rough balance. For over thirty years, slavery had been forbidden north of the 36°30′ latitude. The Kansas–Nebraska Act voided this prohibition, upending the Missouri Compromise and threatening those arrangements that had been holding the Union together, if barely.

Stephen Douglas now proposed that decisions about slavery should be made locally, state by state, vote by vote. Congress debated the matter for months, often with spectacular threats, epithets, accusations. The Act was eventually passed by the Senate in March, the House in May. President Pierce signed it into law on May 30th.

The entire political landscape transformed. A feeling in the North that the South had long wielded too much power over the national politics, that they were expanding slavery into the new territories and perhaps had their eyes on the North itself, resulted in the end of the Whig Party and the creation of the Republican.

The abolitionists doubled their efforts. Kansas became a place of blood and terror. Preston Brooks, a congressman from South Carolina, beat Charles Sumner from Massachusetts nearly to death on the floor of the Senate with his cane. Sumner's recovery from this beating took three years while Brooks became a hero throughout the South, receiving canes as gifts wherever he went. Rather than saving the Union, the Kansas-Nebraska Act hastened the war.

Douglas returned to Illinois to defend himself. He told his friends he could have traveled all night by the light of his own burning effigies. As he began to cross the state, speaking in support of his Act, Lincoln began to follow and answer him.

> . . . we began by declaring that all men are created equal; but now from that beginning we have run down to the other declaration, that for some men to enslave others is a "sacred right of self-government." These principles cannot stand together.
>
> They are as opposite as God and Mammon; and whoever holds to the one must despise the other.
>
> —Abraham Lincoln's
> Peoria Speech, October 16, 1854

vii

John becomes a farmer. Asia can see that he feels the same despair over this that Edwin once felt facing a future as a carpenter. He leaves the house before Asia rises in the morning and often returns after supper is long over, too weary to eat what Ann Hall has set aside for him. He has that gift, to choose a course of action, however distasteful, and give himself over entirely to it. When Asia asks, he's always too busy and too tired to work on Father's biography. Asia struggles on alone and lonely.

She's grown used to his company, to hours spent before the fire, reading poetry and imagining grand futures for him, palaces of fame. Like so many boys of his generation, he'd read and re-read the adventures of Walter Scott and Bulwer-Lytton. He wants to be a soldier, to be tested, to see himself fired like clay in the great kiln of battle. Instead here he is, only just sixteen, grimly torturing grain from barren ground.

Like Asia, Brother John has a great emotional range. He has a temper. He weeps for his losses. In fits of joy, he throws himself onto the dirt, smelling, tasting, inhaling the ecstatic world. Farmer John lives in a narrow box of miserable responsibility. Asia hardly sees him and hardly recognizes him when she does.

A new crew of men are hired to help with the harvest, the cheapest help available, Irish immigrants. These white men won't take instruction from Joe Hall. John must manage them. This he's unable to do.

It's customary for white hands to share the noontime meal with their employer and his family. It's customary for the ladies of the household to join them at table. But John feels a great distaste for these men, distaste they quickly reflect back. They dislike him for his British blood. They dislike him for the free and familiar way he deals with the local blacks. They've heard that he was bastard-born. Who is he to feel superior to them? Most of them are his elders, some by decades.

John refuses to let Mother, Rosalie, and Asia anywhere near these men. By noon, they're often stripped down, dirty, smelly, and sweaty, not *delightsome*, Asia observes primly. Their accents are thick, their conversation uneducated. Dining with such would be an insult to the Booth women, John decides. He makes them keep to the upstairs during the noon meal.

Asia sees in this a beautiful, knightly chivalry. Her own Ivanhoe of the fields. Rosalie is more concerned. She loves and admires John as much as anyone. And she understands that if they ask of him the sacrifice of supporting them, then he must be left in charge, his judgment trusted. A meal with a tableful of male strangers would be a torment to her. Still she worries he's made a mistake and would force herself to dine downstairs if the choice were hers.

The men gather at the kitchen table in the sweltering house. The women huddle in the even more sweltering bedroom upstairs, eating from plates held on their laps. The butter sweats in its bowl, the women sweat in their dresses. Eggs dry from the edges in as quickly as they can eat them. "Father would have made friends with these men," Rosalie says in her whisper. "He would have shared a bottle and a story, played the pirate. And so they would have worked hard for him." She's not criticizing John. She's only anxious that he make a success of this and for his own sake. Rosalie recently returned from town with a new saddle as a surprise for him. "When do you imagine I'll have time to ride?" John had asked her listlessly.

The butter is now completely melted. Mother spoons it onto her bread. Asia watches as Rosalie lifts her hair, wipes her damp neck, and lets it fall again. A single drop of sweat runs along Asia's spine, stopping at the band at her waist.

"Your father had a Northern spirit," Mother says, red-faced in all her widow's black. "A democratic spirit. No man in the North would ask to be called Master in his own house."

However much he might like it, Asia thinks.

"John," says Mother, "has a more delicate sensibility."

Asia is a Northerner herself, which means that John must be one as well, but there is a transactional nature to Northern manners, a mercantilism that she dislikes and he finds abhorrent. It's the Yankee way, she thinks, to value a thing only for the money it might make.

John's own manners and opinions were formed by his classmates at St. Timothy's Hall. Brief as his time at that school was, it marked him for the South forever. He thinks he knows a superior sort of person when he sees one and to pretend otherwise is to dissemble.

Asia hears a man singing downstairs. He has a tenor voice, a voice so beautiful, she forgets everything else and sits, spoon in the air, listening.

> In the old churchyard in the valley, Ben Bolt,
> In a corner obscure and alone
> They have fitted a slab of granite so gray
> And sweet Alice lies under the stone.

Asia thinks if there were a face to match that voice, a woman might fall in love. Not her, of course, but some other woman. Asia can imagine it perfectly.

"Have you ever noticed," Rosalie asks, "that the coloreds are always singing of the coming glory and the Irish are always singing of the glory lost?"

Asia is struck by this observation. She repeats it to John when he comes in, late that night. He's seated in a parlor chair, drinking a glass of their own cider. She's holding his bare foot in her lap, puncturing a nasty blister on his heel with her embroidery needle, draining it into a rag.

John takes from it a lesson she didn't intend. "Of course, the Irish understand nothing about the black race," he says. It infuriates him, how they come to this country and vow to liberate the Negroes before they've even seen a black face. "Patrick in all his meddling ignorance. Nothing will destroy the American black faster than freedom." He was exhausted when he came in. Now he's agitated.

He empties his glass and stares into the fire. Asia wonders if he thinks of the prophecy Mother once saw in the flames as often as she does.

"You're right," she says. "The Irish don't really understand what freedom means. They don't grow up democratic." And maybe she believes this, but maybe she's just placating John, she's not even sure.

"The song was my idea," he says. "They were so angry about you ladies being too high and mighty to join the table, they threatened to express their opinions on the tablecloth in jam and butter. How I wish we could be rid of these men.

"Oh, Asia," he says as she cleans and wraps his foot. "I do feel so desperate. Surely I have talents beyond this."

THE HIRED MEN work too slowly. One day, John and Asia walk together out to the fields and find crowds of birds—turkey buzzards, crows, and magpies—feasting joyously on the unharvested grain. John has his rifle and he brings one of the largest down, the sound of the shot scattering the rest into the air. To Asia's dismay, what John has killed is not a turkey buzzard, but an actual turkey, full-grown and eatable. This turkey has wandered over from the Woolseys' who have never been neighborly. Mr.

Woolsey will surely take Mother all the way to court. Asia and John stare aghast at each other over the bleeding body. Asia was planning to pick some squash. She's brought a bag. She opens it and John lifts the dead bird in. The bag is heavy in her hands. She might as well be carrying rocks. They start for home together. Gloom overwhelms them.

"Nothing for it," John says at last. "We'll take it to Mother and then, if she says so, I'll take the horrid thing to Woolsey."

"No," says Asia. "We'll take it into the woods and dump it there."

She doesn't wait to hear him agree. She leaves the path immediately, stepping and sliding into a small ravine with a rattle of pebbles. She walks along the bottom, picking her way past stones, logs, protruding roots, twists of brambles. She steps in a shallow puddle and mud sticks to the bottom of her right shoe.

She needs both hands to scramble up from the ravine, so she sets the bag down, her skirts catching on one tree root, another tearing her sleeve and leaving a stinging red welt on her arm. John hands the bag up to her and follows more gracefully. When they are deep into the woods, far from the usual paths, they hide the body in some brush, and, carrying the empty bag, make their circuitous, surreptitious way home.

Asia's having second thoughts. John's first impulse was honest and forthright. She's ashamed of having talked him out of it. She's been rereading Thomas Hood's poem "The Dream of Eugene Aram," and she says to John that now, like Aram, they've done a murder and hidden the body. "I hope it's not the gallows for us," she says. She's trying for a light touch, but guilt is pressing upon her. John is silent.

Once home, she goes to her room, shoves the bloody bag

under her bed to be washed later. She scrapes the mud from her shoe, picks the leaves from her hair, covers her torn sleeve with a shawl the day is much too warm for. She cleans her face. When she goes downstairs, no one seems to notice anything amiss.

Mr. Woolsey arrives the next morning. John has already left for the fields. Mother opens the door while Mr. Woolsey is still on the porch steps, beating the dust from his hat against his leg. He's a vigorous, prosperous man of middle age. "I expect to be recompensed for my turkey," he says without preamble and without entering the house. He names a price, twice what the turkey was worth.

"What turkey?" Mother asks. Asia listens from a hidden place halfway down the stairs. She has no trouble hearing him—he's speaking loudly and in anger. Rosalie comes down the stairs, thumping and creaking the wood. She pauses to give Asia a puzzled look, then continues towards the parlor.

"You ask your boy what turkey," Mr. Woolsey says. "Your boy that the whole neighborhood thinks is possessed by the devil. You ask your rude, impertinent girl. They've poached my bird, the two of them. I expect if I look in your midden, I'll find the bones."

Asia feels the widening gap between the person she wants to be and the person she is. How could she have been so cruel to poor Henry Lee, accepting a ring, allowing him to wax on about a life together in an ivy-covered cottage she'd never meant to live in? He hates her now and rightfully so. She's spread gossip about Kate O'Laughlen in retaliation for the stories Kate has spread about her. Although her outward behavior towards her mother has lately improved, that anger still lives in her heart, like the stone in a cherry. And now she's a thief and a liar.

"I don't know what you're talking about," Mother tells him.

"I'm talking about your low common children. I'm talking about theft."

"Asia," Mother calls. "Will you please come here?"

Asia misses a step on her way to the door and narrowly avoids a fall. The hidden scratch on her arm is hot and painful. She suspects that her face has gone white, and she worries that the wrong expression or a sudden tremble will give her away.

"Good morning, Mr. Woolsey," she says, her voice false in her own ears. Mr. Woolsey's thick shock of hair, freed from his hat, is sticking up from his forehead. He has narrow-set eyes. When he looks intently at her, she feels like a bug pinned to a screen. Somewhere far off, Asia hears the little Hall children playing blindman's wand.

"I think your mother is an honest woman," Woolsey says, "despite her criminal offspring. You tell her what happened to my turkey. I think she'll want to make it right."

"I don't know what you're talking about," Asia says. She feels low and common. She feels criminal. She feels the tick of her guilty pulse in her temple. This is the worst thing I've ever done, she thinks.

But Guilt was my grim Chamberlain: That lighted me to bed,
And drew my midnight curtains round, With fingers bloody red!

She makes sure to catch John before he comes home. John is a natural confessor. He has to be stopped.

She meets him in the lane. His shoulders are slumped, his footsteps a trudge. But when she tells him what has happened, his reaction is not what she expects. "Life is so short," he says. "Don't let us be sad. It's a beautiful, beautiful world."

———

MOTHER, WITH A sharp eye at both of them, meets Woolsey's price.

THE NEXT THING John shoots is Woolsey's pig. He does this while seated in the window of his bedroom, his legs dangling, the sun high overhead. There is no attempted cover-up. "Your pig was trespassing," he tells Mr. Woolsey. "You all seem to have a lot of trouble figuring out which land is yours and which is mine."

A week later, from that same window, he shoots Stephen Hooper's dog. Stephen Hooper is a free black man, the father of several half black children, all of whom live with their mother. His cabin is about half a mile off from the farm. John has no particular gripe against Hooper. He just likes shooting things.

Long gone the days when the farm was a sanctuary for all God's creatures. No squirrel, no rabbit is safe here now. "Trespassing," John says again when Hooper comes to ask about his dog.

And yet, John's capable of great tenderness towards anything he can't shoot—flowers, insects, butterflies. He rescues a katydid from Asia who'd planned to pin her under glass. "You're so bloodthirsty," he says. "I won't have it. Katy shall go free and sing in the sycamores tonight."

viii

The harvest is a poor one. As a precaution against this, Mother leased some of the fields to a neighbor, Mr. Hagan, but that also ends badly. Hagan, ambitious and industrious, spends enormous sums on fertilizers and sends Mother the bills. He works the men and the horses to the point of exhaustion. After several weeks of this, Mother can bear no more. She meets him in the field to insist that the working day not start before sunup nor end after sundown. He is driving everyone most cruelly, she says.

"Mind your own business," Mr. Hagan tells her sharply. "If I glean a profit from this worthless land, it will be through hard work and a miracle." His anger grows the more he speaks. He calls Mother a series of names, lewd names, names intended to remind her that she lived for years with Father unmarried, names she hasn't heard since Adelaide stopped following her about.

Mother returns to the house in shock. She tries to tell Rosalie and Asia, but the story is frequently interrupted by her sobbing. When John comes home to dinner, Mother and Rosalie are sequestered in Mother's bedroom. Asia gives him the full and furious report.

He goes immediately out to confront Hagan, then returns more quickly than Asia anticipated. "He said you were a liar," John tells her. "You know he's a friend of Woolsey's." Asia feels her face growing hot. She did lie about the turkey, of course. But does that make her a liar? She doesn't think so.

John doesn't appear at suppertime nor in the dark that follows. A red moon rises over the treetops. The house is hushed, only the fire crackling and whispering in the night. Mother seems to have recovered. She sits with her sewing while Rosalie reads in the yellow lamplight. They appear calm, but, like Asia, they're drawn tight, waiting for the release of hearing John coming home. "I expect he's gone to Bel Air for the evening," Mother says finally, but it can't be true as Cola remains in the stables.

The women put out the lights and go to bed. I won't sleep at all, Asia thinks, but then she does. She dreams of riding into a river, thinking she can cross, but feeling Fanny's feet lose purchase. She dreams she's being swept away, one of a great many unlikely things bobbing in the current—books, cats, hats, chairs, a cow, and a banjo.

In the morning, Asia finds the evidence of John's breakfast, but he'd gone out again before she woke. The sun is high and the dew gone when Hagan arrives in a cariole with Mr. Woolsey and the sheriff. Hagan's head is heavily bandaged. One eye is red with burst blood vessels, the skin around it black. The other is covered by the dressing. Woolsey helps him out of the cariole. The sheriff has a warrant, charging John with assault and battery.

"He near to murdered me," Mr. Hagan says. "And no doubt would have, if he weren't stopped."

THE TRIAL TAKES place in the Booth parlor. Mother sits by the window, the brooch of Byron pinned magnificently to her collar. Rosalie takes the chair beside her. The Hall children crowd the doorway between parlor and kitchen, telling each other to shush.

Asia thinks that John looks splendidly defiant, his black eyes shining. He speaks passionately of the insult to the Booth women. He notes that there is only him to defend them, that his mother is widowed and his sisters otherwise unprotected.

In response, Hagan produces the stick with which he was beaten. It has a serious heft. To Asia's astonishment and fury, John is found guilty, given a fine of fifty dollars, and bound over to keep the peace. Apparently Woolsey has gotten to the judge. Apparently calling a respectable lady a whore is only a trifling matter nowadays.

For weeks afterwards, the Hall children can be heard about the place, singing a song of their own creation. The chorus: "Oh, we's bound over to keep the peace, glory, glory, we's bound over to keep the peace."

Magnanimous in victory, Hagan sends Mother a letter, committing to a shorter, kinder working day. His spelling is atrocious. But then, so is John's. Although Asia argues that Hagan was barely scratched, in a letter to his friend William, John boasts that he beat Hagan until "he bled like a butchr."

ix

Suitors and visitors:

The weather cools, the leaves begin to turn, coins of gold amongst the green. Asia wanders through the woods, her thoughts autumnal. She wonders idly why this leaf is still green, when the one next to it is not. Why does God put his finger on one leaf, yet not another? Why are good people struck down and the wicked sometimes spared?

The lineage of Newfoundland dogs is ended, but the Halls have a litter of big-footed, liver-spotted puppies and Pink Hall, a tall boy, nearly as black as his father, Joe, and about Asia's own age, brings them sometimes to Tudor Hall so Asia can watch them play, hold a snoring puppy in her lap. The Halls seem to think she needs cheering up, but really, she doesn't. Her life is good. She's as contented as she's capable of being. The end of harvest means John has time for her again. Joe Hall manages the cider press and the dairy without much help. John and Asia are back at work on Father's biography.

Although she still prefers her old Baltimore set, she's made new friends. There are teas, the final picnics of the season, an occasional ball. Asia and John attend these together, all heads turning when they enter a room—this handsome, high-spirited couple. John's friends fall in love with Asia. Asia's friends fall in love with John. Bel Air society is not as lively or as elegant as in Baltimore, but Asia makes do.

John tells William O'Laughlen that he has his eye on three girls, and Asia knows who two of these are, but is mystified as to the third. Years later, a fellow actor will say that John Wilkes "cast a spell over most men . . . and I believe over all women, without exception," but he hasn't yet come into his full powers and tells William he only hopes he gets enough.

Asia sends a letter of her own to Jean, tucking a second letter inside. The letter enclosed is for a boy named Walter Scott. Jean is to post this letter so that Walter will look at the postmark and think Asia has visited Baltimore without telling him. It's meant to be a joke. Walter has given her a ring, engraved with a heart and Asia's name. Asia is smitten.

A few days later, she encounters Walter's older brother Dan in Bel Air. He's out riding with his friend Jim Crocker. Asia teases them into racing her home. She can feel Fanny's pleasure at being the faster horse. Her strides lengthen. The ground streams beneath her.

Asia turns into the farm lane, pulls up at the porch, and drops to the ground. She's light-footed, lighthearted, giddy, laughing. Fanny is breathing hard, but triumphant, and Asia takes her soft muzzle in two hands, kisses her. Dan comes galloping on his large bay. He is, or so Asia writes Jean, red, white, and blue with anger.

"You were determined to win, weren't you?" Dan asks her coldly. He thinks considerably less of her for doing so. Later he will ask Rosalie to accompany him into the fields to pick wildflowers. Rosalie can be counted on to know her place.

Asia cares not one whit. "Either that or break my neck trying," she answers gaily. She hands Fanny's reins to Pink Hall, and tells Dan and Jim to sit on the porch steps while she fetches a pitcher of cider. Dan is thin and pale with excellent teeth and wild, curly hair, a thoroughly presentable young man. Asia feels her blood quicken delightfully, brushing past him on her way into the house. She thinks that she can find her way back into his good graces anytime she likes.

For a time, her affections waver between the brothers, though neither relationship lasts. She would have retained a friendship with Walter, had he been willing. As to Dan, she pleads with Jean never to pen his name again. "It looks to me now like a coil of snakes," she says. "A doom upon my happiest dreams," which is the way Asia's romances generally seem to end.

JOHN'S FRIENDS FROM St. Timothy's Hall come to call—Samuel Arnold sometimes, but far more often, Jesse Wharton. Asia is surprised to hear John referred to as Billy. She learns that Billy Bowlegs was John's nickname at school, chosen because John's legs curve like his father's did, and inspired by the Seminole Chief Billy Bolek. It's quite clear that this nickname is meant more affectionately for John than for Bolek, and that John takes it as intended. But Asia suspects that, since he never spoke of this, John must not have liked it much.

Jesse Wharton is a handsome boy, with a wide smile and an open, readable face. He and John and Asia walk through the woods together, the leaves now more brown than red. But the sun is out and the day mild enough to sit on the steps down to the spring, the place where Asia once made Edwin give her all his pebbles.

The boys smoke their pipes and the smell of tobacco wafts about. Asia fills and empties her cupped hand with cold water, listening to the music of it falling, but also to Jesse. He tells a story she's never heard before, a story of a wild river and a day in which John, sucked under by a powerful current, nearly drowned, which makes Asia suddenly remember the dream she'd had. She has a brief image of John, floating face down amongst the books and chairs. For just a moment she can't breathe.

"We thought we'd lost him for sure," Jesse says. "We thought he'd never open those big eyes for us again." He throws his arm over John's shoulders and John lays his cheek briefly on Jesse's hand. A thin column of smoke rises like a charmed cobra from the bowl of his pipe.

"No, I'm not to drown," he says. "Nor burn nor hang, though my sister has long believed I'm marching towards a martyr's death."

Does Asia believe that? She doesn't want to.

Years later, she will write that it was a golden afternoon. She will write of her deep contentment. How she watched the two boys, leaning together in the sunshine, so gifted, so beautiful, so brilliant, and wondered about their futures. Surely both would leave a shining mark upon the world.

EIGHT YEARS LATER, in April of 1862, Jesse Wharton will be killed in the Capitol Prison in Washington, DC. A captured Confederate, he'll be shot by the sentry on duty. Maybe he stuck his head out of the window, refused to retreat, and abused the sentry with awful oaths and the taunt that he was too cowardly to shoot. Maybe he was quietly minding his own business, in fact, had just looked up from his mother's favorite Bible verse, when he was murdered, suddenly and without cause. It all depends on whom you ask.

All this was known to Asia when she wrote about his shining

mark. But on that lovely, quiet afternoon, she was unaware and unconcerned. The war was several years and a handful of verses to the beautiful Miss Booth in the future.

ASIA IS SITTING in the parlor, mending a torn hem, when she hears a horse and carriage coming down the lane. No one is expected and she sets down her sewing to go and see who is arriving, but Rosalie gets there first. Suddenly Rosalie is calling for Mother, her voice uncommonly loud and excited.

Asia hurries out to the porch, just in time to see June taking baby Marion from Hattie's arms and helping her down. He turns to look at the women running towards him, one after another, from the house he's seeing for the first time.

It's been years since Asia saw him. In that time, he's grown to resemble Father so much, her breath stalls in her throat. He looks simultaneously enormously pleased and slightly abashed. "Surprised?" he asks them.

x

The railroad across Panama is nearly complete and that perilous journey now reduced to a comfortable four-hour train ride. June makes it sound as if dropping in unexpectedly from San Francisco will soon be normal, as if they might expect him at any moment. Nancy Hall runs off to find John and bring him back to the house.

June doesn't escape a scolding. Ann Hall is mortified by the dinner she's cooked, which is now too simple and contains none of his old favorites. Mother is appalled not to have a room ready so that poor, exhausted Hattie can immediately lie down. Rosalie has a grip on June's arm that shows no sign of loosening. Asia takes the baby.

Asia loves babies. Marion's face crumples at the sight of her and she sobs for her mother, but Asia's not discouraged. She peeks from behind her hands, sings songs, waltzes Marion about the room, determined to make herself a favorite. She can't wait to give Marion a bath. Right now, Marion smells of urine and spoiled food. Her dress is stained and clean cloths will have to be found to diaper her since the ones Hattie brought, including the one she's wearing, all need a desperate washing. And yet, she's adorable, lots of hair and big brown eyes.

Asia's feelings for Hattie, who also has hair and eyes, are more complicated. On the one hand, Asia hardly knows her. On the other, Asia's awed by this woman, only a few years older than Asia herself, who's already traveled so far and seen so much.

The dinner hour is filled with stories of San Francisco, stories that center on theaters and culture rather than the brothels and murders for which the city is also famous. The notorious Catherine Sinclair has been performing there, often with Edwin as her romantic lead, though she's sixteen years his elder. Catherine Sinclair is a beautiful woman, but her success is due mostly to her divorce from the far more famous Edwin Forrest. Affairs were alleged on all sides, the newspapers all but eaten by the scandal for days on end. *That's* the woman people pay to see.

"And what do we know of Laura Keene?" Mother asks. Edwin has recently left with Keene to tour Australia.

June doesn't understand what's being asked. "Promising, but unseasoned," he says.

Hattie does a better job of cracking Mother's code. "A complete professional. Edwin is safe with her."

This is the answer Asia wants, but she resents Hattie being the one to have it. Hattie can have June if she likes: Asia doesn't care so much about this brother who left the house before she was quite old enough to know he was in it. But Edwin is hers. She doesn't want to hear that he and Hattie are close.

That night Asia asks across the darkness between their beds if Rosalie doesn't find it a little strange, how June and Hattie showed up with no warning.

"Clementina is divorcing him," Rosalie says, which Mother must have told her and not said to Asia. Mother and Rosalie have no secrets between them. It's just Asia left on the outside as if she's still a child. "He needs it done quietly. You know that he's already married Hattie?"

Despite the overabundance of evidence to the contrary, Asia thinks well of actors. For actresses she has nothing but contempt—those women who make public love to men for money. She would never go onstage herself, has never even considered it. Hattie retired from the profession when June pretended to marry her and somehow Asia finds that narrow throughway that allows her to excuse her bigamist sister-in-law while remaining thoroughly shocked by the behavior of Catherine Sinclair.

"Have you ever wanted to travel?" she asks Rosalie. "Just take off and see the world?"

"Never," Rosalie answers immediately, as if she doesn't even have to think about it.

JUNE's VISIT IS a brief one. Three weeks later, his divorce in motion, he returns to San Francisco with his family. Saying good-bye proves hard, especially on Mother. "How many years before we're together again?" she asks. Her eyes are a watery red. She holds the squirming Marion tightly against her breast. "How big you'll be when I see you next! You won't even remember me."

John will ride his horse alongside the carriage into Bel Air and say his good-byes there. Having his older brother around was a wonderful respite for John. The two men had an instant, comfortable rapport, June preferring this younger brother to the other one.

Edwin's drinking is worse than ever, though June never says so. Neither Catherine Sinclair nor Laura Keene had a successful run in San Francisco and in both cases, reviews laid much of the blame on their leading man. Edwin might at least bother to memorize his lines, critics suggested.

June had listened with interest to John's feelings about slavery and the South, which encouraged John to lay them out at some length. Suddenly politics dominated the supper table, the women quiet, the men electrified by all the areas of agreement they find. They both support the South, but they also support the Union. They both support the Kansas-Nebraska Act. Although not actually working out as planned, still they both believe it was a step in the right direction. June believes this because he is temperamentally a moderate on all things, John because he sees the abolitionists as the primary problem, with their righteousness, their intolerance, their intransigence. *They* won't be happy until every slave in the country is free! Such talk is common around Bel Air, such sentiments widely held. But Asia has not heard this before from John, at least not in this detail. She wonders if Mother minds the implied rejection of Father. She looks to her mother's face and sees there only the joy of having two of her boys together at the table where she can see and hear and touch them.

June remembers his own miserable days of farming here and is deeply sympathetic to John's desperation. "It's a terrible property," he says. "Always was. Father was mad to ever lease it." He must see what is plain to all, that they are not thriving. Yet he returns to San Francisco having offered little in the way of assistance.

xi

Then it's Halloween, season of pranks and prophecy.

The house is filled with friends—Miriam Thatcher, George and Charlotte Mattingly, Edwin's old friend Sleeper Clarke, William and Michael O'Laughlen, but not their sister Kate, who has never liked Asia, not even when they were little girls playing in the street together, and stayed behind in Baltimore to show it.

The moon rises, pouring its yellow light over the hushed world, and the women send the men away. They unpin their hair, which falls in ripples to their waists. They leave the house, moving as silent as ghosts (though if anyone asked, Rosalie could tell them ghosts are anything but silent), except for the leaves crackling beneath their shoes. Asia leads the way to a hollow tree stump. A recent rain has left small caches of water in the indents of wood. The women wet their fingertips and draw the moisture in a cross on their foreheads. Then they stand in a silent circle and wait for an apparition of the man they will someday marry.

This is all in good fun, and yet there is some magic in the trees and the spots of moonlight under their branches, in the quiet and the cold, in the sense Asia has of being on the verge of a pregnant moment. Asia begins to tremble, and she clasps her hands together to hold them still. Charlotte, to her right, gasps suddenly and then falls silent again. Asia's hair is heavy down her back. She breathes in the clean smell of pine, the dusty smell of the

Lombardy poplars. She hears a horse in the lane. The dive of a hawk, the brief interrupted cry of prey. She's committed to an unmarried life and yet she's disappointed when no vision appears.

Back at the house, only Charlotte claims to have seen something, a tall indistinct stranger bending towards her. Asia thinks she's made the whole thing up. "Nothing?" Sleeper asks her, his gaze so intense she can't meet his eyes.

"Nothing," she says blithely. "I shall live and die an old maid."

"Not if I can stop it," he tells her, but he's turned away, his cheek as red as if she'd slapped him.

She's pinned her hair back up and they are gathering the implements necessary for marauding. The moon is gone—there when they needed it, gone when they don't—and the stars are out, huge and luminous.

Several children from the cabins join them, including Pink Hall, who seems to grow taller every day. He's holding hands with his little sisters, Nancy and Susanna.

They're quite a large party. Asia is aware that her days as a Halloween bandit are coming to an end, that all too soon she won't be able to think of herself as a child. She feels the melancholy of this, and determines to enjoy every moment of this last sortie. The night is extravagantly beautiful, like a hymn or a poem. In those shadowed gullies the sun never touches, a silvery frost overlays the dead leaves.

Asia's wearing her warmest cloak. Her nose is cold and beginning to run. She has a handkerchief tucked into her muff and uses it with some frequency. Tomorrow, she thinks, my nose will be red as a berry. She has an unexpected thought, that she'd rather Sleeper not see her that way.

Occasionally they pass other groups, all of them bent on errands of mischief. Everyone pretends not to see everyone else. They fall on the neighborhood farms, removing gates, taking down snake fences, making off with carriage wheels, harvesting heads of cabbage and stacking them into pyramids like cannon-balls. They come across one of their own horses, loosed and with a cabbage tied to its neck.

Asia walks between John and Sleeper as they approach Stephen Hooper's cabin. John is just saying something about the profusion of stars, when he suddenly shoves Asia to the ground, throws himself over her. Asia hears the sharp sound of a rifle and slowly understands that Stephen Hooper is peppering them with buckshot.

John's hat has been blown from his head.

The shots continue, striking rocks and mud, echoing in the still night. Little Susanna Hall begins to cry. "Am I shot? Am I shot?" she asks her brother Pink, who kneels to wrap his arms around her, rocks her gently, and says that she is not. No one has been shot.

When firing ceases, John rises slowly and retrieves his hat. "I'll remember this, Hooper," he shouts. "Count on it."

Sleeper helps Asia up, asks anxiously if she was hurt in the fall. She's too angry to know for sure. As a black man, Hooper is not allowed to have a gun. "He had no provocation," Asia says, forgetting his dead dog, incapable of understanding what a black man might feel, living alone in a remote cabin, and seeing a mob of people coming silently towards him in the dark.

It would be as easy as anything to see him hauled away. Asia assumes John will report it. And yet, days go by. She asks John about it. "I don't know," he says, as if he's as surprised as she by his own lack of action. "I seem to have forgiven him."

How is a person able to do this, erase an injury from the heart

as if it never made a mark? Asia can't fathom it. John, so determined, so single-minded about some things, is oddly mercurial
about others.

His restraint appears to unsettle Hooper. Henceforth, Asia
says, he treats them with a smiling hatred. A year later when
some of Hooper's sons are hired to work on the farm, Asia objects. "Remember Halloween," she says.

John puts a hand on her arm. "That was a long time ago."

No, she thinks. *One may smile and smile and be a villain.*

THIS IS THE last time Asia will see Pinkney Hall on the farm. A
few days later he and his sister Mary Ellen run. Aunty Rogers
takes this as a personal insult, a suggestion that they don't take
care of their slaves, that their slaves are not, in fact, practically
family. If anything, Elijah has been too indulgent. Hasn't he let
Pink see his parents more often than a slave could hope? Hasn't
he always behaved with tolerance and generosity when another
owner might have noticed laziness and insolence?

She turns a suspicious eye on Ann and Joe. *Someone* gave
Pinkney and Mary Ellen the money to escape—they could never
have managed without money.

Ann listens soberly to Aunty Rogers' grievances. She says that
this comes as a big surprise to her as well; she had no idea. She
says that she can't imagine what insanity came over her children.
She agrees that they had no cause, assures Aunty Rogers of her
own fundamental goodness. She admits to nothing. The Booths
could take acting lessons from her (and probably any other slave
in the South as well).

Asia would have been entirely convinced had she not, just a
week or so prior, happened on Ann and Rosalie whispering

together in conspiratorial fashion, a conversation that stopped immediately when Asia walked in.

Aunty Rogers remains insulted. She comes less often to visit the Booths, where she is so likely to run into Ann. Asia doesn't want to choose between these two women—she loves them both. She feels there must be blame on both sides. Aunty Rogers should have forced her husband to emancipate Ann's children. But Ann shouldn't have participated, if she participated, in this illegal flight.

John says very little about it, noting only that the Booths depended on Pink to care for their horses and what are they to do now? It's an inconvenience rather than an outrage. He grants the Hall family an exemption from his usual politics.

So two more of Ann and Joe's children are free. But they won't see their mother again until the end of the Civil War. And they have looked on their father for the very last time.

xii

For most of Asia's life so far, the large world of not-Booths has occupied very little of her thinking. Living among slaves, intertwined as they are with the Hall family, she seems strangely oblivious to the great issue of the nation. What does it have to do with her and her brothers? Plus Father always said that actors can't afford to be political. When he wrote his death threat to Jackson, that was a personal, not a political, matter.

This changes.

National politics grow increasingly violent while politics in Baltimore take their own volatile turn. The issue of the moment here is not slavery, but immigration.

John tries to goad Asia, and sometimes Rosalie, into argument. He has a didactic, badgering style and insists on continuing long past the point at which he's either convinced or exhausted his opponent, as he will not quit without winning. Asia begins these arguments full of spirit and ends them drained of all conviction. His beliefs are so much more deeply held than hers.

He's joined the Know-Nothing Party and, finding the opposition at home too tame, begins to frequent the Bel Air saloon in pursuit of livelier game. He's passionate about the anti-immigration sentiments and there are other things that also appeal to his sixteen-year-old heart. The Know-Nothings are a party of clandestine meetings, secret oaths and handshakes. They think and move like spies.

In November, he's chosen as a delegate from Bel Air to a great mass meeting in support of the Know-Nothing candidate for Congress, Henry Winter Davis. The day starts dry, but follows a night of rain that left the roads in great puddles of mud. Asia decides to ride Fanny rather than taking the cariole and so she dresses that morning in her riding habit, short jacket, overskirt. She meets John downstairs and he's wearing a coat Asia has never seen before, red with velvet lapels, over a light vest, and with pale gray trousers strapped under his boots. He's begun to grow a mustache, as yet a faint shadow on his upper lip. He looks magnificent. Rosalie and Mother come into the parlor to exclaim over him.

"Come with us," Asia says to Rosalie, knowing that she won't. She says that crowds give her a headache.

The roads are so jammed, they unsettle Fanny, who prefers to stay out of the mud but also at a certain distance from other horses. She dances about the puddles and, Asia suspects, may even on occasion be hoping to shake her off and go home. Fanny's had a foal that she's now reluctant to leave.

It's discovered that the Bel Air banner, needed to decorate the stage, was left behind so John says he'll ride back for it. He and Cola take off at a reasonable clip, hugging the side of the road rather than weaving through the traffic moving in the other direction. Asia hears the crowd gasp. Cola is on his knees; a bit of ground has crumbled beneath his hoofs. But John leaps off, pulls Cola upright, and remounts without a foot in a stirrup, simply springing unaided to Cola's back. He gives the crowd a quick, careless salute, then urges Cola forward again.

Asia is aware of the fluttering handkerchiefs and hearts around her. "He's *so* handsome," a woman nearby says. "Who is he?"

Asia goes to stable Fanny. A wall of black clouds is forming to the west and they must all hope that the rain will hold off. Only the stage is covered.

There's a parade to the platform. People crowd the sides of the roads to make room for the marching Know-Nothings. She worried that John would not be back in time, but there he is, carrying the flag of the party, red and white stripes and in the blue corner, an eagle spreading his wings aggressively over the ballot box. Superimposed on the stripes are the words NATIVE AMERICAИS, BEWARE OF FOREIGИ IИFLUEИCE.

Had Asia worn her hoop skirt instead of her riding habit, she could have kept a space for herself—hoops are growing larger as bonnets shrink. As it is, she's crowded into a woman who smells of roses and also to a man with a large mole on one cheek who smells of drink. "Please excuse me, miss," he tells her. "I'm being shoved in all directions and having the devil's own time keeping my feet underneath me," but Asia can see perfectly well that it's not the crowd that has him swaying.

She's impressed with Davis' speech, which focuses on the dangers of popery. He speaks simply, persuasively, and from the heart, or so it seems to Asia. She judges him chaste and elegant. He has an abundance of curly hair and a magnificent mustache. But if the crowd around her represents the party, she's less impressed with them.

She's almost home when a sudden downpour soaks Fanny's flanks and mane, her own bonnet and skirt. She arrives on the porch like some drowned thing, her hair and sleeves plastered to her skin, and Rosalie brings her tea and towels, pulls her shivering and dripping inside to stand in front of the fire, stripping off her wet stockings. Thunder rattles the windows. She'd felt quite patriotic, quite engaged, while listening to the speeches. The rain has sobered her up. "I never saw such a queer collection of people," she tells Rosalie, toweling the rain from her face and hair, but she can't put her finger on just what was so queer about them.

John arrives hours later, after the rain has stopped and the sun gone down, with no such concerns. He's been in the saloon with the other Know-Nothings, reliving a day of unalloyed triumph. Asia takes one look at his glowing face and tells him that the time will come when he must choose—politics or the theater. "You can't do both," she says. "Father always said that."

Mother agrees.

HENRY WINTER DAVIS will win his race. John doesn't know that he's just supported a man who will devote himself to keeping Maryland in the Union, who will castigate Lincoln in the strongest possible terms for his leniency towards the South, a plan, he'll say, that, whatever Lincoln proclaims, guarantees the return of slavery in all but name.

Lincoln and the Lost Speech

Come as the winds come, when forests are rended; Come as the waves come,
when navies are stranded.

> —Sir Walter Scott, as quoted by Lincoln,
> as remembered by witnesses to the Lost Speech

In 1856, in Bloomington, Illinois, Lincoln speaks extemporane-
ously at the convention where the Republican Party is being
created. Some in attendance say later that this speech had such
power, was limned with such divine fire, that no one who heard
it was unchanged. "In a brief moment every one in that . . .
assembly came to feel as one man, to think as one man and to
purpose and resolve as one man. Rarely if ever was so wonderful
an effect produced by an oration. It was the speech of his life in
the estimation of many who heard it," Judge John M. Scott
wrote. He was quite safe in saying so, since no text survives to
trouble the matter. Those reporters charged with transcription
claim they were so transported they forgot to take notes.

Or else the speech's disappearance was calculated. It seems
that Lincoln, speaking off the record, allowed himself to express
a more radical form of anti-slavery than his usual. It seems to
have been an angry speech. Lincoln apparently argued that no
compromise with slavery was possible—that the nation must either be all slaveholding or all free.

Friends tell him later that he has gone too far and they believe he's been persuaded. But in two years he will repeat himself and this time for the ages—"A house divided against itself cannot stand," he will say.

The speech establishes him as a leader in the Republican Party and soon he is being asked to speak so often and in so many places it becomes tiresome. He begins to hear from people who want him to run for the presidency.

xiii

Despite Mother's obstruction, Asia has managed to amass a fair collection of materials for Father's biography. She and John work together to wrestle it all into order. The manuscript is always open, always in Asia's thoughts.

Skinner-Street, February 27th, 1817

Sir:

I witnessed your performances of Richard and Iago, and you may, perhaps, not be displeased with receiving a few hints and remarks from a person of old experience in matters of literature and taste.

With your Richard, I was not altogether satisfied. You got through it with much bustle, activity, and energy, and were rewarded with almost unexampled applause; but it appeared to me a representation rather of promise, than of

that full conception and meditation, I long for in a performer. Your Iago struck me very differently: I mean in the
third act of the play for the rest was not excellent. I have
seen Garrick, and most of the eminent performers of the
last age. But I confessed that that evening I saw something
new . . . your tones of insinuation, in particular, when it
was your part to infuse the poison of jealousy into Othello,
were so true that, by my faith . . . I immediately became
impressed with the persuasion, This Booth will make a
real actor. I set down these things because, as you are a very
young man, they may be of use to you . . .

I am Sir, your obedient Servant,
William Godwin

As WELL AS helping with the manuscript, John has begun to pre-
pare for his own life on the stage. He's set himself the task of
memorizing Shakespeare's plays and Cibber's adaptations. A slow
study, he repeats the speeches so often that, passing by on their
own business, one or another of the little Hall children will stop
to supply the word he missed, the line he needs. The whole farm
speaks in iambic pentameter.

Asia doesn't say so, but she worries that he lacks some essential
understanding of the text, something that came quite naturally
to Edwin, even as a young boy. John has a beautiful voice, but
whether his emphases and inflections are right or wrong, neither
he nor Asia can tell. He needs a teacher such as he imagines Father was to Edwin.

Even his physical gifts cause him concern. He worries that
he's too solid and square for the quicksilver Romeo, too jerky

and stiff for the graceful Hamlet. One day, he comes to Asia's bedroom. The sun is coming through the window, but pale and wan. Asia's at the little desk, writing letters, her fingers stiff with cold. John amuses himself by putting on her petticoat, her shawl. He stands in front of the mirror. He says, "'The Thane of Fife had a wife. Where is she now?'"

Asia turns around in her seat. He holds out his hands to her imploringly. "'What, will these hands ne'er be clean? Here's the smell of the blood still . . .'"

He pauses and Asia supplies the prompt. "'All the perfumes of Arabia . . .'"

"'All the perfumes of Arabia will not sweeten this little hand,'" he says. "Don't I make a lovely Lady Macbeth?"

He decides to go further. He takes Asia's old blue gingham and her newest bonnet and disappears. When he returns, he's fully rigged. He walks back and forth in front of her, his hoop swinging side to side, until she's helpless with laughter. He looks at himself in the mirror again. "What will you give me if none of the farmhands recognizes me?"

"Oh, please don't!" she says. "We give the neighbors enough to talk about," but she's too late. She stays at her desk, watching his figure from her bedroom as, wrapped in Rosalie's cloak, he heads over the frosty lane towards the barn.

He returns a quarter of an hour later. She hears him down in the kitchen with Ann and Nancy Hall. There is shrieking and laughter and she hears bold little Nancy ordering him to undress. "Undress right now, Master John," she says. "Undress and wear your own clothes!"

By the time he returns to Asia's room, he's enormously pleased with himself. "Everyone I passed," he says, "raised his hat to me. All greeted me with the respect due such an elegant lady." His confidence is hugely raised by the successful experiment. Maybe he can take on the light, skip-about parts, after all.

IN AUGUST OF 1855, John returns midday from an overnight visit to Baltimore. Asia is out with a basket, gathering the glossy black dewberries so that Ann Hall can make a jam. Nancy Hall is helping by holding the thorny branches to the side with a large stick so that Asia doesn't get pricked while Elizabeth Hall pouts that she *is too* old enough to help. They are surrounded by spotted dogs and farm cats and more children from the cabins.

The spotted dogs see John first, riding in on Cola. They begin to howl with the excitement of his arrival. The children swarm about his horse's hoofs. He holds up a bag of candy, flings its contents. "Get it before the dogs do," he tells the children and the melee commences.

John dismounts and comes to Asia. He takes her basket, reaches over to brush some stray hair from her face. "Guess what I've gone and done," he says. She can see how pleased he is.

"It's something wonderful," she says. "But I can't guess what."

"Last night, I played the role of Richmond at the Charles Street Theater."

When Mother is told, she's not so pleased. Edwin started small and worked his way up to the major roles. He earned his place. While June, when green, had found that companies would hire him on the basis of his name alone. It's a smart business move for them. If a Booth commands the stage, people will pay to see that. If he stumbles, proves talentless, people will pay to see that, too. Mother says, as gently as she can, that John is unseasoned and unready.

The night John appeared was the only night in which the

theater was filled. A capacity crowd had hissed John's performance. The air of triumph Asia detected was the best acting John
had managed. Mother was right. He'd been exploited for his name
and the man who did this was Edwin's good friend Sleeper Clarke.

It all made John remember how, years ago when he was only
eight, Sleeper and Edwin had taken the role of Richard away
from him and offered him Richmond. He remembered their ar-
rogance, their thirteen-year-old bossiness.

Yesterday, he'd been grateful to Sleeper for giving him his
chance. Sleeper's been practically family for as long as John can remember. He wants to believe in his good intentions. The fault is
John's own, his own dreams, his own vanity. Getting above himself. He says nothing to Asia. The next time Sleeper asks, he says no.

xiv

Asia turns twenty. It's an occasion for a good scrubbing of the
soul. What has she done in the past year on behalf of heaven? Has
she avoided becoming what she most fears—scrupulous, prudish,
judging, and cold-hearted? Has she instead been what she most
wishes—generous, merciful, a kindly old maid? How can she do
better? What lies ahead?

"I fear the unfolded page," she writes to Jean. "Promise you'll
always love me."

xv

Letters arrive from Edwin with such adventures! Pirates boarded
his ship near Samoa, trying unsuccessfully to seize the wheel and

run it aground on the coral reefs. There was a mutiny in which the traveling players were forced to defend the captain with their counterfeit swords and wooden guns.

After a successful run in Sydney, the troop moved on to Melbourne, where Edwin celebrated his twenty-first birthday in a manner his letters do not recount. In fact, quite, quite drunk, he attempted to fly the American flag at his hotel, while loudly castigating the British Empire. This roused the Australians to such a pitch of patriotism that they refused to come and see him act. In one drunken spree, Edwin destroyed the whole Australian tour.

Laura Keene, all too familiar with such behavior, fleeing a drunken husband of her own, never forgives him. Eliding the cause, Edwin's letters admit to the rift. He writes that he's "suffering Keenely" as a result. He parts from her and sails on to Hawaii, where he performs Richard III for King Kamehameha, who had once seen his father in the same role.

John can hardly bear to read these letters, so great is his envy. He's desperate to protect his captain from a mutiny—he's better with a sword than Edwin is by miles. Meanwhile, the situation on the farm is desperate. No one since the Hagan debacle has leased the fields. No one has ever teased a good crop of grain from them. In the winter of 1855, the Booths begin to slowly starve.

ASIA IS ALWAYS tired and always cold. She feels brittle and breakable. Her hair loses its gloss, she suffers from constipation, and she understands that nourishing food would cure all of this, but the larder has little of that. Then the cows go dry. Only one continues to yield, but her milk is pink in color, which makes Asia remember how Herne the Hunter comes in his hoofs and horns, shaking his chain, and making *the milch-kine yield blood*. "There is nothing," John says, "that Shakespeare didn't anticipate."

Snow blankets the woods and fields in higher and higher drifts. The world is hushed. The water doesn't flow, the birds don't sing. Only the sound of the thawing and the freezing again. Only the sound of icicles dripping from the tree branches and eaves and windows. Only the wind.

The pump freezes and it takes an axe to fill a bucket at the spring.

Some of the horses have to be sold. This includes Fanny's foal. They can no longer afford to pay Ann Hall and the snow is so deep, she would struggle to reach Tudor Hall anyway. No one is braving the roads; they haven't had a guest in more than a month. Still, Rosalie wants to bring Joe home. Mother says no. She's behind in his school fees, but he's being fed where he is. A growing boy needs food.

Asia has a cage of pet partridges. There is no eating them as they all have names, but there is no feeding them either. Asia lets them go, watches them pick and scatter across the white ground. "They were too pretty to eat," Rosalie says and Mother says, "This is what comes of giving a name to every creature that wanders onto our land."

Asia decides to go with John into the woods to check on some traps that he set the day before, traps for animals without names. More snow in the night, so she opens the front door to a world of blinding white. The porch steps have disappeared.

John must take a stick when he walks, stabbing it into the drifts to be sure of the solid ground beneath. In this way, he finds the snake fence at the perimeter of the property, vaults over it. "Come on," he says to Asia. "One leap will do it."

Surely she would have made that leap on another day when

her belly was full. Instead, she lands short, sinks into a drift up to her neck. She can't move her arms or pedal her feet and by the time John has managed to pull her out, adrenaline has her heart hammering. Snow sticks like burrs to her skirts and she can't shake it all off. "I was drowning," she says. "I nearly drowned." We thought he'd never open those big eyes for us again, she hears Jesse Wharton say.

"I doubt a person drowning would have managed the squawking you did." John is laughing at her panic. He adds, more gently, "I never lost you. I had you safe." She's shivering uncontrollably so he suggests that she go back to the house; he can find the traps himself, but she's too frightened to go alone. The way home now seems to her one continuous and all-too-likely grave.

In the woods, under the trees, the snow thins and they can more easily make their way forward. They've caught two animals, a possum and a squirrel. Whatever horror these animals felt when the traps first sprang has been spent. Both are limp, eyeing Asia with resignation. Both are more starved than the Booths.

John lets them go. "They wouldn't have been a mouthful anyway," he says. "Poor miserable creatures." And then, changing his mind when it's too late, "But they were quite prepared to die. How stupid of me!"

Asia is numb by the time they make it home. The return of sensation in her arms and legs is fiery and painful. She trembles so hard it seems she might break a tooth.

Eventually, she is warm again. But still hungry.

JOHN SELLS SOME livestock and finds a distant neighbor, Mr. Parker, who lets him purchase a lactating cow. John sets off on foot to fetch her. The snow is falling at a slant when he leaves, there is an icy wind, and Asia has a terrible premonition as she watches his figure blur and disappear. She runs after him, but only makes it as far as the family graveyard, where the crosses barely clear the snow, the dead lying deeper and colder than ever.

They expect him back that afternoon, but night comes and he hasn't returned. The wind has stopped, but not the snow, which now falls straight and white from the black heaven. Asia lights the lamps, sets one against each of the chilled windows so that John can find his way home. Branches of frost blossom on the glass.

She retires to the settee and, in the lamplight, tries to pick up the story she was reading . . .

The road grew wilder and drearier and more faintly traced, and vanished at length, leaving him in the heart of the dark wilderness, still rushing onward with the instinct that guides moral man to evil . . .

But the words are meaningless on the page. Mother has set down her sewing and rocks in her chair, her arms tight around her own body. "My boy, my boy, my boy," she says. "My own, my darling boy."

The long night is unendurable. The women grow quiet. No one goes to bed. Asia wraps herself in a quilt and thinks again of the cocoon of snow, how it pinned her arms. She might have died if John hadn't been there to pull her out. She would probably have died. People do die in the dangerous cold, only steps from their own front doors. She hates the cow he's gone to buy. She hates the Parkers for offering her. She thinks that if something has happened to John, she will never get over it.

"I remember," Rosalie says suddenly. "I remember when Henry died."

"Stop that," Mother tells her.

"I remember it perfectly."

"Not another word. I warn you."

It's been years since anyone mentioned Henry's name in Asia's presence. She knows about these dead brothers and sisters, but the world they lived in is an imaginary one, the world before *her*. They don't feel dead to her; they feel like something in a book or a dream.

"You can't have him," Rosalie says.

"What?" Asia asks, but Rosalie isn't talking to her.

"I won't listen to this." Mother's voice is shaky but shrill. She rises, staring at Rosalie. Then she leaves the room, her shoes scraping against the wood floor as if she can't even lift her feet, as if she's forgotten how to walk.

"You can't have him," Rosalie repeats, talking to the air, and Mother returns, wringing her hands together. She barely makes the doorway before she leaves again. Again returns. Asia can see that if John doesn't come home, all three of them will go mad. They will die of starvation here, in the house that Father built, each one madder than the next.

IN THE MORNING, the snow is no longer falling. The sun rises and that pink and yellow is reflected on the clean, white page of the yard. Icicles hang like teeth from the window frames. Asia is leaden with exhaustion. She melts a bowl of snow on the parlor fire, takes it upstairs to wash the night from her face. When she brushes her hair, a knot of it remains in the bristles. She feels as listless and limp, as resigned and hopeless, as the possum they'd trapped. She tries to think of the very last thing she'd said to John, but it was too ordinary to be memorable. Nor can she remember what he'd said to her. What she remembers is how he'd once said that she'd marked him for a martyr's death. Would this be that, frozen to death while trying to feed his family?

She goes into John's bedroom, lies on his bed. She can smell his muddy, smoky scent in the quilt she herself made for him. The antlers, still dripping with their weaponry, hang above her, casting shadows like bony fingers against the wall. She should get up. She should put on her riding clothes, saddle Fanny, and ride out to the cabins, get the men to go and search. But she's too afraid of what they'll find.

She makes it as far as John's window. From there she has the best view in the house of the buried lane. She sees John, tamping down the snow as he comes, leading a cow and making his slow way home. She waits just long enough to be sure that he's real, before running, sobbing, calling for Mother and Rosalie, downstairs to meet him, shoeless out into the snow.

IT TURNS OUT that the women's fears were not exaggerated. His escape was a narrow one. He'd walked for hours, the wind blowing into his face, snow coating his sleeves, encasing his gloves and boots, his hat and the scarf over his face until he must have looked like a snowman walking. The drifts were high. He must wade sometimes and force his way forward, never certain he hadn't lost the road. Suddenly, chilled to the heart, he was overwhelmed with the need to sleep. It seemed like such a reasonable thing to do—rest for a bit, close his stinging eyes—that he had to deliver stern lectures to himself, saying that to sit down for even a moment would be his death. The argument in his head only stopped when, through the blur of snow, he thought he saw a light.

Fairyland, he thought, because he was just that far out of his mind, but the light turned out to be real, the Parker farm at long last. He was taken inside, so frozen he was unable at first to speak or think. Mr. Parker poured brandy down his throat and whipped him about the chest and shoulders with the flat of his hands until John came back into himself.

His plan to take the cow and leave for home immediately was forcibly overridden. While the women had been mad with fear, John had been tucked safely into a warm bed and sound asleep.

The cow is the most beautiful Asia has ever seen. They name her Lady Parker and crowd about her in the barn, drinking glass after glass of warm, foamy milk. Then Rosalie, Asia, and John take turns at the churn. How long since they had butter? Cheese? A cow. A cow. My kingdom for a cow, Asia thinks. And yet, joyous as Asia is, contented and full for the first time in days, she cannot forget that the kingdom they nearly paid for this cow was John's life. A world without John! She can't even bear to think of it.

THEY LIVE THROUGH the winter. Spring feels like a season of plenty, summer the same. John goes about his grim farm work, the harvests as bad as ever. Each year they fall further behind.

The leaves turn color. Another terrible winter looms.

xvi

But Edwin gets there first.

WORD HAS GOTTEN out. Edwin Booth is returned from the gold country. A rich man has come to town. Neighbors are already gathered, waiting on the front lawn, when his carriage arrives, chased down the lane by young men, some of whom were only babies when he left. He swings lightly from the carriage to the ground, and into the cheering crowd. The boys quarrel for the privilege of wrestling his heavy trunks into the parlor.

It's been four years since Asia saw Edwin and though still boyish, he's also completely transformed. He's wearing a velvet cape pinned shut at the top with a brooch of diamonds and nuggets—a parting gift, he will tell them later, from the ladies of San Francisco. His boots are red with swirling designs stitched over the vamp and the uppers. With his dark skin, black curls, and exotic clothes, he looks like a prince from *The Arabian Nights*. Asia can see how shabby and tattered poor John looks beside him. She knows she looks the same. She's suddenly shy, too awed by his magnificence to throw herself into his arms when he comes to hug her.

She sees the effort he makes to adjust his face as he greets Rosalie. Is Rosalie so altered? Asia can't remember when Mother stopped telling Rosalie to stand up straight, but it was quite some time ago. One shoulder is now permanently higher than the other.

The crowd in the yard, half of them black and half of them white, show no sign of leaving. Edwin moves among them, clapping the ones he knows on their backs, shaking hands with those he doesn't. He pays particular court to the little Hall girls, who dance about his legs and stand on his red toes. Laughter and babble and through it all, Edwin looking pleased but abashed, and running his hand through his hair. When he laughs, he throws his head back, a mannerism Asia doesn't remember from before.

Ann Hall appears with a buttermilk cake she's whipped up for the impromptu party. She tells Asia to pass around cups of mint tea, which Asia does with a smiling face, all the while wishing she could make them all go away and leave Edwin to his family.

Luckily their stores of hard cider are insufficient to the day or the men would never have gone home.

As it is, the party doesn't end until dusk. Only then does Edwin make it the last few steps, up the porch and into the parlor. It's the first time he's been inside Tudor Hall. Mother takes him through so that he can admire the size of the rooms, the number of windows. The house looks to its best advantage at just this time of day when the fireflies blink in the grass outside and the time has come to light the lamps in the parlor.

Edwin disappears to wash up, and he's gone so long, Asia worries suddenly that he won't return, that she dreamt the whole thing. But then he's back, his hair and face still damp. She feels so tight with excitement and expectation she can hardly breathe. Edwin was always her favorite! How had she forgotten that?

Finally, he opens his trunks. He shows them first a resolution, printed on parchment, passed by the California legislature, declaring him to be one of the state's great treasures. The state of California, this resolution says, is now generously sharing him with the rest of the country.

He's brought sugar and a large spiraled shell from Hawaii, puzzle boxes from San Francisco's Chinatown and Mexican chaps for John and Joe. A necklace for Rosalie with a green stone shaped like the crescent moon. A silver bracelet for Asia, which she immediately snaps onto her wrist, shaking her arms to see it glitter in the lamplight. Embroidered scarves for all the women, including Ann Hall.

To Mother, he gives the proceeds of his final San Francisco performances, a series of benefits and farewells including his first performance ever of *King Lear* (the Tate adaptation in which Cordelia survives and triumphs). He's earned the nearly unbelievable sum of twenty thousand dollars, much of it in gold. He gives Mother his purse and it's so heavy it falls through her hands. Mother begins to sob.

She's worn herself out, worn herself to the bone, waiting for him to rescue them. Asia hears her long, jagged exhale, as if, ever since Father died, she's been holding her breath and only now can she breathe again.

When Mother cries, Rosalie does the same. Asia feels that the sun has stepped out of the sky and into the Booth parlor. Edwin's shining so brightly, her eyes water when she looks at him. It takes her a moment to understand that she, too, is crying.

AT TWENTY-TWO (nearly twenty-three) Edwin is now in charge. He moves the family back to Baltimore, where he begins almost immediately to perform at the Front Street Theatre. He takes on many of his father's old roles, appearing before the audiences that knew his father best. Perhaps he hasn't yet attained his father's genius. No one cares, they love him so. He plays to packed houses.

IN JULY 1857, the following ad will appear in the *Bel Air Southern Aegis*.

> FOR RENT—the splendid and well-known residence of the late J. B. Booth, in Harford County, about three miles from Bel Air, on the road leading to Churchville. This place will be rented to a good tenant if immediate application be made. There is 180 acres of land, 80 of which is arable. John Booth, Baltimore, Md.

No Booth will ever live on Father's farm again.

BOOK FOUR

The senator from South Carolina has read many books of chivalry, and believes himself a chivalrous knight, with sentiments of honor and courage. Of course he has chosen a mistress to whom he has made his vows, and who, though ugly to others, is always lovely to him; though polluted in the sight of the world, is chaste in his sight;—I mean the harlot Slavery.

—Charles Sumner

Four years have passed since the Booths last lived in Baltimore. In many ways, the city is the same. The O'Laughlens still live across the street; the little Struthoff grocery is still next door. The parlor in which Father's body once lay is still wallpapered in flocked yellow, lace curtains at the window, green shutters outside. Pigs still wander at will and remain a contentious political issue. Are they a public menace? Or are they public servants, keeping the streets free of garbage with their omnivorous ways? Visitors from England find them charming, a touch of the Old World, the fairy-tale village here, in a city sometimes referred to as Mobtown.

Because in other ways, Baltimore has changed. The Cock Robins, the Gumballs, and the Neversweats have grown-up and become the Calithumpians, the Rip Raps, the Plug Uglies, the Blood Tubs, the Rosebuds, and so many more. Streetlights have been installed all over the city and that soft glow now drifts in the windows at night, dimming the stars, and puddling on the floors. These streetlights are intended to reduce the danger of being abroad after dark. Forty-two lamplighters have been hired and they are almost never beaten and robbed as they go about their work.

Since the municipal elections of 1854, the anti-immigration American Party, the party of the secretive Know-Nothings, has been in charge of the city. Their agenda includes reforming the police, improving the water supply, and staying in power. These all require muscle, but especially the last. In polling places controlled by the gangs, only members of the party are allowed to cast a ballot. Others may try on pain of death.

The presidential election of 1856 happens mere days after the Booths return. Kansas remains awash in blood and Senator Sumner has been almost killed in a beating on the Senate floor, and still the level of violence in Baltimore shocks the country. Hours of riot and mayhem leave some thirty people dead, another three hundred injured. The O'Laughlens, coming with raisin cakes to welcome the Booths back, warn them to stay inside on Election Day.

Which is what they do. After all, only Edwin is eligible to vote and he's no Know-Nothing.

When the election is over, the first-ever presidential candidate for the new Republican Party, John C. Frémont, has been defeated despite carrying most of the North. Democrat James Buchanan sweeps the South and Frémont's own state of California. The American Party nominee, ex-president, ex-Whig Millard Fillmore, takes only one state. That state is Maryland.

FILLMORE HAS ONE supporter in the Lincoln household. Not Lincoln, himself—of course, Lincoln supported Frémont. But Mary Todd Lincoln writes to her half-sister, "My weak woman's heart was too Southern in feeling to sympathise with any but Fillmore. I have always been a great admirer of his, he made so good a President & is so just a man & feels the necessity of keeping foreigners, within bounds. If some of you Kentuckians, had to deal with the 'wild Irish,' as we housekeepers are sometimes called upon to do, the South would certainly elect Mr. Fillmore next time . . ."

She is anxious that Lincoln not be mistaken for an abolitionist. Nothing could be further from the truth, she says.

ONE YEAR LATER, Baltimore braces for another municipal election. This time the rioting is mostly contained in the Eighth Ward—that Irish and German district known as Limerick—though some of it spills over into the Fifth and a number of Plug Uglies and Rip Raps travel into DC to menace the voters there.

Large numbers of Baltimoreans have simply stopped trying to vote. "I thought my life of more consequence than voting," says David C. Piquett, a Democratic candidate for office, who was chased through the streets and shot at. The death count on Election Day is down, but a policeman is murdered. Twenty-four gang members are arrested and charged. They all stand trial. None are found guilty.

Baltimore is one of the last remaining bastions of Know-Nothing power. The national party has collapsed over the issue of slavery. Henry Winter Davis, the man John and Asia had gone to hear in Churchville, now a congressman, argues that slavery is so very divisive, the best way to deal with it is never to mention it.

The city government often appears to take that advice. But the local population of free blacks, estimated now to be more than seventy-five thousand, is concerning to slavers in other parts of the state. Even Davis, who opposes slavery, feels that blacks and whites cannot live together. He himself inherited several human beings and freed them all, but only on condition that they move to Liberia. At this time, Abraham Lincoln also sees Liberia as the answer to the slavery question.

This is not the solution the Maryland slaveholders want. They want the free blacks re-enslaved.

In 1860, a bill proposed by Representative Colonel Curtis Jacob outlines a number of mechanisms through which this might be accomplished. He delivers a lengthy speech on the subject. In it, he castigates the Northern abolitionists as "frenzied vampires," "literally crazed and mad . . . with the lust for Southern blood." How long, he asks, must they wait to see someone, anyone, punished for Edward Gorsuch, who went to Christiana to recover his slaves and died there?

He goes on to decry free-Negroism as "an excrescence, a blight," and then, just to be clear, "a mildew, a fungus." The free Negroes have no actual rights of citizenship, he says, pointing out that they cannot vote or carry a gun or testify in court or own a dog or attend a church with a black minister or buy alcohol or sell corn or gather publicly or gather privately. Their condition is a freedom in name only. And yet, by their very existence, they destroy the contentment of those in bondage.

Jacob mourns those happy slaves of the past, now infected with the desire for liberty. Universal re-enslavement is the only path back to black contentment. His bill proposes that every Negro emancipated in the last thirty years be returned to their rightful owners without the cost of litigation or any other vexatious delay.

Jacob's bill is thankfully defeated. But a number of city representatives, including the theatrical manager John T. Ford, spend their own money to publish and disseminate Jacob's speech. They will not accept this defeat. They will get their message out and try again.

THE BOOTHS ARE neither oblivious to nor personally affected by these events. Edwin is scarcely home before he leaves again on tour. John's starting his theatrical career in earnest. June is still in San Francisco with his family. Joe remains at school. The time of the Maryland Booths is coming to an end.

Rosalie

i

In 1856, when Edwin returns from California, Rosalie is thirty-three years old. Re-occupying the house on Exeter entails a spate of housekeeping. November is not the month for these things, and yet the bedding is aired, the curtains washed, the rugs dragged out on the first sunny day and beaten within an inch of their lives. Mother, Asia, and Rosalie work together to polish the house back to their standards. Mother is interviewing candidates for cook and laundress. Someday soon, Rosalie will be a woman of leisure, or at least more leisure than she currently enjoys. In the meantime, she works.

Increasingly, Rosalie feels the need to talk with Edwin on a delicate matter. As she sweeps and dusts, as she runs the tablecloths and curtains through the mangle and returns them to the tables and windows, as she chops the vegetables and grinds the spices and flours the fish, she tries to plan this conversation. She will have to be alone with Edwin—this in itself is difficult to accomplish as neither Mother nor Asia is inclined to let him out of her sight. And then she must find just the right way to say what she wants to say. The Edwin who's come home is bigger, louder, and more colorful than the Edwin who left. Rosalie is not fooled. Was she not, for many years, practically his mother? She could be blunt with this new Edwin if she didn't see through his new clothes and mannerisms. Underneath, he is still that little boy with the big, sad eyes who never asked a question if he didn't already know the answer. Rosalie has never done anything to hurt that little boy and she won't start now.

It's so wonderful, how he swooped in to save them all. He has every right to congratulate himself, although, Edwin-like, he's just as prone to self-flagellation for not understanding sooner how dire the situation was. Why, he asks, didn't anyone tell him? Mother too selfless, of course, but Asia or John or Rosalie herself surely could have written. So he's already feeling guilty when there is no cause. Rosalie fears that he will seize fresh guilt from what she wants to say.

Which is this: Rosalie is worried about John. Edwin hardly knows him. He doesn't understand how abnormally sensitive John is where his own shortcomings are concerned. And Edwin's miraculous rescue wouldn't have been necessary if John hadn't failed so miserably on the farm. This doesn't mean John's not as relieved and grateful as the rest. He hated the farm. He's well rid of it. Everyone knows that he did what he could. No one blames him for the year of trial and tribulation. No one except for John himself.

So Rosalie would like to ask Edwin to consult with John as if they are equals. To try not to provide such a vivid contrast to John's failures. At the very least, Edwin could stop talking about the way poor Mother has been supporting them all, educating, clothing, feeding them on the paltry hundred or so dollars left in Father's estate, as if John had been nothing but another mouth at

the table, another millstone around Mother's neck. Another alba-
tross, just like his sisters.

ROSALIE AND ASIA are working together in the parlor. Outside,
a chilly winter morning. Inside, the bright sunlight is streaming
between and through the lace curtains, dappling the floor.

Outside, the mulberry trees are dripping free of their glittering ice casings. Inside, it's just turning warm enough to let the
morning fire die. One charred log rests on a mound of glowing
ash. Soon enough, when the sun shifts and the chill returns, Rosalie will coax that log into flame. For now, the sunshine suffices.

Asia is standing on a chair, in her work clothes, gingham skirt,
burlap apron. She's pulling books off the higher shelves and
handing them down to Rosalie to be dusted. Asia's talking to the
books as she does this. "Hello, Homer, you old blind fool. Hello,
Byron, you mad, bad man. Come! Let us clean your dirty faces."

The stack of Mother's *Godey's Lady's Book*s can only be handed
down a few at a time, so heavy are they with advice, fashion, and
receipts for the modern woman. "Hello, little Oliver," Asia says
and hands Rosalie her own beloved *Oliver Twist*.

Rosalie blows the dust from the top of the pages. It dances
through the sunlight and up Rosalie's nose. She sneezes three
times. "Bless you," Asia says. "Bless you. And bless you again."

If Asia weren't there, working away, Rosalie would take a
break now. Her crooked back is aching. She would sink onto the
settee, put her feet up like a girl, open *Oliver Twist*, and read it
again from the beginning.

She does this instead. She closes her eyes, asks for advice from
Mr. Dickens concerning her talk with Edwin. She chooses a

random page, and points. The sentences on which her finger has landed are these:

I only know two sorts of boys. Mealy boys and beef-faced boys.

Rosalie can, in fact, make this relevant to her current predicament. What she cannot do is make it helpful.

MOTHER IS CALLING Asia to the kitchen. Asia hops down, graceful as a doe, and disappears. The fire whispers one last time. There's a bright square on the flocked wallpaper where a picture once hung. Rosalie tries to remember which picture it was. Why was it removed? She feels slightly insulted at this implied criticism of Booth taste. Now she remembers it—a young girl feeding chickens. Horses watching with high interest from the pasture behind her. Maybe it wasn't the sort of vista that pulls you inside. Maybe it didn't have the colors and romance of the painting of Niagara Falls that Asia loves so much that she insisted on taking it to the farm and then insisted on bringing it back. Still, Girl with Chickens is a perfectly inoffensive picture. Rosalie will find it, wherever it is, and put it back where it belongs. It will be there to remind her that she's not, in her heart, the city sort.

Because all this time, she's also been thinking of Asia standing on the chair. When she was young, she, too, used to hoist up her skirts and climb. Not the furniture, that was never allowed, but trees all over the farm, the apple trees in the orchard, and most especially the cherry tree at the corner of the cabin. From there, holding on to one branch, feet on another, she'd look down on

Mother and Ann hanging the laundry, Mary Ann and Elizabeth chasing each other around their legs. Henry and Nelson, down by the spring, poking sticks into anthills. June off in the distance, leading the cows to the dairy. She could see them all, but, and this was the best part, none of them saw her. None of them ever thought to look up into her secret, leafy, birdy world.

For whatever reason, her agoraphobia completely disappeared when Father died. These last years on the farm had made her long for the time before the deaths, for a girlhood in which she now felt she'd been practically a dryad, singing to the bees and the frogs and the water. Smoke rising from the cabins, the smell of pine and rain and musk. The rising trill of blackbirds, the rounded call of doves and owls. The forest in springtime. The forest in new snow. Meadows in the stars. Stars in the meadows.

All those pleasures were still there when they returned, but denied her by the endless chores that fell to adult women and the limits of her own body. She'd wasted the last of her girlhood, shut up in the dim room of the cabin, afraid of voices she should have welcomed.

The ghosts were gone now, gone silent, the doorway between worlds shut fast no matter how she bangs upon it. She should have known that she'd miss them, her dear dead brother and sisters, the sticky web of their love. She's lonely without them. She's ordinary without them. They knew her at her best. The same cannot be said of Edwin, Asia, John, and Joe, who, she sometimes feels, have always been so focused on each other, they hardly know her at all.

Sometimes when she watches Asia and John interrupting each other to tell a story or laughing at a joke she doesn't even understand, the way she misses Henry is a roaring in her ears, a bitterness rising in her throat. For just a moment she can see him again, beckoning her forward through the green light into a carpet of lilies. *Hie thee home to me*, she thinks, desperate with love for the ghost who never spoke, but who might, even now, be trying to find his way across the ocean. He'll look for her at the farm. He won't know to come here.

Rosalie climbs onto the chair. She's a little drunk, truth be told. She's found that a small glass of gin in the morning helps the ache in her back and if she stops with just the one, no one's the wiser. Not even Mother, with all her years of honed observation.

Already Mother's making noises about Edwin's drinking. "I can't blame him," she's said to Asia and also to Rosalie when she sees that the level in the gin bottle is down. "It's in his blood. It's the family curse."

It hasn't occurred to Mother that Rosalie is in the same family.

She's drunk just enough now to feel exhilarated rather than frightened when the chair creaks beneath her. Just enough to give her the sense that if she did fall, she would float down like a leaf on a stream.

Through the window, Harriet Struthoff's flowered hat goes by. This is a hat for the young woman Harriet Struthoff ceased to be some years ago. There are so many ways for a spinster to look ridiculous. Rosalie admires Miss Struthoff for not caring. She wishes that she, too, could wear a big and lovely hat now that Edwin is here to buy one for her. Instead he surprised her a few days ago with a writing box, mahogany and brass, linen paper inside for her letters. All very elegant and Rosalie does love it, that very thoughtful, that impeccably appropriate spinster's gift.

After all, Rosalie has no one for whom to wear such a hat. A few weeks back Mother had said, apropos of nothing, "You know that I don't think much of marriage. I didn't like it myself." This was for Rosalie's ears only. Asia must be allowed to believe that

Mother's heart had been broken forever by Father's death. *For where thou art, there is the world itself . . . And where thou art not, desolation.* Whereas Rosalie had always understood Mother's collapse to have been largely a matter of economic anxiety. Now that Edwin is paying the bills and as long as she has her darling John, Mother is content.

Just as Rosalie is thinking this, Mother enters the parlor. Her gray-streaked hair is in a knot at her neck, the center part straight as a nail. There are just a few flecks of dandruff, a light sprinkling of snow on the shoulders of her black dress. She inhales sharply. "Come down from there before you hurt yourself," she tells Rosalie. "What gets into you?" As if she often comes into a room to find Rosalie standing on the furniture.

She holds out a hand to help Rosalie down. There is stumbling and swaying, tottering and thumping. Mother is right, of course. Rosalie should stay on the ground where she belongs. "Poor Rose, the invalid daughter" is not the identity she would have chosen when she was sixteen, eighteen, twenty-three. By thirty-three, she's accepted it. She can play to its advantages as needed. It's better than no identity at all.

ii

Mother, Asia, and Rosalie are all at the table, watching Edwin not eat. Rosalie pours him a cup of coffee, which she knows from experience can set things right. She pours herself one, too. The smell of coffee is stronger than the smell of gin.

He's returned from a two-week tour in Washington, DC, and Richmond, tired, but exhilarated, staggering in after dark, flush and flushed, breath you could light with a match. He rises late the next morning, the jolliness gone, his eyes like black holes. "My head," he says grimly at breakfast, brushing his hair back with one listless hand and staring unenthusiastically down at a plate of corn dodgers and doughnuts. Everyone else ate hours ago and John has already left the house. He's started making himself scarce when Edwin is around.

They can't coax out anything but monosyllables, but Rosalie is left with the impression that Edwin's performances were good. Better than expected. He made money, most of which he gives to Mother.

After three or four days of low skies, the morning is a dazzle of sunshine. "Edwin has brought the sun back," Rosalie says to the table, pretending there weren't several equally sunny days during his absence. Winter keeps losing her grip—coming and going and coming again.

Twenty minutes later, while Rosalie is still washing up, Edwin returns to the kitchen. He's more presentable this time, face washed, curls combed, wider awake. "Rose," he says. "Would you show me Father's grave?"

"Of course," she tells him, all tender and flattered.

Asia, uninvited, insists on coming along.

Only then she doesn't. While Edwin is fetching the carriage, hitching the horse (Roman, a chestnut Morgan), and bringing it all with much clatter to the front of the house, Asia's friend Jean Anderson arrives unexpectedly. Clearly there is gossip of some sort, confidences to be shared. The whispering begins before Jean has even removed her gloves. So Asia begs off and suddenly the tête-à-tête Rosalie wants is being offered without any contrivance on her part.

In spite of the sun, the wind is cold enough to sting Rosalie's cheeks. Her bonnet is too small to provide much protection. She remembers a time when women went out blinkered like horses. Edwin helps her onto the running board and into the buggy, puts a rough blanket over her lap, and takes up the reins. They drive in silence for a few blocks, down a street framed with sycamores, branches trembling, leaves rattling. And then Edwin asks her, "Do you remember my pet lamb? She used to follow me around, just like in the rhyme?"

"Yes," Rosalie says. "I can't remember what happened to her."

"She went back to the farm. One day I was trying to read and she wanted to play. She kept pushing the book out of the way. So I hit her, a good solid crack on the nose with the book. I'll never forget how she looked at me. After that, she never came near me again."

"What made you think of her?" Rosalie asks.

"I don't know. Regrets." Perhaps his head is still hurting. He shakes it vigorously, smacks his own temple with his hand as if trying to dislodge a stone from his brain. The carriage bumps over something in the road, something small, an apple maybe or a potato someone dropped. Rosalie can't lean out far enough to see. Edwin doesn't seem to have noticed. He's in the middle of telling her what it's like to play Father's old roles, how Father ghosts his every move so that with each gesture he can see his father's hand moving through the air and must force his own in a different direction. "Like a rebellious puppet," he says.

Rosalie thinks of suggesting that he not take the roles Father was so famous for. After all, his youth and beauty are more suited to romantic leads and less to glowering villains. But she can see that he's deliberately announcing himself as his father's son.

When, at supper two days ago, John had declared, and not for the first time, his determination not to trade on Father's reputation, but to act under the name of Wilkes, Rosalie had understood this to be a criticism of Edwin. She'd thought, unkindly, that John was more likely to suffer than Edwin by any comparison to Father, but, of course, she didn't say this.

Had it been Edwin criticizing John, her instinctive protectiveness would have been the same. She loves them both. She wants them to love each other.

They arrive at the gate to the cemetery, an elaborate arrangement of twisted iron, black leaves and vines, with real leaves and vines twining between. Edwin helps Rosalie down and ties up the horse. He gives her his arm. The paths are spongy with wet leaves and mud, flanked by tall, thin Normandy poplars. We should have brought flowers, Rosalie thinks and then thinks not, remembering how Father wouldn't suffer a flower to be cut. "This way," she says. She sees that it's hard for Edwin to match her gait. They keep falling out of step.

Edwin hunches against the wind. He looks very young suddenly, as if he's sloughed off five years since breakfast. His hands are bare. He asks her to tell him about the funeral.

"It was cold like this," she says. "Cold and gray. The whole day dressed in mourning."

"This isn't cold," Edwin tells her. "I once had to walk for hours and hours through a blizzard with snow up to my neck." Rosalie waits to see if he wants to say more. He doesn't.

"Well, it was snowing during the funeral," Rosalie says finally. "But not hard, not a blizzard. People still came. So many they couldn't all fit inside. It was the funeral of a great man. We were so proud to be his family." For just a second the shadow of Adelaide Booth falls across the conversation. Then, just as quickly, she's gone.

They arrive at the grave and Rosalie drops his arm. The grass is dead and black and bent flat against the mud. The stone is a white marble, simple and unsentimental. Edwin cleans it with his handkerchief. "It's not enough," Edwin says, "for a man of his stature."

"Father abhorred flash," Rosalie says.

"But he wasn't drab either. I'll put up something better when I have the money." He's crying. When did that start?

"My dear boy," Rosalie says.

"I killed him," Edwin tells her. "I had just one job, to protect our father, and I grew tired of it and let him go off on his own and he died all alone on that ship because of me." Edwin's shoulders are shaking, his hands over his face. A crow calls and launches from a nearby tree. Rosalie watches it skim the blue sky like a stone skipping over water. *Come, the croaking raven doth bellow for revenge.* To the children of Shakespeare all the world's a metaphor.

But she's left speechless. Should she insist that he's not to blame? On what evidence? Everyone in the family has had that same thought, however they try not to. It's been there the whole time, like a fly at the window, buzzing in the back of their boundless gratitude, wonder, and love. She reaches to put her arms around him, but at her touch, he moves away. He won't take his hands from his face. He sobs so hard his whole body shakes. He wipes his face with the same handkerchief he used to clean Father's headstone and now there's a streak of wet dirt on his cheek. Rosalie takes off her glove and erases it with her fingers. She has to rub hard.

She can find no words that might absolve him. "You saved *us*," she says instead. They won't be having that talk about John. Not now, and probably not ever.

Edwin

Years ago, Edwin saw himself as a comic actor, while his friend Sleeper Clarke planned a career as a tragedian. Those roles have flipped. Sleeper never had the face for tragedy—too elastic—nor the hair—a muddle of curls. He comes that close to handsome without ever actually arriving. Whereas Edwin . . . No one, another actor will note someday soon, can stand against those eyes.

Sleeper is currently the principal Low Comic for the Arch Street Theatre company in Philadelphia. He stars in those farces that close the evening, send the audience home laughing. Whether he's good at this or not is debatable. But he is popular.

At Edwin's urging, Sleeper secures a position in the company for John. The spring of 1857 finds John in Philadelphia, rooming with Sleeper and Sleeper's mother. He performs bit parts, billed as J. B. Wilkes. Though everyone in the theater world knows who his father is, it's hoped that many in the audience do not. His performances are hit-and-miss and he's anxious to do nothing that will tarnish the Booth name.

Back in Baltimore, Edwin says to Asia, "What a good friend Sleeper has always been to us!"

Asia sticks out her tongue.

They are up in the boys' bedroom. Asia's lying on John's empty bed with Edwin's pillow under her head, watching as Edwin packs. He's recently been in Boston (where Louisa May Alcott saw him perform and liked him better than his father) and is now headed for New York.

After the years of larking about in California, Edwin has gotten more serious. He has a manager, Benjamin Baker, or Uncle Ben, as he likes to be called. Uncle Ben has great plans (and, it will turn out, sticky fingers). But all Edwin knows now is that he's managed to book a two-week run at Burton's Theatre.

Out in the dark, it's raining hard, a spring rain, the thunder loud and close, the lightning in glaring sheets. Lear weather.

Two lamps are lit in the bedroom but their light doesn't reach the corners. Periodically the window blazes, sharp and dazzling, followed by a drum roll of thunder and a purple square of afterimage. Edwin remembers Coleridge's line about reading Shakespeare by lightning flashes.

Asia is telling him about an acquaintance, a Colonel Green who claims to be married, but Asia thinks he's not. She is laying out her evidence. First off: the state of his collars.

Edwin has never met Colonel Green and isn't listening. He's thinking about a girl. A few months back, during his Richmond engagement, a sixteen-year-old named Mary Devlin had played Juliet to his Romeo, Katherine to his Petruchio. At her young age, she was already a professional—a member of the John Ford's Marshall Theatre company, brown-haired and brown-eyed, not beautiful, but pretty and soft-spoken. She'd only recently acted with the great Edwin Forrest, and yet she'd said she could have acted with Edwin Booth forever. They read each other's minds. It was a dance.

Edwin had been flattered by the implied besting of the man he was named for. He'd liked the way she allowed herself to be led. His usual leading lady was much older and much more experienced than he. These accomplished actresses hit their marks, achieved their moments. His job was to keep up.

Mary Devlin was unspoiled and charming. Yet an attempt on his part to nudge the relationship forward had been sweetly but cleanly rebuffed. She had genuine suitors and he'd had no serious intent. Quite the opposite. Never would he marry an actress!

Probably he wouldn't marry at all. I will live and die an old maid, he thought experimentally, just to see how it felt. If Rosalie can do it, why not Edwin? They can slide into their dotage together.

Asia has stopped talking. Probably she made a persuasive case. Edwin goes to the door of his room. "Mother?" he says. "Mother?" he says, more loudly, though he knows she hates to be yelled for. When there is still no answer, either because she didn't hear or is pretending she didn't hear, he takes a lamp and goes downstairs. The kitchen smells of yeast and rising bread.

Mother and Rosalie are sitting at the table, planning out the next week's meals. The doors to the oven are open. A few red embers glowing inside provide the only light. The sound of the storm heightens the sense of warmth, like a snug berth on a rocking ship. Edwin feels the same wave of anticipatory homesickness he used to feel as a boy whenever he left with Father.

"Mother," Edwin says. "I need Father's Iago costume. Also Richelieu."

Mother looks at but not into his face. "I'm saving Father's

costumes for John," she says. She goes back to her shopping list, apparently feeling this needs no explanation or apology.

Edwin has seen Mother over the past weeks altering the pants, the tunics, the robes. Father was a small but bulky man. Edwin is very slight. He'd assumed those alterations were for him. He'd told his manager as much. Uncle Ben has been cobbling bits and pieces together for him, sewing with great galloping stitches while Edwin rehearses. These makeshift make-do's are nothing compared to Father's jeweled and fur-trimmed elaborations. Who knows when John will play Iago? If ever. Edwin will play him next week. And also the week after that. Edwin is the one Father chose to carry his legacy. He feels the ghost of Father's hand as it landed on his shoulder, dubbing him heir apparent.

"I see," Edwin says. Heat has flooded into his face and neck. He holds the lamp away so as not to show that.

"Some critics would recognize Father's costumes," Rosalie says. "It might be better not to wear them."

"That's right," says Edwin. He's trying not to sound sullen. He leaves the room and goes back up the shadowed stairs. The lamp on the wall throws one shadow, the lamp in his hand another. The result is a misshapen creature, spiderlike, with four arms, four legs. Thunder rattles the windows on the second floor.

He sees Mother's hands, the needle dipping and rising over Richelieu's robes, white skin against the red velvet. Of course John should get the costumes. John didn't kill Father.

My heart, he thinks, is a withered apple.

Asia looks up sleepily when he enters. "Are you all right?" she asks. "You look a little strange."

"I'm flattered you think that's a change," Edwin says.

iv

Edwin and his manager arrive in New York. Uncle Ben's promotional playbills lean heavily on the genius of the father born again in the son. He pushes Edwin to open with Richard III, Father's most iconic role. Edwin's instinct for his first night had been *A New Way to Pay Old Debts*, but he yields to Uncle Ben's persuasion.

This is a mistake. Even those critics who never saw his father perform accuse him of superficial imitation. His voice is too nasal, his performance too halting. He has everything his father had, Walt Whitman says, excepting guts.

Edwin's Lear, his Sir Giles Overreach, his Shylock and Richelieu find better reception and his booking is extended a week. Still, he feels discouraged. He's getting little sleep as Uncle Ben shares his room, snoring loudly and arrhythmically through the night until Edwin, on the point of desperation, pours himself a drink and follows it with another. The spring weather turns bad—rain, wind, and an unseasonal chill. Perhaps this is why the theaters remain half full, the audiences torpid. But Father would surely have overcome the challenges of a small spring squall.

In the middle of his second week, two letters are delivered to Edwin. He's recently risen, but wishing he were still in bed. His toast is burnt. There is a sour, stale taste in his mouth and a headache knocking dully about in his skull. He takes a sip of tea, which turns out to be cold.

One of the letters is from his mother. He opens the other. It's from the critic Adam Badeau. Edwin knows Badeau by reputation. He publishes erudite essays on art under the pen name the Vagabond. He's terribly sophisticated.

Badeau has sent Edwin his recent review. It begins:

I have been several times, of late, to see the young genius
who is playing at Burton's theatre . . .

The review does not suggest that Edwin has no faults. His
acting is described as undeveloped, plastic, and chaotic. He sometimes mars the musicality of his voice by slurring his lines. But
this is only to be expected in one so young. What is not
expected—the moments of complete transcendence. These are
the moments a critic like Badeau lives for. Everything wrong can
be easily fixed. What's right is beyond instruction. There is no
Rubicon Edwin cannot cross with work and study. The review
includes the usual paean to Edwin's eyes.

A note accompanies the review. Badeau would like to meet
while Edwin is in New York. Edwin need only name the time.

Edwin sets the letter aside and opens his mother's. June has
written Mother to say that he's run out of money and Mother is
writing Edwin to be sure that he has that same information. Hattie may be expecting again. June's letter is unclear on this point.

Mother doesn't come out and say that Edwin must now support June and June's family along with everyone else. She merely
wonders where money for June might be found.

As for John, the salary the Arch Street company is paying
won't even cover his cigars. She suspects he's wishing he'd chosen a different profession. Apparently his time in Philadelphia has
not been a triumph.

Edwin already knows this. Sleeper has written, complaining of
John's indolence. Everyone expected more of the son of Junius Brutus Booth, Sleeper says. Sleeper had told John it was time to apply
himself and John had responded by moving out of Sleeper's house.

THE WEATHER IMPROVES and Edwin goes out. He walks quickly through streets much wider than those in Baltimore, past buildings much taller. New York is an important city and knows it. Fewer pigs.

At Washington Square Park, he joins the crowd by the fountain. The sun is shining and the tulip trees just coming into green and yellow bloom. Children chase each other over the grass. A father is trying and failing to launch a kite. A mother is bandaging a skinned knee with her handkerchief. A small boy has stepped behind a tree to piss.

How much money will June need to find his feet beneath him again? Where will Edwin find that money? Edwin runs calculations through his head until the numbers turn sharp-cornered and begin to hurt.

THE REVIEW Adam Badeau sent touches not only on Edwin's performances but on the subject of American art in general. It references a painting of Niagara Falls done by Frederic Edwin Church. This painting is about to be shipped to Europe for various exhibitions, but is currently on display here in the city. According to Badeau, the painting and Edwin both represent something new in the world. American art need no longer mimic the tired forms and sentiments of the effete Old World. The painting is a testament not only to the magnificence of the Falls, but also to the wilderness through which the water first passed, the deep forests and wide plains of wild America. The singular men who will tame her.

Edwin decides to go and see it. There is a line and Edwin takes his place at the back, moving slowly past smaller works—dead pheasants draped over piles of fruit, women reading books in dark corners, ship masts against bloody horizons. When he finally stands in front of the canvas, he struggles to find the words for his feelings. He is so awed as to be undone.

The man behind him is explaining the painting to three young women, possibly sisters. All three have the same sharp nose, the same thick brown hair in braids down their backs. "Look at the energy, the motion," he says. "The sunlight moving on the water. The rainbows rising. You see the power of the water, but you also feel the whole dark wilderness through which the water has moved. Wild America. The continent waiting to be tamed. The singular men who will tame her." Clearly the man has also read Badeau's review. He's read about Edwin then, but has no idea he's standing next to the genius of Burton's Theatre.

He continues to talk, but Edwin ceases to hear him. He's thinking of the painting in the Booths' hallway. He decides that it's too pretty, a bit sentimental. He's ashamed of how much he'd liked it before. Now he's aware of its fundamental lack of a dark and hidden wilderness.

At the same time, he's so tired of always finding himself wanting. Standing before this magnificence of water and light and movement and color, he allows himself, for maybe the first time, to own the full range of his dreams. Somewhere in the city is one reviewer who thinks he has something in common with this extraordinary masterpiece.

There is no Rubicon Edwin cannot cross with work and study. He's not thinking about money at all now. His ambition has arrived at last and it comes in a flood.

Asia

v

Asia is half mad with love for Edwin, who is taking her on a trip to Niagara Falls. She's never been on such an adventure before. Later she will remember this golden interlude as the last and maybe the best of her girlhood.

It's summertime, the theaters closed due to the heat. John has arrived unexpectedly home from Philadelphia and will join them. Since poor Rosalie is obviously not up to the journey, Edwin has suggested that Asia invite her best friend, Jean. It couldn't be more perfect and every bit of it Edwin's idea. He has a sudden need for great, gushing amounts of water, he says.

In a secret drawer in a secret cupboard in her secret heart, Asia has long wished that one of her brothers—Edwin or John, it makes no difference which—would marry Jean. Asia and Jean are already as close as any sisters, much closer than Asia is to Rosalie.

Jean's a petite, bosomy young woman. Not striking the way Asia is; you have to look twice at Jean, but when you do, you see that she has a face worth spending time on. Doll-like eyes, curling hair, a cleft chin. Of course, Asia is prejudiced, but that doesn't make her wrong.

THERE ARE REASONS, just now, why romance is unlikely. John's precipitous return is connected to rumors that, back in Philadelphia, he's left a girl pregnant. He himself thinks he's probably not responsible, but a considerable sum of money was required to persuade the girl to share his doubts.

Edwin is suffering from the clap.

Of course, Asia knows none of that. She has the most wonderful brothers!

ONE TRAIN RIDE and another and then they board the trim little steamer *Our Lady of the Lake.* Asia and Jean see their luggage into their stateroom before joining the boys at the railing. A small gull lands briefly near them, looks at them with one red eye, turns its head to see if they improve from that perspective. There are several passengers on the deck, but Asia is determined to pretend that it's only the four of them and she mostly gets her wish. She cordons off their little party with a barricade of icy politeness. She's gifted at icy politeness.

The boat moves like a dream over the calm waters of Lake Ontario while the sun sets and the stars rise. Asia feels as if she's suspended in place, floating in air as well as on water, as if she's the one still object in a spinning world. She can't remember ever being happier.

She moves closer to Edwin, tucks one hand under his arm. Her fingers are warm; the air is cool. The sky glitters above and also on the lake, the points of light reflecting on the black water in streaks like comets. She's left her hat in the stateroom and talked Jean into doing the same. Her bare head makes her feel girlish, and Jean's brown hair is escaping her knot in fetching curls.

"What a sky," Jean says. "Stars thick as bees."

John looks upward. "'Stars, hide your fires; Let not light see my deep and black desires,'" he says. Is he flirting? Asia can't be sure. Probably she's letting her hopes overrule her good sense. Even John wouldn't use *Macbeth* for a flirt.

"Black and deep," Edwin corrects him. "My black and deep desires." John says nothing. Edwin clears his throat. "'It is the stars. The stars above us govern our conditions.'" This is a game Edwin and John play, dueling Shakespeare.

"'The fault, dear Brutus, is not in our stars, But in ourselves, that we are underlings,'" John says. And before Edwin can riposte, "'I deny you, stars.'"

Asia closes her eyes and she can see again black words on a yellowed page. Once when she was very young, she stood in the branches of the cherry tree with Edwin below her and what she said was: "'Take him and cut him out in little stars, And he will make the face of heaven so fine That all the world will be in love with night.'"

"Well done," says Edwin. "The cup to Asia."

She lets go of Edwin's arm and drops a curtsey that sends the hoop of her skirt swinging like a bell. She takes Jean's soft hand in her own. "'There was a star danced, and under that were you born,'" she tells Jean. She looks from John to Edwin. Both have ceased to pay attention. Both are staring out over the water toward the dark shore. "Don't you think so?" she asks them insistently. "Isn't that our Jean to a turn?"

vi

Edwin has booked them into rooms in Cataract House, an enormous, elegant five-story hotel, which, had they only known it, is one of the last stops on the Underground Railroad. There is no sign of this.

They breakfast in a dining hall with high ceilings and tall windows. Asia's chair gives her a view of the green-and-white rapids rushing past. While they wait for their food, John tells a story about an addlepated actor in the Philadelphia company.

"The play was *Lucretia Borgia*," John says, "and the scene the one in which the four soldiers find her on the street to enact their revenge. So the line is supposed to be 'I am Ascanio Petrucci, madame, cousin of Pandolfo Petrucci, Lord of Sienna, who was assassinated by your order . . .' But this foozler can't come up with it to save his life. He bumbles and stumbles about and finally he just up and says, 'Damn it all, who am I again?' There's old Lucretia on her knees, begging for her life, and everything has to stop, the audience is laughing so hard."

Of course, the addlepate in John's story is John himself. Asia wonders if he really thinks they don't all know this. It was a blunder heard round the world, this son of Junius Booth who turned the tragedy of *Lucretia Borgia* into farce. The actress playing Lucretia will never forgive him for destroying her big scene.

Their guide comes to fetch them, an Irishman named Patrick Burke. Mr. Burke looks to be in his early fifties, with hardened skin like a sailor. He takes them to the top of the American Falls, then down Biddle's staircase to the base. Great clouds are gathered above the water. Asia counts nine rainbows, some bright and in complete rings, some faint and fragmented. Her face is dewy with mist.

Mr. Burke tells them, shouting to be heard, that a few years back an enormous boulder detached from the cliffs and fell into the gorge, narrowly missing the staircase while he himself was inside. A few feet closer and neither he nor the staircase would be standing today. "I felt the careless finger of God," Mr. Burke says, "just scratching an itch."

The splendor of the sun on the crashing water leaves Asia nearly faint with awe, all her senses full to the brim. God the careless? No! God the creator, God the artist wielding his brush of light and liquid.

FROM THE DIVINE to the petty. They ride to the Canadian side through streets lined with tawdry curiosity shops, peep shows, and saloons. They pass by insistent pitches for tours, refreshment, pictures, pamphlets, bits of congealed mist, which Mr. Burke tells them not to buy as they are really just white stones. How is it possible that so many people can gaze on the face of God and see only a place where pigeons might be plucked? Asia watches a workman tip a wheelbarrow full of trash into the translucent green waters.

At John's insistence, they stop on the field where the Battle of Lundy's Lane was fought. Here Winfield Scott commanded the American troops, Gordon Drummond, the British. The fighting was close, more bayonets than rifles, and when it all ended some nine hundred men had died. It was the bloodiest battle of the War of 1812, Mr. Burke says. Every time they put a foot down, they are stepping on some soldier's grave.

John talks excitedly to Mr. Burke about the movements of troops. They studied the battle at St. Timothy's Hall, he tells them. He is showing off. "The armies fought on into the night. You must imagine them fighting by moonlight."

"'Tongue, lose thy light! Moon, take thy flight! Now die, die, die, die, die,'" says Edwin.

Not by moon nor star nor sun, does Asia want to imagine the soldiers gutting each other as if slaughtering hogs. She wants the thunder of the Falls, not the thunder of the guns. She's impatient to move on. But John is focused on getting Mr. Burke to agree that Drummond's bureaucratic stubbornness was no match for Scott's expertise and bravery.

"The battle is generally reckoned a draw," Mr. Burke says mildly, "except for those who feel that Drummond won outright."

John loves opposition. "Only because the American casualties were so high! Only because he started with the superior ground!" Every sentence a thrust. "He didn't outmaneuver Scott, who was by far the superior tactician. He just sent his men forward again and again and again."

Asia wants to tell Mr. Burke to stop arguing. With all his disdain for mere dogged endurance, John's debate strategy most resembles Drummond. He will send his men forward again and again and again until his foe is exhausted.

"Are there ghosts?" Jean asks.

"How could there not be?" says Mr. Burke.

THE AMERICAN FALLS are mere prelude to the Horseshoe. Mr. Burke provides the party with protective gear—sacks of oilcloth that go from neck to ankle and belt with rope, a tight hood that leaves only the face exposed. None of the waterproof boots are small enough to fit Asia. She's forced to shuffle along as if she has boxes on her feet. "We look dangerous," John says. "Brigands."

"We look like walking hillocks," says Edwin.

The path under the Falls is narrow enough to make the fit of Asia's boots a matter of concern. She holds tightly to Edwin's belt as he proceeds ahead of her, from handhold to handhold on the rocky wall to their left. The next moment she is drowning. Water sprays from above and below, filling her nose and throat, blinding her. Her instinct is to turn back, but Edwin pulls her forward through the water and into the air. Wiping her face with her soaking sleeve, she sees that she is in God's own church. She sees the great, soaring stone arch from which a wall of water pours.

vii

Two days later, with one night spent in New York, they're on the train back to Baltimore. It's dark outside and Jean and John have fallen asleep opposite each other, each reflected dimly in the black windows. The train clicks and sways. Asia's more than contented. In the lobby of their New York hotel, John had mischievously leaned down and kissed Jean on the cheek. His apology—she looked so sweet, he said, he couldn't help himself—and Jean blushing into her hands are delightful to remember.

Finally!

Edwin tells Asia a story. He's talking quietly so as not to wake anyone. "One time Miss Hyde made me stay after school. I don't remember what I'd done; no doubt it was dreadful. She set me some passages to copy. I'm sure I was there at least two hours. But when I got outside, Sleeper was waiting for me. He'd never gone home, but watched the whole thing through the window. He had a large rock in his hand. 'If I saw her go for her cane,' he said, 'I was going to put this rock right through the glass.'

"Sleeper is such a good man," Edwin says. "Faithful and steadfast. And he's loved you forever. I'd be so relieved to see you married to him. Then I'd know that you'd be well taken care of no matter what might come."

It's true. Sleeper has been courting her for so long, Edwin working all that same time to bring the match about. Why should her schemes work out and not his?

She surely doesn't want to end up like Rosalie.

So why not Sleeper? She can picture her life with him and it's a good life, a comfortable life. He makes a good living. She believes he'll be a good husband. She doesn't love him the same way she's sometimes been in love, but those passionate feelings led eventually to passionate heartbreak, sometimes hers, sometimes his. Bad feelings all around.

And shouldn't twelve years of tireless devotion be rewarded? And shouldn't Edwin be made happy in the bargain?

She thinks all these things. The sound of the engine and the wheels on the track are a sort of lullaby, singing her home. She's drowsy and happy and she trusts Edwin completely. She trusts him with her heart.

It's time, she thinks. Time to grow up.

"All right," she says. "But tell him I still want to be asked."

NO ONE SEEMS surprised by the engagement. Mother and Rosalie are pleased. Only John sounds a sour note. "He wants the connection to the Booth name," he tells her. "You don't know the extent of his ambition. I do."

There is nothing wrong with ambition, Asia thinks.

"He doesn't love you," John says, but in her mind, Asia is far away, standing before a great stone arch and a thunderous wall of water, and she can't hear a word.

Rosalie

viii

Rosalie is beginning to wonder if Edwin has feelings for Mary Devlin. No one in the family has met her yet and nothing Edwin says is truly suspicious. But her name comes up more often than Rosalie would expect. She thinks they might be writing to each other.

She's not the only one wondering. One day at dinner, when they are all gathered around the table with only John missing, and even Joe home now that his schooling has finished, Edwin mentions that Miss Devlin says that *Romeo and Juliet* now makes her think about what a romance between a girl from the North and a boy from the South might look like in these fractured times. The play seems particularly pertinent. But there are always factions. Perhaps it's always pertinent.

Asia waves past the politics. "Is she pretty?" Asia asks. "This Miss Devlin of yours?"

"More sweet than pretty," Edwin says, "and hardly mine."

"But you do like her?"

"Don't tease your brother," Mother says.

"I wasn't."

The factory whistle blows. A horse and cart go clattering by. Mrs. Murphy, the new cook, a well-worn woman with hands like spatulas, banks the fire and pretends she isn't listening.

"She's a good girl," Edwin says. "And very talented. But I would never marry an actress, you know that. She's like a sister to me."

"You have a sister," Asia says.

"Two," Joe reminds her.

Maybe Asia's been persuaded. Rosalie has not. But why shouldn't Edwin fall in love? Rosalie only wants to see him happy, a condition he rarely achieves as he has no gift for it. And, after all, hasn't Asia done the same? She's certainly been performing the part—rushing for the post, sighing over songs of lovers parted.

The kitchen smells of chicken and ham. Since Father's death, meat has become commonplace at dinnertime and Mrs. Murphy likes to put ham in everything, pile one meat on top of another, frying them together. Rosalie has had more trouble getting used to meat than the others. She looks down at the drumstick on her plate and thinks how very much like someone's leg it still looks. She takes a sip of tea, which she has secretly sparked up with a bit of gin. Mrs. Murphy is the Booths' third cook, the last one having been dismissed for drinking on the job.

Edwin changes the subject. "So, Joe, what are your plans now that school is done?"

"I don't know," Joe says. His knife clicks against his plate as he saws off a great hunk of meat. He lifts it to his mouth, but before it goes in, he says, "I haven't thought."

Joe's less handsome than his brothers, still growing into his nose and ears, his cheeks still plump and cherubic. He's a dreamy, indolent boy of whom a friend will later say that he was either stupid or else had a wonderful knack for counterfeiting stupidity. He's currently working as a ticket taker at the Holliday Street Theatre.

He and Rosalie remain close. She remembers how he used to climb into her lap, the weight and warmth of him on her legs. She remembers the dusty smell of his hair when he was a little boy, how his grubby little hands would snake around her neck. What Rosalie and Joe share is a sort of outsider view of their own family—Rosalie the oldest, since June is never around, and Joe the youngest. What they share is that neither of them is Edwin or Asia or John.

Since Joe appears to have nothing more to say concerning his future, Edwin changes the subject again. Like many melancholics, he can tell a funny story. He describes a recent performance of *The Merchant of Venice*. He was playing in some backwater—a place so small that Edwin can't even remember the town's name, just that the theater held perhaps forty people, so even though every seat was taken, few people were in attendance.

Edwin was Antonio and they were nearing the end, halfway through the trial scene, when they heard the steamboat whistle. If they missed the boat, they'd miss their next engagement. Edwin saw Uncle Ben in the wings, gesturing wildly for Antonio and Shylock to wrap things up, quick as they could.

"So I said to Shylock, 'Would you take ten ducats and a fine pig?' and Shylock said, 'I guess that's as good an offer as I'm going to get,' and Portia said, 'How about we all dance the Virginnie Reel then?' and we dropped the curtain. The audience had heard the whistle; they all understood. We left them laughing and legged it to the docks just in time to board."

"Who was playing Portia?" Asia asks.

ix

Edwin's obsessed with a guilt-induced plan to put up a grand new marker for Father's grave, an expense he can only manage with an exhausting season. Uncle Ben has booked him everywhere. The year is 1858.

Edwin's chosen the sculptor Joseph Carew of Boston, the same man who, with his brother, designed the beautiful monument for the Reverend Charles T. Torrey, an obelisk with Torrey's likeness in bas-relief on one side and a grieving woman at the base. If you didn't know to look for them, you might miss the shackles on the woman's feet. Torrey had been jailed in Baltimore for helping fugitive slaves and died a martyr in the prison there.

Arguably, Edwin has hired the lesser of the Carew brothers.

It's his only economy. Father's tombstone will also be a marble obelisk, only bigger, almost twenty feet high, with the name BOOTH also unusually large and, on the far side, an epitaph from *Julius Caesar*:

> His life was gentle, and the elements
>> So mix'd in him that Nature might stand up
>> And say to all the world—This was a man.

Edwin lays out all these plans as he makes them. Rosalie sees how much he wants Mother to be happy. "You're such a good son," Mother assures him, reaching over to pat his hand. Privately, to Rosalie, she worries about the expense.

Rosalie has her own plans. In a quiet moment, she asks Edwin, could the bodies of Frederick, Mary Ann, and Elizabeth be moved from the farm to the Baltimore cemetery? "Father loved them so," she says to Edwin. "I know he'd want them gathered about him."

Edwin is instantly agreeable, even enthusiastic. Yet nothing is done to make this happen. He continues to talk about Father's stone which he plans to unveil on Father's birthday, and never mentions the lost children. It seems to Rosalie that he forgot his promise the moment he made it. Perhaps it was a mistake not to have had Mother there as witness. Rosalie refuses to nag, but a little worm of anger eats at her. Let Edwin meet a ghost or two and see how soon he forgets them.

She's at the cemetery one day, talking to Father about this, when she sees a pale, thin man she thinks she recognizes as her half-brother, Richard Booth. He's walking in her direction, but veers away at the sight of her. She wonders if he was also visiting Father's grave.

She's surprised to think he might do this, as she's never seen him there before and, really, he has good reasons to be angry with Father. The way Father had taken him on tour, shown him a fatherly regard and affection, only to snatch it all away the minute Adelaide arrived. How hurtful that must have been. And then those years when they all lived in Baltimore without Father taking the trouble to see him, find out how he was doing. She can almost understand why he fought so hard to take Father's estate away from them.

But that evening, just before she goes up to bed, Mother tells her Adelaide has died, so it must have been his mother, not his father, who brought Richard to the cemetery. Mother's voice is colorless when she delivers the news, poking at the fire with her back turned so her face is hidden. Her posture makes it clear that there will be no conversation regarding this matter.

Although Rosalie has vivid memories of the harridan who followed them, spitting and shouting through the streets, the news of her death softens Rosalie. There's no denying that Father treated his first wife abominably. What a sad life Adelaide led. She wonders if Mother feels guilty about it. Rosalie has no reason for guilt herself, but she's ready to acknowledge blame on all sides.

This generosity of spirit vanishes the first time she sees Adelaide's gravestone. It reads:

> JESUS MARY JOSEPH
> PRAY FOR THE SOUL OF
> MARIE CHRISTINE ADELAIDE
> DELANNOY
> WIFE OF
> JUNIUS BRUTUS BOOTH TRAGEDIAN
> SHE DIED IN BALTIMORE
> MARCH THE 9TH, 1858
> AGED 66 YEARS
> IT IS A HOLY AND WHOLESOME THOUGHT
> TO PRAY FOR THE DEAD
> MAY SHE REST IN PEACE

Wife of Junius Brutus Booth, indeed! The fact that this stone rests only a short stroll from Father's own grave, in the same cemetery, under the same poplars, adds to the insult. Here lies Adelaide, reaching out from beyond the grave to spit on them one last time. Her claim to Father is apparently deathless.

So Rosalie's enmity will be the same. She decides that she will not be praying for this particular soul.

Old Spudge sends them her obituary as it ran in New Orleans under the quite mistaken assumption that they'll be amused.

No less than three persons died, at Baltimore on Tuesday of disease of the heart. Mrs. Mary Booth, a divorced wife of the celebrated tragedian Booth, aged 65 years; Mr. Joseph Lokey, a messenger at the Mt. Clare Station, rather advanced in life; and a man unknown, apparently 50 years of age, who fell dead in the street.

The obituary goes on to identify Father and "Mary's" only surviving child as Edwin.

ON A SUNNY afternoon, Rosalie sits in the Exeter kitchen with Joe Hall. They are both drinking coffee—his with two big spoonfuls of sugar, hers with a splash of gin. Joe has stopped by with some of the spring produce for Mother—slender carrots and pale radishes and green onions—but Mother and Asia are out ordering wedding clothes. Rosalie tries to talk Joe into staying until they return, but he says he can't. He says that Ann would fret. He just has time for the coffee.

"I guess you've heard that Asia is to marry Sleeper Clarke," she says.

"It's good news," Joe Hall says. "Mighty good news. Fine man. She'll be living in Philadelphia then."

"She will."

"Do you think she would look in on our Pinkney and our Mary Ellen? I expect they're in Philadelphia now. Ann and me, we'd sure like to know how they get on. I don't have an address," Joe says.

"Of course she will." This is a lie. Rosalie can't imagine how Asia would find the two Halls if they're in hiding. But perhaps they're not. Perhaps they count on Aunty Rogers and her husband not tracking them down.

Outside there's a sudden battle, dogs against pigs, by the sound of it, barking and squealing, and several men shouting for it all to stop. The noise moves down the street at a run.

Across from her, Joe Hall has closed his eyes. He sits, swaying slightly, as if he's gone to sleep while upright at the table, his two hands wrapped around his cup. Since his eyes are closed, Rosalie feels free to examine him closely. The sun is falling hard on him, deepening every line on his face, and there is a mass of those lines, a map of years and worries. One of his front teeth has gone yellow. He's still a big man, but his chest has caved in and his shoulders curved. Rosalie used to ask him how old he was. That's something I never did know, he'd say.

She's known him all the years of her life. His was one of the first faces she'd ever seen, looking down as she lay in the wicker cradle he'd made for her. In that time before memory, his face was already there.

It occurs to Rosalie that someday she'll see him for the last time and that this could be that very day. What will his grave marker look like? It won't even have a birth date.

Rosalie will be proved prescient in all of this. He'll die two years later, neither the date of birth nor death on his stone. He'll never again see his son and his daughter, the children who fled.

"Do you think there'll be war, Miss Rose?" He's opened his eyes again and his fingers now tap on the scarred surface of the table. A song of some sort. She remembers one that he taught her when she was a little girl:

They put John on an island
Hallelujah
They put him there to starve him
Hallelujah
But the angels came and fed him
Hallelujah
They fed him on the bread of heaven
Hallelujah

"No. I don't think there'll be war," Rosalie answers. She doesn't explain herself, but the truth is that she can easily imagine white men who will fight and die to keep their slaves. She knows these men. Joe Hall knows them, too. They live all around the farm in Bel Air. They went to school with John. John is one of them.

But she can't think of a single white man she knows who would fight and die to free the slaves. The ones who believe in slavery have so much more conviction than the ones who don't.

"We surely miss our girl, our boy. They can't come home; we can't get there. Change is hard," says Joe. "But change is life."

And death, Rosalie thinks. Death is a mighty big change, too.

x
—

Rosalie has suffered a shock. She's come to her bedroom and closed the door, hoping to be given some privacy. She's combing through her wet and tangled hair with more vigor and less care than usual. It's as if she wants it to hurt.

Moments ago, she and Mother and Asia were all in the kitchen together, washing their hair. They use rainwater, which they collect in basins and save for the weeks between washings. It's a major undertaking and the boys, if any are around, are shooed from the house for the duration so the women can proceed in their undergarments. Today is warm and the upstairs bedroom actually hot. Rosalie is in no hurry to put her skirts back on and she wants the tangles gone from her hair before it dries.

Asia was talking, as usual, not even stopping when Mother poured a pitcher of water over her head. Rosalie was toweling the ends of her own hair when she heard Asia say something that began, "When we're all in Philadelphia . . ."

All, she had said. We all. All of us. Rosalie was so surprised she missed the rest of the sentence.

"Are we all going to Philadelphia?" she'd asked.

Mother rubbed the rainwater through Asia's hair. "We wouldn't keep this big house just for the two of us. The boys are hardly here now and when Asia goes . . ."

The minute Mother says this, Rosalie sees how inevitable the move is. And yet it hadn't occurred to her. Her eyes had suddenly filled so she'd left the kitchen as inconspicuously as she could and come upstairs to be alone and cry. But somewhere on the stairs, the tears had vanished without falling, her eyes parched and stinging instead.

She's never loved Baltimore, but this is where her life is. She has friends—the Cole sisters, Nelly Morgan, Kate Greene—and she gets together with them every couple of weeks to gossip and sew shirts and aprons for charity. Maybe she doesn't really care for Nelly, but she likes the Cole sisters.

She's lived with Asia, they've shared a bedroom, for the whole of Asia's life, but always under Mother's roof. In Philadelphia, Rosalie will be a permanent guest in Asia's house, an intruder on the young couple. Efforts will be made to make her feel welcome and Asia will make sure that she sees those efforts. Rosalie will feel a constant pressure to be both out of the way and useful. She will never feel that the house is hers.

Rosalie knows better than to imagine she'll be given a room of her own. She'll be sharing with Mother now, the widow and the spinster. She can see how it all will go.

But she can also see that nothing else makes sense. Unhappy as she is, she can't come up with a single argument in favor of the expense of remaining in Baltimore.

A timid knock on the door, and Mother enters. Water has dripped down the front of her chemise, soaked into the shelf of cloth over her heavy breasts. Her graying hair is wrapped in a large white rag. "I guess we took you by surprise," she says. "I didn't mean to. I thought it was obvious."

"It is," Rosalie says. "I don't know why I was surprised."

"Philadelphia is a wonderful town. Sleeper says he'd much rather live there than here. So much to do!"

"I'm sure I'll get used to it." Rosalie can't say out loud, not to anyone, but certainly not to Mother, how much she dreads the daily witness of Asia ruling her little kingdom. It puts her in mind of those novels in which the younger married sister leapfrogs in status over the older unmarried one.

Sleeper's visits have been hard enough. You can't enter a room without seeing the two spring apart, Asia's face flushed, hair in disarray. But probably once Asia is married that will stop. Mother and Father had a baby every two years like clockwork, and yet there had been no canoodling for Rosalie to interrupt.

Mother takes the comb from Rosalie's hand and stands behind her. Her pale face floats in the pocked mirror above Rosalie's own. Rosalie's hair is thick and combing it out requires patience. Mother's being much gentler than Rosalie, untangling the knots

at the ends first, only making the long strokes from the scalp
when there is nothing left to snag on. "You know I'll always take
you with me, wherever I go," Mother says. "You know that
you'll never be left alone and uncared for as long as I'm alive."

Ever since the deaths of Mary Ann and Elizabeth, Rosalie has
believed that her job was to care for Mother. Perhaps she's been
waiting all those years to hear just this, that Mother is caring for
her. Now the tears come and this is not because she's unhappy
over the move, which she is, but because Mother is there, with a
face full of love, combing out Rosalie's hair as if she were just a
little girl.

xi

Eleven years after Edwin first made the offer, John has finally
agreed to be Henry, Earl of Richmond, to Edwin's Richard III.
They appear together, one night only, at Baltimore's Holliday
Street Theatre, recently bought by John T. Ford. Mother, Rosalie, and Asia are all in attendance. Joe makes a show of demanding their tickets.

A box has been reserved for them, with three rocking chairs
threaded with ribbons and a good view down to the stage.
They've dressed in their best—Asia in a violet silk and Rosalie in
dove gray. Mother is sticking to her widow's black, but has
dabbed her wrists and neck. The powdery scent of Héliotrope
Blanc, a gift from Edwin, floats through the air along with the
hum of the audience settling into their seats.

All three are determined to love both performances in absolutely equal measure, but this is complicated by the fact that they
must wait so long for John to arrive onstage while Edwin is

everywhere, and playing Father's old role. The more he deviates from Father's delivery, the more Mother whispers that she can't help but feel that he's doing it wrong. She just knows Father's version so well. She could do it herself. Pause here. Sweeping hand gesture.

Edwin falls to his knees. "'Take up the sword again, or take up me.'"

Rosalie hears Asia whispering the answer along with Lady Anne. "'No! Though I wish thy death, I will not be thy executioner.' I did that scene in school once," Asia says, "after the first time I ever saw Father perform. I got a spanking. At home, not at school."

"I remember," Mother says.

Rosalie wishes they would stop talking. Edwin's voice is so intense. "'Then bid me kill myself, and I will do it.'" It's romantic, or it would be if Mother and Asia would be quiet, if Richard weren't so evil and Edwin not her little brother.

Finally, finally John appears. "'Thrice is he armed that has his quarrel just; And he but naked, though locked up in steel, Whose conscience with injustice is corrupted: The very weight of Gloster's guilt shall crush him . . .'"

Rosalie hears Mother catching her breath. She thinks she knows why. "He looks so much like Father," Rosalie whispers. The resemblance is so strong as to be startling.

But Mother says no, he looks like Edwin. So very much like Edwin.

This isn't true. John is taller. John is handsomer. The handsomest man in America, some are saying. A woman in the audience compares him to a new-blown rose, its petals still beaded with the morning dew.

In future, it will be a rare review that doesn't make these comparisons: Edwin to Father, John to Father and Edwin. Few argue for the sons over the legend of the father, but between the brothers things fall out more evenly—Edwin the better elocutionist, John with more fire. Edwin with more poetry, John with more passion.

Of course, Edwin is working under the handicap of so often performing drunk.

On this particular night, J. H. Stoddart, the actor playing Buckingham, declares both performances splendid. "I shall never forget the fight between Richard and Richmond in the last act, an encounter which was terrible in its savage realism," he says.

That fight ran so long and was rendered with such ferocity that certain members of the audience feared they were about to witness actual and serious injury. Certain members like Rosalie.

Edwin

xii

Edwin's career benefits from a lucky advantage with regard to timing. Back in 1853, only a year after Father's death, the legendary tragedian Edwin Forrest retired from the stage. Forrest had gained early notice through his popular Indian roles, particularly the last of the Wampanoags; shot to notoriety by rudely hissing William Macready as he played Macbeth, a feud that later culminated in the deadly Astor Opera House riot; responded to the exposure of his own infidelities by accusing his wife of the same (she claimed he had mistaken a phrenology examination for lovemaking); brutally whipped one of the men he held responsible for the destruction of his marriage, a man in such ill health he was utterly unable to defend himself; sued his wife for divorce in a six-week trial the public followed avidly and which he eventually lost; and then lost a later suit for the assault. He was tired.

His absence left an opening Edwin was able to exploit—the old greats dead or gone—and only Edwin at the gate. If this opening was mere luck, the use Edwin made of it was the product of hard work and careful planning, not all of it his own. Two

other people—Adam Badeau and Mary Devlin—devoted themselves to Edwin's advancement.

Adam Badeau:

Since that encouraging review back in his first New York run,
Edwin and Badeau have grown close. Adam refers to them as
Romeo and Vagabond, Edwin calls them Ned and Ad. Adam is
older than Edwin by only two years, but he's better educated,
more sophisticated, better connected, and smarter. He's a short
man, as is Edwin, but stout and ruddy where Edwin is thin and
pale. He wears glasses. His clothes show the kind of subdued taste
that only money can buy. His offer to mentor Edwin is eagerly
accepted. Soon Edwin is studying French and Latin for elocu-
tion, history and philosophy for interpretation.

"You know he's in love with you," Uncle Ben tells Edwin and
Edwin does know this. Adam often complains of Edwin's emotional distance, his coldness, as if Adam has a right to something
different. Sometimes this makes Edwin uncomfortable. Sometimes he loves Adam right back.

The two spend hours discussing the state of the theater. The
old ranting, referred to now as the Bowery style, remains popular
in the cheap seats, but the upper classes want subtlety. "No acting
is great which pleases only a single class," Adam tells Edwin.
"The gods of the gallery are as good critics as the blues of the
boxes." Still, the professionals, including Badeau, are working to
transform the popular taste. Sometimes people have to be taught
to want what they should want.

The war will intensify the growing preference for suppressed
over expressed emotion, especially when the suppression comes
with evident (though delicately played) struggle.

Badeau admires innovation. He longs to see something new.
This desire is, in and of itself, innovative. For years, actors have

been applauded for imitation. Every part, however old now, had once debuted with the author there to provide guidance. The less things change over the generations, the closer a performance comes to the wellspring, the true quill. Shakespeare as directed by Shakespeare.

As rewritten by Cibber. Adam and Edwin begin to put more of Shakespeare's own lines back into his plays. This, too, is innovative.

Adam takes Edwin to libraries and museums to research costumes. They read plays together, stopping to analyze who the character is at each moment, how he develops over the course of the play, and how a quiet line might be read to convey this.

In the old style, actors were evaluated on their delivery of the big speeches, the ones the audience knew and were waiting for. This was called *making the points*. Reviewing Edwin's Hamlet, a later critic will write, "From first to last, he not only does not make points where points are usually made, but he does not make a point at all."

IN THE SUMMER of 1858, Ned and Ad, Romeo and Vagabond, take a trip to Tudor Hall, which has stood empty since the Booths returned to Baltimore. This trip is Adam's idea. Edwin will show him the farm where he grew up. He'll share stories of his childhood and his famous father. Adam will turn the whole thing into an essay for *Noah's Sunday Times*. It will feed the public appetite for backstage stories about actors. It will remind readers who Edwin's father is. It will solidify his position as a rising star.

Their departure is delayed by Mother's insistence on serving Adam breakfast and keeping him talking around the table. Keeping Adam talking is the world's easiest task. "We have a long drive ahead," Edwin says finally, as if his family doesn't know exactly how long it takes to get to Bel Air. Even that doesn't bring the gab to a close. Edwin swallows his annoyance with his third cup of coffee.

They don't get on the road until noon and then they encounter a series of further delays. A harness breaks and has to be knotted together with shoelaces. A wheel gets stuck in a puddle and Edwin must hand the reins to Adam, by far the better dressed of the two, and leap down, add his shoulder to the work of the horses. Now his boots are muddy as well as laceless. Edwin begins to feel that the whole trip has been a mistake, as if he cannot run faster than the earth turns and will end farther from his destination than he began.

But when one of the horses loses a shoe, the whole adventure tips to comedy. What can they do but laugh? "A farrier, a farrier, my kingdom for a farrier," Edwin says. The sun is hot and high and the horses' backs show dark streaks of sweat. Edwin's shirt is damp and soiled.

When they drive at last through the trees on the long approach to the house, the temperature drops. In that coolness, Edwin feels his welcome. "Your foot is on your native heath," he hears his father say. These woods, these streams are home to him.

A man comes to take the horses. "Master Edwin," he says. "It surely is good to see you," and Edwin returns the pleasantry, hoping he's managed to conceal the fact that he can't, for the life of him, remember the man's name. He retrieves his shoelaces.

The old cabin is now occupied by the Hall family, but no one has lived in the main house since the Booths left. The windows are dark and reproachful, the grass entirely gone to weed, sedge, and bramble. Rosalie's mint has escaped its bed and spread over the path, turning their steps to perfume. Edwin picks a dandelion,

closes his eyes, opens them, and blows the stem clean. The seeds
float away. "What did you wish?" Adam asks.

"No ghosts," says Edwin. "Did I ever tell you I was born with
a caul?"

"I wasn't," Adam says. He's taken his glasses off to clean them.
His bared eyes are intense, making Edwin acutely aware that
they are spending the night together. "You'll save me from
drowning. I'll protect you from ghosts." He hooks his glasses
back over his ears.

"We used to have a lawn," Edwin tells him, but Adam has
held up a finger, hushing him. He seems to be listening to a dove,
calling over and over in its three-note song. "Dactyl," Adam
says. And then he tells Edwin that everything is perfect, that it's
all beautiful, that he prefers the wildness of weeds to the most
beautifully planned and maintained gardens. No better land-
scaper than nature.

The sun is setting. The frogs come out. Edwin unlocks the
door.

They walk through cobwebs. The air is stale and still. Adam
wants nostalgia for his article, but Edwin lived only a few weeks
in this house; he struggles to provide it. This is where his family
lived without him. This is what happened while he was in California. He can't wipe the feel of cobwebs from his skin. This is
Father's dream house empty of dreams.

That turns out not to be true. In every closet and cupboard
treasures have been left behind. Books in many languages, some
with corners turned, passages circled, others with the leaves un-
cut. Plays familiar and unknown. Lope de Vega, Jean Racine,
Byron, Shakespeare, the Koran, and the Bible.

They've come equipped with candles but not with candlesticks.

As it grows dark, Edwin finds a basin in which to prop one candle, an old shoe for another. Adam produces two cigars and they pass the shoe to light them, breathe in the dank smell of tobacco.

In the wavering light, their excavations continue. Asia appears to have left much of her research here. Edwin finds drawers of Father's playbills and even some letters and journals. He picks up one of these and realizes that what it advertises is the first time Father and Edmund Kean appeared on the same stage. Decades ago and miles away. He can so clearly imagine the curtain call, the audience in thunderous applause and all of them, every person in every seat, now dead. In his mind, he watches as they go, one by one, winking out of existence. The last left is a pale woman with rouged cheeks and a feathered hat clapping heartily as she ages before his eyes.

Adam and Edwin sit on the floor together, flicking the ash from their cigars into the basin with the candle, passing their discoveries hand to hand, exclaiming over every find. They'd bought sandwiches on the road, but have forgotten to eat them. Suddenly Edwin is too tired for food, his exhilaration turning in a moment into exhaustion. He takes his watch from his pocket, reads it, and then claps his hand over its face. "Guess the time."

"Ten," says Adam, his round face swimming in candlelight, but it is half past two.

Time for bed. They carry the candles up the stairs and find an old mattress in John's room. The antlers still hang on the wall, empty now of their armory. Edwin opens the window and the breeze is cool and smells of cedar and ash. He finds some moldering bits of costumes in a closet. He gives Adam Macbeth's cloak, keeps Lear's for himself. They blow out the candles and lie together. Edwin is nervous and unsure so he keeps on talking.

"One time," Edwin tells Adam, "one time in Boston, I was resting in the room, when my father came running in, dropped to the floor, and rolled under the bed. 'I've gone out!' he told me. Seconds later there was a knock on the door. I went to get it and the sculptor Tom Gould was standing outside. Gould had once done a bust of Father and adored him, but Father found Gould tedious. 'Father's out,' I said, but he walked in past me, sat on my bed to wait for his return. I took a seat above Father. Now I was the one stuck with making conversation and I've never been good at that. Soon enough I'd run dry. It made for a long silence, which Father misunderstood. I heard his voice, singing out from under the bed. 'Is that old bore gone?' he asked."

"Marvelous," Adam says softly. He yawns, a great, cracking yawn that makes Edwin yawn, too. Adam shifts to his side, his back to Edwin. Edwin is looking up through the moonlit forest of antler tines.

"Did I ever tell you about my trip to Hawaii?" he asks. "We performed there on our way home from Australia. We were only men then. I'd been drunk and stupid and the women had all quit us and gone back to California. We tried to talk the captain's wife into taking a role, but she just stood on the stage and laughed hysterically the whole time, though it might have been sobbing; it was hard to tell. So we made Lars Roy our leading lady instead. He was a little man with a beard he refused to shave so he wore a scarf across his face like a lady in a harem. Which he had! He married three of the island women and we left him behind. I think about him sometimes. Wondering how paradise worked out for him.

"My God, but Lars Roy was the ugliest Juliet you ever did see."

Adam says nothing. Perhaps he's asleep. Edwin lowers his

voice. "I mistook what they eat for breakfast for paste and used it
to put up the playbills. Worked just fine," he says. No answer.

Edwin can't calm down. He feels rattled and jangled and
aroused. Adam smells of cigars and also sweat, and also the mildew of the cloaks. An owl calls. A dog barks. Edwin remembers
the great black dogs of his childhood. They were his first horses.
Rosalie would set him on their backs and hold him by the arm so
he didn't slip off. He remembers the bullfrog, realizing there'd
been no sound of it this evening. Perhaps its reign of terror has
ended. He wishes he were in the cabin instead of this house, in
his real bedroom where the sound of the streams was his original
lullaby. They can't be heard from John's room. How can he sleep
without that?

He thinks about Father's playbills and about time passing and
how the things you can keep really only serve to remind you of
all that you've lost. He feels the permanence of trees and stars, his
own life galloping by. He thinks about Mary Devlin, her brown
eyes, her soft hair. Adam accepts Edwin's drinking. He understands that the price of Edwin's friendship is forgiving and forgetting the things he says and does while on a toot. Mary is not so
resigned. Promise me you'll be a good boy, she says. Promise me.
Promise me.

Edwin should be the one wrapped in Macbeth's cloak. Edwin
is the one who's murdered sleep.

FROM ADAM'S ESSAY:

I warrant you, some of his fair admirers would not have
slept, so long as he talked, and doubtless they envy me my

snooze on his arm. But 'twas dark, and I couldn't see his eyes; besides I had seen them all day.

MARY DEVLIN:

The first time Edwin and Mary met, sparks flew. He spoke up to her balcony and her lovely voice drifted down to him. Although he insists otherwise to Asia, she's uncommonly pretty. Usually when Edwin acts, there's a part of him standing aside, critically watching his own performance. Suddenly, he was too immersed in hers to think about himself. His heart raced giddily in his chest, he felt all of Romeo's agony should his love not be returned.

"You were wonderful," she told him at the curtain and he stumbled through returning the compliment.

She reminds him a little of June's wife, Hattie. Same abundant brown hair. Same pink-and-cream complexion. Same sympathetic manner. The next morning, he'd bought an expensive turquoise bracelet and given it to her after their final show. "I want you to remember me," he'd said. She'd come out from her dressing room, fully dressed, her hair only half-pinned. He would have given anything to bury his hands in that hair, but a bracelet won't pay that toll. He wrote to his mother—"I've met a young woman who could almost make me forget my vow to never marry an actress."

Mary's family had produced more children than they could afford to keep, so when Edwin first meets her, she's the ward of the actor Joe Jefferson and his wife, Margaret. Jefferson knows Edwin and likes him. He also knows Edwin's reputation for bedding, in the words of Adam Badeau, "singing chambermaids," and that he does not like. He makes Mary return the bracelet.

Edwin takes it from her hand, their fingers touching. "It's still yours," he says. Her eyes are big and brown. "I'm just keeping it for you." And soon she has it back again, in a package in the post containing two bracelets, hers and an identical one for Jefferson's wife. "I hope you will both accept these as they are intended," Edwin writes, "a sincere expression of admiration and friendship."

He's gone by then, less dangerous. Mary is allowed to keep the gift.

And then the sparks flicker out of their own accord. The two fall out of contact and Edwin does nothing to change that. He's preoccupied with his family's finances and his career. He thinks of Mary constantly, and then less, and then hardly at all.

MARY STARTED ACTING at age twelve. By seventeen she's a leading lady at the Marshall Theatre in Richmond, Virginia, the same company John's just joining. Most of the Devlin family lives in Philadelphia, where her father works as a tailor and makes costumes for the Arch Street Theatre, the company John's just left. Both her parents are Irish immigrants.

An engagement to the wealthy lawyer R. S. Spofford is expected and encouraged by her family and friends. Edwin tells some people that she's already spoken for. To others he says, Don't believe in this marriage; it will never happen. To all he says, She's like a sister to me.

Mary doesn't have Adam Badeau's education nor his flashy brilliance. Everything about her is muted, not a swan, but a sparrow. And yet, in her quiet way, she's as smart as he is. She has her own feelings about the new naturalism. She, too, loathes the old histrionics, the ranting, the railing.

But she also feels that naturalism can go too far. No one wants to pay for a performance of everyday life, scenes from the supper table. Her ideal is an elevated naturalism. Lines with cadence, not overpowered by their delivery, but allowed to echo in their own intrinsic power. Scenes and situations with weight and moral significance.

Gorgeous tragedy. Art that inspires. Art that feels like art.

The prejudice against actresses remains strong. Coarse and forward—if not actually prostitutes, they bring prostitutes to mind. Asia, herself about to marry a low comic, is convinced that any association between Edwin and Mary will destroy the good name of the family. It will remind everyone of the days in which Mother was called a whore.

She needs constant reassurance that nothing of the sort will happen, which Edwin is happy to provide. But after a long interval, he appears with Mary again. And then again after that. Now they are corresponding. Still he promises Asia she has nothing to worry about.

There's nothing coarse about Mary. Her manners are delightful, her innocence palpable. In temperament, she's Edwin's opposite—the incarnation of sunshine. Edwin feels the sweetness of that sunshine whenever he sees her. Still his determination not to marry her is unshaken, for her sake if not his own. Would her bright spirits survive his violent melancholia? He can't think so. Marriage to him would only destroy her happiness.

Such selfless abnegation is irresistible. To Mary, Edwin's melancholia is one of his most attractive features. In the long tradition of young women and wounded heroes, she aches to heal him with her steadfast love. The poor Byronic lamb.

On some level, Edwin must know this. He's no fool.

Lincoln Running

I suppose the institution of slavery really looks small to him. He is so put up by nature that a lash upon his back would hurt him, but a lash upon anybody else's back does not hurt him.

—Abraham Lincoln describing Stephen Douglas

The Lincoln-Douglas debates continue throughout 1858. Douglas is still advocating for popular sovereignty with regard to slavery; he's been neither converted nor silenced. He argues that this is what the Founders intended, a claim Lincoln devastatingly rebuts, one signer of the Declaration of Independence at a time.

They also clash repeatedly over the Dred Scott case, which denied citizenship rights to freed slaves in perpetuity. "Lincoln thinks he knows more of the law than Chief Justice Taney," says Douglas, or words to that effect. Applause. Laughter. "Lincoln has declared war on the Supreme Court."

He accuses Lincoln of believing that the Negro is his equal and his brother.

Lincoln pleads not guilty.

. . . anything that argues me into his idea of perfect social and political equality with the negro, is but a specious and fantastic arrangement of words, by which a man can prove a horse chestnut to be a chestnut horse . . . There is a

physical difference between the two, which in my judgment will probably forever forbid their living together upon
the footing of perfect equality, and inasmuch as it becomes
a necessity that there must be a difference, I, as well as Judge
Douglas, am in favor of the race to which I belong, having
the superior position.

But this he does openly confess to believing:

> . . . there is no reason in the world why the negro is not en-
> titled to all the natural rights enumerated in the Declaration
> of Independence, the right of life, liberty and the pursuit of
> happiness.
>   . . . in the right to eat the bread, without leave of any-
> body else, which his own hand earns, he is my equal and
> the equal of Judge Douglas, and the equal of every liv-
> ing man.

The debates continue. Douglas has long been known as the
Little Giant because he is short, but forceful. Lincoln is now
called the Giant-Killer.

More and more people are urging him to declare his candidacy.

In 1859, the likeliest choice for the top of the Republican
ticket is William Henry Seward, former governor and also senator of New York. Seward appears to want the presidency desperately. "He will die if he doesn't get it," friends say. But he's
considered an extremist on the issue of slavery and any attempt
to alleviate those fears alienates the abolitionists. It's a hard needle to thread.

The second major contender is Edward Bates, a lawyer and

politician from Missouri. On the subject of slavery, Bates is conservative. He was once a Know-Nothing, which counts against him, and he has a sort of schoolmarmish air that no one likes. His base of support is solid, but unexcited.

"No man knows, when that presidential grub gets to gnawing at him, just how deep in it will get until he has tried it," Lincoln says.

THE DRED SCOTT decision is now generally agreed to be the worst Supreme Court ruling in all of American history though not for lack of competition.

xiii

As 1859 begins, Edwin is touring. Rosalie and Asia are still in Baltimore, with Asia's wedding day approaching. Joe is preparing for medical school. John has moved to Richmond, Virginia. He sends Edwin a letter, full of his usual apologies for being such a slow and dismal writer. He finds spelling a particular challenge.

Things are going well for him, he writes. He's getting decent parts. Richmond society is very much to his taste. But something about the climate doesn't agree with him. He's been ill ever since his arrival and the medication he's on makes him too dull-witted to learn his lines.

Plus, his identity is not the secret he would like it to be. "I sometimes hear the name of Booth called out from the gallery," he writes.

THE AMERICAN THEATER world at this time operates primarily on the star system. Edwin is a star. He travels from city to city, performing with one company and then another. Like his father, he'll arrive for an engagement, perform in seven different plays over a two-week period, and then move on.

The company does not travel. They provide the sets, the staging, and the rest of the cast. This is where John is. He's called a ute, a utility player who can take on whatever part is required. The plays are familiar to all. One day of rehearsal to manage the blocking is usually all that's needed once the star arrives. The sets are no more than serviceable. A rustic cabin one night becomes a ship's interior the next.

Staples include *The Marble Heart, A New Way to Pay Old Debts, The Last of the Mohicans,* and *Richelieu.* These performances are augmented before and after with dances that show the women's legs, tableaux, and short farces. Not-art that looks like not-art.

Meanwhile, off in New York, Laura Keene—the same Laura Keene who once took Edwin to Australia—is shaking things up. She's managing her own theater now, an unusual thing for a woman. At the suggestion of Joseph Jefferson, Mary Devlin's guardian, she produces a play called *The Sea of Ice. The Sea of Ice* is an extravaganza. It lasts three and a half hours and demands some difficult staging. A family is stranded by mutineers on an ice floe and the audience must see the floe break apart before their eyes. The Keene company performs *The Sea of Ice* night after night to packed houses from early November through Christmas.

Her next endeavor, also urged by Jefferson, is even more popular. In 1858, she purchases *Our American Cousin* from its author, Tom Taylor. She reworks it considerably and it remains a work in progress even as it's being performed. Bits of physical comedy are added nightly, lines ad-libbed and altered. The relatively minor role of Lord Dundreary expands to the point of madness and suddenly everyone is buying Dundreary scarves, shirts, and collars, speaking in Dundrearyisms (the nonsensical mashing together of two aphorisms as in *too many chefs gather no moss*). By the time Keene's play settles into its final form, it's a phenomenon. *Our American Cousin* runs for an almost unheard-of one hundred and fifty nights.

This is advantageous for the theater. Keene is making massive amounts of money, much of which she spends improving the sets and costumes. Her productions become gorgeous.

But it's ominous for the company. Before these long runs, players were unconcerned if the night's show had no role for them as tomorrow night's surely would. Now months might go by in which half of the company never sets foot onstage. There's little point in keeping them, none in paying them.

For one hundred and fifty nights, Jefferson plays Asa Trenchard, the leading man. When *Our American Cousin* is finally followed by *A Midsummer Night's Dream,* Jefferson plays Bottom. This latter role doesn't suit him. And Keene has begun to find working with him difficult.

So Jefferson leaves her company and goes to the Arch Street Theatre in Philadelphia. Unbeknownst to her, he takes her version of *Our American Cousin* with him. When Keene learns that the Arch Street company is performing her play, note by note, gesture by gesture, she sues for copyright infringement. At issue—does the performance of a play constitute its publication? Can a person own the words? Can a person own the way the words are said? These questions will occupy the court for the next nine years.

With none of that settled, Sleeper Clarke brings the play from Philadelphia to Richmond, where he takes the part of Asa Trenchard and John plays the buffoonish Lord Dundreary. Sleeper tells Asia, who tells Edwin, that he introduced himself to the company as John's newest brother. This expression of familial affection pleases Edwin even though it's a month premature. It doesn't please John. *We'll burn that bridge when we get to it,* as Lord Dundreary would say.

ON APRIL 28TH, 1859, Asia and Sleeper are married at the old St. Paul's Episcopal Church, in Baltimore, Maryland. The church has been recently rebuilt in the soaring Italian style after a fire damaged the original. Asia's family is all there, minus only June, to witness the union. Asia's wearing a new dress, a pale rose silk, the bodice covered with Brussels lace. Edwin thinks she looks very beautiful, her cheeks pink with excitement, her dark hair carefully curled around her temples.

She's borrowed Mother's Byron brooch, perhaps not the smartest token to wear to your own wedding. Edwin guesses Rosalie never talked to Asia about Byron the way she once talked to him. He can feel how keyed up Asia is. She's so nervous she thrums with it. There's no need. Sleeper is no Byron. She's perfectly safe.

John had to ride through the night to attend. "I'm bringing so little to the marriage," Asia says. She's waiting between her brothers, trembling on Edwin's arm, on John's arm, between the sandstone columns of the portico. Above them, light flashes suddenly off the stained-glass window of the risen Christ.

"He's the world's happiest man," Edwin tells her.

"You're bringing the Booth name," John says, "which is

dowry enough and the only thing he wants from you. You're just a professional stepping-stone to him."

John seems tired. Perhaps from the overnight ride, perhaps from his persistent ill health. He's pale and his eyes are shadowed. But he can't be allowed to spoil Asia's wedding day. Edwin won't have it. "You've never liked him. I've never understood why."

"You don't know him the way I know him."

"I've known him for years."

"Please," Mother says. "We won't send Asia off with a quarrel."

xiv

Two months later, Mother moves to Philadelphia to live with Sleeper and Asia. Rosalie and Joe follow soon after. Edwin and John arrive when the summer heat has closed the theaters. So they are all there together in August when they learn that June's wife, Harriet Booth, has died in childbirth along with the baby. Asia's already suffering through the earliest stage of pregnancy—the days of exhaustion and nausea—so the news carries a special horror.

Mother's and Rosalie's sorrow seems to settle on poor bereaved June and little Marion. "They'll have to come here," Mother says, and if Sleeper has just a moment in which he wonders how to fit ever-increasing numbers of Booths into his house, who can blame him?

Edwin is the only one who really knew Hattie and the loss lays him low. He remembers her courage on the trip over the Isthmus, her kindness to him after Father's death. He'd found her an ideal wife, mild-tempered and yielding, and now that June is so unenviable, he's able to admit having envied him. The way his family is talking, as if she'll be missed only as a wife and mother, is adding to his grief. He leaves the house to walk with his own memories, grieve in his own silence. He sits on a park bench in the shade of a maple tree. Above his head, a breeze moves with focused precision through the branches, fluttering one green leaf and then another. Squirrels dash about the grass, halfway up the trunks and down again, engaged in a game whose only goal is quickness. He opens his flask, thinking of his wild California days, his days among the dunes and saloons. He wonders if Hattie was disappointed in him. She never said so, but how could she not have been? What would Mary think if she knew half the things he's done?

He leans forward, elbows on his knees, head in his hands. He closes his eyes. He hears birds, the murmured stream of conversations, children laughing as they run. It's a peaceful scene, offensively so. He rejects it, this thin skin of happiness over the dismal world. Say good-bye to it, Hattie, and go straight to God. I'm going to need you there, making me coffee and toast, when my turn comes.

When Edwin lifts the flask, his hands are shaking like leaves.

LOSS FOLLOWS LOSS. When he hears, through a rumor he thinks reliable, that Mary is to wed Spofford after all, the news destroys him. He's performing Richelieu in New York, so drunk he falls onto the stage like his father before him. The problem, he decides, now that humiliation has been added to heartbreak, is that he's not drunk enough. He goes to work on that in earnest. Eventually Uncle Ben has to roll him to his hotel and into bed, where he rouses himself sufficiently to have another couple of drinks.

The night passes, the sun is stretching its afternoon fingers into his room, and Mary Devlin is laying a cool cloth onto his forehead with a gentle pressure to the temples. He seizes her by the wrist. "If you marry anyone but me, Mollie, I'll die," he says. He might die anyway. He feels awful. His teeth ache.

He likes her less when she refuses to get him another drink. The horrible sobering begins.

Later, he remembers proposing, but dimly. He thinks she accepted. But maybe he was hasty, maybe she was. He takes a cold, deliberate look at his wishes. He finds them unchanged.

When he asks again—neither thinks the first time counted— his offer is conditional. He's decided that her background on the stage is actually an advantage to him. She'll understand his life as no other woman could. But he hasn't changed his mind about marrying an actress. If she wants to be his wife, she must give up her career.

His second condition is that she go into nine months of seclusion, nine months in which she will better herself with lessons, reading; she will improve her musical talents; she will learn French. Under Badeau's tutelage, Edwin is now an acceptable addition to the more elevated parlors. Mary must undergo this same polishing. It's an insulting offer, should Mary take it that way.

She does not. She's seventeen years old and desperately in love. She writes to Spofford.

She writes to Edwin.

Everything will I study, to charm and interest you, and although a brilliant education, has never fallen to my lot, I am sufficiently well-informed to appreciate the good, and beautiful—the rest will come, I doubt not. Forget if possible, as I shall, that the Stage, ever claimed me as its votary—and any love I may have had for the Art I transfer to *you*—

Coincidentally, the time of her seclusion is just the amount Edwin needs to complete a course of medication for venereal disease.

NOT EVERYONE IS pleased with the engagement. Adam Badeau is extravagantly miserable. "I have seen for some time growing evidence enough not only of her importance, but also of my own eclipse. I wish to God I'd never seen you. It's a frightful thing to live out of one's self; to be buried alive in somebody else."

And from Asia: "I'd like to write a letter on her face with this pen . . ."

Asia

xv

No one is doing anything Asia wants them to do. Jean's last letter hints at an infatuation with a wild Australian. Asia writes back immediately: "No! John has his eye on you, so I understand," and even as she writes it, she knows it's not true. John has his eye on a diminutive elf of an actress down in Richmond. Asia seems to be the only one who remembers that he once kissed Jean.

She and Sleeper have a nice, clean house on Franklin Street near the square, with a large room for Rosalie and Mother, and Rosalie is acting as if it's some sort of prison, skulking about at all hours, looking for the way out.

Worst of all is Edwin. He's to marry Mary Devlin in a year's time. Asia forgives him his drinking, as it's a hereditary condition and his only failing.

But she cannot forgive this misbegotten romance. Mary has already asked to borrow money—it is all money with her, Asia says to Rosalie, to Mother, to anyone who will listen. Mary's inveigled her way in by rushing off to New York to nurse him when he was particularly vulnerable. How can Edwin be so blind to her scheming? She'd wanted to love Edwin's wife like a sister, but she cannot, will not ever. This designing artful actress, this obscure daughter of Irish immigrants, deserves only contempt.

Her own marriage is perfect, her husband loyal and true. She thanks God for him every day. And yet, everyone, including Sleeper himself, knows she only married him to please Edwin. If Edwin had changed his mind, raised the slightest objection, she would have canceled the wedding instantly. She's astonished that he won't do the same for her.

She feels that the dark days of Father's bigamy are returning, despite all her efforts to keep herself free of taint, to protect and burnish the great name Father left them. It's as if she met a wild beast in the forest and ran and ran and ran only to arrive home at last and find it waiting there. Her usual tempestuous moods are alarmingly amplified by the hormones of pregnancy. She drowns her pillow in storms of tears.

She writes Edwin to make it clear that when he brings Miss Devlin back to her family in Philadelphia, there will be no welcome in the house of Sleeper and Asia Clarke.

She writes to Jean:

. . . Oh Jean—you don't know the trials I bear, little annoyances, rising merely from the fact that I cannot adore Miss Devlin, a quiet ladylike reception would be as Ned terms it—a wet blanket. He has written some sharp letters inferring that I am not a lady—At any rate I am not a fool . . .

In the midst of all this family tumult, down in Virginia, John Brown and twenty-one men under his command—sixteen white, five black—take control of the Harpers Ferry armory.

Caution, Sir! I am eternally tired of hearing that word caution.

It is nothing but the word of cowardice!

—John Brown

OCTOBER 16TH, 1859.

The five black men who accompany Brown are Osborne Anderson, John Copeland, Shields Green, Lewis Leary, and Dan-
gerfield Newby. Brown's plan is to distribute the guns to slaves
throughout Virginia and then to lead a slave rebellion. God has
commanded this.

But His ways are mysterious. Brown holds the armory only a
short time before it's retaken by Colonel Robert E. Lee's ma-
rines. Most of the insurrectionists are killed, including Brown's
sons. Brown himself is wounded and captured.

The magnitude of this event temporarily shocks the Booths
out of their private concerns. They are all, despite their differences, despite their general aversion to politics, passionate about
the preservation of the Union.

Off in Richmond, where John is, people talk of nothing else.
John's become a frequent and popular guest at Richmond's balls,
shooting ranges, whorehouses, saloons, and salons. Everywhere
he's assessed approvingly, despite his connections to the theater
and his Maryland upbringing, as a real Southern gentleman.

WEEKS PASS AND the rest of the family return one by one to personal issues and grievances. Rosalie is finding the move to Asia's
house every bit as bad as she'd feared. Sleeper kisses Asia's shoes,

her gloves, her shawls—anything that's touched her body finds its way to his lips. It's an appalling thing to witness.

Edwin works to stay sober. He's focused on his career, on his intended, and on his health. He's never been political.

Asia returns to her terrible pregnancy and her search for new adjectives to hurl in the direction of Mary Devlin.

Only John remains obsessed with the John Brown affair. Asia is, as always, the one he confides in. Once again, he's remembering Christiana, the Gorsuch family, his happy nights spent at Retreat Farm. Mostly he remembers how no one was held accountable. But Virginia is not Pennsylvania, praise the Lord. This time will be different, he tells Asia. This time blood will pay for blood.

Sure enough, John Brown is condemned to the hangman's noose. Rosalie was quite wrong to think no white man would die to bring about the end of slavery.

ON NOVEMBER 19TH, at about six p.m., Virginia governor Henry Wise receives an urgent telegram from the colonel tasked with guarding Brown. Five hundred soldiers must be sent immediately to Charlestown as an armed force of abolitionists is marching to Brown's rescue. It seems the North admires the man. Several Northern states have petitioned for mercy.

Wise has been smarting for weeks over the fact that he and his state militia were not the ones to retake the armory. He blames President Buchanan for not informing him immediately of the attack. He plans on being the next Democratic nominee for the presidency. That battle would have been just the thing.

But now he has this second chance. Within the hour, the bells in Capitol Square have rung the muster and the militias are gathering. So is the rest of the city. Crowds line the streets, cluster at the telegraph offices and the train depot. Another three hundred abolitionists are added to the rumored army. All is confusion and chaos, marching bands and waving handkerchiefs. One thing is clear. The theaters will be mostly empty this evening. All of Richmond is out to see the militias off. And this is the moment when John enters the story.

HE TELLS ASIA all about it when next he visits. It's been a long time since she's seen him so excited and also so serious about anything. Mostly he's just her brother, but occasionally Asia really looks at him. How can Jean resist? He's so handsome, his bright eyes, his animated face. "It's a wonderful thing," he says, "to be right in the middle of something so momentous. To feel that you've touched history and history has touched you." Asia can see what he's feeling though she's never felt it herself. When has she ever touched history?

Outside, it's dark and the wind is loud. Sleeper is at the theater, Rosalie and Mother have gone to bed. Asia had also retired, but then risen again as she's being kicked and punched from the inside and can't sleep. She finds John downstairs, sitting in the lamplight of the parlor, his hands cupped behind his head. His face is a harlequin mask, half lit, half dark.

She and John haven't had a moment alone together so she doesn't begrudge her lack of sleep. She lies on the sofa, stretching out to give the baby more room. The thought of her as a mother makes John laugh—she can't imagine why nor can she say exactly why she likes his amusement. Maybe it's his insistence on seeing her as the same person she's always been.

John finds a shawl and lays it over her. He sits on the end of the sofa, swinging her feet into his lap. "Poor Asia," he says.

"You've been invaded." And then, as she closes her eyes, he tells her what he's been doing with himself.

THE NIGHT OF November 19th, he was out walking with other members of the company. They were about to perform *The Last of the Mohicans*, the curtain only an hour away. But the excitement on the street was intoxicating. One minute he was going to the theater to paint his face and shout his lines. The next, he'd spun on his heel and walked in the opposite direction. His companions called to him, but he waved them away. "I'm off, boys," he told them.

He hurried to the depot, where a special troop train had been commandeered for the civilian soldiers and was just about to depart. They'd had to wait for the governor. Without that, he'd have been too late. But he managed, with only minutes to spare, to talk his way onto the train. Several other men were trying to do the same. He was the only man to get through.

"I know people," he says to Asia vaguely, and then shows her a calling card with the signature of O. Jennings Wise, the governor's son, on the back. He retrieves the card from Asia, returns it to his breast pocket. He'd spent the next eighteen days as a soldier in the Richmond Grays, he says.

Asia has a fleeting memory of sitting on his bed at Tudor Hall, listening to him talk about the insurrection at St. Timothy's. His excitement is just as boyish as then. "The best time in my life," is what she remembers him saying. And now he's had a better.

THE GRAYS GO first to Washington, where they have enough time between trains to march on the city in a spirited display.

John's borrowed some bits of uniform, a musket, and he marches
directly behind the governor. The man next to him carries the
Grays' flag with the state motto in curling letters: *Sic semper tyrannis*. They circle the White House three times, expecting every
minute that President Buchanan will come out to salute them.
This doesn't happen. He appears to be asleep.

Wise gives a speech. When he's president, he says, he will
never sleep through an invading army. It's the least, really, one
can ask of a president, that he be awake when troops descend on
the Capitol.

They leave Washington, unheralded. The total trip takes
twenty-one hours. They ride on three trains and one steamship,
crossing through Maryland, over planted fields and plantations,
then through wild gorges and tumbled rocks. Harpers Ferry lies
at the juncture of the Potomac and the blue necklace of the
Shenandoah. "Remember Niagara?" John asks Asia. "Almost
that beautiful. Almost forgot how tired and hungry I was. Almost."

Finally they arrive at Charlestown. Rain is bucketing down,
the ground a churn of mud. They must stand at attention in this
storm, water streaming from their hat brims, while Governor
Wise gives more speeches from the shelter of a nearby porch.
Then the Charlestown city leaders make barracks for them out of
houses and schools.

No abolitionists ever arrive. It now appears there was never an
army on the way. The sortie turns social. The young women of
Charlestown insist on a ball so that they can meet the soldiers.
One red-haired flower tells John over a glass of punch that she
feels as if she's in an Austen novel.

He's given the position of quartermaster sergeant, for which
he draws a salary. He keeps a military discipline, drilling in the

mornings, helping to manage provisions in the afternoon. In the evenings, he tells stories and performs soliloquies on command. He couldn't have enjoyed himself more if there'd been actual fighting.

JOHN BROWN ASKS to be spared the steady stream of visitors come to gawk at him. He doesn't wish, he says, to be a monkey show. And yet, on December 1st, John manages to enter his cell. He doesn't tell Asia what they said to each other and she doesn't ask. But she can see that the experience has moved him deeply. "He was a brave old man," he says. "I could see him scanning the horizon for his rescuers when he stood before the scaffold. His heart must have broken when he felt himself deserted."

John has a souvenir for Asia—John Brown's spear with the words *Major Washington to J Wilkes Booth* written on the handle in ink. He swings her legs aside, runs upstairs to fetch it. Asia lies very still, waiting for him. Outside some men pass, singing drunkenly some song about the pleasures of being drunk. Irish by the sound of them, no surprise there. Probably relatives of Mary Devlin's.

She sits up when she hears John's footsteps. There's a moment of dizziness, a brief blackness before her eyes, and then John puts the spear in her hand and she feels the weight, the reality of it. John Brown's spear! Had he used it? The wood is splintering slightly. A tiny piece, like a thorn, goes into her palm. Not deep enough to make her bleed, just a prick. John pulls it out easily with his fingers.

He's kneeling by the sofa, the lamplight shining on his black hair. "Give the spear to your son," he says. "When he's old enough to value it." He's still appalled by the raid, the lives lost, the terrible idea of slaves with guns. He's glad Brown went to the gallows. But he can't help but note the old man's stoicism. He admires men of action, men who live their principles without apology or compromise. Brown is an instrument of evil, but also a Shakespearean hero.

On December 2nd, John was there, in the crowd to see Brown hang.

HE RETURNS TO Richmond to learn he's been fired from the theater for desertion. But his brothers-in-arms, the Richmond Grays, lay siege to the Marshall until he's hired again. Though he says to Asia that he's less interested in acting now. Maybe being a soldier is his true vocation. "He's wild to do it," she tells Mother and Rosalie next morning.

Mother responds with alarm. War seems more likely with every passing day. She should never have said a word to anyone about that long-ago night when, baby John at her breast, the harbinger of an anointing arm rose from the fire. She really can't bear to lose him. It makes her hysterical to think of it.

She tells him it would kill her if he enlisted. "I love my children above my country," she says. "I love my children above all." She sobs into her hands. From behind the screen of tears, she whispers the names of Frederick, Mary Ann, Elizabeth, and Henry—her sad roster of lost loves. By the time she's finished, he's promised never to go to war.

Lincoln Goes to Kansas

John Brown has shown great courage, rare unselfishness . . . But no man, North or South, can approve of violence or crime.
— Abraham Lincoln, December 1859

As Brown is being hanged, Lincoln is traveling to Kansas, braving the weather and the uncertain roads. This is much appreciated, all the more so since the audiences are small and hardly worth the effort. Few politicians come to Kansas in December. Fewer have Lincoln's national profile.

So the Republicans there are gratified, but also firmly Seward's people, their own feelings about slavery radicalized by the boil of terrorism and murder in which they've been living. They see no reason to switch to Lincoln, much as they like him. Despite this, Lincoln's chances for nomination have materially improved and their own John Brown is responsible.

In the shock of the insurrection, Seward is suddenly too extreme. Every effort must be made to disassociate the Republican Party from Harpers Ferry. John Brown, it is said, has killed the Seward presidency dead.

If Seward is too radical for the conservatives, Bates is too conservative for the radicals. What's needed now is a moderate. What's needed now is Lincoln.

LINCOLN'S PRIVATE OPINION is that Brown, while right in his beliefs, was wrong in his actions.

LINCOLN'S PRIVATE OPINION is that Brown was insane and those
slaves who did not come to his side when called were not.

xvi

The following winter is severe. Snow drifts against the front door
during the night and Sleeper has to push with his shoulder to
crack the seal of ice in the morning. One morning he can't do it,
and has to leave through the kitchen, where the stove has already
warmed things up. Rosalie, going out for groceries, takes a bad
fall and is helped home by two men, each so drunk at ten in the
morning as to make it unclear who is holding up whom. Rosalie
mentions several times the fact that, in Baltimore, the grocery
was right next door—it was a matter of a minute to fetch the eggs
and bread no matter what the weather. If this is intended to ir-
ritate Asia, it works. They have servants to go for the groceries.
There was no need for Rosalie to leave the house.

Asia hasn't been outside for weeks. The air is an arctic blast in
the lungs. The ground is too icy—if she fell she would never get up
again. She would lie there like a turtle on its shell. And yet, inside
the house, she sweats at night, the baby burning in her belly. She
takes off her clothes and stands before the bedroom mirror. She

can make out the shape of a foot, kicking out against her stretched skin. A dark line extends up from her navel. Shiny streaks of skin fan over her hips. Her nausea has never completely gone away and the only thing she can eat with any pleasure is flavored ice.

The Philadelphia house is larger than the one on Exeter Street, but it's also older and darker. Sleeper has promised Asia a better house after the baby comes, something out in the country where a child can run. In the meantime, Asia spends much of her time in the only room downstairs that gets full sunlight in the morning. She lowers herself onto the sofa. It doesn't seem possible that her stomach could swell so much without bursting.

She's there, with a book she isn't reading in her hand, listening to the fire eat itself in the fireplace when, for no obvious reason, she thinks of Hattie and is overwhelmed with dread. She rises and hoists herself up the stairs to the nursery. The preparation of blankets and toys and tiny clothes is something Asia would have expected to enjoy, but she's left it mostly to Mother. In truth, she's hardly been in this room. She pauses in the doorway, because Rosalie is already there, sitting in the window where the light is best, doing the uninspired but necessary sewing that a great many diapers require.

Rosalie looks up at Asia. "We'll be ready when the baby comes," she says and then she looks at Asia again. "Are you feeling all right?"

Since Asia first learned she was pregnant, she's had many moments of joy and anticipation. She's always loved babies. Won't it be wonderful to have one of her very own? She pictures herself kissing a round knee, singing a lullaby, sleeping in a chair with the baby breathing softly against her shoulder. But her dreams have turned strange—birds underwater and fish in the air—and she startles awake several times a night gasping for breath. Sometimes these bouts of panic spread into the daylight and then keep on spreading, like a shadow that eventually consumes the figure that cast it.

She looks now at Rosalie, whose crooked back probably means she could never carry a child and anyway she's too old and anyway who on earth would the father be? Asia wishes she were Rosalie now, crooked back and sad future and all. She's always had such a calling to the convent. Goddamn Edwin anyway for making her marry.

Asia drops into the rocking chair and starts to rock. The wooden floor creaks beneath her. Outside the sky is a pale, grim gray. "Are you all right?" Rosalie asks again and Asia stops rocking by putting her feet down hard.

"I'm afraid I'll die," she says and then, realizing that her voice was so soft, Rosalie can't possibly have heard, she says it louder. "I'm afraid I'm going to die. Don't tell Mother."

Two months back, she'd made a study of the gravestones in Father's cemetery. She'd been methodical, one section at a time. Of course, not every woman who dies in her twenties or thirties dies in childbirth. Her mind is full of angels with frozen wings.

"I don't want to die," she says. She's weeping now, which she didn't expect, and it makes her cross. She was right to think this shouldn't be said aloud. Now it sits in the chair beside her, now it starts the chair rocking again, now it has her by the throat.

She certainly hadn't planned on telling Rosalie, but, here, she's done it and really whom else could she have told? Not the boys—it would be almost cruel how ill-equipped they'd be. Not Jean, because she still wants Jean to envy her married state and join her in it. She needs the company.

Not Mother, who is surely suffering these same fears, as any mother would. Mother made John promise not to go to war because she couldn't bear to lose him. Why didn't she make Asia promise not to marry? Why does the extraordinary courage of ordinary women go so unsung? Asia would go to war in a minute. She'd come home with medals.

Rosalie puts down her hemming. "You were too little to remember John's birth. Or Joe's. But I remember them. Mother had ten babies and no problems. You'll be exactly the same," Rosalie says. She bites the thread off, knots it. Her hands are the most graceful thing about her. "I was just now remembering how you used to go flying down the roads on Fanny. Sidesaddle and faster than all the boys. I used to worry you'd break your neck. But nothing scares you."

The two women look at one another. Then Rosalie stands and crosses the room. She puts her arms around Asia. They don't often touch and this embrace can't exactly be accomplished—Asia with her big belly, Rosalie with her Richard III spine, and the chair rocking spasmodically beneath them. It's a hug made up of sharp elbows and stumbling. And yet, it's all the nicer for the awkward unfamiliarity of it. She can feel Rosalie loving her, which is not a thing she often feels. The solace of having an older sister.

Rosalie's cheek is lying on her hair. Rosalie smells of something almost like gin. "You are Asia Sidney Booth Clarke," Rosalie says. "And nothing scares you."

BY THE TIME she goes into labor, Asia's more than ready to trade in the tiresome little aches and exhaustion for the Big Agony. A false alarm brings the nurse to stay for two days and then go away again. The doctor begins to call daily. Then one morning in late March, she wakes to a stabbing pain in the back of one shoulder. The pain moves down into her lower back, where it feels like a great spiked ball, levering her spine apart. It hurts so much she doesn't even notice when her water breaks.

Joe goes for the doctor. Mother and Rosalie help her out of her soaking nightgown into a soft old one, move her to Mother's bed, where the blankets are dry. Sitting is impossible; it even hurts to lie down. She tries one side and then the other, curled in agony around a pillow.

She'd been told that her labor, while painful, would be sporadic—there would be moments to rest between the waves. She's aghast to find this was a lie—the back pain never lets up. It begins to twist, wringing her spine out like a dishrag.

The nurse comes first, followed shortly by the doctor. Everything is going splendidly, they say. Everything is just as it should be. The nurse forces Asia to get up and walk about the room. Asia is a knot of burning fury.

She lies down again. The doctor puts her on her back, palpates her stomach. She has a moment of screaming wonder—I've never actually been in pain before, she thinks—and then all thoughts leave her mind.

The nurse gives Asia a tincture of opium. It has a curious effect—Asia splits in two. One of the Asias lifts up out of her body to watch the whole debacle from the ceiling, her body spread out and pawed over like a carcass at an autopsy. The other Asia is left behind to feel everything just as before.

Hours pass in hellish torment. The doctor leaves—the room, the house, the city? Asia doesn't know. The floating Asia goes with him and sends no message back.

Night falls and the baby is no closer to being born than it was twelve hours ago. The doctor must have come back, because he's leaning over Asia, explaining things to her. There are bread crumbs in his beard.

The baby has lodged its head against Asia's pelvic bone. "All we need," the doctor says, "is for Baby to tuck its chin."

Baby does nothing of the sort. Asia is given more opium. She's rigid with pain and exhaustion, and also hungry. Her throat is raw.

Finally, the doctor grows tired of waiting. He reaches one horrid, enormous hand inside her, rummaging about, while the other bears down onto her stomach. Mother sobs quietly beside the bed. Asia feels the baby being shoved back inside and thinks they've decided not to have it, after all. This seems a good decision and perhaps the only way she'll survive this.

But then, finally, the baby slides downward, and, with a great deal more effort and pain, in a tidal wave of gore and shit, Asia Dorothy Clarke (they'll call her Dolly) enters the world. Everyone— Mother, Rosalie, Asia, and the baby—is crying. The nurse washes little Dolly and passes her over, wrapped in flannel, squinting and howling. She's wrinkled and red and hideous. Asia's first thought is that she's embarrassed to show her to Sleeper. After all that work! Her second thought is that she would die before she let anything hurt this tiny person. Dolly stares into Asia's eyes. So this is what love feels like, Asia thinks. That's her third thought. Dolly nuzzles about her breast, but before she latches, Asia is already asleep.

xvii

Dolly's an active baby, prone to runny noses and sleepless nights. Asia spends hours holding her in the rocking chair, the only light filtered in from the street outside. She's mesmerized by the kaleidoscope of Dolly's expressions—fear, worry, joy—a full rehearsal for the day when they'll be attached to actual emotions. After her unpromising debut, she's turned so pretty. Asia doesn't suppose there ever was a prettier child.

She fits perfectly in Asia's lap, her head on Asia's knees, her toes digging into Asia's collapsed stomach. When a fever lays Asia low for a few weeks, she misses that dimly lit time in the rocking chair. Becky, the nursemaid, takes over the nighttime shift, feeding Dolly with a bottle, and by the time Asia recovers, her milk is gone.

She celebrates her wedding anniversary. So much has changed in a year. Asia's a wife and a mother now and her role as sister is relegated to her lesser tasks. This might not have happened if she and Edwin hadn't grown so cold, if John weren't always so far away.

The Booths are all moving about these days. Edwin is on tour, as usual, and Joe is accompanying him, performing the tasks Edwin once performed for Father. This is a temporary arrangement as Joe will soon be leaving for Charleston, South Carolina, where he's enrolled in medical school.

Edwin rents a place in Philadelphia for himself and Mary, though they're not even married yet. Mother and Rosalie move in immediately, which makes Asia suspicious that Rosalie asked Edwin for a house. She can just imagine the way Rosalie and Edwin must whisper about her behind her back.

Rosalie and Asia have been sniping at each other over trivial, daily annoyances for weeks. Even Mother's legendary patience has been tried. Asia is glad when they leave. And also hurt. She doesn't mind so much for herself—no truer expression than *familiarity breeds contempt*. But she's surprised they're willing to leave Dolly.

She's hurt that they're willing to miss even a day of the Dolly show.

This evidence that Mother plans to keep house with the despicable Mary Devlin is another blow. Obviously, Asia's the only one who cares about the family name. She can't, all by herself, protect the great reputation of the Booths.

But she'll also soon be moving. Sleeper's found a place in the country, which he's in the process of enlarging. Asia looks forward to living with frogs and bees and rabbits again. She hopes that she'll be able to ride by then. It will be like being back on the farm only without the horrid farming.

Meanwhile, John is tiring of the Marshall Theatre. He tells Asia the city is too easily pleased by his performances and he's come to believe their enthusiasm is once again for the memory of Father and not for his own accomplishments. There are additional considerations he doesn't share with Asia. He's entangled himself with more than one young woman—actresses and prostitutes. He's made proposals he won't honor, promises he won't keep. And he has debts. He's unwilling to live on his income and too proud to ask Edwin for an allowance.

Edwin helps in other ways. He persuades Matthew Canning, a manager from Philadelphia, to take John on. Canning stipulates only that John must perform under the Booth name, to which John agrees and then does not do. He's making his move now from stock player to star. He begins to tour. His emotional attachment to Richmond, however, remains potent. Even more than Baltimore, Richmond is the city of his heart.

"MY HEAD IS full of Marry Mary marry marriage," Edwin says to everyone who is not Asia. Asia is pretending an unlikely concern over the feelings of Adam Badeau. Poor Adam—wandering alone and forlorn. Quite given up. Undone by Edwin's cruelty.

Adam is threatening a retaliatory marriage himself. He's chosen a woman educated in the French way, which he explains to Mary means a woman without a heart. Mary is distressed by this vision of marriage, so he offers a bizarre counter proposal: He'll forgo his own wedding, if only Edwin will agree to play London.

Edwin already has plans to do this so it's an easy promise to make. The woman with no heart is saved.

On July 7th, in New York City, Edwin and Mary are wed. It's a short ceremony on a gold and silver summer morning. Mary wears a crown of white flowers, her hair loosely knotted low on her neck, tears of joy dampening her face.

Few are in attendance. Not Mother, not Rosalie, not Joe, certainly not Asia—only John is there, and Adam. Adam's touched to see John's unabashed happiness for Edwin; how he throws his arms around his brother and kisses him. Asia hears this and thinks that she is glad, glad, glad not to have been a witness. Her whole family is made up of fools.

For their wedding trip, the couple rents a house on the Canadian side of Niagara. Niagara, where Asia was once so happy, is being taken away and given to Mary instead. Edwin invites Mother and Joe to join them.

Asia goes out into the mild summer evening, pushing Dolly's pram through the square. The sparrows and pigeons are hopping about as the glare of day shades into a rosy twilight. Dolly's hand has made it into her mouth. Sometimes her sucking is so loud, Asia can hear it over the sound of the pram wheels.

She's thinking about that happy trip to Niagara. It wasn't all that long ago and yet, in her own memory, she seems like such a girl. She remembers the godlike feelings she had looking down on the Falls, that sense of perspective and power. She remembers the rainbows hovering about the water by the dozens. The cup to Asia, Edwin had said, but maybe he'd never meant it, maybe he's never loved her the way she's loved him.

THE THIRD GUEST in Niagara is Adam. He says that both Edwin and Mary are taking pains to prove that their affection for him is unchanged. But this is a story for public consumption. In fact, tensions are rising. Mary is that much more sure of her claim on Edwin, which makes her bold enough to say openly to him that Adam's a bit of a bore. Adam talks and talks and talks over anyone who might redirect the conversation. He's far too interested in hearing his own opinions. What a shame he's not "like other men," she tells Edwin, "for then your friendship could be secure." Implying that since he's not, it's not.

How quick Asia would have been to take Adam's side if only she'd known. Her letters to Jean contain fantasies of Mary going under the Falls or taking a swim in the whirlpool. Every Hamlet needs his Ophelia. *When down her weedy trophies and herself Fell in the weeping brook.*

xviii

Asia tells herself that she's contented with the small doings of her own establishment. Dolly is endlessly engrossing—she has two teeth and can pull herself to standing!—and Sleeper as attentive as ever. They go to the seaside. She revels in a trip to Baltimore to see old friends. She has trouble making new ones. My heart's a poor soil for it, she says, and longs only for the dear old faces. She takes Dolly in her pram to see her aunt and grandmother. No

one mentions Mother's time at the Falls. No one speaks of Mary
Devlin at all. Mary Devlin Booth.

Asia's succeeded in driving Edwin and Mary from Philadelphia. Edwin decides he can't subject Mary to her ferocious enmity and they never do occupy the house he'd rented, leaving it
to Mother and Rosalie. Asia tells herself she's glad of it, so very
relieved, although there's no real victory to be had from an opponent who simply quits the field.

Instead Edwin and Mary move into the new and opulent Fifth
Avenue Hotel in New York City. Joe goes to see them and comes
back with tales that, Joe-like, he seems unaware will cause her pain.
The hotel is where the rich and connected stay. It has an enormous
dining hall, lobby, and common rooms, all fitted out in deep green
and red curtains, rosewood counters, white marble columns, and
masses of gilt. In order to access the upper floors, guests ride in the
astonishingly modern vertical screw railway, an elevator operated
by a steam engine that rotates a gigantic screw to raise and lower
the car.

Mary's developed her own style, which Joe is unable to describe to Asia's satisfaction, but he does say that her gowns are all
in deep blues and wine reds, and that she has a lot of them. The
hotel staff refers to Edwin as the Prince and Mary (the daughter
of Irish immigrants!) as the Princess, a particular triumph since
the Prince of Wales has also stayed there and been found insuf-
ficiently royal to take Edwin's crown. Joe talks of glittering
friends and grand parties.

It's clear to Asia that Mary is living rich. She has no idea how
hard Mary is working for this money. Mary's taken the artistic
advancement of Edwin's career on as a calling. She makes notes
on every performance. They discuss these over dinner. She is my
severest critic, Edwin says, and therefore my kindest.

But keeping his spirits up is hard work. Keeping him sober is harder work. Had she only known it, her life bears some slight similarity to that of the boy Edwin, the Edwin who followed his father through the moonlight, trying to keep him out of bars. But with less resentment and more gratitude. Mary knows that she's lucky. Still, on occasion she feels the same loneliness as that sad boy.

His growing success has one unexpected outcome—it brings Edwin Forrest out of retirement. Forrest would never admit that he's competing with this younger Edwin, as he sees nothing there worthy of competition. "Good voice, good eyes, and his father's name," Forrest says.

They perform in New York City on the same nights, Forrest at Niblo's and Edwin at the Winter Garden. They both play Hamlet. They both play Richelieu. Forrest goes to see Edwin in *Macbeth*, although if asked he would have said he was there for Lady Macbeth, being now portrayed by the great Charlotte Cushman. This is the role Abraham Lincoln once told Cushman he most wished to see her play. But Cushman and Edwin make an almost comical pair—she so much older and bigger than he is. It takes all their skill to move the audience past this visual and Edwin is sometimes unable to forget it himself. He tells Adam that when Cushman urges murder on him, he's tempted to say, Do it yourself. You're much bigger and stronger than I. He refers to Cushman as the Colonel.

Forrest is fully alive to the comedy of it. He laughs when Cushman says: "'All the perfumes of Arabia will not sweeten this little hand.'" Cushman's hand is as big as a cod. And as to Edwin, why does he scuff along the ground like that as if he's looking for some coin he dropped?

The critics are split in their judgments. One who favors Edwin says that Forrest represents "the biceps aesthetic; the tragic calves; the bovine drama; rant, roar, and rigmarole." Later, when Edwin's Hamlet is described as slightly feminine, Edwin will be pleased. That is just what he was going for.

Meanwhile, in Columbus, Georgia, moments before John is to go onstage and play Hamlet, Matthew Canning, his new manager, shoots him.

xix

John's relatively short career as an actor is replete with accidents and illnesses. His energetic sword fighting will regularly result in injury, either to his opponent or himself. In the course of a single play, he will stab a fellow performer and fall on his own sword, bleeding copiously but continuing his scene.

He will suffer a voice-threatening bronchitis, a life-threatening streptococcal infection, and a large tumor on his neck. His extremely active love life will occasion bouts of venereal disease, and one lover, cast aside for her own sister, will slice open his face. And he will carry always the bullet from Canning's gun in his body.

Asia first learns of the accident when she reads about it in the paper. One of the peculiarities of the Booth family is how often they communicate via article and review. The article has a winking sort of quality, a certain delicacy in the wording. Asia gathers that John has been shot in the buttocks. In fact, the bullet is in his thigh.

By the time she rushes to Mother with the news, Edwin has already wired. He's expected to live, Edwin says consolingly, but rather than calm Asia down, this alarms her. Nothing in the article suggested the injury was ever anything but humorous. She understands now that it's much worse than she'd thought.

How exactly it happened remains unclear. Either John or Canning was careless with Canning's gun. Either John had taken the gun from Canning's pocket and it had fired as Canning tried to recover it, or Canning was laughingly threatening the whole troupe to perform well or else, and had inadvertently hit the trigger. Or something entirely different. Accounts vary. Accounts vary wildly.

John was lucky that the bullet missed the femoral artery. He had an excellent doctor, who decided against removing it; it had gone too deep for that. The doctor cleaned and bandaged the wound, had John transported to his bed with instructions to remain there. The show went on, with John's understudy playing Hamlet. John's recuperation lasts several weeks.

A couple of months pass, and he goes to his mother's house in Philadelphia, still not entirely recovered. He visits Asia, who sees a cautiousness in the way he moves that tells her he's still in pain. He's lost weight and is less energetic than usual. But he's gratifyingly delighted with Dolly. She's crawling now. The knees of her clothes are always gray with dust and betray the fact that Asia's not stayed on top of the housekeeper.

Dolly is at an enchanting age, with round cheeks, four teeth, and a smile like a jack-o'-lantern. She laughs hysterically when John pops up from behind his hands, sobs when Becky comes to take her away. John dines that evening with Asia and Sleeper, then Sleeper leaves to go perform. John's feelings towards Sleeper have not changed. He's barely civil.

He's expected back at Mother's. Instead, much like that wintry evening many months ago, they take up positions on the sofa. This time, he's the one stretched out; she's the one with his feet in her lap, the smell of his socks faint in her nostrils. She's stirred the fire into a blaze and it cracks and snaps and sighs. She has a dull, underwater feeling. The wind outside tosses the tree branches. Their shadows wave like seaweed on the walls.

He tells her a little about the end of his tour. While he was still bedridden, the company moved on to Montgomery, Alabama, where slaves are building a new theater for Canning and his players. John caught up two weeks later, on his feet, but not at his best.

His arrival happened to coincide with a rally for Stephen Douglas, one of four men currently running for the presidency. Douglas' candidacy is bitterly opposed by William Lowndes Yancey, who controls the Democratic Party in Alabama. Locals call Yancey the prince of the Fire-Eaters. "We want Negroes cheap and we want a sufficiency of them," he says.

Politics in Montgomery are at a rolling boil—book burnings, bonfires, and effigies, militias arming and training. Yancey is demanding war. It took considerable courage for Douglas to come. He's pelted with garbage on his way to the venue, and lucky the missiles weren't something worse.

At this time, John's still loyal to the Union, his fury split, though not equally, between the abolitionists and the secessionists. Neither, he believes, has the right to threaten the nation, and one night, at a popular bar, he says so. The bar is crowded and smells of hops and ale, tobacco and sweat. John has to speak loudly to be heard. His words occasion a brief silence, then the hubbub of a dozen conversations resumes.

He's misread the room. At a table in the darkest corner, a plan is immediately hatched to kill him, a plan overheard one table over. Word reaches Canning, who contrives, with the help of Samuel Knapp Chester, a supporting actor in the company, to smuggle John out of town. "I owe Sam my life," John tells Asia. Asia tries to remember which one Sam is. She thinks he's a large, balding man whose mustache ends in sharp points. She could be wrong.

John's made this into quite an exciting story, all politics and devilry and spy-craft. But there's something hectic in his manner when he tells it, a high-pitched emotion she can't identify. He seems feverish. She wonders if he's been this way since he was shot or maybe since he learned some of his beloved Southerners want him dead. She thinks that *something* has happened and she thinks he hasn't told her what. She counts on being his confidante. This is her first inkling of a whole world of things he doesn't tell her.

She'd be even more concerned if she knew that he's begun to drink. For years, with the examples of Father and Edwin before him, John's been careful around liquor. That's all changed. Now John's the loudest drunk in the bar. When he'd railed against secession, he'd been disgustingly squiffed.

He's not drunk this evening, but whatever turn in his spirit overrode those years of caution is there when he's sober as well. It unsettles Asia just enough that she lets him go to Mother's without sharing her own awful news. Asia is pregnant again.

"I dread it with such terror," Asia writes Jean. There's been no time to forget the horrors of Dolly's birth and, as she's never recovered fully, this one is bound to be worse. She blames the nurse who pressured her to stop breastfeeding during her fever, despite the pain in doing so. No one explained to her that once her milk dried up, she'd be ripe for pregnancy again. It was a cruelty to both mother and child and not one she'll soon forgive.

Along with the familiar nausea and exhaustion, depression has wound tightly around Asia like a web she can't escape. She snaps at Sleeper and Becky and even at Dolly. She cries herself to sleep. She'd believed that John's visit would raise her spirits, but apparently nothing will do that.

BOOK FIVE

Doesn't it strike you as queer that I, who couldn't cut the head off a chicken and who was sick at the sight of blood, should be cast into the middle of a great war, with blood flowing all about me?

—Abraham Lincoln

The Election of Abraham Lincoln

But you will not abide the election of a Republican president! In that supposed event, you say, you will destroy the Union; and then, you say, the great crime of having destroyed it will be upon us! That is cool. A highwayman holds a pistol to my ear, and mutters through his teeth, "Stand and deliver, or I shall kill you, and then you will be a murderer!"
—Abraham Lincoln, Cooper Union Speech, 1860

Prior to the election of 1860, politicians in the Deep South warned that if Abraham Lincoln prevailed, they would take it as a declaration of war. His name is kept off the ballot in every Southern state but Virginia. And yet, due to a dysfunctional and divided Democratic Party, on November 6th, Lincoln is elected.

Seven states—South Carolina, Mississippi, Florida, Alabama, Georgia, Louisiana, and Texas—immediately secede and Jefferson Davis is named president of the Confederacy. This all happens so quickly that Davis' inauguration precedes Lincoln's by two weeks.

Lincoln's route to the capital starts in Springfield and goes through Baltimore, where he's expected to make a few remarks between trains. But Allan Pinkerton, charged with his security, hears of a plot to assassinate him there. Much of Pinkerton's information comes from Kate Warne, a member of a new unit of female detectives, specially formed to gather intel through "methods unavailable to men."

There is much disagreement on the way to handle this threat. Finally, Pinkerton persuades Lincoln to pass through Baltimore secretly on an earlier train and to do so in disguise. It's a decision Lincoln will quickly regret. Caricatures and newspaper columns make a mockery of his costume and his cowardice—his enemies never forget how he sneaked into Washington. Evidence of the assassination plot seems suddenly thin. All this may partly explain why Lincoln was so often careless about the possibility of assassination later.

On April 12th, 1861, the South Carolina militia takes Fort Sumter and the war begins. The first battle is essentially bloodless. Following Lincoln's call for volunteers, Virginia, Arkansas, North Carolina, and Tennessee also secede.

The killing starts in Baltimore. Although Maryland does not secede, pro-secessionist sentiment is strong there. So is pro-Union sentiment. The city is a powder keg.

On April 19th soldiers from Massachusetts are on their way to Washington to answer Lincoln's appeal. Like Lincoln before them, they must pass through and change trains in Baltimore. They are met by a well-heeled mob; not the Plug Uglies and Blood Tubs, these are men of property and standing. Four soldiers are killed—two of them shot, one beaten to death, and one hit by the storm of stones thrown his way. Twelve rioters also die.

The governor decides that the best way to keep the peace is to prevent Lincoln from routing more troops through Maryland. He orders the railroad bridges to the north and northeast burned, an aggressive move that cuts the capital off.

Troops from Philadelphia sail into Annapolis and take control. Lincoln suspends the writ of habeas corpus and Maryland becomes, essentially, an occupied land. Officials with Southern sympathies are arrested, the municipal police disbanded. Henry May, who represents Maryland in Washington, denounces the occupation—his people are in chains, he says, meaning, with no sense of irony, his white people. He is himself arrested on suspicion of treason, only to be released some months later without charges.

The first line of the first verse of the Maryland state song references Lincoln:

> *The despot's heel is on thy shore,*
> *Maryland!*
> *His torch is at thy temple door,*
> *Maryland!*
> *Avenge the patriotic gore*
> *That flecked the streets of Baltimore*
> *And be the battle queen of yore,*
> *Maryland! My Maryland!*

And here is how the song ends:

> *Maryland!*
> *She is not dead, nor deaf, nor dumb—*
> *Huzza! she spurns the Northern scum!*
> *She breathes! she burns! she'll come! she'll come!*
> *Maryland! My Maryland!*

The song was written in 1861 by a friend of one of the dead rioters. Attempts to rewrite or replace it as the official state song were made in 1974, 1980, 1984, 2001, 2002, 2009, 2016, 2018, 2019, and 2020. These efforts finally succeeded in 2021.

IN 1861, JUNE is still in California. Now a widower with a young child, his finances are increasingly precarious. His sympathies lie with the South, but he's loyal to the Union. The war is far away.

Mother, Rosalie, and Asia remain in Philadelphia. Asia's had a little boy and, at Sleeper's insistence, as an olive branch, named him Edwin. She has two children now under the age of two. She calls them her trotters. Between the nursing and the feeding and the diapers and the need to sleep whenever any brief window presents itself, she doesn't have time for the war.

The sons of Philadelphia are leaving in great numbers for the battlefields. None of the Booth men enlist on either side. The women of Philadelphia are organizing donation drives and working with the wounded at the Satterlee or Mower hospitals. None of the Booth women participate. Rosalie or Mother could do so—they have the time—but they don't know how they'd explain it to John.

John's transforming into a secessionist. He spends days, weeks—writing comes so hard to him—working on a speech for a Northern audience. He has no venue nor occasion for this speech. He will never finish nor give it, but in it he lays out his thoughts concerning the wrongs being done by the North to the South. He quotes Shakespeare. The North is robbing the South of her good name. And for what? he asks his imaginary audience.

"Why, nothing but the slavery question!"

Slavery is not a sin, he insists. And if it is a sin, it is not *your* sin, so why do you care?

"You know it is not a sin. and if it was. the Constitution forbids you to interfere with it." That strange stutter of periods. It's not a sin, but if it's a sin, it's not a sin, but if it is . . .

He is working his way towards his climax, which is, once again, the Gorsuch story. How the father of his dearest childhood friend, Thomas Gorsuch (whose name he seems to have forgotten since it appears in the speech as Thomas Gorruge), was killed retrieving his runaway slaves in Christiana.

He writes, "I begin to hate my Northern brothers." He writes, "If abolitionists held the whip, slaves would be beaten double."

These opinions put him at odds with the rest of the family. But, given his promise to Mother not to fight, no one is much perturbed. Let him say whatever he likes. What's the harm? Mother, who once angrily told Aunty Rogers that in her house the natural dignity of every person God made was to be respected, makes no such objection when the sentiments come from her favorite son.

Besides, John tells his family, the war will be over soon enough. Recollect how Lincoln slunk into Washington. Lincoln doesn't have the guts for a protracted campaign.

EDWIN ALSO BELIEVES the war will be short. Edwin's faith is in the great general Winfield Scott, who will surely wipe out secession in a single battle. In fact, Scott is already retiring and George B. McClellan taking his place. McClellan, who will conduct the war so disastrously, some will suspect him of secretly working for the South.

Edwin and Mary are still in New York, but he's been invited to star in the fall season at London's Haymarket Theatre, so they're making plans to sail for England. Meanwhile one friend after another goes to war. Richard Cary, to whom Edwin is particularly close, enlisted immediately and is already encamped outside the capital.

Another intimate is Julia Ward Howe, whose husband, although he escaped prosecution, is widely understood to have supplied John Brown with guns and money. Julia is unhappily married and a little in love with Edwin. A few years back she published an ode to his Hamlet, celebrating his beauty and genius.

> *And thou, young hero of this mimic scene,*
> *In whose high breast*
> *A genius greater than thy life hath been*
> *Strangely comprest!*

Now she is writing new lyrics to "John Brown's Body," lyrics that will become "The Battle Hymn of the Republic." She travels from Boston to Washington with her husband and other abolitionists in the hopes of persuading Lincoln into emancipation.

Adam Badeau is off in Louisiana, serving with Brigadier General Thomas Sherman. Edwin writes to Adam, and a bit defensively—"Cold steel & my warm blood don't mingle well," he says. He makes a joke of being too cowardly to be a soldier. In fact, the only thing on his mind is how a successful London season will accelerate his stardom.

Joe is in South Carolina at medical school when the first shots are fired at Fort Sumter. He manages to attach himself to one of the Confederate medical staffs working there and is wildly excited about it. When the battle ends, he deserts and travels to Baltimore.

He takes a room at the Barnum Hotel. Meeting the actor

William Howell on the street, he invites him back, shows him a large, locked trunk. With an air of secrecy, he opens it. Inside are a great many grisly souvenirs from medical school and from Fort Sumter. Exploded shells, split rifle stocks, bits of skull and bone.

Howell will shortly be sharing a Baltimore room with John, the brother he far prefers.

JOHN HAS FRIENDS among the Baltimore rioters and is outraged by the federal reaction. He and Howell fantasize about enlisting and rising to prominence within the Confederate ranks, but neither does anything of the sort.

John tells Howell that a victory gained simply through larger numbers and greater resources would be hollow, would be no victory at all. Such an outcome seems to him unsporting, insupportable, and therefore impossible.

> If we are marked to die, we are enough
> To do our country loss; and if to live,
> The fewer men, the greater share of honor.
> God's will, I pray thee wish not one man more

is pretty much what John thinks.

Edwin

i

By the time Edwin and Mary leave for England, Mary is expecting. The sea journey is a trial. It hurts Edwin's heart to see her rosy face gaunt, her appetite gone. He makes continual efforts to tempt her with one food after another, and she says that she likes being fussed over, but if he doesn't stop right now, the contents of her stomach will soon be on the deck. Nevertheless, she writes her friends on arrival, assuring them that the ten-day journey was delightful.

In London, he finds rooms on the fashionable Bloomsbury Square, an area with trees and grasses, the street where the prominent politician Benjamin Disraeli had lived as a child. Still, the air is an oppressive mixture of smoke and fog. Edwin feels it in his throat; it makes him worry for his voice. An organ grinder chooses their corner for a daily butchering of some lovely tune. Carriages clatter up and down the street. It's never quiet.

Edwin walks to the Haymarket Theatre, imagining his father a young man on these same streets, passing many of these same buildings. He enters through the columns edging the portico, goes up the stairs and onto the dark stage. The green curtain falls in folds before him. Everything he sees feels heavy with history.

He's introduced as the star of the season to the rest of the company. He's not imagining their unfriendliness. Edwin's kept his hair long so that he can play Hamlet without a wig. "Is that how men wear their hair in America?" a man who might play Falstaff asks and Edwin understands that it's not a question but a mockery. Someone is quoting Shakespeare—"'There's many a man hath more hair than wit'"—but he can't quickly locate the source. He thinks it came from a man who, were casting left to Edwin, would play nothing but ghosts.

He hasn't been bullied since he was a boy, but oh, how quickly the feelings come back. "'They have a plentiful *lack* of wit,'" he says, but only to himself.

"It was fine," Edwin tells Mary that night. His head is in her lap and she's rubbing his temples. He's relieved to see her radiant again. His cheek lies next to the slight curve in her belly that is their baby. He sees her hair coiling over her breasts. "But they think me a bumpkin. They told me that in England no one spits on the stage, as if I were about to do that."

Edwin set such value on wowing London. As the days tick towards his opening, his nerves snap and twang. He can't sleep without drinking, though drink only works for an hour or two, and then he's awake again, lying stiffly immobile so as not to wake Mary as well. He's never seen the dark come so early nor stay so late. He can see that Mary is worrying about him.

With good reason.

The season does not go well. The audiences are appreciative. He finishes each evening stepping forward to acknowledge the sustained applause. He returns to Mary well satisfied. And then morning comes and with it his reviews. The critics are muted in their praise—"good, but not great"—except when they're savage—"bobbing fiercely hither and thither like a dumpling in a boiling pot." He tells Mary that only the audience matters, and he tries to believe it, but he's losing his way onstage. He needs her and her notes. He needs someone outside himself to tell him what he's done. Mary is too advanced in her pregnancy for this. He has his first understanding of how the baby will usurp her attention.

Other circumstances conspire against him.

The popular Charles Fechter opens opposite him at the Princess Theatre. Edwin takes a week off, hoping the enthusiasm for Fechter will ebb, but it doesn't. He goes to see Fechter's Othello and dislikes it. Fechter builds his characters visually from a myriad of physical moments. His Othello shakes hands with everyone who steps onto the stage, like an overly friendly dog. He sits through one whole scene, writing at his desk, waving a feather pen about. Edwin builds his characters through motive and emotion. The constant busyness onstage annoys him. "Bobbing fiercely hither and thither like a dumpling in a boiling pot," is what Edwin thinks, yet the critics are rapturous. Charles Dickens seems to attend every performance. All London is agog with Fechter's "new Hamlet," his "new Othello."

In early November, the war back home comes to England. The USS *San Jacinto* intercepts and boards the RMS *Trent*, removing, without permission, two Confederate envoys from her. This aggressive action inflames the British public. That it doesn't result in Lincoln's second war is partly due to the patient efforts and diplomacy of Prince Albert. The rise in anti-American sentiment further sharpens the tongues of Edwin's critics. He's out one day for a brisk walk through the streets, when a young man in a shining top hat mutters in passing, "You have a lot to answer for." The man is houses away before Edwin understands that what he has to answer for is the *Trent* affair, that, even for people who've never seen him onstage, something in the way he dresses or walks marks him instantly as American.

The calendar turns to December with all her chill and dark. One morning Edwin wakes to find the windows coated with frost inside as well as out. "My legs are aching," Mary tells him and he massages each in turn, trying to stir the blood.

They've moved to a villa in Fulham, small, but charming. The air is better, the street quieter, and Mary loves it. She sings in her lovely alto voice as she goes about the house. This is the house in which their child is born, one week old when Prince Albert dies.

At the time of the *Trent* negotiations, Albert was already very ill. A pall settles over the streets. The theaters are never full, rarely half-full. The baby is small, but hearty. The villa is a little spot of joy inside the great sad city.

The more London fails to love him, the more Edwin loves America. When Mary goes into labor, he tacks an American flag on the wall above her bed. His baby may be born in England, but will enter the world under that flag.

Mary screams throughout the delivery, and Edwin's terror appears to amuse the doctor. "All perfectly normal," he tells Edwin. "Seen it a hundred times," but it doesn't seem possible to Edwin that the very first act of every single person he sees on the street, the milkman, the beggar, the lord, and the lady, is to produce a searing pain in the one who'll love them most.

The baby comes and Edwin's allowed to tiptoe into a room smelling of blood and kiss them both briefly. Then he's shooed outside so that everyone can clean up. He steps out into the icy garden. His terrors have melted away. He's a father. He's a father!

He looks about him to see what's changed, now that he has a father's eyes. There is the horizon of chimneys, all streaming with smoke, the thin, bare branches of trees, three rosebushes cut to their ugly stumps, two large crows fluffing their feathers, Mary's muddy boots, a path of white stones with old bits of snow melting at the edges, a gray scrim of clouds. The world seems very full, not a patch neglected, not a space left blank. It's incredible really, the work, the detail, God put into His creation. Edwin thought he'd come outside to smoke his pipe. Instead, he cups the cold bowl in his hand and sobs with exhaustion and relief and gratitude and awe.

He spends the dark afternoon writing letters by gaslight, interrupted twice by the baby's cry, a sound never heard in this world before. To his mother he writes that Mary is safe, but weakened. To his friend Tom Hicks, the painter, Edwin says that he won't tell him the sex, but if he paints the baby using nothing but red and makes it not a boy, he will just about hit the mark. I am right mad with joy, he writes to everyone.

Mary sees what a terrible mistake she made in wishing for a son. What a narrow escape she's had! They name the baby Edwina. (Did you ever hear the like?! Asia says, unmoved by mutual motherhood.)

BEFORE EDWIN LEFT, he could scarcely be bothered with the war. Safely abroad, he and Mary are desperate for every bit of war news they can find. He has friends on the battlefields. He carries his poor broken country in his heart.

But the British press can't be counted on for clarity or accuracy or nonpartisanship. He spends hours upset by stories that turn out not to be true. By now it's clear that the war will not be short and that the suffering will be great. The Battle of Camp Allegheny. The Battle of Rowlett's Station. The Battle of Dranesville. The terrible, terrible Trail of Blood on Ice. No sooner do they hear of one victory than the details of an agonizing defeat arrive. It's impossible to know what to believe. It's impossible to know who is winning. He has a terrible feeling it's not the Union.

Mary is struggling to nurse Edwina and failing. The doctor diagnoses broken breast syndrome. She weeps over her breakfast of egg and sausage. "I know," she tells Edwin, "that in the big world, this is such a little matter. I'm going to cry for three more minutes, and then I'm going to stop." She's as good as her word. Edwina goes onto the bottle.

Edwin travels to shows in Manchester, then Liverpool. Outside of London, his reviews are excellent, except for one Shylock and one Hamlet on consecutive nights. These two performances are described as truly painful, and the cause, the critic says obliquely, is both lamentable and reprehensible. Edwin has again taken to the stage drunk. But he sobers up, rights the ship, and is forgiven.

Everywhere he goes, he sees the vehement preference of the British for the South. He hadn't expected this. Most of the British people oppose slavery. And yet it seems that their dearest wish is to see the South prevail and the Union dissolve. His fellow actors tell him that the North is not interested in destroying or confining slavery, but merely in continuing to participate in its profits.

I'll get no justice here, Edwin thinks. And neither will my country.

Lincoln and Willie

He was too good for this earth . . . but then we loved him so. It is hard, hard to have him die!

—Abraham Lincoln on the death of his son, 1862

Edwin gains a child and Lincoln loses one.

On February 16th, 1862, Ulysses S. Grant won the first major victory for the Union, taking Fort Donelson in Tennessee and earning the moniker Unconditional Surrender Grant. Washington, DC, celebrated with bells and cannon fire. Lincoln immediately promoted Grant to major general. More celebrations were planned, but canceled due to the death four days later of Lincoln's son. Willie is just eleven years old, dying at the same age as Henry Byron Booth, another golden child.

Willie has been sick since January, his condition improving and worsening capriciously, allowing his desperate parents to continue to hope. When his death finally comes, it's more than his mother can bear. Mary never recovers. She clears the White House of everything that might remind her of Willie. She never again enters the room in which he died. She asks his friends not to visit, and since they were little Tad's friends as well, Tad's loneliness and loss are extreme. He begins to cling to his father. Lincoln conducts the war with Tad in his lap. Nighttime finds

Tad sleeping, curled up like a cat, beneath his father's desk, his head on his father's shoes.

ii

In April Edwin receives a letter from Mother, the handwriting slanted with haste, the page often blotted. It seems that Joe has disappeared.

He'd joined the Union army, but left his post on learning he was not to be immediately made an officer. It's a distinction not many can boast—to have deserted both the Confederate and the Union armies in less than a year.

He'd then come home to his mother, saying that he was troubled in his mind. When Mother's ministrations began to annoy him, John took him off to New York to work as his personal assistant and valet. Joe didn't actually do the tasks he'd been hired to do and, despite this, complained ceaselessly about the stinginess of his wages. John, he said, was a money-grabber. It ended in a terrible row and he'd stormed away.

No one has seen him since.

John has searched the hospitals, spoken to the police. Not a hair has been found. Mother is, of course, collapsing. She'd given him money, June had sent him fifty dollars, and he'd helped himself to the salary he felt he deserved from John so he's not without funds. By the time Mother's letter reaches Edwin, Joe's been missing for more than three weeks. John writes that initially he'd feared suicide. Now he thinks Joe has gone to sea.

One morning, Edwin decides to see J. M. W. Turner's final

works. He stands for a long time before each one as others come and go, their voices hushed, their footsteps tapping on the marble floors. The critics have uniformly hated Turner's whales and Edwin uniformly hates the critics so he'd hoped to see genius. Instead, he likes them no better than anyone else. All bosh and whitewash.

Springtime is here, the sun mild. He takes a long route home, through the park under an arch of greening plane trees. A line of carriages passes, a woman wiping her nose with a handkerchief, a man walking as he reads the paper, oblivious to the fact that Edwin has had to step around him. Somewhere in the city is an oak mentioned in the Domesday Book. He should find out where, go and see it. He should write to Rosalie and ask where Henry is buried. He should do a great many things. But it's too late to love London now, he doesn't want to. He came with an open heart and London has served him cruelly. So mostly what he should do is leave.

He and Mary will have a two-month holiday in Paris and then go home to New York.

Stepping through the door into the Fulham cottage, he has that familiar sense of shelter, for no other reason than that Mary is inside. Apparently she has a guest—he can hear the bustle in the kitchen, the murmur of voices. He hangs up his coat and hat and goes to see. There, at his kitchen table, Mary is serving tea to his brother Joe. "Hello, Ned," Joe says. "I like your baby."

Joe is on his way to Australia, having decided to make his fortune and buy a cattle ranch. He knows nothing about ranching, but he says he guesses he can learn it easy enough.

Edwin sends a hasty note to Mother: "Wandering boy sleeping in the guest room. Hale and hearty."

Mother's letter back is overjoyed. She hopes he'll take Joe to

Paris when they go. She hopes he won't let Joe out of his sight. She tries to turn Joe's flight into an impulsive lark. "I wish you all had money and could travel about," she says. Yet she can't stop herself from complaining that Joe hasn't written himself.

She diverts briefly to the war. She thinks that Joe will want to know there is fighting near Richmond, but the city hasn't yet fallen. Five thousand seven hundred and thirty-nine Union dead— our dead, Mother says, leaving no doubt as to her loyalties—and Philadelphia flooded with the wounded. Then this is how she closes: "Joe says I treat him as if he were still a baby. He don't think that I love him just the same as if he were."

Joe isn't quite on London time and Edwin never sleeps. Mary goes to bed with a kiss for each, and he and Joe settle in to make a night of it. It's raining now, a steady patter and, in spite of the lovely day, they are feeling London's chill damp. Edwin builds a fire and they pull two chairs up to it. The red light flickers over Joe's thin face; his cheeks, once so cherubic, have sunk. He stretches his legs, sits low and curved in his chair. All is quiet except for the fire, the occasional sizzle of a drop falling through the chimney onto the coals, and the clock ticking on the mantel. Edwin produces some brandy and the two share family stories. It begins light-hearted, but turns quickly otherwise. Soon Joe is running, piece by piece, through a carefully curated argument in favor of himself as the most aggrieved, the most abused of the Booth siblings.

"When I was at Mother's, I met Asia's friend Lizzie Markson," he tells Edwin. "And do you know what she said to me? She said she never knew there was a brother younger than John. Not the first time this has happened, mind you. Half your friends don't even know I exist. They know of all the rest of you."

Edwin has no ready excuse, but it doesn't matter because Joe is moving on. "Whenever you all were together," he says, "I was off at school. Even when John and I were at school together, he came home nights and I was boarded away."

"Did it ever occur to you that you were the better off?" Edwin asks. "I always envied you your schooling—nothing to do but study and be with your friends."

"I didn't have friends," Joe says. "I didn't have friends and I didn't have family. I was the loneliest boy in the world."

Edwin will not give up his own status as most put-upon Booth without a fight. He's astonished to hear Joe talk about his golden path to riches, the sunny idyll that has always been Edwin's life. He tries to set Joe straight, telling him about the loneliness of the years on the road with Father, the way Father's death still haunts him, how, brandy in hand, his current life is one long struggle with drink.

Joe reminds him that, at seventeen, he'd had so many teeth pulled, he'd had to wear a horseshoe-shaped wooden brace in his mouth for more than a year to preserve the shape of his jaw.

To this, Edwin has no answer. Asia, hearing some version of this evening later, tells June that they quarreled, because it suits Asia now to imagine people are quarreling with Edwin. In fact, it was all quite cordial. They just didn't in the end agree about the rank of their suffering.

Edwin turns to trying to talk Joe out of Australia. "Why not go to June in San Francisco?" he asks. "You want a family? You have one. San Francisco is just as wild as Australia."

This is advice Joe will take eventually, but only after Australia fails to magically manifest his dreams.

June writes to Edwin:

> I would not say so to Mother but I am afraid [Joe] is not
> sound in his mind . . . I do not say positive insanity but a

crack that way . . . which I fear runs more or less thro' the
male portion of our family myself included . . . I recd a letter from Asia pleading in Joe's behalf & excusing his conduct, putting it down as sensitiveness and innate modesty,
but I am afraid my surmise is nearer the truth . . .

I am sorry you & Asia are not on more loving terms—
but I feel Asia has a little of the family taint . . .

The actual subject of this letter is the fact that June owes Edwin
nineteen hundred dollars, some of which he has lost in mining
speculation and some of which he has spent on a house, but none
of which he can repay. He's explaining his profligate and unsanc-
tioned use of Edwin's money. Not guilty by reason of hereditary
insanity.

iii

In September, Edwin and Mary return to New York after an
absence of nearly a year. Edwin finds the war simultaneously
present—few untouched by loss and grief—and strangely absent.
The city is as full of gaiety as it's ever been. The theaters and
restaurants are thriving, the bars boisterous, the streets bustling.
In the midst of death we are in life, Edwin thinks. Although he
once enjoyed this same disconnect, it now seems unfathomable
that things can simply be going on as before.

The Prince and Princess move back into their rooms in the
Fifth Avenue Hotel, with the Princess now in Parisian gowns and
the royal child with a Parisian nanny. One of the splendors of the
Fifth Avenue Hotel is its bathrooms. Claw-footed tubs and flush-
ing toilets! Edwin goes immediately to fill the basin with cold

water and soap his cheeks for a shave. He's only half done scraping his face when he hears a cry from Mary. She's at the bathroom door, holding a letter in her hand. Her sweet face has gone white, her eyes big and shining like glass. "Oh, Ned," she says. "Oh, my darling! Your friend Dick is dead."

Richard Cary, the first of Edwin's friends to enlist, had been killed back in early August and the letter informing Edwin has been waiting here these weeks. Richard was shot in the leg at the Battle of Cedar Mountain. The wound was not instantly fatal, but his men were unable to transport him to the field hospital before he bled out. The letter is from his sister, who also writes that an unfinished letter to Edwin was found in his pocket. Richard Cary was twenty-six years old, two years younger than Edwin.

Edwin feels the whirlwind rise around him, the deafening sound of his own blood. "Mollie," he says, dropping the blade and groping towards her. She puts her arms around him, rocking and petting him, and he cries without restraint or control, slightly embarrassed when he straightens up to see that he's left the bodice of her dress soaked with suds and tears.

Edwin will never experience a loss free from guilt. He remembers the letters he'd written to Richard, which seem now egotistical, as if Richard, facing one battle after another, could possibly be interested in the advancement of Edwin's career. He writes a letter of condolence to Richard's wife and then, having sent it, immediately writes another. But what, really, can be said?

A second letter is also in the pile, this one from Adam Badeau, all about the horrors of the Battle of Antietam. At first this seems strange—Adam is still in Louisiana and nowhere near Maryland. But James Harrison Wilson was there. Adam has fallen in love. "I can tell no one but you, dear Ned," he writes. By God's grace, Wilson is not among the twenty-three thousand dead.

Edwin, newly sensitive to the danger Adam is in, writes back that he's praying for the God of Battles to spare his Ad. He consults with Julia Ward Howe as to what he can do for the war effort and she proposes charity performances, the proceeds going to medical supplies or to the Union's indigent widows and orphans. He does several of these.

He can't seem to go to sleep at night and he can't wake up in the morning. Mary often brings Edwina, freshly bathed, to do the deed, so his day can begin with the pressure of her tiny hands, levering herself up and over the rumpled bedclothes, up and over his body. He opens his eyes and she's inches away, staring intently into them, her sparse hair haloing her head. When she sees him looking back, she grabs for his nose. She smells of milk and powder. He holds her, kicking and laughing above his head. It's so easy to make her happy. It's all he wants to do.

Lincoln and the Emancipation Proclamation

This government cannot much longer play a game in which it stakes all, and its enemies stake nothing. Those enemies must understand that they cannot experiment for ten years trying to destroy the government, and if they fail still come back into the Union unhurt.

—Abraham Lincoln, 1862

Abraham Lincoln writes a short statement threatening to free the slaves in the Rebel States. He reads it to his cabinet. Some in the room have been waiting years for these words. Still they are stunned to actually hear them. This will change everything. The war will no longer be fought to restore the old Union, but to establish a new one. The end of slavery will be, henceforth, the primary purpose of the Union forces.

William Seward, once his rival for the Republican nomination, now Lincoln's Secretary of State, advises him. A move so momentous must not be seen as an act of desperation, a last throw of the dice by a losing army. Lincoln should announce it only after the Union has won some substantial victory.

Lincoln agrees. He waits.

The Battle of Antietam is a horror. More men are killed on this single day than the fatalities in all of America's other nineteenth-century wars combined. The dead cover the ground like grass. The mud turns red.

Nevertheless, it is a victory. Lee has been driven back out of Maryland. Five days later, Lincoln issues his ultimatum. He gives the Confederacy until January to return to the Union. If they refuse, he will free every slave in the rebelling states. He tells his cabinet that he'd promised this to God if He delivered a great victory. "God has decided this question in favor of the slaves," Lincoln says.

Lincoln and the Dakota War

You have asked for my advice. I really am not capable of advising you whether, in the providence of the Great Spirit, who is the great Father of us all, it is best for you to maintain the habits and customs of your race, or adopt a new mode of life. I can only say that I can see no way in which your race is to become as numerous and prosperous as the white race except by living as they do . . .

—Abraham Lincoln addressing the fourteen chiefs in
Washington, DC, March 1863

In September of 1862, at the very same moment as his ultimatum to the South, Lincoln is also warring with the Dakota Sioux in Minnesota. When Sioux leader Taoyateduta agreed to the sale of land in northern Minnesota, he believed the deal he'd made meant his people would never again be poor. But the monies promised did not arrive and the Sioux began to starve. Taoyateduta made the following entreaty:

We have waited a long time. The money is ours, but we cannot get it. We have no food, but here are these stores, filled with food. We ask that you, the agent, make some arrangement by which we can get food from the stores, or else we may take our own way to keep ourselves from starving. When men are hungry they help themselves.

The response was to suggest that the Sioux eat grass or their own dung. Defrauded of, at one estimate, nearly one hundred thousand dollars by dishonest agents and officials, and facing starvation, warriors attacked numerous settlements throughout the Minnesota River Valley. The surviving settlers spoke of unimaginable tortures and cruelties. Preoccupied by his other war, Lincoln did not send federal forces until early September.

The Dakota Sioux surrendered in late September after their defeat at the Battle of Wood Lake. The uprising was then criminalized. Military tribunals conducted hasty trials with none of the niceties of due process or legal representation. Three hundred and three men were sentenced to death.

Lincoln reviews these case by case, weeding out those who participated in the massacres from those who fought as soldiers. In this way, he commutes the sentences of two hundred and sixty-five. The remaining thirty-eight are hanged together on December 26th. They go to the gallows singing.

This remains the largest act of presidential clemency in United States history. Also the largest mass execution.

iv

Through a friend they met in London, Mary and Edwin become acquainted with Elizabeth and Richard Stoddard. Richard is a poet and critic. Elizabeth has recently published a successful novel, *The Morgesons*. The Stoddards run a literary salon in New York and they come to meet the Booths for the first time in the library of the Booths' hotel. The room is elegant—high windows with the light streaming in, tall bookshelves with a ladder to reach them, gleaming silver plates and candlesticks, the tapers gold, and an enormous mirror above the mantel from which, at certain angles, the sunlight flares.

Edwin feels an instant electric connection to Elizabeth. She's about ten years his elder, dressed rather drably, a small brown bonnet encircling her face. The furrow between her nose and lip is unusually deep, as if God ran His finger down it. "Elizabeth," he says, taking her hands, which are warm and soft.

"Edwin," she answers. Everyone in the room turns to watch. Everyone in the room feels suddenly invisible, as if a footlight has illuminated the couple and left the rest in darkness. Edwin drops her hands and slowly undoes the strings to her bonnet. He lifts it from the wings of her dark hair. He leads her to a chair. He hasn't taken his eyes off her. These are intimate gestures yet something about her makes him feel free to take them. Of course, she falls a little in love with him. How could she not?

Fortunately she falls a little in love with Mary, too. Like calls to like, Mary says. Edwin and Elizabeth have very similar personalities—volatile, passionate. She and Richard provide the ballast. Soon the Stoddards are their most intimate friends.

Adam Badeau provided Edwin's first entrée into New York's literati, but what the Stoddards can offer is a cut above. He's the only actor included in their salons, marking him out as an artist first and foremost. Critics begin to note the intelligence and sophistication of Edwin's audience. Now when he's onstage, he's continually aware of the Stoddards sitting with Mary in her private box. He knows that when the applause dies away, he'll be headed to some gathering where the adulation will continue, where his performance will be discussed in admiring detail. The trip to England was a disappointment, but not a waste. New York's critics see a new maturity in his work that they credit to his time abroad. It's a strange thing, to be enjoying such heady success while his country is swimming in blood. He doesn't quite know how to feel about it. His mood changes moment to moment.

Then there is Mary. It seems to Edwin that she's been a little sick ever since Edwina was born and is now a little sicker. She still comes to every play and she makes it through the late nights after, but he can see that she's exhausted. She talks more to Elizabeth about her symptoms than she does to him. All Edwin knows is that she's suffering in the places where women suffer, that there is an unnatural heat in her abdomen, and no diagnosis.

He's well aware that the reason Mary pushes herself to accompany him everywhere is to keep an eye on his drinking. He'd promised her when they married to control it. But he can't perform, not at his best, without. He sweats and shakes; his thoughts muddle. He feels desperate for a way out of his own skin. He can't remember his lines and all this is put instantly right with just one drink or maybe two. All he needs is enough liquor to get through his performances.

And maybe a glass or two after to calm him down. He begins to dislike the pressure of her hand on his arm as she steers him away from the bottles and glasses. She fails to keep him sober as often as she succeeds.

Asia notes that Mary's influence over him seems to have waned. The rest of the family might choose to believe that love is stronger than liquor. As to herself, Asia's never doubted the outcome.

EDWIN, MARY, and Elizabeth Stoddard travel to Boston, where Edwin performs for a week. While there, they hear of a brilliant physician who treats women for women's problems, a Dr. Erasmus

D. Miller. Miller's practice is in Dorchester, so if Mary is to be among his patients, Dorchester is where she must live.

Edwin buys a house on Washington Street, a cozy nook with windows in the back overlooking the slope down to Dorchester Bay. Edwin likes the house better than Mary does. He can sit for hours, smoking his pipe and watching the light play over the water, turn it silver or green or black with the moonlight spreading its shining road. Two trees in the yard go a vivid yellow, blazing like candles.

He pulls Mary into his lap, her head against his chest. Her hair falls from its knot. He combs his fingers through it. "When the snow comes," he says, "we'll take a sleigh ride in the dark. I'll hold you just this way. Your hair will catch the starlight." He imagines her ruddy with cold, a red scarf around her neck.

He thinks they'll spend many winters here. He thinks this is a house that they'll return to over the years. A good place for Edwina and her brothers and her sisters to grow. Better than New York City.

To Mary it's just a place to be lonely. Edwin's engagements often take him away.

In order to diagnose Mary, Dr. Miller must perform the very examination she'd hoped to avoid. He takes a good, long, painful look inside. Then he goes to find Edwin, standing by the parlor fire, smoking his pipe. Dr. Miller is encouraging. He tells Edwin that Mary's condition is serious, but not dangerous. Edwin's been telling himself that Mary will, of course, recover, but how wonderful to hear it confirmed. He's surprised by the physicality of his relief. His legs give way and he must sit down, but maybe he doesn't even need legs. He's so light with joy that he's floating.

"I'll return her to you in the glow of health in six months' time," Dr. Miller promises. "If she does exactly what she's told."

Edwin is about to leave for another run in New York. Mary will rest here and recover, well cared for by Dr. Miller. And Edwin can drink unimpeded. It works for everyone.

Dr. Miller's prescription is for absolute rest. No outings, no visitors. Even Mary's time with Edwina is strictly limited. The boredom cure. A good time to learn Sanskrit, one of her friends says jokingly.

There are other aspects to Dr. Miller's treatment that leave Mary in tears after every visit and make her dread the next one. She never tells Edwin what's being done to her and he never asks.

WHENEVER HE VISITS, he can see how very dull her life is. It's not like Mary to complain, but rather than improve, she seems to him to be wilting. When John comes to town, Edwin takes her to the theater against her doctor's orders. What Dr. Miller doesn't know can't hurt him.

John is playing the villainous Duke Pescara in *The Apostate*.

> *O Fortune,*
> *Thy smile still follows me, and each event*
> *Swells the deep rush of Fate, in whose swift tide*
> *I'll plunge the man I loathe.*

It all seems quite normal, to be sitting with Mary in the dark, the sound of the audience shifting about them, a cough or two from the boxes, or the silence of the audience spellbound. As he watches, he takes her hand, wonders what her sharp mind will see in John's performance.

Edwin himself is impressed. A few rough edges, he thinks, but he'll make his mark. He's worth a dozen polished, bloodless players. John is full of the true grit.

Mary doesn't disagree, but she adds that John still has much to learn and more to unlearn. This is just the outcome Edwin would have chosen, for John to be good, but not as good as Edwin.

John's career is flourishing. He's using his full name now, and his playbills say, "I Have no Brother. I am no Brother. I am Myself Alone."

His audience is rougher than Edwin's, his reviews more mixed, though mostly good. Where he really excels is swordplay. He can fight right- and left-handed. He can make it so real he frightens his fellow players. There are some who buy tickets just to see him do that. Others come for his handsome face. Managers have taken to appearing onstage before his appearances to plead with the ladies in attendance to act like ladies. On leaving the theater, John's had gloves ripped from his hands, buttons from his coat, hair from his head. Notes with unladylike offers arrive daily in his dressing rooms.

He's making great sums of money. It's not clear where it's all going.

WHENEVER HE'S ALONE in New York, Edwin drinks. His friends are increasingly concerned. In February, at their insistence, he moves in with the Stoddards. Richard puts together a team to watch over him, a schedule so that he's never left alone. Within a day, Edwin sees what they're up to. They don't know with whom they're dealing!

Edwin's been trained to give people the slip, trained at his father's knee.

Richard reasons, remonstrates, pleads, and threatens. He takes hold of Edwin, but just say the word *poet* and the picture that comes into your mind will be Richard Stoddard. He's a fragile, ethereal man. Edwin's no head-knocker, but he can best Richard Stoddard.

He shakes loose and goes on a bender. By the time Richard finds him again, several hours later, he can hardly stand and it takes two men to lift him into the carriage. He's dimly aware of a crowd of people watching. He tries to throw Richard off, but liquor has leveled the playing field. It makes Edwin furious, because who asked? Who asked for Richard to involve himself?

Attempts are made to sober him up for his performance—coffee inside, cold water out. He stumbles through *Hamlet*. One critic says: "It is to be regretted that in his present weak and nervous state he should attempt to act at all." The disappointing performance is politely blamed on ill health.

FEBRUARY 19TH: A telegram arrives from Orlando Thompkins, a family friend and manager of the Boston Museum theater. It says that Mary is improving steadily.

Another telegram, later that night: Mary continues comfortable. Dr. M says there is no need for you to come.

Edwin has passed out in his bed at the Stoddards'. He wakes in the dark with a strange fancy. Someone has just blown a puff of air on his right cheek and then another on his left. Ghost kisses, he thinks. He rises onto one elbow, but he's still not sober. The room revolves around him, the furniture moving past, tipping and whirling like a carousel. He hears a woman's voice, soft but distinct and full of desperation. "Come to me, darling," she says, "I am almost frozen."

By morning, he remembers this only dimly. A strange dream, he thinks. He can't quite call it to mind. It hovers at the edge of memory, but will come back to him fully later.

February 20th: Mary no worse. Dr. M says you should come tomorrow, arriving in the afternoon. Stay on through Sunday.

Edwin prepares to cancel his Saturday performance. But then doesn't, because a second telegram arrives. Mary doing better. No need to worry.

He's already on his fourth bottle of porter in anticipation of a dry weekend. That seems to have been unnecessary, but what's done is done. He'll see Mary soon, and he'll stop drinking then. He hasn't forgotten his promises. This is just one final indulgence.

More telegrams arrive while Edwin is onstage playing a boozy Richard III.

Half of them express an urgency. Mr. Booth must come at once.

The other half reassure Edwin that Mary is improving and there is no need for alarm.

These aren't given to Edwin until the play has ended. By then, he's missed the last train of the evening. He and Richard leave at eight the next morning. The train moves slowly, makes many stops. Whenever Edwin looks out he sees an apparition of Mary in her shroud, floating over the snowy towns and fields. Eight in the morning is almost exactly the time that Mary dies.

In Mary's last letter to Edwin, she writes of going to watch John and finding him more melodramatic than before. His great drawback, she says, is that he cannot transform. Her final words to Edwin are these:

The snow is falling beautifully to day: & the sleigh-ride you will miss. Babe talks of Papa—kisses his picture—& cries in her pretty half complaining style . . .

. . . write me all that you do & hear & above all things love me dearly . . .

EDWIN'S GRIEF IS a terrible thing. It devours him. He spends the first night locked in the bedroom alone with Mary's body, lying next to her, feeling how cold and heavy she's become. He weeps and prays to die himself. He weeps and remembers his strange dream. He begs her for just one more of those ghostly kisses.

EDWIN WILL LIVE a good many more years. He's far from done with tragedy and grief.

But two things he is done with. One is the Stoddards. This doesn't happen quickly. In the aftermath of Mary's death he depends on them completely. Richard arranges the funeral. Edwin writes daily heartbroken letters to Elizabeth, castigating himself for his sinful nature—a drunkard by eighteen, a libertine by twenty.

But then, among Mary's things, he finds a letter. Elizabeth had written to Mary telling her that, sick or well, she must come to New York at once.

Mr. Booth has lost all restraint and hold on himself. Last night there was the grave question of ringing down the curtain before the performance was half over, lose no time. Come.

Edwin believes that worry over his drinking hastened Mary's death. Her disappointment in him was so profound as to be fatal.

Two people are to blame for this: the man who drank and the woman who told. He sends an angry letter to Elizabeth. She responds with an equal measure of wrath. The friendship is at an end.

The other thing he's done with is liquor. Never after February 21st, 1863, will anyone ever again see Edwin drunk. "To take a drink—it would be as if I killed Mary all over again," he says.

Rosalie

v

Every winter seems unusually bitter in these days of war. Edwin stays in Dorchester, snow packed deep around the little house, chilled in his heart and his spirit. Mother, Sleeper, and John attend the funeral, where Mary, never to be older than twenty-two, lies like Ophelia surrounded by flowers. She wears a painted miniature of Edwin's face on her breast.

Everyone is worried about Edwin. So Mother stays on, which means they give up the rental in Philadelphia, which means Rosalie goes back to Asia's.

Asia would have liked to attend Mary's funeral with her brothers and husband, but given her unrelenting animosity towards the deceased, it was unthinkable. She seems to Rosalie to be moping. Of course, it's terribly sad, she tells Rosalie, but all things considered, Mary's lucky to have died. Since Edwin has returned to his old wild ways, nothing but misery lies ahead. Mary's better off out of it.

"Don't say that to Edwin," Rosalie says. She's thinking of a memorable line only recently read—*'Tis better to have loved and lost*. She believes it.

"I'm not an idiot," Asia tells her.

By May, Edwin has decided that Dorchester is too quiet to drown out his reproachful, mournful thoughts. He and Mother make a plan to settle in New York City. Edwin will buy a large house, one that can accommodate the whole family and be a real home for Mother, Rosalie, John, and also Joe, should they ever see him again. "Strange, wild, and ever moving," Edwin says about his youngest brother. "He causes us all some degree of anxiety."

While Edwin looks for a suitable place, the publisher George Putnam offers his fully furnished house as a rental. This beautiful home is on 17th Street, in the fashionable and prosperous Gramercy Park neighborhood.

Once again, Rosalie is being cast upon the winds. Just shy of forty years old and she still has no say in where or how she lives.

Probably if she'd kicked up a fuss, she could have remained with Asia. She's grown very fond of Asia's children—Dolly and little Eddy. But she misses Mother. And Edwin will let her go her own way without comment—that's appealing. She thinks there will be plenty of liquor in the house. About this, she is mistaken. She packs her things.

Any resentment vanishes when she walks through the door of the Putnam home. She's never lived anywhere half so magnificent. She has a room to herself on the second floor, a blue room with a window seat for reading, soft rugs, a high bed, and a wardrobe with forget-me-nots painted on the china knobs. She writes her letters on the very desk where Washington Irving once wrote "Rip Van Winkle."

Edwina is a dear little thing, gay as a flicker for all the tragedy

about her. And one child in the household is ever so much easier
than two.

Marie, Edwina's Parisian nurse, turns out to be good with
hair. One day, she offers to do up Rosalie's and the results are so
pleasing, Rosalie asks her to do this every morning. Edwin gives
Rosalie the name of one of Mary's dressmakers and soon she has
three new dresses in the same deep blues and reds that Mary favored. "You look so elegant!" Mother tells her.

A letter soon arrives. Asia is pregnant again. Rosalie has had a
very narrow escape.

Edwin's friends are desperate to keep him occupied. They
visit often, so the house is filled with interesting and accomplished people, famous people, important people. Rosalie is too
shy to speak, but now that she feels presentable in her looks, she
likes to sit and listen to the politics and the gossip. She's never
wanted to be at the center of a story, not even her own, but she
likes very much being near the center. If she stays seated, no one
sees her awkward gait. Her life is suddenly interesting. Also, the
brandy comes out. Edwin does not drink himself, but he won't
deny his friends.

One evening Julia Ward Howe, a frequent visitor, brings a
friend from Boston, the Unitarian clergyman James Freeman
Clarke. Clarke takes the seat beside Rosalie, introducing himself.
She knows who he is. She's read his sermons in *The Atlantic
Monthly.*

Like Mrs. Ward, Reverend Clarke is a prominent abolitionist.
Rosalie thinks he has a comfortable, likable face, his beard
streaked with gray and neatly trimmed, his hair long, white, and
unruly as if he combs it only with his fingers. "I met your father
once," he tells her immediately. Perhaps he took the seat beside
her for just this purpose. She stiffens slightly. "When I was a

young man in Kentucky. Just starting in my first posting. He asked me to officiate at a funeral for some pigeons."

Rosalie hears Grandfather's voice. *Is there no end to your freaks?* Is there no end to the Booth children being reminded of them? "I believe he was arrested," she says just so she can be the one to say so.

But Reverend Clarke pats her hand reassuringly. "He was such a lovely, gentle man. He read *The Rime of the Ancient Mariner* to me. The power of his voice—uncanny. He wrote me a letter afterwards forgiving me for refusing. I wanted you to know that it's a memory I treasure."

The group around him has been growing and next, at Mrs. Ward's request, he begins to describe their delegation to President Lincoln, shortly after his inauguration, back in 1861. He and Mrs. Ward and several of the other abolitionists had gone to urge complete emancipation. They'd come away disappointed. Lincoln had evaded their requests with his meandering stories. His high-pitched voice, his rustic accent—an unsophisticated bumpkin, they'd thought, too small for the moment he finds himself in. "Never have we so misjudged a man," Mrs. Ward says.

Reverend Clarke leaves then for a group at the dining table. What she can hear of that conversation is all about the war. Edwin brings her a sweet tea. He doesn't know how much she wants something stronger. They suffer sobriety together, she invisibly, he by continual smoking. His voice has taken on a rasp, but it doesn't matter as he has no desire to return to the stage. "It would choke me," he says, "to deliver one of Shakespeare's speeches."

ONE MORNING SHORTLY after her arrival, she and Edwin walk the few blocks to Gramercy Park together. She leans on his arm. He matches her stuttering step. They pass through the black gates into the green and blooming springtime. Sunshine turns the tender leaves to pale gold, dapples the pavement. Pigeons walk in the delightful way pigeons walk, with their funny, jutting heads, and the city squirrels are zestful. She takes a deep breath and everything she smells is young and green.

"I can't believe," Edwin tells her, "for the millionth part of a minute that Mollie's deep love for me is buried in her grave."

"I don't believe that either," says Rosalie.

Edwin takes her hand and squeezes it. "I believe that she who sat beside me only a few scant weeks ago is still living and is near me now. But why doesn't it make me happy to think so?"

Edwin tells Rosalie that, when they were in Dorchester, he and Mother often talked about ghosts. Mother had seen Father twice around the time of his death, though not to speak to, and Edwin saw him once, back when he was in California. Rosalie wonders what she might have said if she'd been present for this conversation. She's never seen Father herself. She doesn't want to see him, but it's hard not to be just a little hurt.

EDWIN BEGINS TO visit a New York medium named Laura Edmonds, daughter of the prominent spiritualist John Worth Edmonds. Laura operates through trance. Edwin invites Rosalie along, but the advantages of summoning ghosts are not as clear to her as they are to him.

He brings back reports of sessions in which Mary and sometimes Father and even once Richard Cary occupy Edmonds' body and speak to him through her. Mary assures him that she is still his and always will be. It was so hard, Laura tells him when she's got her own body back, not to seize you and cover you in kisses.

Father is proud of his stagecraft; Richard is at peace. Death seems to turn everyone so pleasant. Rosalie thinks that these banalities are not the way any ghost she's ever spoken to talks. But it comforts Edwin, so she says nothing. "I'm *almost* convinced," he tells her. "I wish I could banish all doubt."

With all the war dead, mediums are enjoying a bull market. John comes to visit and the brothers spend several evenings together with this mystic or that. They return to the house full of the strange and wondrous things they've experienced. Edwin's faith seems to be growing. "It's making a Christian of me," he tells Mother and Rosalie. "Not that I wasn't before. But now I *really* am." For a brief period after each session, Edwin seems almost merry. He visits the famous Fox sisters, where ghosts touch his legs beneath the table, rock his chair nearly out from under him.

He hosts his own séances under the crystal chandelier in the long dining room of the Putnam house with no medium in attendance. Rosalie reassures herself that if there are ghosts about, they are Putnam ghosts. There's no reason to think they'll want to talk to her and, as it turns out, they don't.

One evening, from her dark corner, Rosalie overhears Edwin's friend Adam Badeau, who is visiting on a temporary leave. "Touching Ned's fingers," he says, "I received a strong nervous influence like nothing I've felt before. My right hand and arm began shaking more rapidly than any human being can shake, so rapidly that you couldn't see my hand. My hand was then slammed repeatedly down on the table until I'd hurt myself. Afterwards, it assumed the position of a hand writing. A pen was put into it and marks were scratched onto the paper, but they amounted to nothing. This went on for more than an hour."

The experiment was repeated the next night with the same results. "It was very strange," Adam says. "I suppose it was just a sort of nervousness on my part."

No. It had all been Edwin, Rosalie thinks. Edwin's gift is to make people believe.

JOHN IS FOLLOWING the war news hungrily. Off in Pennsylvania, triumphant after his victory at Chancellorsville, General Lee attempts his second invasion of the North. He brings 71,000 men across the Potomac into Maryland and then to southern Pennsylvania. On July 1st, they meet the Union forces in the town of Gettysburg. Three days later, the Union casualties number 23,000, 28,000 Confederate. Lee has lost more than a third of his army. There is a day of thundering rain in which Lee is allowed to retreat. John goes grim and glum.

Edwin has returned to hardly noticing the war, so preoccupied with his own misery and his explorations of the world beyond the veil. Everything but his own grief seems remote again and, honestly, unimportant. As Rosalie comes upon him one morning in the breakfast room, sun streaming merrily through the windows, Edwin says, "I never knew how much I loved her," and then flees upstairs without another word.

When Rosalie mentions Gettysburg to him, he tells her that the war is a mere matter of bodies. *His* interest is in souls.

Perhaps this is just as well, Rosalie thinks, now that John is in the house. It's always best if he and John stay away from politics.

vi

The storm moves from Gettysburg to New York City. In its aftermath, the summer heat is unbearable. Rosalie goes about the large house opening every window at night, closing them and pulling the drapes every morning. She's sitting in the parlor, holding her book to her face in the dim and curtained room, when Edwin comes to talk to her. She closes the book with her finger inside. It's *The Wide, Wide World*, which Rosalie has taken from Mr. Putnam's shelves. She's read it before, but never in such a handsome edition. The book's main message is to meet life's troubles with Christian faith. There's also a romance, which is the part Rosalie is rereading.

"I've asked Adam to come and stay while he recovers," Edwin tells her. "He can take my room."

Adam Badeau was wounded in the foot in the Battle for Port Hudson. When Edwin first heard, Rosalie had found him oddly dismissive. She'd said so and he'd turned those haunted eyes on her. "Which is deeper," he'd asked, "my wound or his?"

"Don't say that to him," she'd said, but too late; the deed is done.

A letter later and Edwin understands that Adam's injury is serious. His foot was shattered and has had to be surgically reconstructed. He will walk again, but not for many weeks. "Ad should be with people who love him," Edwin says and Rosalie can't say no—the house is Edwin's. Besides, no one should stand in the way of friendship and charity. She does worry that Edwin will get the friendship while, as a woman, the charity will fall to her. That she'll be the one expected to play nurse.

She doesn't love Adam. He's too obsequious where Edwin is concerned. Also quite vain for such a stout little man. And will John behave himself with a Union soldier convalescing in the house? John's the one Edwin should be asking.

"The world is still beautiful to Ad," says Edwin wonderingly.

ADAM'S CARRIAGE ARRIVES. His foot is an enormous lump of bandages and bracing, and he looks older than Rosalie remembers, more lines scratched into his round red face. He has to be carried from the street to the house, put down in the parlor so his bearers can rest, and then taken in one tremendous go up the stairs to his room. John and Edwin carry him together, their hands clasped in a sling beneath him. Rosalie follows with one of his bags.

He's made comfortable, propped with pillows. His glasses are set on the small nightstand, his face bare and strange without them. Rosalie fetches a pitcher of water with ice in it and the brothers move two chairs alongside the bed so they can sit with him. The day's heat is coming on and the air in the room is very still. Rosalie can smell the medicine under Adam's bandages, something sharp like eucalyptus. John's and Edwin's faces shine with sweat from the work of carrying him. John and Adam reminisce about their meeting at Edwin's wedding. Such a joyous day, they all agree mournfully. No one could have predicted this unhappy future. "'Our wills and fates do so contrary run,'" says Edwin.

"'O God, that one might read the book of fate And see the revolution of the times,'" says John.

The men settle in. Rosalie can see what a relief it is to Edwin to talk again about Mary with someone who knew her well and she likes Adam better for his patient listening. He's had a long journey in a weakened state. He must be exhausted. Edwin has said all these same things to Adam before, and yet, he encourages Edwin to keep talking. He himself says lovely things about Mary.

Their contentious, competitive relationship is forgotten. Now that she's dead, Mary and Adam were the best of friends.

Adam's wound still needs care, twice daily cleaning and re-dressing, but he's brought a servant to do this. Randall is a young black man with wide eyes and a scar on one cheek that no one asks about. He moves about the room, preparing the basin, un-packing Adam's clothes and medicines, answering Rosalie's ques-tions in his musical accent. He's from New Orleans. He's been with Captain Badeau for nearly a month. He has four little sisters back home and it shows in the way that Edwina takes to him. Rosalie has to physically remove her from the sickroom. She leaves the men to their talking and herds Edwina down the stairs to the kitchen for a slice of buttered bread as compensation for the loss of Randall's attention.

I order that a draft be made in the said Sixth District of the State of New York for the number of men herein assigned to said District, and fifty percent in addition.

IN WITNESS WHEREOF, I have hereunto set my hand and caused the seal of the United States to be affixed.
—Abraham Lincoln

ADAM ENTERS THE house on Saturday, July 11th. The following Monday, the 13th, as Rosalie is taking a solitary breakfast of ap-ples and cheese, she hears a strange sound outside. It's a bit like an enormous audience clapping and cheering, but not exactly. It's a bit like a howling wind, but no wind is blowing. John appears in his shirtsleeves, drops of water still clinging to his mustache from his morning's shave. The noise continues. Now it's clearly human.

"What in the world?" Rosalie says.

"I'll go see," says John. She follows him to the door, where he grabs his hat and disappears. She doesn't even think to tell him to be careful; she has no sense that care is needed.

Edwin and Mother have come downstairs. "John's gone to see," she tells them. She goes to check on Edwina. "Keep her out of Adam's room," she tells Marie and Edwina's lip comes out. She's only starting to speak, but there's a surprising amount she understands. She stamps her tiny foot. It's adorable.

Almost three hours pass. The noise has receded by the time John returns. Fire bells ring in the distance and then abruptly stop. The smell of smoke is in the air. "It's a riot," he tells them. "It's a working man's riot."

New York City has just begun the new draft. There've been mutterings ever since its announcement, much of the anger focused on the fact that three hundred dollars buys your way out. The war will be fought, by design, only by the poor.

According to John, a crowd of German and Irish immigrants marched from Central Park to the Ninth District Office, growing in numbers and anger as they went. They moved like a wave or a fire, destroying everything before them, howling their fury. He saw several men break into a store and steal axes with which to arm themselves. He saw women prying the tracks of the Fourth Avenue railway off with crowbars. He saw a policeman set upon and beaten until his head was as swollen as a melon. And he saw the Black Joke Fire Brigade torch the Ninth District Office and refuse to put out the fire they themselves had started. They'd assumed the traditional waiver for firemen would apply to the new draft. They'd found out otherwise.

He's only come home to give them this report. John is eager to get back out there. Edwin thinks of going, too, but John says no. Edwin's sympathies are too well-known. "The streets are full of Lincoln haters. It's Jefferson Davis country now," John says.

Initially, Rosalie is not alarmed. The fire and the crowds seem to be moving away from the house. She still thinks of war as something tidy enough to happen on prearranged battlefields, the women left out of it, their only role to nurse the wounded and mourn the dead.

She wonders a little about John. He seems exhilarated. Is he truly only an observer? He has always had this need to be *in* the story. And she has no doubt that agents of the Confederacy are working the mob, stoking the rage, whispering a word in someone's ear, handing someone an axe. She tries to remember how Dickens described the mob in *A Tale of Two Cities*—something about a howling universe. Surely John, despite his sympathies, would never be part of that?

Edwin goes upstairs to sit with Adam. Rosalie begins a letter to Asia. "We are all well here," the letter begins, "though suffering considerably from the heat."

By ELEVEN-THIRTY A.M., the draft has been suspended. This has no impact on the rioters. John's periodic reports grow more alarming. They've torched the Eighth District Office. They're destroying the Lexington Avenue homes of wealthy Republicans, smashing their windows, chopping up their sofas and paintings, emptying their pantries. Looting stores, destroying telegraph lines. A policeman was stripped of his clothing and murdered with paving stones.

Five thousand frenzied rioters are right now swarming First Avenue, armed with pistols and hatchets. They're looking for more policemen. They're looking for rich men. They're looking for abolitionists. They're looking for Negroes. They attack the first two black men they find—a man selling fruit from a cart and a little nine-year-old boy. By suppertime, the Colored Orphan Asylum on Fifth Avenue has been sacked, the beds, the children's clothes, carpets, and desks carried off and the building now nothing but embers. The police presence held out just long enough to get the more than two hundred children to safety.

The smoke has thickened. "We should leave," Rosalie says. She's been thinking this for the last couple of hours, waiting for someone else to say it. She's worried about the fires, worried about the difficulties of moving Adam in a hurry should it come to that. Better to go too early than leave it too late. Surely Edwin has friends in the country who would welcome them.

John says that the railways and the ferry slips have all been destroyed. No one is working. "There's no one to take us," he says. "Besides, it's too dangerous to go out."

"Stay home tonight," Mother tells John and he complies. The decision is an easy one. Another storm has moved in.

RAIN DROWNS THE fires and tempers the heat. Rosalie hears it through her open windows, a calming, tranquil tapping, clearing the air and, she thinks, also the streets. Surely the worst is over. She loves the way rain smells. She has no trouble going to sleep.

But she has a vivid and frightening dream. She's on a train, the sound of the storm becoming wheels and engines. She's on her way home, through unfamiliar scenery, thick trees crowding close to the tracks and then suddenly, a man's grinning face is right next to hers, just the window glass between them. In her fright, she turns to the other passengers, only to realize that they are all dead. She's been riding in a car full of corpses.

She wakes from this in the still dark, her heart going fast. The rain has stopped and the streets are silent. She falls back asleep and in the morning, the events of the day before and the dream occupy the same space in her mind. Neither feels real.

John goes looking for ice and is back in short order. According to his assessment, the sober German immigrants have left the streets and only the Dead Rabbits, a rabid Irish gang, remain. He's just seen a group of boys—boys!—behaving with a cruelty he won't describe. "We have to hide Randall," he says. "They're going house by house now, forcing their way in, looking for soldiers and Negroes. And here we sit with both."

Randall is moved to the basement along with anything that identifies Adam as a Union soldier, though nothing can be done about his incriminating accent and wound. John and Edwin will take over his care. Randall's not to move.

Rosalie's fright was well managed yesterday. Today, her chest locks around her heart every time she hears a noise from the street. She watches from the upstairs window. No one is there. No rioters, but also no carriages, no deliveries, no pedestrians. One black dog passes the house. That's all she sees in an entire morning. She waits in a panic for John to come home with his report and then panics even more wondering what's happening while he's at home. Her flask is empty. Her hands shake.

She tries to help Marie with Edwina, reading books, building towers of blocks, pretending all is well. The day passes slowly in a strange mix of terror and tedium.

RANDALL AND ADAM have the worst of it—Randall unable to leave the basement and Adam unable to leave his bed. Adam is acutely aware that he's brought danger to the household and also that he's in no condition to help defend it. A man named O'Brien, a soldier much like him, has been killed by a gang of women and they took six hours to do the job. A girl who protested was beaten and her boardinghouse destroyed. A druggist who offered the dying soldier a drink of water was beaten and his store destroyed.

John continues his forays outside though Mother begs him not to. "I'm careful," he says. He tells her that a loyalty test is being administered on the street. All he has to do is say he's for the South and he can walk unmolested. Nothing is easier for John than to say he hates the president.

He scavenges for food and information. He gives the first to Mother and Rosalie, but has become miserly with the second. Now he shuts himself up with Adam and Edwin whenever he returns. Rosalie only knows that the police have been overwhelmed; there's no militia in the city as they've been sent to distant battles, and so, if the mob chooses murder and arson, which they do, there's no one to stop them. That there are details beyond that, details worse than what John has already shared, details so dreadful no woman can hear them—well, that's the most frightening part of all. She takes Randall his meals, both of them frustrated by the vagueness of her information, frightened that there is no better place to hide him.

By Wednesday the gangs have moved towards the wharfs, attacking the brothels and shaking down the bars and groceries for drinking money. In the afternoon, they are back, close enough to hear their voices again, only two blocks away, John says, but they turn north and the shouting fades. Still forcing their way into homes in the Gramercy Park area on Thursday, though John says the military has arrived at last. He says that a howitzer and an artillery unit just returned from Gettysburg now occupy the park. The tide is turning at last.

The riots end on Friday. Colonel Thaddeus Mott clears the Upper East Side and follows the retreat to the tenements, where his soldiers force their way in with the points of their bayonets. One group of rioters, driven to the roof, choose to jump to their deaths. By the day's end, the barricades and bodies are being removed and the streets are secure. There is no reliable estimate as to how many have died.

ADAM AND RANDALL leave under army escort for the safety of a friend's house in Rhode Island. "I'll always be grateful," Adam tells the Booths, "for the way you stood by me. I'll never forget it."

EDWIN'S SALONS RESUME, his friends emerging from their holes, shocked and traumatized. It's over, Rosalie tells herself, but what she hears makes her wonder if such a thing can ever truly end. So many buildings burned and looted, so many women molested in their houses, so many people murdered cruelly and capriciously, especially the Negroes, hunted like animals, shot down, hanged, burned alive, tortured, and mutilated with no one daring to help. Black families are leaving the city as fast as they can.

She's unsurprised to learn that the old familiar gangs from Baltimore, the Plug Uglies and the Blood Tubs, as well as the Schuylkill Rangers from Philadelphia, had raced in to take their share of the spoils. Were the riots a criminal enterprise, a secessionist attack, a racial massacre? Or something else, something more formless and ancient? People, stripped of restraint and consequence, to be what they really are. *The Town is taken by its rats*, Herman Melville will write.

The abolitionists believe that the governor, a Southern sympathizer, deliberately emptied the city of all military units prior to the draft. These soldiers then had to return, including some four thousand troops from Gettysburg that might otherwise have pursued General Lee's retreating army. A complete victory for the South, is the conclusion of most of Edwin's friends.

Hell is empty and all the devils are here.

THE RIOTS HAVE roused Edwin from his catatonic grief. He buys a brownstone on 19th Street. He tells Mother to furnish it as she pleases; he has the money for comfort and taste. They can't match the magnificence and history of the Putnam home, but somehow the riots have spoiled Rosalie's pleasure in that. There may be such a thing as too rich. She would never feel completely safe in that house again.

In small and larger ways, Rosalie is changed. At the same time that Edwin is finding his faith, Rosalie is deciding it might be easier not to believe. Her relationship with God has always been transactional. She thinks now that God would be a fool to love us, rotted as we are, and she is too proud to believe in a foolish God.

Asia

vii

Years later, when Asia feels quite desperate to hear someone, anyone, say something nice about John, she'll discover a newspaper article in which Adam Badeau's been asked about this time with the Booths, and about John in particular. John saved my life, Adam will say. He treated me with great gentleness. He gave no indication of deep Southern sympathies.

Reading this, Asia will manage to forget what John once told her about these same events—"Imagine me forced to save that Union soldier with my rebel sinews!" And also how they'd both disparaged Adam as a "deceptious mortal" on account of his homosexuality. In this article, Adam is being kind when Asia has all but forgotten what kindness feels like. It will make Asia weep for an entire afternoon.

HIDING HIS SOUTHERN sympathies is something John seems increasingly less inclined to do. Sleeper and John arrive in Philadelphia on the same train. The minute they enter the house, Asia can feel . . . something. Sleeper is curt. One quick kiss and he's in the kitchen asking for something to eat. John is gay in his new feverish, unpersuasive way. Asia pretends not to notice this palpable tension.

That night while she and Sleeper are lying next to each other, he tells her that while on the train he'd made a joke about Jefferson Davis. John had seized him by the neck and flung him side to side like a dog with a sock. He shows her his bruises. He asks her to rub his shoulders. Under her fingers, his muscles shift about like rocks.

When they're alone, she asks John about this. "I only come here to see you," he says. And in magnificent understatement, "Clarke and I, we are as the antipodes."

The Clarkes have moved again, out of the country, which Asia decided she hated, and back into Philadelphia, to a house on 13th and Callowhill. Sleeper's an enormously popular player by now. His favorite role is Timothy Toodle and he's gone off to do that when this conversation takes place. The children have scattered books and shoes and toys about the parlor. Asia is tidying up while John starts the fire. The wood is too green and the room gets smoky. The night is dark and so dry that the packed snow whistles in the wind.

Asia and John sit by the fire. Asia's hands are cold. She holds them close to the flames. "If you feel so strongly, why don't you go and fight for the South?" Asia asks him. "Every Marylander worthy of the name is doing so." She regrets the words the moment she speaks them. She has no desire to see John go for a soldier.

There's a long pause before he answers, so she feels she's shamed him. He stares into the fire, which is burning more cleanly now, though the smell of smoke lingers. His face is thin and shadowed.

"If I had only my arm to give, I would. But my brains are worth twenty men, my money worth a hundred," he says. "I serve the South best as I am. Thanks to Edwin and his friends in high places, I have General Grant's pass. It's a passport to anywhere. Little does Grant know what a good turn he's done the South."

His meaning is just coming clear to Asia. John is a spy, a smuggler, a blockade-runner. Any one of these carries the penalty of death. She hadn't known this. She doesn't want to know it. She begs him to stop, but he sits, smiling at her, shaking his head. She reaches across the distance between their two chairs to take his hand, surprised by its heat and hard calluses. She runs her thumb along them. "Many nights of rowing," he says in answer to the question she doesn't ask. He tells her that his thigh-high boots hide pistol holsters. He's chosen his shabby coat—he who once was considered quite the dandy—deliberately to keep attention off him. His hat has a brim that covers his face. Against his promise to his mother, he's joined the Knights of the Golden Circle, a fanatical group dedicated to raising an army, conquering Mexico, and making it part of a slaveholding Confederacy.

Upstairs the baby cries out. Asia feels a mother's disappointment. She should have slept another hour at least. She hears Becky's footsteps going in to her. The milk comes prickling into Asia's breasts and if she doesn't go up, her dress will soon be soaked with it. She stands. "Please don't go back to the South," she says.

He sounds surprised. "Why, where else should I go?" He begins to sing softly—"in 1865, when Lincoln shall be king."

"That will never happen," Asia says.

"That will never happen," he agrees.

The baby's cry is loud now and heartbroken. Becky's unable

to soothe her and Asia worries she'll wake the others. She hurries up the stairs.

She'll share none of this conversation with her husband. If she must choose between the two, the choice is easily made. Booths are Booths above all. She'll share none of this conversation with her other brothers, a decision that will haunt her the rest of her life.

Lincoln and Shakespeare

Some of Shakespeare's plays I have never read, while others I have gone over perhaps as frequently as any unprofessional reader. Among the latter are Lear, Richard Third, Henry Eighth, Hamlet, and especially Macbeth. I think nothing equals Macbeth—It is wonderful.
　　　　—Abraham Lincoln to the actor James H. Hackett, 1863

John T. Ford has renovated his theater in Washington, DC, hiring James Gifford, the same architect who built Tudor Hall. In November of 1863, at the express invitation of his good friend Ford, John Wilkes Booth does a two-week engagement there. Abraham Lincoln goes to see him play Raphael Duchalet, Europe's greatest sculptor, in *The Marble Heart*. Among the guests in his box that night is Mary Clay, the daughter of the US ambassador to Russia. She begins to feel that Booth is directing some of Duchalet's threats and oaths directly at the president. She mentions this to Lincoln. "He does look pretty sharp at me, doesn't he?" Lincoln replies.

Booth credits Lincoln with this one thing—that he loves the theater. In fact, Lincoln often uses it as an escape from the constant entreaties and interruptions of his daily life. His wife complains that he's not watching the play at all.

On this occasion, he applauds heartily. He sends Booth an invitation to visit the White House, an invitation that is rebuffed.

Lincoln hardly notices. He has other things on his mind. Ten days later he'll be delivering the Gettysburg Address.

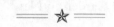

viii

"I'd rather have the applause of a Negro," John says later that same night. He glories in saying such things right in the heart of Lincoln's Washington. He's in a bar, drunk, and everyone around him is drunk. The cigar smoke is thick as fog.

There is at least one Lincoln lover present. "You'll never be the actor your father was," a man with a great bushy red beard says.

John sets his glass onto the table. "I'll be the most famous man in America," he tells them all.

Meanwhile . . .

Edwin's popularity continues to grow. The sculptor Launt Thompson has done a bronze of him as Hamlet. Edwin tells Adam the result is worthy of Mike Angelo. Soulful photographs, his hair long and loose about his shoulders, are sold in the New York shops, the purchasers largely but not entirely female.

He also plays Washington, DC, not Ford's Theatre, but Grover's. Lincoln sees John once. He goes six times to see Edwin. Secretary of State William Seward gives a dinner in Edwin's honor. The conversation is so lively, so congenial, that when Seward walks him to the door, he says he hopes for many such occasions. He hopes for a long friendship. His nineteen-year-old daughter, Fanny, has the obligatory heart-flutter in response to Edwin's eyes. She retires to her room to write about them at length in her diary.

Edwin and Sleeper have gone into business together. They've bought the Walnut Street Theatre in Philadelphia and then, adding in a third partner, the manager William Stuart, they've taken the lease on the Winter Garden in New York. Asia is becoming very rich as a result.

She's also seeing more of Edwin, hearing his adventures and triumphs. She's desperate to return to the old intimacy they once had when he was the brother she loved the most. Mary's been dead for months. There's no reason the rift should continue.

But Sleeper is always about, behaving as if Edwin has come to see him. When Sleeper leaves the house, Edwin usually goes along. They are planning on purchasing a third theater in Boston. They are full of plans. "I can't give Edwina back her mother," Edwin says. "But I can make her an heiress."

Although he talks of money, Asia can see that the Winter Garden is a labor of love. For too long, the New York audiences have been fed the thin gruel of Laura Keene's melodramas when they need the hearty nutrition of Shakespeare. Edwin's planning to do *Hamlet*, and the theater is undergoing a long and expensive renovation, scenery and costumes commissioned by real artists, floating footlights, velvet seats, until it becomes the perfect setting, from tip to toe, from greenroom to gallery. Sleeper is mostly focused on the Walnut. The Winter Garden is for Edwin. Neither suggests including John in these profitable ventures.

As EDWIN RISES, John sinks. He is drinking heavily, fighting with people in saloons, whorehouses, and onstage. He's getting a reputation as volatile and violent, and it's harder for him to get bookings. There are several actors, Edwin Forrest among them, who refuse to perform with him.

He takes a tour to Leavenworth, Kansas, in the middle of winter and is trapped by a blizzard on his way back East. Forced to travel for four days by horse-drawn sleigh through frostbite weather, he becomes seriously ill. In Louisville, Kentucky, he collapses mid-performance.

He recovers, but his general condition is weakened. Specifically, he's left with a persistent bronchitis, which some are whispering will mean the end of his stage career. It's possible that, though he can still manage a single performance, his voice will never again survive the night after night after night. I'll be fine either way, he tells Asia. The theater has never mattered to him the way it does to Edwin. Besides, he can make more money elsewhere. He's started his own enterprise—the Dramatic Oil Company—and is buying up oil wells.

ASIA SHOULD HAVE known it would be Edwin to raise the Booth name again. Look at him, the coveted guest of the most consequential men in Washington, admired by the president himself.

Look at her, married to his business partner and closest friend. She begins to make frequent visits to the house in New York, intent on reestablishing her own centrality in the family. She's a Booth through and through and no one should forget it. It's insupportable that Rosalie should know more about family matters than she does.

ix

June has left California for good, selling his house and quitting his theater. His finances have forced him back on the road—he's been touring since May. He, too, makes many visits to the New York house, one of the family again after so many years away. His daughter, whom they call Molly, is a lively addition. A hoyden, a handful. Asia adores her niece. She reminds Asia of Asia.

These visits, with her children (all but Joe) and her grandchildren under the same roof, may be the happiest time in Mother's long and difficult life. She loves to walk into a room and find a group there, planning an outing or laughing about something one of the children has said. Edwin's house comfortably holds them all and they're gathered there one day in August of 1864, expecting John, who is late.

When he finally arrives, his condition is shocking. He staggers through the door and faints dead away in the entryway, his head hitting with a bang on the gleaming wooden floor. June picks him up too easily. He's thinner than Asia has ever seen him.

Edwin runs for the doctor while the rest of the family crowds around his bed. Asia thinks that he looks like a beautiful marble statue, a gravestone angel. This image takes strong hold of her— her brother's pale, dead face. Since she'll never actually see him dead, this is the picture she'll carry. It will come to feel later as if she saw his ghost while he was still alive.

When he comes to, he's in terrible pain. He's suffering from an infection—St. Anthony's fire, or erysipelas—in his right elbow as a result of one of his vigorous sword fights. "For God's sake, die!" his exhausted opponent, Richmond to his Richard, had told him. "Either you die or I will!" His arm is a bright, angry red, the skin raised. He's running a high fever, has chills and shakes. The doctor comes and cuts his arm open to allow the pus to drain. The doctor doesn't say so, but the possibility of amputation is on everyone's mind.

Instead, under his mother's care, John improves quickly. Soon enough, it's clear that both his arm and he will survive. Still he's weak and bedridden for another three weeks. Asia enjoys visiting the sickroom, seeing John turn into the little boy he once was. She reads him plays and poetry, makes him lemonades and teas, keeps his cut clean and dry.

Now he's the sun around which the family revolves, everyone acutely aware of how close they came to losing him again. He seems tired, but contented, two states he seldom visits. He's always had an easy, comfortable friendship with June, and Edwin is anxious that everything that can be done is done. His sisters make a pet of him, his nieces crowd his room for as long as they're allowed. A rocking chair is brought into the bedroom for Mother so that she can sit in the dark, watching him sleep. Such a rare gift to know exactly where he is.

The day he comes down to breakfast is celebrated with constant fussing at him to eat more. He used to be so hale.

He spends his first day of returned health writing letters to various young women who have probably missed hearing from him. It takes the whole of the day and much of the night as he wants these to rhyme. June is amused by his agonies of composition until John wakes him for help with spelling and word choice. But in the light of morning, even that seems funny. All goes swimmingly for three whole days. And then John and Edwin have a terrible fight.

It starts at breakfast with everyone there to witness it. John's chair has been pushed into a little puddle of sunshine as Mother wants him to put some color back in his cheeks. He blinks sleepily. Molly has begged the cook for a bread pudding with currants and the kitchen is filled with the familiar smell of scalded milk. They are all tucking in when Edwin mentions that he plans to vote for Lincoln's reelection. He's never voted in an election before. He's proud of this remarkable display of civic responsibility.

John's response is immediate. "You'll see Lincoln crowned king and have only yourself to blame."

Edwin started the fight. John escalates it.

"That baboon has no right to the presidency." John is already shouting. He's not well enough for such passions. Asia puts a hand on his shoulder and he slaps her off. "His pedigree, his coarse, low jokes, his vulgar similes . . ."

Edwin starts to respond and John raises his hand. He's not done yet. He will *not* be interrupted. "And he's a mere puppet of the North. Greater minds than his play on his overweening vanities. People who want to crush out slavery by any means—robbery, rapine, slaughter, and bought armies—makes no difference to them. People without honor and goodness." It's a speech. Clearly he's given it before.

Rosalie rises and takes Molly and Edwina out of the room. They do not go silently. "No," Molly says firmly, "I want to see," but Rosalie has the sleeve of her dress gripped in her hand and is not stopping. "No!" says Molly.

Edwina echoes her. "No! No!"

"You're distressing Mother," June says to his brothers. He's the oldest, but he's been away so much. It's Edwin's house and he's used to being the oldest, Rosalie clearly not counting. John is the only son here with no standing beyond the power of his conviction.

"I so love having you all visit," Mother says, her voice trembling, her eyes red. Her gray hair hasn't been done up yet this morning. She looks disheveled, an elderly waif. "We've had such a lovely time."

That should have been enough to stop them, but Edwin and

John don't even seem to notice. They've risen from their chairs and stand, staring each other down. John is still holding his fork. He points to Edwin with it. The tines circle menacingly in his hand. "'Tis the time's plague when madmen lead the blind,'" he says.

"'The fool doth think he is wise,'" Edwin answers.

Edwin's never been a brawler. But John's only barely able to use his right arm. Asia can't guess how this will end. However it does, it won't be good. She is a mother of three. Breaking up fights is practically her profession.

She moves into the space between her brothers, forcing them apart. There is a momentary tableau. She sees the stubble on Edwin's chin, the shadows under John's eyes. She smells the stale smell of sickness still on John's breath. Then John drops his fork onto the table, where it hits his plate with a loud crack and bounces onto the floor. He leaves the room.

Asia wonders what just happened. Surely John would never have stabbed Edwin. Suddenly her intervention seems unnecessary and she wishes she hadn't done it. It's almost as if she doesn't trust her brothers. Everyone sits back down and pretends to go on eating. No one speaks.

Whatever pretense of peace was achieved proves temporary. Later that morning, the quarrel starts again. Asia hears it, the voices, not the words, rising from the parlor. By the time she's downstairs, Edwin has ordered John from the house. In an instant, John's packing his bag. In an instant, he's out the door.

June runs after him. Asia watches from the window. They're three houses down, talking together, June's arms in constant motion, John hunched stubbornly into himself.

The weather is changing, the air dry, but crackling with electricity. Asia feels her hair lifting, on her arms and neck. In the distance, lightning stretches in large white sheets. She can smell a storm coming. There's a yowling right under the window, that strange unearthly call of a cat in heat. It feels all portentous to Asia, but of what she couldn't say.

John walks away. June comes back to the house.

Asia meets June at the door. "He says," June tells her, "that if it weren't for Mother, he'd never set foot in Edwin's house again. He says he's going to leave the North entirely and live in Virginia. He says that he knows none of us agree with him, but he really can't bear having his dearest principles denounced as treason inside his own family. He says every day here is a new stab in his heart.

"And he's finished with anyone who takes Edwin's side."

Asia won't take Edwin's side. But she won't side against him either. There must be a way she's allowed to love them both.

JOHN DOESN'T GO live in Virginia. Weeks pass. He and Edwin put a flimsy patch on their wounds. He continues to visit his mother, saying as little to Edwin as possible. Edwin tries to reach him with talk about acting, a subject on which Edwin can be encouraging, even admiring. "You'll do great things," Edwin tells him. "You've got the true grit."

John's not interested. "It's not in my stars," he says.

x

Edwin comes to play Philadelphia and he and Asia finally have the intimate, private conversation she's been longing for. Edwin has met a woman here. A woman so sweet, he tells her, that he can only imagine Mary has sent her.

Perhaps he's feeling guilty. Mary's only been dead a year and a half. Asia's the last woman to defend Mary, but really! Wasn't that the world's great love affair?

The new woman is Blanche Hanel. Her father is a wealthy shipping agent and a patron of the arts. She's tall for a woman, about Edwin's height, and blond, which is new for him. He asks Asia to call on her, which Asia does. Blanche has none of Mary's disqualifications. She also has none of Mary's sharpness of mind.

She makes up for being less smart by being more rich.

A flirt, is what Asia thinks, but good-hearted and obviously smitten. Asia won't risk opposing another of Edwin's choices. If she makes him happy, then Asia has no objection. Edwina should have a mother. It will probably work out very well.

Edwin's old friend and new enemy Elizabeth Stoddard is not so generous. Having written passionate odes to Mary's death and Edwin's grief, having called him a noble soul and sensitive genius, she feels she's been made a fool. She writes that she pities the woman he marries next, whomever she is, as Edwin is incapable of fidelity and sincere feeling. Only when drunk, she says, did he manage to be even half a man.

AROUND THIS SAME time, Edwin has a curious adventure. He's in the depot in Jersey City, waiting for the train to Philadelphia, when he sees a young man inadvertently jostled off the platform into the space between two moving train cars. Edwin is able to grab the young man by the collar of his coat and hoist him back to safety before there is any injury.

The young man recognizes him. "Thank you, Mr. Booth," he says, with a bit of an awestruck stammer. "That was a narrow escape."

"Not at all," Edwin tells him and then his train arrives and he boards it. It wasn't, Edwin thinks, really a narrow escape as the train was moving so slowly. He gives the matter no further thought.

xi

In late November, the Booths are all back in New York again. The three brothers are to appear together at Edwin's Winter Garden Theatre in *Julius Caesar*. This has been long scheduled, but after the Great Fight, Asia worried John would back out.

It's to be a one-night-only event, a benefit performance. All profits will go to a fund to raise a statue of Shakespeare in Central Park. They've never all been onstage together before. They never will be again.

Asia comes to the brownstone, bringing her three children, Dolly, Eddy, and Adrienne, and returning June's daughter, Molly, after an extended visit. Molly's little cousins are mesmerized by her. Those who can walk follow her everywhere—raids on the kitchen and rampages about the house. It's lucky they're no longer at the Putnam place. The potential damage to Washington Irving's desk is dreadful to contemplate.

John arrives soon after. He and Edwin do their best to avoid open warfare. From John's perspective, there's plenty of cause. Lincoln recently won reelection, the first president to do so since Andrew Jackson in 1832. Never in John's lifetime have eight whole years been given to any one president. It's unnatural. It's a monarchy.

Adam Badeau, now fully recovered, has been promoted to Grant's staff and is helping Grant conduct the Siege of Petersburg. This is very close to John's beloved Richmond and a poor thank-you for John's kindness to him.

And Edwin has taken the best part for himself.

He will be Brutus. June will be Cassius, and John, Mark Antony. Edwin Varrey, from the original cast of Laura Keene's *Our American Cousin*, is playing Caesar.

This is the event of the season. The theater sells out instantly, some seats, having sold for the unheard-of price of five dollars, are scalped for as much as twenty. Several policemen are on duty to handle the crowd before the doors open. It's all too much for Rosalie, who takes one look, says she feels ill, and goes straight back home in the carriage.

Asia has a seat in the orchestra. The theater is stifling, especially coming in from the New York November. People are crammed into every available space, some sitting, many standing, and Asia has to force her way forward, her cheeks burning.

She struggles out of her coat, so crushed on both sides that she strikes the hat off the elderly woman next to her when she shakes her arm out of her sleeve. While apologizing, she identifies herself as the Booth sister. It has the desired effect. "Oh, my dear, we're just so excited about this evening," the woman says. She's wearing choking amounts of lilac perfume.

Mother is seated above in a private box. Asia can't see her face, but there is her glove on the rail. The theater darkens and the play begins. The woman next to her is whispering and Asia is just about to ask her to stop when she does. Her brothers come onstage in the second scene, strolling in together. The play pauses as the audience shouts and claps. If only Father could have been here. He could have played Caesar.

John has shaved his mustache just for the performance. "He looks like a young god," Asia overhears someone behind her say, someone with a strong Southern accent. She wonders if Edwin is feeling the challenge of comparison. At the end of the first act, her three brothers emerge from behind the curtain. They bow to the audience. They bow to their mother. The bravos are deafening.

Act 2 begins. Scene 2. Caesar's House. Varrey has only just told the audience that a coward dies many times before his death when fire engines are heard outside. Although more than a year has passed since the riots, they're in no way forgotten. The people around Asia begin to stir uneasily. No one can leave quickly, it's much too crowded. Asia stands to look towards the door and when that doesn't work, she climbs onto her chair. She can see a scrum at the back, like a school of fish trying to force its way through too narrow a channel. The smell of smoke penetrates the lilac.

The woman next to her has risen and is standing in front of Asia's seat, blocking her from getting down. Onstage, Varrey steps forward. "Please stay calm," he says. "All is well," but how can he know that? "Please! Keep to your seats." More people in Asia's row are pushing past her into the crowded aisle.

"Please let me down," she asks the top of the top hat now standing in her way. "I have to help my mother." She has a vague plan to go onto the stage instead of towards the doors, find her brothers, exit with them. But Mother is in the wrong direction. She remembers Father talking about a long-ago theater fire in Richmond. Nearly a hundred people killed, most of them in the boxes and above as the cheap seats were nearer the doors.

The crush at the back has turned to pandemonium. Asia can see this clearly from her high vantage point, the shoving, the shouting. A theater critic is knocked to the ground and writes later of the forest of legs, the trampled furs and hats. Edwin joins Varrey on the stage. "There is no fire," he shouts. "There is no fire." His voice is loud enough in a silent theater. Not loud enough for this one. Asia thinks she's the only one to hear him.

A man runs onstage with a large flat piece of scenery—a Roman column. On the back he's written in enormous red letters Edwin's exact words—*There is no fire*. He hoists it above his head. "Oi, Oi!" he shouts.

A squad of policemen have managed to hold their ground against the fleeing crowd. One of them calls out, "There's no danger. The fire is already out. It's only a drunken man! It's only a drunken man." His words are a pebble tossed into water. The panic subsides, first in the small circle around him and then in expanding rings. The words finally reach Asia. "Only a drunk. Only a drunk."

It takes half an hour to completely restore order. Asia is far too hot now, sweating under her dress collar. The man in the top hat has helped her down. The people who made it to the aisle now step on her feet as they return. The play resumes.

Julius Caesar is not a play often performed. It's widely thought to read better than it plays and it has an insufficiency of female roles. So when, during his most famous speech, Mark Antony adds a line, few notice. *Sic semper tyrannis,* Antony says. The motto of Virginia. It makes sense in the context. Asia doesn't even wonder if that's the way Shakespeare wrote it.

The applause at the end is thunderous. Asia claps until her palms sting. The Booths come back and come back again. They step forward individually. The applause for John is louder than that for Edwin or June. The Booths step forward together. They raise their hands towards their mother in her box and she, too, is applauded. The next day's reviews will liken her to Cornelia, the Roman mother whose sons were her jewels. How proud she must be, the papers will say, with such jewels as these. No one will note how badly things went for Cornelia's sons. Or that she also had daughters.

Two events mar the evening's end, though Asia only hears of them the next day. William Stuart, the stage manager, is responsible for both. Stuart is the personification of bonhomie. Also of duplicity. First, he neglects to invite John or June to the after party. By the time Edwin realizes, June has already left, escorting Asia and Mother home. He begs John to come. An oversight, Edwin says. Please come.

But John leaves. William Stuart has never liked him and the feeling is mutual. He pretends to believe that Edwin is not behind this insult.

On the following evening, Edwin is due to begin a run as Hamlet. Stuart has posted the playbills all over the lobby. BOOTH, they say. Edwin finds Stuart to object. "There are three Booths."

"After your Hamlet, there will only be one," Stuart tells him. In any event it's too late. John and June have already seen them.

IN 1867, THE uninsured Winter Garden will be destroyed by fire, along with all the carefully commissioned sets and costumes. Edwin's wardrobe alone is valued at sixty thousand dollars and all of it ash. "It gets me out of my contract with Stuart," Edwin will say. "I won't complain."

FROM THE NEWSBOYS that night, they learn that the fire in the Lafarge Hotel next to the theater was set by a Confederate agent.

From the newspaper next morning, they learn it was only one of nineteen fires set that night in a plot to overwhelm the fire department and burn New York City to the ground. As a plot it was better in theory than execution. All nineteen fires were easily extinguished.

Next morning, while Edwin sleeps in after his late night, Asia, June, and John take the children out front to play in the snow. June and John pelt each other with snowballs. The children demand a snowman.

As they comply, June and John talk about last night's performance. No one says so, but Asia feels an undercurrent of resentment that when all three are onstage together, Edwin is understood to be the star, even when John gets most of the applause, even when June is the novelty on the New York stage where Edwin is a fixture.

They get to the panic about the fire. June says, "If this were California, the arsonists would have been strung up without a trial."

"They're just trying to show Northern cities one fraction of what's been done to cities in the South," John says. "Little enough return for what's happening right now in the Shenandoah Valley."

The family is increasingly worried about John. He's become monomaniacal. He rejects any news of Northern victories. "I haven't heard that," he'll tell June when faced with evidence as if, since he hasn't heard it, it can't possibly be true.

"It's a family quarrel," June says. "North, South—we're all still family. We quarrel, we make it up. Don't drive yourself mad over it."

Here's the thing about John. You can talk to him. But you can't make him listen.

Still since it's June and not Edwin saying these things, there's no reason to spoil the day over it. Asia goes inside to find a hat for the snowman. When she comes back, Molly is chasing John with a handful of snow, the other children shouting, laughing, and dancing like monkeys.

xii
———

The next night the Winter Garden Theatre sees the debut of *Hamlet* with Edwin in the title role. The play runs for two weeks, three, eight, until Edwin feels the exhaustion of playing the same part, night after night. He begs for a change, but Stuart says no, the play is still selling out. This run, which will last one hundred nights, is the final making of Edwin's name. Ever after, he will be America's Hamlet. Edwin refers to this as "my terrible success."

It was a shame Shakespeare couldn't see him, the critics write, he was so exactly what Hamlet ought to be. In outer aspect composed and gentle, inwardly filled with a fierce passion, Booth's Hamlet inspired a sort of worship. It was more than a calling, almost a cult. One morning little Edwina is offered an omelet. "That's my daddy," she says.

The role of Claudius is played by Samuel Knapp Chester, the same man John credited with saving his life in Montgomery. Night after night, Chester stands onstage with Edwin, saying nothing beyond his lines. "'God hath given you one face, and you make yourselves another,'" Hamlet tells Ophelia, and no one knows better than Chester how true this is.

Unbeknownst to anyone else, John has made repeated attempts to enlist Chester in a plot he is forming against the president. It's to be a kidnapping. Lincoln will be bundled into

Richmond, Virginia, and held there until he can be traded for Confederate prisoners.

John has applied every pressure at his disposal on the frightened, but unyielding, Chester. Chester need only show up with the carriage. He never even has to see Lincoln. John is asking so little.

"I have a family," Chester says, but so does John; this excuse holds no water. John insists. He cajoles. He threatens.

In the face of Chester's intransigence, he's sorry to have ever divulged his plans. He holds a gun under Chester's chin. "If you mention this to anyone," John says, "I will send Confederate agents after you. They will hunt you down. Wherever you hide, they will find you. *And* your family." Chester feels the barrel of the gun pressing into his neck. He finds it persuasive. He regrets having saved John's life, but cannot say even that to anyone.

EDWIN GETS A letter from Adam Badeau. Adam is in the middle of his second great heartbreak. His intimate friend, James Wilson, has cut him off, alluding to a single night Wilson now regrets. Adam blames jealous fate for this, "jealous fate which cannot bear that men should be so purely happy, and so happily pure—so nearly good . . . I'd give ten years of my life to annihilate one day and its consequences," Adam writes to Wilson.

None of this agony is in his letter to Edwin. To Edwin he says that the young man Edwin saved on the train tracks a few weeks back was Robert Lincoln, the president's son. Robert is also on Grant's staff and has told them all the whole story. Grant would like to do something to thank Edwin. He may have saved Robert from serious injury.

It takes Edwin a moment to even remember this incident.

Still, it is gratifying. He tells Adam that all he needs is for Grant to drive the nail straight into the Southern head.

Edwin tells Asia and Rosalie about the rescue on the train tracks.

He assumes they won't tell John and they don't.

IN JANUARY OF 1865, the Thirteenth Amendment passes, abolishing slavery in the United States forever.

IN FEBRUARY, WHILE Edwin struggles with exhaustion in the midst of his historic run, June arranges his schedule to spend a day with John in Washington, DC. Rosalie, Edwin, and June have had a tête-à-tête-à-tête about John.

Asia is home in Philadelphia. She is so much better informed on John's activities than the rest of them. If she'd been there, if she'd been consulted, things might have gone differently. Or not. Asia is John's most intimate connection to the family. Her instinct is to admire and support him.

The other three are concerned at the way his passion and febrile certitude are erasing every other thing he used to be. They're not thinking about anything he might do so much as who he is becoming—Father's madness without Father's genius to excuse it. And how will he react when his beloved Richmond falls, as it surely will and soon?

June volunteers to go and talk to him, play the big brother. Obviously this task can't fall to Edwin. John is currently in the capital so June meets him there at the Surratt boardinghouse. They sit together in the overstuffed parlor, full of geegaws, vases and candlesticks and figurines. June feels oddly spied on by Mrs.

Surratt and her daughter, oddly unsettled by the ticking of multiple clocks. He suggests going out.

Twilight is just falling and they walk together along the darkening streets. They follow the lamplighter for a block or so, seeing the lamps flare, yellow and haloed in the misty evening.
June's trying to find a place to begin when John suddenly provides it. "Virginia! My Virginia!" he cries out tragically. He turns
south, his face wet with tears.

Obviously, sober sense is in short supply here. "John," June
says. He grabs John's shoulders, looks him in the eyes. "The
North will win and there's nothing to be done about it. You
would do best to concentrate on your profession."

He can see the condemnation in John's face. "I'm not so
bloodless as you," John says.

June's second attempt goes better. They find a bar and over
whiskies, June learns two things he didn't know. One: John's
been boasting for months of big profits from his oil wells. The
truth is that he's lost nearly everything. June scolds him affectionately for pretending otherwise. Time for him to recommit to
the stage.

Two: John, like Edwin, is in love. He's secretly pledged to a
senator's daughter, the beautiful Lucy Hale. Senator Hale is a
committed abolitionist, recently appointed ambassador to Spain.
He'll be taking Lucy with him when he goes. Rough waters
ahead—Romeo and Juliet to be sure—but June is reassured. He
encourages John to wax on about Lucy's many perfections, until
he can see the old John coming clear again.

He returns to New York with a favorable report. John is making plans for the future. He's determined to deserve Lucy and he
understands, he agrees with June, that to do so requires steadiness
and industry. John doesn't come right out and say that he loves

Lucy more than his dear old Virginia, but surely he must. They are so eager to be reassured, they ignore the revelation that John has been lying to them for months.

MOTHER WRITES JOHN a letter, complaining that he's not been to visit, telling him that she's miserable and lonely in Edwin's house without him. "I always gave you praise," she writes, "for being the fondest of all my boys, but since you leave me to grief I must doubt it. I am no Roman mother. I love my dear ones before country or anything else."

xiii

So there they all are: Edwin is engaged to be married. Asia is pregnant. June is touring. John appears, disappears, reappears. He seems to have been frequenting Montreal, a hub of Confederate scheming, but is also, often, in Washington. They assume that he keeps returning to the capital because Lucy Hale is there. They find these repeated visits encouraging. A good woman will soon put John right.

He still comes often to Philadelphia. Asia might see him at any hour. He arrives, sleeps on the sofa in his clothes, and leaves before dawn. When he goes, Asia removes all evidence of his visit. Sleeper is none the wiser.

Men stand at the sill in the darkness, and whisper for him to come to the window. They keep their faces hidden. Some of their voices she knows—little Michael O'Laughlen, who used to live on the other side of Exeter Street and trailed after John wherever he went. Sam Arnold, John's old mate from school. But when she greets them, they tell her, No, no, that's not my name. You've mistaken me for someone else.

Most of the voices are strange to her.

One night John takes her hand. "I need to show you a cipher," he says. His plans are changing, the kidnapping of Lincoln replaced with something more dreadful.

She pulls her hand away. "I want no knowledge of it."

He waits in silence for her to change her mind. She doesn't.

He then takes a packet of letters from his vest, gives them to her. "Keep these until I return," he says. "Lock them in the safe." He kisses her on the cheek, on the forehead, on the hand. He leaves. She sits staring at an envelope labeled *Mother*. Before she's risen, he's back. "Let me see you lock them up."

The safe is in a cold, stone, windowless room. Asia keeps the keys; Sleeper never goes inside it. The room has two doors. She opens the first, the heavy door. She opens the second, the iron door. When the packet is secure, they return to the couch. She sits. He kneels.

He puts his head in her lap. "'I dare do all that may become a man,'" he says. "'Who dares do more is none.'"

She strokes his hair. "I'm going to name the baby after you if it's a boy. Then I'll have my very own Edwin and John all over again. Promise me you're being careful. I need you to teach the children to ride. To sword fight. Recite a poem."

"Make it a boy then," he says.

SOME THINGS LAST. There will always be a place on her cheek, her forehead, her hand where he kissed her. She will always be able to conjure the feel of his black hair under her fingers. "Be patient. This war will end," she tells him.

The country is burning, the dead and the grief, the terror and the bloodshed piling higher every day, unfathomable numbers, immeasurable sorrow. General Lee will surrender on April 9th at the Appomattox Court House. Church bells will ring and a dizzying joy will spread through the North. Winged victory will arrive.

None of this will end the war. Some things last.

"Keep yourself happy, my dear," he says.

"Not until I see your face again."

And then he's gone.

Lincoln and the Final Act

This war is eating my life out; I have a strong impression that I shall not live to see the end.
—Abraham Lincoln to his friend Owen Lovejoy, 1864

But also:

I expect to go back and make my home in Springfield for the rest of my life.
—Abraham Lincoln to Mary's cousin
John Todd Stuart, 1865

Lincoln wakes from a familiar dream to an unfamiliar emotion. The dream is of being on board a ship, moving rapidly towards a distantly glimpsed shore. The emotion takes him a moment to identify. If not happiness, at least the absence of unhappiness. Five days have passed since General Lee surrendered.

He breakfasts with his oldest son and they talk about what Robert might do now his military career is ending. Perhaps the law? To speak hopefully with Robert about his future, to know that he'll have one, is a great joy. He imagines the same conversation over breakfast tables all across the country.

AT ELEVEN A.M., General Grant arrives for the weekly cabinet meeting. Grant is worried about Joseph E. Johnston's army in North Carolina. Lincoln can't share his concerns. He tells Grant about his dream, the same dream he had before Sumter, Bull Run, Antietam, Gettysburg, Vicksburg, Wilmington—almost all of the great battles. The dream portends a momentous occurrence. It portends good news. "Those were not all victories," Grant reminds him.

The problem of what to do with the rebel leaders is discussed.

Lincoln hopes they'll all flee the country, removing the need to do anything. He wants no more violence, no trials, no retributions to add fuel to the fires of resentment. Later in the day, he receives the news that the rabid secessionist Jacob Thompson has been spotted en route to Maine and from there to England. Edwin Stanton, the Secretary of War, is preparing to arrest him, but Lincoln says no. "When you have got an elephant by the hind leg, and he's trying to run away, it's best to let him run," Lincoln says.

AROUND THREE P.M., he and Mary ride to the Navy Yard to tour the USS *Montauk*. Mary expresses surprise on finding just the two of them in the carriage, but he tells her he wanted it that way. He takes her hand, so much smaller than his own.

"You almost startle me by your great cheerfulness," Mary says. They are driving through the springtime, dogwoods and redbuds blooming in the streets beyond the carriage windows, the sun bright, the air warm.

"And well I may feel so, Mary," he answers, "for I consider this day the war has come to a close. We must both be more cheerful in the future. Between the war and the loss of our darling Willie we have been very miserable."

On their return a few hours later, he spies a group of old friends from Illinois just leaving the White House. He insists they come back inside; he has time for a comfortable chat. He's been reading the comic letters of Petroleum V. Nasby, now he shares some of these aloud. He's enjoying this so much, he ignores the first two calls to an early dinner. Lincoln has never been much interested in food though he does like a chicken fricassee.

Around seven-thirty, he meets with Schuyler Colfax, the Speaker of the House. Colfax has plans to travel West. They discuss the rich mineral lodes of the western mountains and Lincoln feels a wild desire to go to California himself. When his term is over, why not? Anything is possible in these wondrous days of peace.

HE WOULD RATHER skip the theater that night, but John T. Ford had invited Mary personally and Lincoln's attendance has been advertised. Grant, also advertised, has already begged off, Mrs. Grant unwilling to endure a night with Mary. The Stantons have likewise declined. Stanton feels it's dangerous for Lincoln to go about in public and he won't condone it by accompanying him. Lincoln's usual bodyguard is away on business in Richmond. His replacement, John Parker, a large man with enormous whiskers, is famously fond of drink.

Lincoln invites Clara Harris and Major Henry Reed Rathbone. Clara is a particular friend of Mary's, the daughter of a New York senator. Rathbone is a survivor of Antietam and Clara's fiancé. Her father is married to his mother so they are also, technically, brother and sister.

Mary is wearing her black and white silk with the embroidered flowers. Lincoln rarely notices her clothes, but Clara is full of compliments he wishes he'd thought to give. They arrive at the theater late by half an hour, enter the hushed and darkened auditorium. The performance stops so the orchestra can play "Hail to the Chief" while the audience claps and cheers. Lincoln is glad he overruled his reluctance and came.

John Parker leads them to a box stage left, decorated especially for them with flags and bunting. He then stays outside it to guard the entrance. Mary takes a seat beside Lincoln, Clara across. Henry sits on a small sofa to Clara's left. The play resumes.

Mary has caught Lincoln's happiness. She rests her hand on his knee, moves closer to him. She smells of bergamot and lemon. "What will Miss Harris think," she whispers, "of me hanging on you so?" and Lincoln assures her Miss Harris will not mind it at all.

THE THIRD AND final act begins.

Scene 2:

Harry Hawk as Asa Trenchard is alone on the stage. "I guess I know enough to turn you inside out, old gal—you sockdologizing old man-trap," Harry says. He hits hard on the *sock* in *sockdologizing*, turning towards the wings where Helen Muzzy, playing Mrs. Montchessington, has just exited. His back is to Lincoln.

This is the evening's most reliable laugh line and Mary's pealing laughter can be heard above everyone's. How wonderful to hear Mary laugh like this! It's that pleasure, more than the line, that starts Lincoln laughing himself. Then he hears something else, but there is no time to understand what it is.

BOOK SIX

What's past is prologue.

—W. Shakespeare, *The Tempest*

April 15th, 1865

i

Edwin is in Boston, where he and Sleeper have been talking of purchasing a third theater. The previous evening, he'd played Sir Edward Mortimer in *The Iron Chest*. "Where is my honor now?" he'd asked the sold-out house. The city is exuberant, the men in the streets ecstatic to learn they aren't going to die on some battlefield, after all. Edwin is in love and General Grant's great task is ended. Edwin feels as happy as he's ever been since Mary's death.

When he makes his way home, word is already spreading, the mood turning from joy to disbelief to anguish. But Edwin is tired and will hear nothing until a servant wakes him the following morning.

Edwin's first thought is not a thought, more like a blow to the head, a sense of falling, the crashing of the sea in his ears. His second thought is that he believes it. He wishes he didn't. He wishes he could say that this is utterly impossible.

He weeps for his president, bleeding in the lap of Laura Keene. His own life going forward is suddenly unimaginable. He moves from room to room, chair to chair, but there is no escape from this.

Before the morning is over, a message arrives from Henry Jarrett, the manager of the Boston Theatre, to say that he prays what everyone is saying about Wilkes will yet prove untrue. Still, he thinks it best and right to cancel all further performances. Of course it's best and right. What's best and right is that Edwin never set foot on a stage again. *The rest is silence.*

ASIA LEARNS WHAT has happened from the newspaper. She opens it and the first things she sees are the paper's black borders and a sketch of her brother's face. Sleeper, rushing to her side, tries through her incoherent cries to understand what's wrong. He can't. Asia is screaming.

Soon enough she's in control again, all ice and iron. Yet the hysteria returns and returns, never triumphant, never vanquished. She wishes she were dead.

At the first opportunity, she goes alone to retrieve John's packet. One letter she burns. One name she feels she must protect. She does this in the cold fireplace, blowing the ashes apart, so no scrap remains to be read. The other letters she takes to Sleeper, who'd never known they were in the house. During her continual breakdowns, he's been solicitous. The appearance of the letters makes him angry.

A US marshal arrives, forbidding them to go outside. Asia thinks they're being imprisoned, which they are, but also protected. An angry crowd is gathered in the street. In an excess of innocence, Sleeper gives the letters to the marshal, including the one addressed to Mother. He stresses that only his wife had known of their existence. The house is searched, even the

nursery with its crying children, in case John is hiding in a wardrobe or under a bed.

A guard is placed at every door.

JUNE IS ON tour in Cincinnati. He gives the desk clerk a cheerful
wave as he sets off for a morning walk. "So you haven't heard,"
the desk clerk says and then wishes he could bite the words back.
He doesn't want to be the one to tell.

June turns around. "What do you mean by that?"

One of the housekeepers comes into the lobby on the run.
"Upstairs," she says, seizing him by the arm. "Quick. Quick!" A
mob of some five hundred people is right behind her. They've
stripped the lampposts of June's playbills and come to hang him.
June is still on the stairs when he hears them cramming into the
lobby, shouting his name. If this were California, he'd be swinging from a lamppost before day's end.

But the clerk manages to convince them that June left in the
night. June spends the day hidden in a stuffy attic room, saved by
the hotel staff, every one of whom holds his life in their hands,
not one of whom gives him away.

JOE IS ON the *Moses Taylor*, headed for Panama. After Australia,
he'd worked in San Francisco, in a job June got for him at Wells
Fargo & Company. He's been away three years. The authorities
find it suspicious that he chose the date of April 13th to start
home.

On arriving in Panama City, he hears of the president's death
and the murderer Booth, but many men are named Booth; he
thinks little of it. At the next stop, Aspinwall, he hears the name

John Wilkes. By then he's had more time to think. By the time he hears, he feels he already knew.

From the transcript of his later interrogation:

Q: Have you ever been insane, Mr. Booth?
A: Yes, sir.

Q: For how long a time?
A: For several months. I was insane in Panama.

Q: On your return?
A: Yes, sir. That news made me insane.

MOTHER AND ROSALIE are in New York. For more than a week, bells have been ringing, horns blowing in the giddy city, and the celebratory noise is only now starting to subside. The war is over. All the boys are home or coming home. Mother says that Ann Hall will be united with her lost children at last. All of them free now! If only Joe Hall had lived to see it. She says that all any mother wants is to be with her children. They make plans for a visit to Tudor Hall.

The doorbell rings and the Aldriches are on the doorstep. Thomas Aldrich is an editor and writer, a man of sincerity and compassion. Rosalie has never liked his wife, an opinion shared by Mark Twain, who called her a dithering blatherskite and worse. "Lord, I loathe that woman," Mark Twain says.

The Aldriches are friends of Edwin's. "Edwin's in Boston," Rosalie tells them. She's surprised they wouldn't know that.

Mrs. Aldrich seizes Rosalie's hands so tightly that her rings dig into Rosalie's flesh. "We're here for your poor mother," she says. Through the open door, Rosalie hears the newsboy calling. "The President's Death! The President Foully Murdered! The President's Death!"

A moment of shock. "The president is dead?" she asks.

"Oh my dear," Mrs. Aldrich says, still clutching her hands though Rosalie has tried to extricate them.

At least John will be happy, Rosalie thinks. She'll remember always how that was her first thought just before she heard the newsboy call, "John Wilkes Booth arrested."

She looks at Mrs. Aldrich, who has taken the time this morning before coming to the house to pin her best hat onto her head, powder her cheeks, and arrange the curls about her face. "Oh my dear," Mrs. Aldrich says.

Mother has heard the cries from the street. She joins them at the door, white and faint. Mr. Aldrich steps forward to lend his arm, help her to the couch. Rosalie hasn't seen the face Mother is wearing since Henry died. All those years ago, and yet she recognizes it immediately. Unspeakable sorrow mixed with madness. She always knew she'd see it again. "Mother, it's a mistake," Rosalie says. "You know John. He would never do this to you."

"Of course, we all hope it turns out to be a mistake," Mrs. Aldrich says, the doubt evident in her voice.

"We must wait and see," Thomas Aldrich says.

More friends of Edwin's arrive—the Osgoods, the Taylors. These people have never spoken two words to Rosalie before. She's stiff with resentment. She sees through their postures of sympathy. This is the most exciting thing ever to happen to them, tourists to the land of grief. And she feels the insult to John, that anyone would believe such a thing. Worse, she can see that they're persuading Mother.

The doorbell rings again along with the postman's whistle. He's delivering a letter from John. There is a terrible power in that letter arriving at that minute. Mother's hands are shaking so that she can't open it. She hands it to Rosalie. Rosalie wishes she and Mother were alone.

April 14th, two a.m.

Dearest Mother:

I know you expect a letter from me, and I'm sure you will hardly forgive me. But indeed I have nothing to write about. Everything is dull; that is, has been till last night. (The illumination.)

Everything was bright and splendid. More so in my eyes if it had been displayed in a nobler cause. But so goes the world. Might makes right. I only drop you these few lines to let you know I am well, and to say I have not heard from you. Excuse brevity, am in haste. Had one from Rose. With best love to you, I am your affectionate son ever,

John

Is that the letter a boy writes to his mother on the very day he means to murder the president? Rosalie doesn't think so. She holds the paper out with an emphatic shake. The letter is passed from hand to hand until it comes back to her.

Mother is still sobbing on the couch. "Oh God, if this be true, let him shoot himself. Let him not live to be hanged! Spare us that at least, that disgrace to our name. Have that one ounce of pity, God." Edwin's friends are clustered around her, Thomas Aldrich kneeling at her feet.

Why is everyone behaving as if this is true? Rosalie's conviction becomes agonized, defensive, less like conviction. She holds the letter against her bodice, as close to her heart as it can be. John's own words in John's own hand. Her proof of his innocence.

All day long, they hear the newsboys calling from the street that Abraham Lincoln is dead and John Wilkes Booth arrested.

ROSALIE IS RIGHT to think this is wrong. She's wrong as to which part. John has not been arrested. He escaped the theater on horseback and is currently in Maryland at the surgery of Dr. Samuel Mudd, having the bone in his leg set. He'd broken it the night before, leaping from Lincoln's box to the stage to deliver the most shocking conclusion *Our American Cousin* will ever have. It was a big scene, with blocking and a speech—*sic semper tyrannis*—and everything. He'd choreographed it carefully, all but the broken leg.

In his diary he writes: "Rode sixty miles last night with the bones of my leg tearing the flesh at every jump. I can never repent it, though we hated to kill . . . God simply made me the instrument of his punishment."

ii

Edwin returns to New York on the 16th, anxious about his mother, but otherwise dead in his soul. He finds Mother in her bed, unable to rise. "I truly think this will kill her," he tells his friends. "I think her heart is so broken, she may will it to stop altogether."

Rosalie is once again her mother's inadequate comfort. Perhaps there is some special love reserved for the child who has never given a moment's worry. Rosalie doesn't feel it. Her own grief is unacknowledged, submerged in her mother's, but it does, from time to time, choke her unexpectedly as she tries to eat her breakfast, read a book, lie sleepless at her mother's side. John's face rises in her mind and she hates him as much as she loves him, in both cases, too much. "Remember him as he was," Edwin tells her, but who was that? Did she ever really know him? Has she only just lost him or did that happen long ago?

JOHN ENTRUSTED A friend with a manifesto he wanted printed in the papers. On hearing of the assassination, this friend opens, reads, and burns it. What does appear in the papers are the letters from Asia's safe, the ones Sleeper gave the federal marshal. Rosalie tries not to look at them. She lasts three whole hours.

The first is to his mother. It's odd to think that this was written many days before the letter they'd received at the very hour of the newsboy's calls. This one is full of protestations of his deep love for his mother, the best, the noblest mother in the world. Still, he owes a duty to his country, he says. He complains, with no sense of irony, that he's lived a slave in the North and can bear that no longer.

And here is the part that especially angers Rosalie: "And should the last bolt strike your son, dear mother bear it patiently . . . my Brothers and Sisters (Heaven protect them) will add my love and duty to their own, and watch you with care and kindness until we meet again."

As if any one of them can substitute for John! As if even all together they can conjure half of Mother's love for him! As if he doesn't know that he's consigned Rosalie, for the rest of her life, to try to be enough for Mother and to fail.

The second letter is addressed To Whom It May Concern. "This country was formed for the *white* not the black man," John says.

> And looking upon *African slavery* from the same stand-point, held by those noble framers of our Constitution, I for one, have ever considered *it*, one of the greatest bless-ings (both for themselves and us,) that God ever bestowed upon a favored nation. Witness heretofore our wealth and power. Witness their elevation in happiness . . . *no one* would be willing to do *more* for the Negro race than I, could I but see a way to *still better* their condition . . .

LIKE MOTHER, EDWIN finds it impossible to sleep alone. His friend William Bispham shares his bed at night. During the day, Edwin stays inside, afraid to be seen in public. After dark, he walks the streets with Bispham and Aldrich. Everyone who loves him is afraid that he will drink, but he doesn't.

He speaks often of the day he saved Robert Lincoln at the train station. The story, which he'd hardly remembered, has become one of his great comforts.

He tells Bispham he doesn't know when it all went wrong for John. He was a loving child and so full of fun. They'd all adored him. He wonders what Father would have said. June writes with his usual stolid pragmatism that he expects they all will recover in time with the exception of Mother, who will clearly never recover.

At the suggestion of Thomas Aldrich, Edwin writes an auto-biography of his childhood as a gift to Edwina, who has been with Asia since before the assassination. This fills a few days. As soon as he finishes, he destroys it.

He writes letters.

He writes to Asia daily: ". . . imagine the boy you loved to be in that better part of his spirit, in another world."

He writes to Adam that he takes comfort in the knowledge that one great heart will never forsake him. He doesn't mean Adam though no heart is more his than Ad's. He means Blanche Hanel.

He writes to the American people:

> . . . It has pleased God to lay at the door of my afflicted family the life-blood of our great, good and martyred President. Prostrated to the very earth by this dreadful event, I am yet too sensible that other mourners fill the land. To them, to you, one and all go forth our deep unutterable sympathy; our abhorrence and detestation for this most foul and atrocious of crimes . . .

He receives letters.

Blanche Hanel writes to end their engagement.

The American people write, one at a time and anonymously, that his life is forfeit; there is a bullet waiting for him, they hate the very name of Booth, and that his next performance will be a tragedy.

THE FAMILY EXISTS in a kind of twilight where the full dark can't come on until they know where John is and what will happen to him.

iii

June and Sleeper are arrested together at the Clarke house in Philadelphia on suspicion of conspiracy. They're taken in hand-cuffs to Washington and the Old Capitol Prison, where they share a cell. Sleeper spends one month there, June two. Roaches and rats, June says, and intolerable heat. And interrogations.

Others have been arrested as well. Michael O'Laughlen and Samuel Arnold are also in custody here. Each withdrew from the plot when John moved the planned kidnapping from some remote country lane to Ford's Theatre, where, he said, Lincoln would be subdued, handcuffed, and lowered on ropes from his box to the stage. This was a preposterous plan—suicidal, Arnold told him—and the fact that John couldn't see that shook them. They were both out by the time the kidnapping became an assassination.

As a result, they'll escape the noose. Instead, along with Dr. Mudd, they'll be sent to the prison of Fort Jefferson in the Dry Tortugas, where O'Laughlen, the little boy who once trailed after John and the Bully Boys up and down Exeter Street, will die of yellow fever.

Also arrested: George Atzerodt, an immigrant from Prussia, whose mission on the 14th was to kill the vice president. He'd lost his nerve and spent the night drinking instead.

A Confederate soldier named Lewis Powell, nicknamed Lewis the Terrible for his savagery, and sent by John to kill the Secretary of State. Seward had already been hurt in a carriage accident and was in bed under a doctor's care, when Powell forced his way in. He beat one of Seward's sons senseless with his pistol, stabbed another. He struck Fanny, Seward's lovely daughter, with his fist, climbed onto Seward's bed, and stabbed him five times in the neck and face. He left six people bleeding, then ran from the house, shouting, "I'm mad! I'm mad!" only to discover that David Herold, the twenty-three-year-old pharmacist's assistant who was supposed to be waiting with the horses, had already fled.

Everyone in the Seward household will survive. Atzerodt, Powell, and Herold will not. They will hang, along with Mary Surratt, at whose boardinghouse the plotting is suspected of taking place.

AS TO JUNE and Sleeper:

The government has letters from June to John about the oil business, which in June's case means the oil business, but amongst co-conspirators has meant the plot. The government has nothing on Sleeper beyond Asia's concealment of John's comings and goings, but this seems to be enough to hold him. June is philosophical. Sleeper is furious. Why is he locked up when Edwin is not?

Asia is kept out of prison by her pregnancy. She remains under house arrest, an agent placed inside to watch her every move. This agent wants to add his wife to the household. He's disturbed that Asia isn't crying. He thinks she needs a woman's sympathy. Asia needs nothing of the kind.

She needs her mother. She's learned that she's carrying twins and either from that or the tragedy her life has become, the pregnancy is at risk. The nurse who's been tending her refuses now to do so because she's a Booth. Her doctor sends word that he's too frightened to come. Only Becky, the nursemaid, has been willing to stay. Asia is all but alone except for the children and the federal agents.

Probably nothing else could have gotten Mother out of bed. On hearing of Asia's distress, she rises silently, packs her bag, and asks Edwin to take her to the train. She's on her way to Philadelphia when she learns that John is dead. Sitting, looking out the window, pretending she sees the fields and copses, the towns and churches, the whole brutal charade passing, while the other passengers whistle and cheer.

iv

There are so many times John Wilkes Booth could have died. He could have drowned while at St. Timothy's Hall; he could have frozen while fetching a cow. Matthew Canning's bullet could have severed his femoral artery. Secessionists could have murdered him in Montgomery, Alabama. He could have been killed in the New York draft riots. He could have died of St. Anthony's fire.

Instead it happens thirteen days too late and in this way: He's fled with David Herold who, having abandoned Powell at the Sewards', reconnoitered with John. They're tracked to a barn near Bowling Green, Virginia, before dawn on April 26th. Herold surrenders, but John won't come out. He seems to think he should be given a sporting chance. "Be fair and give me a show. Draw your men off fifty yards," he shouts, a courtesy he didn't extend to Lincoln. Nor is it given to him.

A torch is thrown inside the barn. The straw catches immediately, illuminating the scene as clearly as if he were onstage. "I saw him standing upright," one Colonel Conger says later, "leaning on a crutch. He looked so like his brother Edwin I believed for a moment the whole pursuit to have been a mistake."

He's shot through the neck by Sergeant Boston Corbett on instructions from God. "Tell my mother I die for my country," John says. But when the dying takes more than three hours, he says, "Please kill me now."

HIS DIARY, FOUND on his body, becomes part of the court record. On April 21st, he wrote:

After being hunted like a dog through swamps, woods, and last night being chased by gunboats till I was forced to return wet cold and starving, with every man's hand against me, I am here in despair. And why; For doing what Brutus was honored for, what made Tell a Hero. And yet I for striking down a greater tyrant than they ever knew am looked upon as a common cutthroat . . .

. . . I think I have done well, though I am abandoned, with the curse of Cain upon me. When if the world knew my heart, *that one* blow would have made me great, though I did desire no greatness.

To night I try to escape these blood hounds once more. Who who can read his fate. God's will be done.

I have too great a soul to die like a criminal. Oh may He, may He spare me that and let me die bravely.

I bless the entire world. Have never hated or wronged anyone . . .

v
———

All that remains is the going on.

EDWIN IS SUMMONED to the capital to testify to John's insanity. Apparently his testimony isn't what was hoped for. He's never called.

He thinks briefly about visiting the Sewards, with whom he once spent such a lovely evening, offering his sympathy. But the promises of continued friendship are surely moot now. Seeing him will only hurt them more.

He visits June and Sleeper in their cells. He offers to let Sleeper out of their partnership; in fact, he urges this. Sleeper tells him no. He doesn't tell Edwin that the partnership he wants out of is his marriage. He's decided that the only way to restore his honor is to divorce his pregnant wife. When finally released, he returns home to tell Asia so. She won't do it.

He speaks to the press. The Booths, he says, are a nest of vipers. A family of Iagos, a house of secrets. He himself is not a Booth, thank the Lord, never has been, never will be.

Six months later, he and William Stuart mount a production of *Our American Cousin* at the Winter Garden in New York. Sleeper takes on the starring role. Edwin's feelings about this are unknown.

Only Laura Keene publicly objects. What could be more tasteless than this rank cupidity? The play runs for a month to full houses.

Keene will actually suffer more than Sleeper from the assassination. She'd made her way to the box, held Lincoln during the doctor's initial examination, since his wife was unable to do so. His blood soaked her skirts and petticoats.

The public is deeply uncomfortable with the thought of their dying president in the arms of an actress. Her career is as a comedienne. No one finds her funny anymore.

JOHN ONCE GAVE Rosalie the courage to leave her house. Now he's taken it back. She no longer even wishes to sit and listen to Edwin's friends. There is no one she can ask to share her bed now that Mother is gone to Asia and, with no one there as witness, she sobs through the night, her hands pressed against her face. Her books no longer engage her. Her grief is a well with no bottom. Each day lasts longer than she can endure and night is no respite.

All the Booths, though mostly Edwin, continue to receive threatening letters. But another sort of letter comes as well. More than one young woman writes to say that she was secretly married to John, or secretly engaged to John, or has secretly had John's child. All have pressing financial needs. Edwin deals with these claims swiftly and coldly.

One letter contains the picture of a child. A girl—her name is Ogarita Rosalie Booth. Rosalie feels that the resemblance is undeniable. While Edwin is in Washington, Rosalie asks Ogarita's mother, Izola, to bring the child to the house. Izola is an actress, darkly Spanish in looks, and she shares the details of her secret and passionate marriage. Rosalie hadn't realized how consoling it would be to talk about John with someone who still thinks he's wonderful. She becomes uncharacteristically loquacious—telling stories about John as a boy, a rapscallion, for sure, but delightfully so, an imp, a larker. They agree that John was a mere tool of greater forces, pressured by the Knights of the Golden Circle into a thing he would never have thought of on his own. This is as close to happiness as she's come since April 15th.

Ogarita looks less like John in the flesh, but her coloring is his, and maybe there is something about her eyes?

Rosalie feels that Izola's grief is real and if that's real, it follows that the rest is also. John left Rosalie some oil stocks. They don't amount to much, but, at forty-two, it's the first money she's ever had that's all her own. She presses some of it into Izola's hands. They agree to meet again.

Edwin is angry when he finds out. What he sees is a scheming woman preying on Rosalie's kindness and her fairy-tale heart. He tells Rosalie that six pictures of women were found in John's diary and Izola wasn't among them. He shows her a letter from Lucy Hale, the senator's daughter with whom John had an understanding. "Read the words of this broken-hearted woman to whom our brother promised such happiness," he tells her. Surely that's put a stop to it.

In fact, Rosalie merely changes the address to which Izola's letters are sent so that Edwin never sees them. The two women continue to correspond until a few years before Rosalie's death. In letters, Rosalie refers to her as "my dear sister," and signs "your loving sister, Rose." She gives Izola personal items she thinks John's child may someday want—his playbook, his gloves, a photo of him as a boy. When, in 1877, Izola has another child, a son, she tells Rosalie she wants to name him after John. Rosalie can't imagine the child's father will agree to that. Anyway, it's a bad idea. She asks instead that he be named after her great love, the lion tamer. Harry Jerome Dresbach is close enough to Jacob Driesbach to satisfy her.

Rosalie's not the only one who loves a good fairy tale. Ogarita will grow up to tell her children that Driesbach died when his own lions ate him. Or perhaps this story also comes from Rosalie. Better dead and eaten by lions than married and running a hotel with his wife in Apple Creek, Ohio.

vi
———

Asia's twins arrive, one boy, one girl. They do not name the boy for John. The girl lives less than a year. After their daughter's death, Sleeper goes to London, where he proves a great success. He writes to Asia that she should come and bring the children, but she delays, reluctant to leave her mother.

Meanwhile, those who knew John (and many who didn't) are selling their stories. He's called a cad, a cheat, and a violent drunk. That he was all those things is no comfort.

"North, East, and West the papers teemed with the most preposterous adventures, and eccentricities, and ill deeds of the vile Booth family. The tongue of every man and woman was free to revile and insult us," Asia says, and then, and in almost exact echo of John's diary, "Every man's hand was against us."

Reporters swarm the little town of Bel Air, which seems to have been and still be Copperhead country. Yet it is possible to find many who do not like John Wilkes Booth. Mr. Hooper, whose dog John once shot, is interviewed. Their old neighbors the Woolseys divulge his penchant for killing marketable fowl and lying about it. Mr. Hagan recounts being beaten near to death.

Some friends remain. Aunty Rogers tells Mother that, while John was on the run, she'd kept a hamper of food for him on the front porch. A reporter found Ann Hall to ask, if John showed up wanting her help, would she give it? "I'd give him anything he needed. I'd give him anything I have," she'd said, and closed the door.

When as a child Asia had learned of her father's bigamy, she'd protested the unfairness of it reflecting on his children. "It's not as if *we* did anything wrong," she'd said. She tries to hold that same conviction now, but it's more difficult. In their hearts, each Booth must be asking: What did I do to cause this? What did I not do to stop it?

Asia's guilt is more specific. Should she have read his letters? Should she have told Edwin about them and the nighttime visitors? Yet who could ever have suspected this?

Finally unable to bear it longer, Asia moves to England. But no one leaves unhappiness behind so easily. She never grants Sleeper his divorce, though he ceases to pay the marriage any mind, behaving in all ways as a single man. He treats Asia with the disrespect he feels her family name deserves. She loses another child at two and a half months. "I am, like my mother, getting hardened to sorrow," she says.

For a year or so, she enjoys being away from America. She feels she can breathe again. But her husband is a philanderer, her mother is an ocean away, and her favorite brother is the dead one. She can't make new friends; she finds the English people impossibly self-satisfied. Everything they do is the best way to do it, she writes Jean, now married without Asia's permission, but still her steadfast friend. No one can tell them anything. This is particularly hard on Asia, who likes telling people things.

She busies herself by finishing the book she'd long planned about her father. She writes a second about Edwin. These focus primarily on their theatrical achievements.

But then she writes a third book, without telling Sleeper or anyone else. Her secret book about John is much more personal.

She doesn't try to publish it. She knows she can't. It remains unseen and unread until fifty years after her death when G. P. Putnam finally brings it out. Although she decries her brother's great crime in principle, on the page, she makes him the hero he thought he was.

She blames Lincoln for having gone to the theater that night.

With Richmond so recently fallen, the surrender so raw, the suffering so great, surely he should have been in church instead. To go out for a vulgar entertainment suggests a callous indifference Asia cannot excuse. The theater! The devil's den. It desecrates his death.

She writes:

> There is no solidity in love, no truth in friendship, no steadiness in marital faith . . . Those who have passed through such an ordeal—if there are any such—
> . . . they never relearn to trust in human nature, they never resume their old place in the world, and they forget only in death.

vii

Edwin's determination to leave the stage wanes. First he vows never to return. Then his retirement must last at least a year. Then, nine months later, in January of 1866, he appears at the Winter Garden as Hamlet again.

He has too many people to support and too little to do to relieve his mind. No one can promise him safety. The letters still come. They will come for years.

I am carrying a bullet for you.

Your life is forfeit.

We hate the very name Booth.

Your next performance will be a tragedy.

At least one local paper is outraged. "The blood of our mar-
tyred President is not yet dry . . . still a Booth is advertised to
appear!"

Once again crowds are gathered in the street before the theater opens. Some are supporters of Edwin, but many are not. The
police anticipate violence and are on hand in numbers to prevent
it. Some without tickets manage to force their way as far as the
lobby before they're ejected.

The play begins. From his dressing room, Edwin Booth knows
when the ghost has made his entrance. Marcellus: *Peace, break thee
off! Look where it comes again.* And then Bernardo: *In the same figure
like the King that's dead.* Edwin can't actually hear the words. He
knows the lines from their stress and inflections. He knows the
moment of them. He knows exactly how much time remains until he takes his place for the second scene.

Edwin leans into the mirror to stare past his own painted face
into the space behind him. On the wall to the right of the small
dressing-table mirror is a coat rack, so overwhelmed with hats
and capes that it looms over the room, casting the shadow of a
very large man. Swords of all sorts lie on the tabletops, boots on
the floor, doublets and waistbands on the chairs.

A knock at the door. His old friend, dear Old Spudge, has
come to beg Edwin to reconsider. What is out there, he says,
what is waiting for you is not an audience so much as a mob. Yet
Edwin can't hear them at all. It seems they sit in a complete, uncanny silence.

No one in his family dared to come. His daughter, Edwina, arriving home under police escort, is now safe in her bed, unaware

that this *Hamlet* is different from any other. He's called for the second scene, but finds he can't make his legs move.

Now he can hear the audience, stamping their feet, impatient at the delay. William Stuart knocks a second, a third time. "Ned? We're waiting."

"I'm coming," Edwin said, and having said so, he's able to rise. He leaves the dressing room and takes his place on the stage. The actors around him are stiff with tension.

One of the hallmarks of Edwin's Hamlet is that he makes no entrance. As the curtain opens on the second scene, it often takes the audience time to locate him among the busy Danish court. He sits unobtrusively off to one side, under the standard of the great Raven of Denmark, his head bowed. "Among a gaudy court," a critic had written of an earlier performance, "'he alone with them, alone,' easily prince, and nullifying their effect by the intensity and color of his gloom." On this particular night he seems a frail figure, slight and dark and unremarkable save for the intensity and color of his gloom.

The audience finds him in his chair. Claudius is already speaking when someone begins to clap. And then someone else, and then someone else. The audience comes to their feet. The next day's review in *The Spirit of the Times* reports nine cheers, then six, then three, then nine more. The play cannot continue and as they clap, many of them, men and women both, begin to sob.

Edwin stands and comes forward into the footlights. The audience sees that Edwin, too, is weeping. It makes them cheer him louder. It's as if he's taken on all the suffering of the nation and is carrying it for them, along with the heavy share that is his alone.

Few actors, if any, have embodied so much and been so beloved. His fellow players gather tightly in, clapping their hands.

Hamlet has his father's ghost, so why not Edwin? In the midst of the applause, he smells his father's pipe and his father's whisky and beyond that, the forest of his childhood home. He hears his father's voice beneath the clapping, low but close and clear. "There, boy," his father says. "There, boy. Your foot is on your native heath."

viii

What is it like to love the most hated man in the country? Loving John is something the world simply will not have. Not loving John is something Rosalie and Asia simply cannot do.

Edwin tries. For many years, John's name is forbidden in Edwin's presence. A young actress asks him one day how many brothers and sisters he has. She realizes her mistake the moment she makes it by the sudden hush that falls over the room. But Edwin is kind. "Let's see," he says, and he counts each name on his fingers. John is not among them.

He blames John for the complete and final crushing of their mother's spirit. He blames John for the damage to their father's name. He blames John for the death of the president he loved and for all that the country suffered as a result. All of it down to John.

But as often happens, the years pass, and his memories move backwards. He remembers John as the only family member to attend his wedding, so filled with happiness over Edwin's happiness. He remembers their game of dueling Shakespeare: *The skies are painted with unnumbered sparks; They are all fire, and every one doth shine.*

Younger still: He remembers their summers on the farm, digging for Indian treasures, knocking together rafts that last only long enough for a single go. He remembers the high-spirited boy with a head full of quixotic dreams, dashing about with his wooden sword.

Still younger: He remembers fireflies and tadpoles, clouds of pigeons, trees to climb and streams to cross, and John begging to come, tagging along behind, running to keep up. "He was my *brother*," Edwin reminds an intrusive reporter who seems to have forgotten this.

ix

Eventually, Rosalie reads the many newspaper accounts of Lincoln's death that Mrs. Aldrich has so kindly given her—as if she might make a scrapbook!—accounts she's wanted to burn, but been unable. Eyewitness accounts.

They tend toward the lurid. They read like a play, a melodrama. Rosalie is an excellent reader. She sees it all vividly. John and Edwin both always preferred to play the villains.

There was a standing ovation for Lincoln when he and his party arrived, somewhat late. Was John already there? No one says so.

Third act. The theater must not have been very dark, because now John is seen at the back of the parquet by one of the actresses onstage. She recognizes him, all in black, she says, his face as pale as death. Moving towards the stairs, but then she has a line or two to deliver and stops watching him.

People in the dress circle take up the story. He ascended the steps and wove through the seats. He's well known to many. No one thinks it's odd that he's there. He's heard to be humming.

Two army officers are in his path, but move aside for him. The president's guard has gone out for a drink, but his messenger, Charles Forbes, is near the door to the president's box. Helen DuBarry, seated nearby, overhears John tell Forbes he has a communication for the president. He gives him the card of a US senator, quite likely the father of Lucy Hale. Forbes recognizes John. He waves him on, a decision he'll regret the rest of his life.

John makes it to the president's box, then stops. He removes his hat and stands for a few minutes, leaning against the wall.

Then he takes the final step down, pushing the door open with his knee. The shot comes instantly, sound and smoke. He shouts something as he shoots. He muddles the line; the audience disagrees as to what he said, but Major Rathbone, the president's guest in the box that night, says it was *sic semper tyrannis*.

Rathbone's turn with the story: The assassin is preparing to leap from the box to the stage, when Rathbone seizes the back of his coat. Suddenly there is a bowie knife in the assassin's hand. "Let me go or I'll kill you," he says. He stabs Rathbone in the arm, a deep cut; Rathbone's own blood sprays into his own eyes. The assassin jerks free.

The single actor on the stage—Harry Hawk—has fallen silent mid-speech and, like everyone else, is looking for the president. The audience belongs to the assassin now. Most of them think this is part of the play, though they hadn't known Booth would be performing that night.

He vaults from the rail, but Rathbone makes one final grab that throws him off balance. The spur on his boot catches in the festooning that decorates the box and he crashes onto the stage. He's up in an instant, staring into the face of the bewildered Harry Hawk.

Hawk hears him speak. "I have done it," he says. "The South

is avenged." He's moving towards Hawk with a bloody knife above his head and an odd, stagey gait.

"I ran," Hawk says simply. For this, for quite some time after, he will have to live under an assumed name.

One more person is injured, the orchestra conductor, shoved out of the way with the blade of the knife.

The assassin has hired a fast Thoroughbred, a spirited mare, now circling the reins. He makes it to the alley, but she can't be mounted; she's too excited. It takes another full minute to bring her under control. Mrs. Lincoln is screaming, and all is pandemonium until soldiers arrive and clear the theater with their bayonets. No one knows where the killer has gone.

The president is carried to a boardinghouse, where he's pronounced dead at 7:22 a.m. Ten thousand federal agents begin the largest manhunt in the history of the country. Reading this, reading one account after another, makes Rosalie frantic with grief, no escape, stuck in this horror like a fly in molasses. How happy, how rich her life once was! John has murdered them all.

FOR MORE THAN a year, before she sleeps, Rosalie will replay this scene, stopping right at the moment when John takes off his hat and leans against the wall. People say that he was waiting for a particular line and the laugh he knew would follow it; he was waiting for noise to cover his shot.

But in Rosalie's version, he's changing his mind. After that pause, she makes him turn, thread his way back through the dress circle and out into the alley where his horse is waiting. For more than a year, Rosalie tells herself this bedtime story. She can only sleep if she believes as hard as she can that he's on his way home. That he loved them enough to change his mind.

That pause is the last place she can find her brother. All she has to do now is begin again from there, begin the rest of her life at that pause, when John is still John, Rosalie still Rosalie, and the world has better things to do than notice either one.

x

In 1883, Rosalie will see Major Rathbone's name again in the newspaper. He had been serving the Arthur presidency in Germany when he suddenly attacked his wife, Clara. She dies protecting the children from their father. He then stabs himself five times in the chest.

He will spend the remainder of his life in an asylum for the criminally insane. He was never the same, friends will say, after the assassination. One more entry in John's account.

xi

Mother won't admit it, but she can't forgive Edwin for throwing John from his house. She believes that this was the moment, the turn. If John had only been supported by his family, loved and welcomed, how differently everything might have gone. After Asia leaves for England, Mother takes Rosalie to live with Joe, who is between wives and finishing his medical degree. Joe has a house in New York City and also a cottage in Long Branch, New Jersey. The women live sometimes in one and sometimes in the other until Mother's death in 1885.

Joe remains as he's always been, argumentative and aggrieved. One day in New Jersey, while Rosalie is answering a knock, a brick is thrown at her head, missing her by inches and denting the doorframe. At the same time, handfuls of smaller stones are thrown by unseen assailants against the windows of the house, spattering against the glass like hail. She staggers, she scuttles inside as fast as she's able, her back by now so continuously painful that only drink makes life bearable. She calls the servants, locks the doors, and hides like Randall in the basement until Joe's return. She believes the vengeance of the nation has come for her at last.

But Joe says no. This was all aimed at him and nothing to do with Lincoln. Joe's in the middle of suing his neighbors. He's building a twenty-foot fence around his property over the outraged objections of all who live near him. He's never been popular and he's not about to start now. It will take more than a brick thrown at his sister to stop him!

Joe was the one who went to Washington to identify John's body, Edwin having been rejected as too recognizable and June still in prison. John had been sewn inside two horse blankets, a thing no one tells Mother.

It then takes Edwin four years to get the body released from the Old Penitentiary, where it's been warehoused. President Johnson finally agrees to turn him over on condition that no gravestone ever mark him. None does. Still, everyone knows where he is. He's buried beside his father in Green Mount Cemetery in Baltimore.

Rosalie succeeds at last in moving Frederick, Mary Ann, and Elizabeth to the same plot. They are mostly together there now— not Henry, buried in England, not Edwin, buried in Boston with Mary, and not June, buried with his third wife in Manchester-by-the-Sea, but all the rest. For once, Joe isn't the one left out.

ASIA LEFT US her books. Rosalie left nothing but a few lines in the stories of her siblings. Edwin left the Players, a club and home for actors in which he lived the last years of his life.

He lasts long enough to see his style of naturalism become unnatural—too mannered, too formal, fossilized.

He dies on June 7th, 1893, at the age of fifty-nine. His funeral is held on June 9th. Joe, his only surviving sibling, is there and three of his nephews, along with his daughter, Edwina, and her husband. Joe Jefferson, Mary Devlin's old guardian, attends though he's been ill and looks it. New York's judges and politicians and clergymen.

Artists and actors. So many actors.

At nine a.m. a huge floral tribute arrives with this banner: *From brother actors of England. We all loved him.* It wasn't true in 1861. In 1893, it was. Good night, sweet prince.

The New York Times describes it as the most remarkable funeral ever held in New York City. Hundreds of men and women gather on the sidewalks outside the Players and around Gramercy Park to watch as his coffin is taken into the church, all of them reminiscing about how, on this night or that, they themselves were there to see the legendary Edwin Booth take the stage.

xii

More than a century has passed since they clapped and shouted and cheered him. All of them, every person in every seat in every theater, now dead. One by one, they go, winking out of existence.

The enslaved . . . *though only ten years old I sold for* . . . and the free, the civilians, the soldiers . . . *wherever they fired on our boats we burnt everything that would burn* . . . the spies, the thieves, the overseers, the auctioneers, the nurses . . . *I have forgotten how to feel* . . . the clerks and the clergy, the critics, the poets and politicians, the profiteers, the postboys, the lion tamers, the pigeon killers, the mummers, the mourners, the farmers, the famous, the failures, the fortunate, the fallen, Frederick, Mary Ann, Elizabeth, Henry, John, June, Asia, Rosalie, Edwin, Joe. One by one, they go.

ARE THERE GHOSTS?

How could there not be?

Author's Note

I began thinking about this book during one of our American spates of horrific mass shootings. Among other things, like other writers before me, I wondered about the families of the shooters—how would such a family deal with their own culpability, all the if-only's? Would it be possible to rejoin the devastated community? What happens to love when the person you love is a monster? This led me to the family of John Wilkes Booth. I knew he had brothers and sisters. I didn't know much else.

Immediately, a conundrum. I did not want to write a book about John Wilkes. This is a man who craved attention and has gotten too much of it; I didn't think he deserved mine. And yet there is no way around the fact that I wouldn't be writing about his family if he weren't who he was, if he hadn't done what he did. The tension over this issue—how to write the book without centering John Wilkes—is something I grappled with on nearly every page.

Researching the Booths was an adventure. I discovered whole communities fascinated by this family, particularly those online at LincolnConspirators.com (formerly BoothieBarn.com) and those in the flesh who maintain the Booths' old home, Tudor Hall. There was no shortage of material. But separating fact from fiction was often impossible. A number of stories about the Booths have been told and retold, appear in many sources, yet have doubtful provenance. One result of having a brother who ranks with history's great villains—a lot of mythology.

Donald Trump was elected to the presidency while I was still in the early stages of research. The shock and despair of this waylaid me for more than a year. It seemed pointless to be writing about anything else and it took much longer than it should have for me to realize that I wasn't writing about anything else. The more I read of Lincoln's warnings concerning the tyrant and the mob, the more I immersed myself in the years that led to the Civil War, the more brightly lit the road from there to here became.

The Lost Cause may be temporarily mislaid, but it has never been lost. Whenever Black people exercise genuine political power in this country, the assassin appears, the mob rises. This is the history of America and there is no escaping it. Abraham Lincoln told us so.

I was in the midst of my final edits when, during the violent insurrection of January 6th, 2021, I saw the flag of the Confederacy carried through the halls of the Capitol for the very first time. Let it be the last.

Afterword
and Acknowledgments

It is only natural, when reading a historical novel, to want to know which parts are true. But the question here is a complicated one. There is an enormous amount of material, both primary and secondary, regarding the Booth family. Some of it is confusing; some of it is contradictory; all of it is fascinating. So there are things here that I am confident are true and things that I know I made up. But there are also things I did not make up, yet am uncertain are true.

Of the characters in this book, Rosalie is the most fictional. She left only a slight mark on the world—one or two letters, and occasional references to her in the books and letters of her siblings, usually referring to her as poor Rose, the invalid sister. It was a great frustration to never be able to settle the question of what exactly her infirmity was. In the end I chose scoliosis, which is referenced in her death certificate. And because, for obvious reasons, Richard III was in my head.

(A parenthetical note on *Richard III*. Lovers of Shakespeare may be startled when some quotes from the play are not as they should be. But the *Richard* being performed is the Cibber adaptation, not Shakespeare's own text. I offer this reminder because I myself so often had trouble remembering it.)

Despite the troubling lack of material, I needed Rosalie to tell the story of the early years, most critically of the children's deaths that so deformed this family. My Rosalie sections are as accurate as I can make them in terms of things that happened, but the character is largely invented.

I was on more solid ground with Edwin and Asia. Many of their letters survive, along with Asia's books. I didn't get to their later lives—Edwin's troubled second wife, the fate of Asia's children, et cetera—so for those interested, there is much more to go and see.

I am indebted to Ann Smith for procuring Asia's letters to her lifelong friend Jean Anderson for me and to the Maryland Center for History and Culture for allowing me to use them. I'm indebted to Sarah Pinsker and Zu Tudhope for providing a comfortable bed, good food, and great company while I visited the sites around Baltimore. I am indebted to Evie Wilson-Lingbloom, who did odd bits of research for me over several years. And many thanks to the Folger Shakespeare Library and to Hedgebrook, two places so close to my heart, I would take up permanent residence in either if I could.

I LEARNED SO much from those who've studied the Booths longer than I. My greatest gratitude goes to Terry Alford, author of *Fortune's Fool*, a magnificent and meticulous biography of John Wilkes Booth. In answer to a random question over e-mail from me, a complete stranger, Terry immediately offered to share with me some thirty years of research he'd done on the family. Unbelievably generous, and I could never have written the book without him. But he is so careful himself, I can only hope he isn't appalled by some of the liberties I've taken.

Among many other materials, he gave me the delightful manuscript *The House That Booth Built* by Ella V. Mahoney, a woman who lived in Tudor Hall after the Booths did and compiled a great deal of neighborhood gossip about them. Terry also took me to Tudor Hall and introduced me to Tom Fink, president of the Junius B. Booth Society. I've made much use of the society's newsletters and publications as well as attending lectures at Tudor Hall.

Terry also introduced me to Jim Chrismer, a Booth family historian who helped me find my way through the Historical Society of Harford County. He put me in touch with Daniel Watermeier, author of the completely wonderful *American Tragedian: The Life of Edwin Booth*. Watermeier opened his archives to me, answered questions, and pointed me towards other sources. I am so very grateful to all of these.

FOR THE WRITING itself, many people were kind enough to listen patiently as I struggled through the book, or to read early drafts and provide help as needed—Jane Hamilton, Gail Tsukiyama, Elizabeth George, Nancy Horan, Ruth Ozeki, Kelly Link, Holly Black, Kim Stanley Robinson, Andrea Hairston, Micah Perks, Melissa Sanderself, Susan Sherman, Jill Wolfson, Tatjana Soli, Peggy Townsend, Liza Monroy, Kathleen Founds, Meg Waite Clayton, and Elizabeth McKenzie.

I had brilliant feedback from my wonderful agents, Molly Friedrich and Lucy Carson, as well as crucial editorial input from the incomparable Sally Kim at Putnam. The enthusiasm of my

Serpent's Tail team, most especially Rebecca Gray and Hannah Westland, as well as my British agent, Anthony Goff, kept me afloat. My assistant, Molly Zakoor, has been helpfully keeping me on track throughout. And my husband kept me sane (or at least as sane as it's sane to be in these insane times).

Of course, none of these people can be held accountable for any mistakes I may have consciously or unconsciously made. Those are entirely of my own doing and I expect to answer for them in the years to come.

Discussion Guide

1. *Booth* is a story about the family of John Wilkes Booth, an infamous figure in American history. But author Karen Joy Fowler doesn't center the narrative on John, instead choosing to tell the story of the Booth family—from the struggles of his parents to his many siblings. Why do you think Fowler chose to write this story as such?

2. Fowler's last book, *We Are All Completely Beside Ourselves,* was organized around a secret, a secret that the characters know, but the reader does not. *Booth* operates in the exact opposite way, being organized around something the reader knows but the characters do not. How did your awareness of Lincoln's assassination impact your reading?

3. The Booths live in a two-story, two-room log cabin, which was manually relocated to Beech Spring, miles away from any major city. How are the Booths perceived in their insular neighborhood? What effect do you think this had on their development, particularly that of the children—particularly Edwin, John, Rosalie?

4. According to Booth family lore, soon after John was born, "a flame rose from the ashes and, shaping itself into an arm, stretched toward the baby as if to knight him" (pp. 61). In that flame, John's mother read the word *Country,* followed by John's

name—a promise of a glorious fate. How aware do you think John, growing up, was of his own prophecy?

5. On page 220, Fowler writes, "Asia dreams she's being swept away, one of a great many unlikely things bobbing in the current—books, cats, hats, chairs, a cow, and a banjo." Would you describe Asia as a dreamer? How so? How do you think these qualities led her to live her life outside convention? To see her brother, John, through a certain lens?

6. What was the role of women in the Booth family? Why was it respectable to be an actor, but not to be an actress? Were you surprised, during the interlude on the farm after Junius's death, that three grown women would leave the survival of the family entirely in the hands of a fifteen-year-old boy?

7. How much of Rosalie's lion-tamer romance was real and how much do you think it was just a fantasy that sustained her? Why did she believe that John had had a secret marriage and left a child behind when none of the other siblings believed this?

8. Edwin and Joe each believe that they are the Booth sibling with the worst childhood. Which Booth would you argue had the most to feel aggrieved about? Do you think Mary Ann was a good mother?

9. Junius Booth, as the most famous stage actor of his day, held onto his vast spotlight, both on the stage and at home. Talk about how the Booth children tried—and often failed—to come out from under his shadow. What made Edwin so determined to follow in the footsteps of his father? Do you think John pursued theater for the same reasons?

10. Slavery was the great issue of the day and yet, with the exception of John, the Booths seldom seem to have spoken of it. How is it possible to ignore something so ubiquitous and contentious

and unjust, especially given their deep connection to the Hall family?

11. Were you surprised by Lincoln's professions of white supremacy?

12. Fowler weaves many Shakespearean elements throughout the story, often quoting from the plays. Talk about Junius and Edwin's many attempts to conquer their famous roles. How did their adventures on the stage often foreshadow tragedies in their personal lives?

13. As John becomes increasingly embroiled in the political scene, his family reminds him "that the time will come when he must choose—politics or the theater" (pp.236). Why do you think the Booths believed that politics and theater were to remain separate? Is it possible that John's theatrical pursuits fueled his political goals? How so?

14. Fowler illustrates many moments of deep comfort and intimacy between the siblings throughout this book. Why do you think these are just as important as the bigger, more dramatic moments and events?

15. At what point in the story did you start to discern a change in John? To what do you attribute this change? When do you think his family noticed this shift, or was it more gradual? What are some marked things in John that his family failed to see in him?

16. Despite knowing it was coming, and despite not seeing the action on the page, talk about your reaction to the assassination when it happens in the story. Which sibling do you think was most affected by John's crime? Why? And why did Ann Hall remain so fond of John even after the assassination?

17. Through this family story, Fowler explores what it feels like to

be brutally betrayed by a loved one, but also to grieve their loss while the world can only spew hate. How does this make you think about love and pain, especially when it's so closely tied up with right and wrong?

18. It is inevitable to read this period through the lens of our modern-day context. How do you think it sheds light on current events?

PHOTOGRAPH OF THE AUTHOR © NATHAN QUINTANILLA 2021

Karen Joy Fowler, a PEN/Faulkner and California Book Award winner, is the author of six novels (two of them *New York Times* bestsellers) and four short story collections. She has been a Dublin IMPAC nominee and was shortlisted for the Man Booker Prize in 2014. She lives in Santa Cruz, California.

VISIT KAREN JOY FOWLER ONLINE

karenjoyfowler.com